THE CHIEFTAIN

HIGHLAND HEROES SERIES PREQUEL

MAEVE GREYSON

MAEVEGREYSON.COM
Magical Romance Sizing Through Time

To those who dare to dream with their eyes wide open.

And to dear sweet Jasper—I miss you still.

ALSO BY MAEVE GREYSON

My Seductive Highlander

THE MACKAY CLAN

Beyond A Highland Whisper

The Highlander's Fury

A Highlander In Her Past

OTHER BOOKS BY MAEVE GREYSON

Stone Guardian

Eternity's Mark

PROLOGUE

THIRTEEN FEBRUARY 1692 - GLENCOE
SCOTLAND - CLAN MACDONALD'S KEEP

*D*awn broke with blood-curdling shrieks and shouts. Gunfire fed into the chaos. Though the bitter winds of winter howled outside, scorching hot air, thick and stifling to the lungs, filled the halls of the stronghold.

Acrid smoke, heavy with the oily scent of pitch and burned flesh, hung low across every room. Tarred brands embedded deep wherever they'd landed crackled and blazed as their black oozing fuel took hold and gained strength.

Alexander MacCoinnich rose from his crouched position behind a bullet-riddled column, stealing a glance beyond its cover. Relief washed across him as he peered through the choking haze and located his brother. Graham hurried in his direction, was almost to him, in fact. Duncan and Sutherland, the youngest of the four MacCoinnich brothers, followed close behind.

Thank God he found them. A bullet cut Alexander's thankfulness short as it burrowed bone deep into his upper thigh. He staggered back against the column, struggling to remain upright. Teeth clenched, he leveled his pistol, took aim, and downed the bastard that had shot him.

His brothers reached him. Alexander motioned toward the end of the room where the chieftain's overturned table was consumed by fire. "Behind that table. Past the burning tapestry. A passage. We canna win this." Another shot bored into the meat of his shoulder, almost taking him to the ground. Burning pain radiated through his body. "Move! Now! I'm feckin' tired of getting shot!"

"Graham, carry the great hulking beast!" Duncan flinched and glanced about for the source of closer gunfire. "Sutherland and I'll guard your backs."

A man, wild-eyed and screaming Clan Campbell's battle cry, plowed toward Duncan who, with the agility born of countless battles, side-stepped away from the man's bayonet then took the intruder down with a single swipe of his claymore. Sword held at the ready, Duncan backed closer to his older brothers. "And ye ken Sutherland and I'll be reminding the both of ye that from this day forward the youngest MacCoinnichs bested the eldest brothers, aye?"

"Aye," Sutherland said, chiming in as he ducked under the arm of another raging swordsman and plunged his dagger deep into the man's side. He yanked the dying man's sword out of his hand, admired the weapon, then secured it into his own belt. "Never hear the end of it if we let Alexander die. The nagging bugger would haunt us the rest of our days, ye ken?"

"I'm no' dead yet," Alexander said as he shoved his pistols into his belt. Ammunition gone and pistols useless, a sense of doom tightened deep in his gut but he wouldna give it free rein. *This isna the end.* He drew his dagger from its sheath, wishing he had the strength to heft the weight of his claymore hanging at his side. Wishes were futile in this hell. The bullet robbing his shoulder of its strength was the reality.

His sight dimmed for an instant and the steady high-pitched ring of blood loss hummed in his ears. Palming his dagger, he blinked hard against the suffocating fog of agony threatening to overtake him. Past battles had been worse. He'd push through this and get his brothers safe and tended to afore he relented and gave in to the darkness threatening to knock him on his arse. *I'll be damned if I pass out and let Campbell and his bloody regiment take me.* He staggered to one side.

Graham hitched himself up under Alexander's arm and clenched him tight around the middle. "Ye can do this, damn ye. Dinna let them win." Gunfire sounded close behind them. The smell of spent gunpowder followed as quick as thunder follows lightning. Graham grunted and jerked a step forward. He bowed his head and grimaced, pain evident in his scowl.

Bullet-riddled columns and upended tables provided little cover. One arm clutched around Graham's shoulders, Alexander stumbled and half-crawled the remaining few feet to the blazing chieftain's table. They made their way past it, then pushed into the shallow alcove concealed behind the flaming tapestry. Duncan and Sutherland stayed close behind, then took up guard on either side of the alcove.

Heat from the ignited tapestry threatened to sizzle his flesh and the sharp scent of burnt hair surrounded him. Alexander pushed away from the support of his brother. Roaring against the excruciating torture of his wounds, he slammed his hands against specific stones inlaid in the wall and shoved. The hidden doorway opened. *Thank God.* He staggered into the darkness, sagging back against the rough slab of the inner wall and pulled in a deep breath of the cool dank air. He motioned at the still open door as his brothers dashed into the tunnel with him.

"Those stones," he said as he struggled to remain upright. "Push the two stones at the base and it will close. The bastards willna be able to follow." He sent up a silent prayer of thanks to MacIain, Clan MacDonald's chief, for sharing the keep's secrets before the attack. The hidden tunnel bettered their odds of surviving.

Duncan and Sutherland shoved at the blocks Alexander had pointed out before they lost the light of the blazing tapestry. Stone ground and gritted against stone and inky blackness blotted out all light as the massive door settled back in place. Alexander slumped against the wall then fisted his hands so hard his knuckles popped. He'd failed. Failed in their mission to protect Clan MacDonald of Glencoe as hired to do so by MacIain's kin, the Lord of the Isles himself, the chieftain of Clan Donald of Islay.

The bile of defeat burned the back of his throat. Alexander closed his eyes a scant moment, pulling in deep breaths and blowing them out. *Now isna the time to wallow. Must move on.* They had but one choice. Save themselves. Live to fight another day and perhaps, if God so willed it, avenge those murdered this day. For that was what this was: murder. Not battle. Not war. Not a skirmish between clans. This attack had been a calculated act of cold-blooded murder.

Alexander shifted in the darkness, a darkness that played hell with a man's equilibrium. He turned to hitch his way forward, deeper into the tunnel. "This way." He forced himself to sound a damn sight stronger than he felt. "MacIain said the tunnel leads to the back of the keep. If the way is clear, we can make it to the trees and then to the cave."

"Horses?" Graham asked. His pained wheezing echoed in the dank, cool darkness.

"Do ye truly think they left the stables untouched?" Alexander couldn't help biting out the words. His wounds were pushing him to the edge of sanity. "The bastards probably set fire to them first. Ye ken that as well as I."

He dragged himself along, right shoulder scraping against the rough, grainy surface of the wall. Feet shuffling, he made a careful sweep of his boot before each step to avoid whatever surprise the darkness might hold. He was growing weaker, his injured leg heavier. He concentrated on breathing, remaining upright, and ignoring the burning stab of agonizing pain radiating from several places on his body. Three times he'd been shot. Four if ye counted the grazing across his ribs, and he'd lost track of how many wounds he'd earned courtesy of swords, bayonets, and daggers. Best talk of something to keep the pain at bay. "We best thank Almighty God and all the saints for revealing that cave to us on our way here to Glencoe. 'Twill give us shelter to rest," he said to anyone willing to listen. "And tend to our wounds."

"And then?" Duncan asked from somewhere behind him in the darkness.

"Leave 'then' to God," Alexander said. "Only He kens that answer and I'm a damn sight too weary at the moment to ask Him." One hand feeling his way, he sent up a silent prayer that his strength would hold until they reached the cave.

Alexander blinked hard at the cold sweat running into his eyes and setting them on fire. Sight was useless in the dark tomb of the tunnel. It felt as though they'd been crawling through this clammy black hell for hours. The sounds of the attack had grown quieter—at least as far as he could tell what with the roaring of his blood pounding in his ears. He didna ken if it was because they'd made their way well past the belly of the keep or if Campbell's troops had finished their massacre of the entire clan. *Damn Robert Campbell and his men straight to hell.*

"I feel fresh air," Sutherland called out. "Take care, brother. Who's to say they're no' waiting for anyone trying to escape."

"Hold fast." Alexander stopped and leaned back against the solid wall, gulping in deep breaths to rally his waning strength. He'd emerge from the tunnels first. A winged bird. An easy target in case danger lay ahead. "The lot of ye stay here until I deem it safe and call out to ye to follow, aye?"

"Nay," Graham argued. "I'll go. I've shot left in my pistol and my wounds are no' so bad as yours."

"Ye will stay here." Alexander adopted the growling tone he'd oft used to keep his brothers in line when they were lads. Aye, his wounds pained him something severe, but he wasna dead yet and as eldest, they best remember he was still verra much in charge. "I'll no' go to my grave with your death on my conscience, ye ken?"

"But ye'd burden me with your death on mine?" Graham took hold of Alexander's arm and wrapped it around his shoulders for support. "We go together. The pups can stay behind."

"Like hell, we will," Sutherland said. "And I'm no' a damn pup, ye condescending bastard."

"We all go," Duncan interjected. "Or none of us go, aye?"

"God's bones, every last one of ye pains me." But his brothers filled him with pride. Alexander held Graham's shoulder tighter and pushed himself forward. "Come then. Mother bore us all years apart but if we die today, we die together."

An icy gust of wind swooshed into the tunnel just as Alexander spotted daylight winking in the darkness up ahead. They'd made it through the keep. If what MacIain had said was true, the tunnel opened a few yards out at the mouth of a shallow ravine. He'd said a burn was nearby and 'twas sheltered by a thick stand of pines. Water from the burn would be most welcome about now. Alexander swallowed hard, his mouth dry. He'd relish one last drink before he died. If he had his druthers, whisky wouldha been his first choice, but water would have to do.

He and Graham pushed their way through the ramshackle door. A circle of dense spiky hedging concealing the exit of the tunnel greeted them. Alexander stumbled, then cursed under his breath as the wicked gorse and its relentless spikes tore across his flesh.

A horse snorted and grumbled just beyond the barrier of thorns.

"Christ Almighty," Alexander said in a strained whisper as he grabbed hold of Graham and pulled them both down into a low crouch. He hissed out a barely stifled groan with the effort. "We're found."

"Ready yourselves." Alexander lifted his dagger. Faint shuffling sounded behind him. The metallic shushing of drawn steel. The click of pistols armed to fire.

"If ye shoot me or cut me, I'll no' save your sorry arses, I grant ye that."

Relief flooded so hard through Alexander that it staggered him to one side. He clutched at a gorse branch for support. 'Twas Magnus. His closest friend. "Magnus, ye wily bastard. When the hell did ye arrive and how in the name of all that's holy did ye know of the tunnel?"

"Ye can see the black smoke as far as Fort William. I got here as fast as I could." The branches of the stubborn gorse bushes rattled as they shook then gave way as Magnus de Gray, dubbed 'Ghost' due to both his stealth and his looks, hacked them aside with his sword. "And never underestimate what secrets ye can discover about a keep by befriending lovely maids with a bone to pick with their former master." Magnus grew quiet as he reached Alexander and Graham still crouching at the heart of the bushes. His mouth tightened into a grim line when he saw their wounds. "Hurry. From the looks of ye, we've no' much time and rumor has it there be at least two more regiments coming to ensure there are no survivors and that no one escapes the glen from either of the passes."

"There's a cave. Higher. Above the northern rise." Alexander winced, and a groan escaped him as Magnus and Graham helped him to his feet. *Ignore the pain. Must make it to the cave.* Darkness whirled around him, knocking him off balance and making him stumble to one side. "Shelter in the cave. Higher. Must go higher into the mountains."

"Ye'll ride my horse. The stables are nothing but smoldering ash and no' a beast in sight. The rest of us will have to walk." Magnus took Graham's place under Alexander's arm. He, Duncan, and Sutherland hefted Alexander onto the horse.

"I owe ye a bottle of the best whisky in Scotland," Alexander said as he sagged forward in the saddle. It felt good to sit, or at least as close to good as he could get right now through all this worrisome pain. If he could just remain upright until they reached the cave, then he'd lie down and if anyone disturbed him, he'd damn well shoot them.

With more effort than he thought he could muster, he hitched forward in the saddle, breaking out in a cold sweat as the need to retch washed across him. He swallowed hard and pulled in deep breaths against the nauseating pain. "Put Graham behind me. He's wounded as well and mighty Stoic can haul us both." He leaned forward and patted the great horse's shaggy neck. "Ye willna mind toting us both, will ye, Stoic?"

At the sound of his name, the large black horse tossed his head and responded with a friendly grumble and a stomp of one of his great hairy feet.

"I can walk," Graham said in an insulted growl.

"Ye think I'm being generous but I'm not, dear brother. With your arse in the saddle behind me, ye'll block that icy wind and keep me warm."

"We must go," Magnus advised with a concerned look around.

Dark smoke billowed from every orifice in the once grand castle behind them and flames licked out around the blocks of stone. Unmistakable sounds of pillaging and men on the move grew closer.

"Verra well then." Graham feigned a bow that ended in a flinching grab of his wounded side. With Magnus's and Duncan's help and a great deal of cursing, Graham pulled himself aboard the huge horse and settled in behind Alexander.

Alexander grunted as Graham shifted behind him and wrapped the length of his kilt around them both. The slightest of moves pained him. Perhaps staying warm wasna the best idea. At least if he grew cold, he might grow numb as well. As if in answer to this thought, a sudden gust of icy wind cut across him and huge clusters of snowflakes filled the air. Snow. A double-edged sword. It could hide their tracks or grow so deep they'd founder.

With a hard wince that stole his breath, he hunched forward in the saddle and urged the horse into a faster trot toward the cover of the dense thicket of pines. Magnus, Duncan, and Sutherland fanned out, dashing into the woods on either side of the horse.

"God be with us," Alexander whispered, a pained grunt escaping him and his breath fogging in the frigid air. Agony pounded through him with every jolt of the horse's gait. He blinked hard, head swimming and vision fading in and out of focus. He peered up into the murky sky, not even bothering to blink as the heavy, wet snowflakes plopped into his eyes.

"God get us to safety—or at the verra least, save my brothers and Magnus." His breath steamed across the frosting folds of the kilt bunched at his throat. He dragged the sign of the cross against his chest then sagged to one side, the world around him fading into a fog of darkness. "Please…"

CHAPTER 1

FEBRUARY 1692 - CLAN NEAL'S KEEP - BEN
NEVIS SCOTLAND

"Ye tied these laces tight enough, I give ye that." Gaersa yanked at the leather strips snugging the fur shaft of the boot around Catriona's calves. The old woman bent lower, scowling at the knots as she plucked at them with her thick, crooked fingers.

Catriona Neal clenched her fists in her lap to keep from brushing Gaersa's stiff, knobby hands out of the way and untying the boots herself. Stubborn Gaersa Aberfeldy, housekeeper to Clan Neal as far back as Catriona could remember. She reckoned the old woman would best the task in her own time. 'Twould hurt the housekeeper's feelings o'er much if Catriona took the job from her.

I'll ne'er be free of these boots.

Catriona forced herself not to fidget. If she moved, Gaersa would try to hurry then fumble at the chore all the longer. The door to the turret room burst open and banged against the wall, startling all thoughts of footwear out of her mind.

Gaersa yanked the boot off Catriona's foot and threw it at the red-faced young lad hopping in place in the doorway. "Sawny Fitzgerald, I'll box your ears for ye, I will! Gave us such a fright, ye did. What do ye mean blowing into a room like that?"

"Hunters," Sawny said between huffing gasps. Eyes wide and hands held high with fingers outspread, he skittered back and forth like a wee scarecrow caught in a strong wind. He swallowed hard, sucked in a great gulp of air, then blew it out. "Hunters are back and…" he paused to draw another deep breath.

"And what?" Catriona prompted. If the boy had just startled the life out of them to tell her the hunters were back and they'd managed to find meat, she'd box his ears herself.

"Men!" Sawny dragged the back of his hand across his mouth then thumped it to the center of his narrow chest. He leaned forward, bobbing his shaggy head in such an excited jerking nod 'twas small wonder that he didn't snap his spindly neck. "They found men. Near dead they are."

Sweet Jesu, now what?

Catriona yanked off her other boot and shoved both feet into the everyday shoes she'd left in the turret room before going outside to walk the path atop the skirting wall. "How many?" She rose from the bench and shook her heavy woolen skirts down into place.

"Two, mistress." Sawny grew more animated as he fidgeted in the doorway. He edged his way back out into the hallway, waving for Catriona to follow. "But Mr. Murtagh says there be more still out there in the snow. He said to fetch ye with great haste."

"More?" Catriona shooed the boy forward, hurrying down the hall beside him. "Are ye telling me they left some out there to die in the cold?" She knew Murtagh was no lover of his fellow man but he wasna heartless.

Sawny's blue eyes rounded even wider. He gave a dismissive shrug as he scurried along beside her. "I'm only saying what Mr. Murtagh said say to ye, mistress." He scuttled and hopped, struggling to keep up with Catriona's long-legged stride. "I be begging your pardon if it offends ye, mistress, but I swear on me mam's grave that's what he said say."

Catriona bit back her words to keep from quashing the young boy further. It wasn't the lad's fault. He was naught but twelve years old and small for his age. A child. He adored Murtagh Aberfeldy and shadowed the stable master's every step when he wasn't tending to his duties as a kitchen boy helping Cook. "I thank ye for fetching me. Now hie back to the kitchen. I'm sure Cook will be looking for ye to help with the evening meal."

The lad's shoulders sagged, and his round face fell as they hurried down the last winding curve of stairs leading to the main floor of the keep. It was quite plain to see that Sawny would much rather return to Murtagh than see to his responsibilities. His forlorn expression pulled at Catriona's heart. She set a hand on his shoulder and paused their descent down the winding stairwell. "If your sister Jenny can do your share in the kitchens, just this once, ye may come and help Murtagh rather than help Cook."

Sawny's little mouth twisted to one side. His pitiful look shifted to one of guilt. "I dinna ken if Jenny will do my share as well as hers for Cook. She's still a bit red-arsed about..." Sawny's words trailed off and the lad seemed quite unable to look Catriona in the eye. After a deep breath, he peered up at her through his shaggy fringe of unkempt hair and drew his shoulders into a cringing shrug. "I dinna think she'll help me."

"What did ye do to Jenny?" Catriona had four brothers. She was well acquainted with young boys' antics.

"Me and Tom caught a rat and put it in Jenny's room." Sawny shifted sideways with a guilty twitch. "But it was mostly Tom's idea." Sawny drew closer and lowered his voice to a secretive tone. "I think he likes Jenny."

Catriona rolled her eyes and shook her head. *Males.* "If ye canna find a way to make things right with Jenny so she'll do your chores, then ye canna come and help Murtagh, ye ken?"

"Aye," Sawny said in a dejected tone as he plodded down the remaining steps. By the time he'd reached the main landing, determination squared his narrow shoulders, and he darted off toward the kitchens. Sawny was not a lad to give up on an opportunity.

Skirts fisted in both hands and held high above her steps, Catriona hurried into the heart of the keep: the clan's meeting hall. Just inside the front entrance to the great room, closest to the tall double doors that led outside to the bailey, six of Clan Neal's hunters and Murtagh stood clustered together. Amid the hunter's hulking fur-wrapped forms lay two men. They had been placed across a pair of benches pulled together to keep them up out of the muck and wet snow tracked inside. The men appeared dead, so still they were and so absent of color. Murtagh turned at the sound of her approach and the rest of the hunters shuffled back a few feet.

Catriona circled the unconscious men stretched across the benches, apprising their grim condition. *Sweet Jesu. Look at them. Barely drawing breath. So near dead.* She looked up at Murtagh. "Sawny said there were more?"

"Aye. Found them on the northern ridge between here and Glen Coe." Murtagh frowned down at the pair as he shrugged off the heavy fur cloak from around his shoulders and tossed it across a nearby table. Strong, healthy fires crackled in the two great hearths of the long hall, making the high-ceilinged room too warm for outdoor clothing. "Old MacAlpin's cave. Seven of them." He dipped his grizzled chin in a single nod toward the lifeless men. "These two were the worst, so we brought them here." He locked eyes with Catriona, a grim look of finality on his face. "They've but one horse betwixt them all and the drifting snow be too deep for them to walk here in their condition. Might survive another few days. A fortnight at best. They've no food or water. Ill prepared, they are."

"Gather additional men and whatever ye need to fetch the rest. We'll no' be leaving anyone to suffer and die." Peering under the bloodied plaid wrapped around the man on the left, Catriona cringed. Gunshot wounds. Cuts. Deep slashes in dire need of stitching. She pressed the back of her hand to the side of his neck. *Fever.* The man burned hot to the touch even after traveling in the frigid weather. She checked the second man. He was overly warm, too.

"Storm's a coming," Murtagh said, as he retrieved his fur cloak and the gloves he'd tossed on the table beside it.

Catriona knew Murtagh wasn't arguing with her request. He was merely stating a fact. She looked up at him and nodded. "Aye, I saw the clouds to the north of us. Ye'd best hurry." She turned to the hunters still hovering close by. "We canna leave those others to die. Think how ye would feel if it were your own kin lost in this weather." She stood taller and lifted her chin. "A storm doesna exist that a Neal hunter canna best. I ken ye will all be safe enough, aye?"

The biggest and burliest of the group, Ranald, stepped forward. "Aye, mistress. We'll get them all fetched afore the storm hits. Ne'er ye fret." He turned and glared at the other men still skulking back in the shadows beneath the gallery running the circumference of the great room. "Ye heard Mistress Catriona. Each of ye fetch an additional man and be quick about it. Extra supplies as well in case the storm delays us."

"And rig up some sledges. Five of them," Murtagh said. "I willna be taking extra horses just to risk losing them in the pass." He turned back to Catriona, scowling at her with a pained expression. After a stolen glance at the hunters scattering to gather supplies, he leaned in close and lowered his voice. "Ye will light a candle and say the words for us, aye? As your mother always did?"

"Aye." Of course she'd light a candle and say the words. She just wished she'd inherited her mother's talents when it came to the mysteries and influencing the way of things. She'd yet to see any results from uttering words, lighting candles, or burning bundles of herbs.

No time to mourn lost abilities now. Catriona motioned forward the ever-growing cluster of servants peeping into the room through multiple arched doorways lining the great hall. "Come. The lot of ye. We've work to do. Our healing room will be here in the hall."

Gaersa emerged from the turret stairwell, her face round and shining with sweat and her plump arms pumping at her sides. She waddled as fast and furious as her matronly form would allow. With a swipe of her fingers across her forehead, she tucked in the strands of gray hair escaping out from under the ruffles of her white cap. After a deep intake of air, she clapped her hands and barked out her orders. "Blankets. Linens. Hot water and basins. In front of the hearths. Off with ye now!"

Servants mobilized. White-capped maids scurried to fetch the required items and scullery lads rushed to pull the long dinner tables and benches out of the way.

Catriona gazed down at the two wounded men, concern, compassion, and indecision fighting for supremacy within her. *Who in God's name did this to ye? And will they follow ye and do the same to us?*

"Are ye tetched?" The familiar bellowing sneer echoed from across the room.

"No worse than yourself, dear brother." Catriona spared a glance back at her belligerent twin. "I've no time to deal with ye, Calum. Take the boys and go if ye're no' inclined to help us tend to these men."

"We can help." Twins Murray and Dougal sprang out from behind their older brother. The pair of nine-year-olds grabbed hold of a nearby bench and started wrestling it toward the wall.

"Fine boys, ye are, the both of ye." Catriona gave them a proud nod. At least her youngest brothers were still her allies. She waved a hand toward them as she turned her attention back to her other two siblings who would just as soon feed her to the wolves. "The two of ye could take lessons from Murray and Dougal. Willing to help their fellow man, they are. It might do both your souls some good to learn their ways, I grant ye that."

Calum and her fifteen-year-old brother, Angus, glared at her from where they stood beside the chief's chair on the raised platform at the head of the room. Both stood with chests puffed out like insulted birds of prey, glowering at the readying of the hall for the wounded.

"Dinna worry after my soul, dear sister," Calum said. A low growl added a deeper level of hatred to his words. He made a pompous sweeping motion with one hand, encompassing the entire room. "The dead of winter and ye're taking in more mouths to feed?" He glared at her and took a threatening step forward, fisted hands trembling at his sides. "Damned foolish, it is. Ye're showing complete disregard for the well-being of your own clan."

Catriona ignored him as she directed Geordie and Tamhas, two men from the hunting group, to place the injured men on tables the servants had padded with blankets and placed close to one of the hearths. "Gentle as ye can, lads. Gentle as ye can."

"Ye will do me the courtesy of listening when I speak, Catriona. Do ye hear me? I willna have ye risking the survival of our clan by taking in complete strangers who look to have been involved in who knows what sort of ill-gotten venture. Did it ever occur to ye that ye could endanger all of us by taking in possible traitors to the Crown?" Calum glared at her as though she mattered less than the scraps thrown to the dogs. "'Tis damned foolish and I'll no' permit it, ye ken?"

"Aye," young Angus chimed in, taking another step forward to keep himself shoulder to shoulder with Calum.

I've no time for your arrogant arses, dear brothers. Catriona drew in a calming breath and released it in a slow, controlled hiss, determined to hold her tongue and not rise to Calum's bait. She'd learned long ago that ignoring Calum was the surest way to vex him and she did so at every opportunity.

"Fetch Elena," she said to Sawny as she tended to the man who seemed to be in the worse condition of the two.

Sawny bolted toward the door, barely pausing long enough to bundle up with an extra plaid before rushing out into the bitter cold weather to follow his mistress's orders.

"I bid ye respond, sister!" Calum slammed a hand down hard atop the chieftain's table. "In fact, I demand it!" His deep voice boomed with barely held fury. Calum's temper matched the flaming red of his hair and his cruelty knew no bounds. All in the keep feared him. All except Catriona.

Spoiled bastard. Mother had always coddled him, justified it by saying he'd nearly died at birth whilst Catriona had thrived. Catriona squared off and faced Calum. "I hear your words, brother. Since it's obvious ye'll be of no help, I bid that ye at least stay out of my way. Can ye manage that, Calum? You and your wee shadow there?" Teeth clenched, she lifted her chin and glared at her brothers, daring them to challenge her. She was in no mood to try to keep Calum appeased today.

"Come, Angus," Calum said with a dismissive huffing snort. "We shall deal with Catriona later, after I've apprised Father of this fool-hardiness. Last I checked, he still led Clan Neal."

15

Angus shot Catriona a taunting sneer before trotting off to catch up with his older brother.

Fools. 'Twould do little good to run to Father. Their sire's only concern of late was how quickly he could drown himself in whisky and port. He cared even less about kith and kin than he had when he was strong enough to emerge from his rooms—and then he didna give a tinker's damn.

Catriona returned her attention to her deathly still patient. As gently as she could, she peeled away the man's blood-encrusted *léine*. A low hiss escaped her as the clotted wounds fought to hold tight to the weave of the cloth then oozed with fresh blood when she pulled the material free. *Judas, so much blood and damage. How could one man survive such?*

She unsheathed the blade she kept belted to her waist and cut away the soiled bloody garment bit by bit. Bile rose at the back of her throat. A hard swallow kept it at bay as she clamped her lips tight against the sight before her. She refused to flinch or turn away.

"Blessed Mother," Gaersa whispered from the opposite side of the table. "The man's a bloody mess. How does he still draw breath?"

Catriona agreed. 'Twas small wonder this great brute of a man still lived. His body looked as though he'd fought an entire regiment.

"Best prop his injured leg a bit higher," Catriona said as she uncovered the vicious wound in his thigh. "'Twill ease the stress off the wound as we work." She pulled away the remainder of his kilt, revealing his man parts in the process. *Sweet Jesu, Mary, and Joseph.* Her breath caught in her throat at the increased pace of her heartbeat. The braw comely warrior was quite blessed indeed.

"My my...a giant of a man and no' lacking beneath his kilt either. That's for certain." Gaersa hurried to drape a linen across him and gave Catriona a stern shake of her head. "'Tis no' proper for a lady, a maiden, mind ye, such as yourself to be seeing such. Ye tend to his wounds from the waist up. Elena and I will tend to his injuries from the waist down."

Elena Bickerstaff, Clan Neal's healer, appeared at Gaersa's side. The frail crone shrugged off her wraps and cloak and handed them to

Sawny without taking her eyes off the man stretched across the length of the table. "This warrior has seen great troubles." The old woman stretched her bent frame up on tip toe to peer closer at the man. With narrowed eyes and sparse white brows knotted together, her thin, bony hands flitted all across his body, examining every wound.

She finished with a sharp shake of her head. Her knobby hands planted on the side of the pallet, she straightened as much as her twisted back would allow and scowled across him at Catriona. "Still full of lead, he is, and some of his wounds already set to festering. We'll have to get the bullets out of him and cauterize the wounds." She gave him another slow sweeping, up and down look. The silver-white wisps of hair peeping out from under her cap fluttered about her wrinkled face like cobwebs. "He's a great beast of a man, he is. Muscled. Strong. 'Tis probably all that's kept him alive." She hitched her way over to the second man and began her examination of him.

"They're both huge," Gaersa said as she toddled over to the hearth, swung an iron bar out from the fireplace, and hung a kettle of water on it before swinging it back over the roiling coals. "We'll be needing plenty of boiling water, that's for certain."

Catriona stayed by the man with the more severe wounds, smoothing his dark hair away from his face and resting her palm across his burning brow. *So many wounds. What horrors have ye seen?* The thought of the pain he'd already endured and the agony of healing yet to come grabbed hold of her heart and twisted.

"Ye're safe now, lad," she whispered to him. "Safe and warm." It didna matter that he might no' hear her words. She needed to say them. Perhaps 'twould somehow help him.

She wrung out a cloth in the basin of warm water and set to the task of washing him, cleaning away the blood and dirt from his great hulking body with as gentle a touch as she possessed. She had to ensure they didna miss the tending of a single wound. Even in his disabled state, the man was a wondrous sight indeed. A chest broader than any she'd seen. His entire body so muscular, it felt rock hard to the touch. The silent strength of him beneath her hands mesmerized her as she ran the soft, wet cloth across his ridges of muscle. Catriona swallowed hard, strange warm flutterings surging through her. What was he like when he was whole and awake? What sort of man might he be?

While Gaersa and Elena tended to the other unconscious man, Catriona was quite aware of their glances her way, watching to ensure that she didn't tend to any part of the man that a maiden shouldn't touch unless that man happened to be her husband.

"Have ye e'er seen so many scars?" Gaersa asked as she hefted another steaming kettle of water from the fire and sat it on the bench between the two men. She waved for the two maids carrying candelabras with fresh candles to come forward and place the additional lighting on benches at the heads of both men. "These lads have seen their share of battles afore whatever happened this time. Some of those scars are old. And they favor each other. Reckon they're kin?"

"Hair black as soot and both the size of great hulking bears? Aye. They're kin. I'd wager maybe brothers even." Elena covered her patient with a light blanket, then bent with a stiff shuffle and scooped up the cloth sack she'd brought with her. "We'll be needing a mighty poultice for the both of them once we rid them of their bullets." She hitched her way toward the kitchen, then paused and turned back, shaking a crooked finger at Catriona. "I'll no' have ye about whilst we cut out the bullets and cauterize the wounds. I ken you're the lady of the keep since your mother's death and ye've guided this clan during your sire's ill health, but ye're still a maiden and it's no' proper for ye to witness such." Elena waved away any possibility of argument as she walked away. "Content yourself to lighting a candle for them and saying the words."

A fool candle and strange words willna heal this man. Prayers? Aye. But I'll no' waste my time mimicking my mother's dabbling in the ancient ways. Elena's advice heated her blood, made her resolve to help the man beneath her hands all the stronger. She meant to tend to this poor warrior and Elena's druthers were better directed elsewhere. Catriona drew in a deep breath and eased it out as her gaze settled on the man's large hand resting at his side. Two of his fingers swelled with a hideous purple coloring and were more than likely broken. With as gentle a touch as possible, she repositioned his arm and propped his injured hand atop a folded cloth. They'd have to splint those later. So many wounds. Braw mighty man or no', how could anyone survive this? She feared all their care and mending might be for naught.

"Do ye hear my words, Catriona?" Elena repeated in a tired but firm tone. "I'll no' have ye seeing such."

She met Elena's scowl with a defiant tilt of her chin. "Ye will be in need of my help." She looked over at Gaersa to include her in the conversation. "Your combined wisdom is great and I respect the both of ye more than ye'll e'er know but the both of ye are older and your strength wanes. I'll be helping with the tending of these men. I dinna believe in shirking duties no matter how unpleasant. These two need attention as fast as we can give it." As if to cement her vow, Catriona pulled the linen back, uncovered the man in front of her, and dabbed away the blood and grime from the wound high on his upper thigh. "And I verra much doubt that the washing of an unconscious man is a grave danger to my maidenhead, ye ken?"

Inwardly, she smiled. Aye, her maidenhead was quite safe, but in all fairness to Gaersa and Elena's reservations, the sight before her did set her to musing. What might it be like to be wanted by such a comely made man? She blew out an excited breath and swiped the back of one hand across her forehead. The hall seemed overly warm, and she wondered at the prudence in placing the men so close to the hearths.

For the sake of her own temperature, she drew the linen back across the man's middle and busied herself with tending to his other wounds.

CHAPTER 2

*H*is screams shattered the nighttime peace of the hall, but the word *scream* didna provide an accurate description of the heart-wrenching sound. The warrior's growling roars sounded more like unimaginable pain unleashed from the depths of his anguished soul. 'Twas a hellish sound that echoed off the rafters.

Jolted awake, Catriona sprang up from her pallet and rushed to the thrashing warrior's side. Thank the saints, they'd strapped him to his sickbed or he would have tumbled to the floor by now. The man's safety demanded restraints. There had been no choice. He'd never survive another round of bleeding.

"Shh…'tis all right. 'Tis all over. Ye're safe now." She wrung out a cloth in a basin of cool water and sponged it across the suffering man's forehead, daubing the sweat from his brow with slow, gentle movements. She laid a hand to his cheek, against the side of his neck, then rested it on the center of his broad heaving chest. Her heart lifted at the cool, clammy touch to his skin. "Praise be. Your fever's broke at last."

A relieved breath escaped her as she pressed the damp cloth along his throat and collarbone, wiping away the sheen of sweat the fever left in its wake. *Praise the Almighty, 'tis at last broken. Fierce thing it was.*

They'd rid his body of bullets, staunched his bleeding with red-hot irons, and sewn closed the worst of the damage left by the blades, but the fever had held to him with the stubbornness of a life-sucking demon. The man, nay, *Alexander* had faired no better for so long that Catriona had feared they couldna save him. She'd feared he'd die within days.

"Alexander," she said his name in a soft whisper, praying it would pull him from whatever dark terrors he still battled. "Alexander MacCoinnich, rest ye easy, lad. All is well and ye're safe here at *Tor Ruadh*."

Sutherland, the youngest MacCoinnich brother, had revealed Alexander's name. Catriona stole a glance around the hall. 'Twas as quiet as a tomb and dark as the maw of a cave except for what bit of golden light flickered from the hearths. A single candle sputtered on the mantel next to Alexander's makeshift bed. The shadowy forms on pallets scattered around the room remained still. The other men had grown accustomed to Alexander's outbursts during his fevered fits.

"Back to sleep with ye, my fine warrior. Find your rest. All is well." Catriona had discovered that the more she spoke to him, the calmer the great bear of a man became even in his unconscious state. As before, Alexander stilled, relaxing into his blankets and ceasing his attempts to snap the bindings around his arms.

Catriona shuddered, struggling to push the troubling memory of cleaning his wounds back into the darkness where it belonged. Elena and Gaersa had been right. Catriona hadn't been prepared for what they'd had to do to save him. 'Twas the stuff of nightmares. She cradled his face in one hand, the stubble shadowing the man's cheek tickling against her palm. Sympathy for him swelled within her heart. *God bless ye, my poor suffering lad. God bless ye and keep ye.* Tending to Alexander's injuries had cost him dearly, but it had been a case of damned if ye do or damned if ye don't.

Catriona combed her fingers through his dark, sweat-soaked hair and raked it back from his face. She pressed the cool cloth along the side of his neck and across his collar bone. A tired smile tickled the corners of her mouth as Alexander's breathing returned to a peaceful, steady rhythm with a gentle rise and fall of his chest. *At last.* The poor man rested. Stifling a yawn, she returned the cloth to the basin and turned away.

"Stay," whispered a deep voice, hoarse and rough but still so weak she strained to hear it.

Catriona whirled about, fearing she'd imagined the sound. She eased closer to the head of the bed. His eyes were open, dark and confused, but clear and lucid rather than wild with fever. She leaned over him so he could better see her in the weak light. "I'm right here. I'm no' going anywhere."

Even in the faint glow of candlelight, Catriona saw the uncertainty and leeriness in his eyes. Such dark eyes. Black as ebony but when the candlelight hit them just right they flickered to a shade of the deepest, richest brown.

"This…place?"

"*Tor Ruadh.* The keep of Clan Neal. Ye're safe here."

Eyes narrowing, Alexander's dark brows knotted into a fiercer scowl. "How?" The word croaked out from between his dry, cracked lips, his unblinking gaze searching her face.

"Our hunters found ye in MacAlpin's cave and fetched ye back here afore the lot of ye froze to death." She poured cool water into a wooden cup, soaked the folded corner of a clean cloth, and held it to his mouth. "Here. Wet your mouth with this for now and if that goes well enough, we shall try a wee swallow or two of water, aye?"

Alexander didn't answer, just allowed her to press the cloth to his lips, watching her with an unnerving look as she guided a few drops of water into his mouth.

Catriona squeezed the cloth against his parted lips, dribbling the water in a slow, steady stream until no more came from it. She took the cloth away and wet it again in the cup. He kept her locked in a fathomless, unblinking stare, scrutinizing her until her cheeks grew warm.

"Your kin are here, too," she said. Surely, he'd be worried after them. "Four brothers and two cousins."

"I dinna have four brothers." Alexander's voice still rasped rough as wagon wheels in gravel but seemed stronger for the water. He blinked hard and fast. His brow creased and his eyes narrowed. "Magnus. I remember Magnus being...there."

"Aye." Catriona nodded. "Magnus is here." Catriona nodded toward the wide hearth on the other side of the room. "He sleeps even now. Over there."

Alexander tried to rise, then halted with a jerk, emitting a low rumbling growl in tandem to falling back to his pillow.

"Be still with ye now!" Catriona grabbed the candlestick, holding the flickering light high as she checked the bandages wrapped around his thigh, shoulder, and midsection. "Shame on ye, sir! Ye canna afford more bleeding! I bid ye lie still this instant!"

Alexander rolled his head back and forth on his pillows with a frustrated groaning huff. At last, he stilled and the hint of a smile lifted the corners of the fine full lips that Catriona had noticed more than once. She'd even dared to wonder what those lips might be like if they ever touched hers. She'd ne'er been kissed before. Not really. Liam Bickerstaff had attempted a stolen kiss once when they were little more than children but that had been a clumsy bumping of lips, teeth, and noses. She blinked away the memory and forced herself back to the matter at hand.

"Daren't ye smile at my scolding." Catriona retrieved a cloth-covered crock from the bench. "Ye've shifted Elena's poultice wrap from your shoulder. Lie still now whilst I apply another." *Stop being the fool about this man. What ails ye?* Time to stop silly daydreaming about this fine warrior and concentrate on getting him healed.

Alexander's smile grew as he pulled in a deep breath, winced, then released it. The smile disappeared when he attempted to lift his arms. He jerked his forearms against the bands of cloth securing him to the table. "Why am I restrained?"

Amazing how a man could sound so strong and in charge even when he spoke in a rasping whisper. Catriona removed the cloth cover of the jar and stirred the poultice, her eyes watering at the rotten oniony smell. "Ye were wild with fever and we feared ye would throw yourself from the table and reopen your wounds." She removed the dislodged bandage from his shoulder and discarded it in a bucket under the bench. As she smoothed a generous amount of the stinking gooey paste on a fresh cloth, Catriona forced back a gag. The stuff stank like a rotting dung heap, but Elena swore it drew poisons out of the body.

"God's teeth." Alexander made a choking sound as he tried to shift away from her. He wrinkled his nose in disgust and turned his face away. "What the hell is that stinking mess?"

"A poultice. Draws out poisons." Catriona drew in as few breaths as possible and took care to breathe through her mouth. "Once your fevers are gone and dinna return, we willna have to use it." She forced herself not to smile as Alexander's nostrils flared and his strong jaw clenched whilst he stared up into the darkness.

"There. All done." She and Alexander exhaled together. The poultice still reeked, but the stench was bearable now that she'd covered it with several layers of linen.

"My brothers. Graham. All are here? And well? Graham's wounds. He lives?"

"Aye." Catriona rinsed her hands in the basin then dried them on a linen towel tucked into the belted waist of her apron. She nodded to the left of Alexander's bed. "Look over yon. Graham sleeps right there. His wounds were bad but not so bad as your own."

Alexander turned his head toward Graham then seemed to relax even more while he watched the rise and fall of his sleeping brother's chest. After a long moment of silence, he returned his focus to Catriona. "How long?" He paused and cleared his throat, flinching from the effort. "How long have we been here?"

"A wee bit less than a sennight." Catriona eased a fresh blanket up over him. "Are ye warm enough? Or do ye need another blanket?" With his fever broken, she didna wish for the man to become chilled.

"Untie me."

Catriona pondered the request. 'Twas true the fever had broken for now but who's to say it wouldna return? It had taken herself, Gaersa, and four strong stable lads to hold Alexander down and tie the bindings the first time. At this unholy hour, everyone was asleep and needed their rest. What if the fever returned and Alexander had another fit? She shook her head. "I think not. This is the first time ye've been sane enough to speak and cool to the touch. I fear the fever might yet return."

Alexander huffed out a frustrated cross between a snort and a groan. "I am fine. Untie me."

"When I tell ye 'no', I mean it," she said in the same tone she used when scolding her youngest brothers. "Now rest a while. When dawn breaks, if ye've remained cool to the touch, we'll remove the ties and change your bedding, but I dinna wish to wake Gaersa or any of the lads at this late hour to help me, ye ken?"

Alexander didn't respond, just glared at her with the muscles in his cheeks rippling as he gritted his teeth. It was all Catriona could do to keep from laughing out loud. Master Alexander MacCoinnich wasna happy with her at all.

Her heart went out to him. The man had to be suffering from lying flat of his back on a blanket-covered table. They'd done their best to cushion his legs and shoulders with blankets but they couldna turn him due to his injuries. An idea to console him came to her. Willow bark tea would ease his aches and if that went well enough, a wee bit of whisky could follow. *Best see if he can keep down water first.* She picked up the cup of water from the bench and held it where he could see it. "Will ye risk a swallow of water rather than the dribbling of a cloth?"

Alexander's face lit up as though she'd offered him a keg of whisky. "Aye, lass. That I will."

A belated thought dawned on her. Catriona realized she'd have to cradle his head and shoulders upward for him to drink without disturbing the stitched wound across his stomach. A sudden flush of warmth rushed through her. *Aye, well, there's no helping it.* She swallowed hard then slid her arm beneath his head and shoulders and held him propped against her. "Small sips, mind ye, your belly's been empty a great while." She thanked the stars above that she sounded a great deal calmer than she felt, what with a man's head and shoulders cradled up against her breast like a reclining lover. She did her best to concentrate on giving Alexander tiny sips.

"Ye're trembling," he said between sips, the look in his eyes sending an even hotter tingle through her.

"I'm having to stand on the tips of my toes," she lied. Aye, 'twas a bold-faced fib and she prayed he wouldna realize the truth. "One more sip and then I'll let ye lie back down for a while before we try the willow bark tea, aye? Elena's been ready to serve ye a tonic but ye've been too ill to drink it." She swallowed hard. Damned if she didna sound as breathless as a maiden caught in the gardens with a suitor.

Alexander gave her another look that took quite the toll on her already rapid heartbeat, then took one more long, slow drink from the cup. Damn him. 'Twas almost as though the man could see into her thoughts.

"Thank ye, lass," he said with a satisfied sigh that let her know he'd not only relished the drink but maybe the giving of it even more.

The feel of him in her arms and the way he rumbled against her when he spoke made it difficult to draw breath without shuddering. With a slow careful shifting, she lowered him back to the bed and slid out from under him with a smile and a quick nod before turning to set the cup away and attempt to regain her composure. She'd ne'er held a man that close before and it disturbed her to admit that it had been rather nice.

"Lie ye down," he said in a low tone that was no longer a rasping whisper. Replenished by the water, his voice was deep and strong yet quiet in honor of the darkness and all who slept around them.

"B-beg pardon?" Catriona turned back to him, heart now pounding so hard it almost choked her. She feared even Alexander could hear it. "What say ye?"

Alexander shifted on the pillow, turning his head her way. "I said, 'lie ye down.' Ye look weary and I fear I'm the cause."

Catriona dropped her gaze to the floor, not knowing how to respond. No one ever worried after her. Never had. Well, no one but Gaersa. The housekeeper had shown some concern for her well-being, but nothing over much. Even when her mother yet lived, everyone expected Catriona to be the strong one. She'd been born to it, or so her mother had often said. Catriona raised her head and forced a smile. "Dinna let it trouble ye. I assure ye I'm well. Thank ye."

Alexander watched her with those damned dark eyes of his that seemed to peer into her soul. After a brief moment, he gave her the barest nod and a smile. "Lie ye down, lass. I'll be fine."

"Call out if need be, aye?"

"Aye," Alexander said, his voice like a gentle caress she'd craved all her life.

Catriona stretched out on her pallet then curled to her side with her back to Alexander, every fiber tensed as taut as a fiddle string. Catriona's stomach knotted. *Sweet Jesu, what ails me?* She'd prayed for the man to awaken ever since he'd arrived and now that he had… She swallowed hard. Now that he had, she wasna all that certain how she felt about it. Granted, she was more than pleased that Alexander fared better and the fever had at last broken, but the man stirred a great many feelings within her, feelings she'd ne'er be able to share or embrace.

"Lass?"

"Aye?" Catriona lifted her head and waited.

"What be your name?"

"Catriona."

"Catriona," Alexander repeated. The way he rolled her name off his tongue with a deep gentle burring of his 'r's' made her shiver. He gave it a sound it had ne'er before possessed. "Catriona?"

"Aye?"

"Thank ye." Alexander paused for a heartbeat then said, "Thank ye for all ye've done. For me. And my men."

"Aye, now go to sleep." Catriona's cheeks warmed along with her at heart at such appreciation. "Dawn will be here in but a few hours and ye need your rest."

"Aye, lass. Rest ye well."

Not bothering to answer, Catriona breathed in a deep breath to calm herself, then let it ease out in a silent sigh. *If only.* She winced at the thought, squeezing her eyes shut as though blocking out the possibility. *Ye daren't hope, fool. Clan Neal is your husband and family.*

The tightness of unshed tears made her throat ache. Tears she'd held at bay ever since her dying mother had made her swear to watch over her younger brothers and see that her drunken brute of a father didn't destroy the clan with his foolhardy ways.

Mother had protected them all before that, protected them from Father's drunken tirades and shielded the clan as much as she dared. Catriona couldn't hate Mother for the burden she'd left her. Mother's vow of *til death do us part* had kept her married to a man she'd hated. A man whose cruel and calculating nature intensified with drink. Father was a soulless man who couldna make the right decision if his life depended not it. Mother had told Catriona that right before she had died. She'd also warned Catriona to always keep her chamber doors locked when she retired. Mother had ne'er said why. Catriona had suspected but ne'er asked. 'Twas easier to pretend an evil didna exist rather than speak about it.

And now a legacy Catriona ne'er wanted trapped her like the biting steel of a hunter's snare. The legacy to protect Mother's clan. Catriona's clan now. There would be no husband for her. What outsider would wish themselves bound to such a remote clan? What man would spend his life at *Tor Ruadh*, ever in the shadows of a drunk, inept chieftain and then under Calum's cruel leadership while Catriona did her best to protect her people?

Aye. I'll always be alone. I can ne'er leave Clan Neal.

She'd given Mother her word.

CHAPTER 3

*A*lexander stared up into the quiet darkness, finally aware of all that surrounded him in what felt to be a verra long while. The place, this high-ceilinged room that looked to be the main hall of the keep, hummed with the comforting noises of a safe place in the night. Burning logs popped and crackled. Embers shushed and hissed as the wood settled deeper into the beds of ash. A faint tang of wood smoke filled the air, mingling with the scents of the last meal cooked and the musk of slumbering men on their pallets. Life. The warm air of the room reeked with life.

Snoring. Alexander listened harder. He'd recognize that irritating nasal whistling anywhere. 'Twas cousin Alasdair. He huffed out a silent laugh, regretting the movement as pain shot across his middle. Who wouldha thought the sound of Alasdair's annoying snores would ever be a source of relief? Worry over his cousin's loss in the massacre had plagued him but thank the Lord above he'd survived and found his way back to them. Good. He hoped Ian, his other cousin, Alasdair's brother, had made it. The two brothers always fought side by side. Where one went, the other followed just as surely as the rising moon chased the setting sun.

He turned his head to the side and watched the steady rise and fall of his brother's chest and felt the better for it. He couldna remember the severity of Graham's wounds, but he knew for certain his brother hadna escaped unscathed during their dash to the tunnel.

A muscle spasm wrenched through him with vicious ferocity, interrupting his study of all around him. The cruel twisting burn knotted in his left thigh, seared its way up through his buttock, then ripped across the small of his back. Alexander grit his teeth and lifted his left leg, arching and flexing as much as he could to overcome the wicked cramp. He hurt from the tips of his toenails to the verra last hair on his head. He swallowed hard and did his damnedest not to groan aloud. *Lore a'mighty, what I wouldna give for a dram or two to dull the pain.*

After what seemed like an eternity, his knotting muscles eased to a bearable level. He tested the bindings around his forearms again. While they appeared to be nothing more than folded strips of linen, the infernal things held strong. A disgruntled snort escaped him. He needed to move about to relieve this damned cramping. He pulled at the ties again, straining against them. Sharp pain, a burning rip, deep and excruciating, radiated from his shoulder down to his middle, convincing him of the error of his ways.

Out of breath as though he'd just run across the glen, he sagged back into his pallet of blankets. "Sons a bitches," he said in a hissing whisper into the peaceful darkness. She had said lay still. Mayhap, he should heed the lass's advice.

The lass. Aye, as strong-willed a woman as he'd e'er met. Catriona.

The thought of her brought a smile and somehow lessened the torture of his discomfort. Memories of the last few days flickered broken and dim as a waning candle, but one thing he remembered well was the soothing sound of her voice telling him all would be well.

And then he had set eyes on her. Fair skin all aglow in the candle-light. Saint Bride herself had surely touched those fiery tresses that framed her face and shone like polished copper. The first time he'd opened his eyes, before he'd freed himself of that hellish fevered dark-ness, he'd thought for certain she was an angel sent to halt his suffering and guide his soul to the everlasting. He looked forward to the morning's light when he could better see her in all her glory.

He turned his head toward her pallet and listened. The rustling of blankets and uncomfortable shifting had finally stopped. He prayed that meant she'd found her rest. Regret shaded his thoughts. He hated that he'd caused the poor lass so much trouble. He closed his eyes and drew in a deep breath, remembering the tempting scent of her while she had helped him drink. She smelled of fresh linen, lye soap, and vibrant woman. He'd sip water 'til Hell froze over if she'd cradle his head against her that long. She'd been soft and warm, so much more comfortable and easing to his aches than any pallet or pillow.

A high-pitched sob followed by a rattling crash at the head of the hall interrupted his pleasant musing. Alexander shifted, turning his head and squinting to see through the heavy veil of shadows across the room. There were two figures. One slight of frame. A woman. The dim light flickering from the hearths made her white shift shimmer with the glow of a restless ghost. She cowered and pulled away from the larger figure. A man. He held tight to one of her arms.

"If ye had brought the port as I instructed, I wouldna have to punish ye!"

The lass cried out again, sounding piteous and lost. "Please..." Scuffling sounded. Benches overturned and hit the floor with a bang. The woman jerked and pulled away, struggling to free herself from the man. "Forgive me, sir. Please...ye're hurting me. Please let me go."

"Let ye go?" The man barked out a low, malicious laugh. "Not until I've corrected ye and ye've serviced me proper." A loud smack echoed through the room followed by the woman's heartbreaking cries. "My belt awaits ye in my room, now get the port and we'll carry on with the night's entertainment."

Alexander yanked against the bindings imprisoning his forearms. A sense of urgency and rising fury made him roar. "MacCoinnichs!" By damn, if he couldna help the women, his brethren could. "Mac-Coinnichs to arms!"

"Sweet Jesu!" Catriona shouted. She sprang up from her pallet and stormed up the length of the room toward the raging man and the sobbing woman. "Calum! Let her go this instant!"

Alexander wished the hearths cast more light. He struggled to make out the figures at the end of the room. One of them he knew to be Catriona. The one she'd called Calum was taller, towering over both the women, but the man's lanky form was narrow. Ignoring the ripping pain across his stomach, Alexander lifted his head and scanned the entire room, searching for someone able to assist the women. "Duncan, Sutherland, Magnus—get that bastard!"

"What the hell do ye think we're doing?" Duncan said with an irritated growl from somewhere deeper in the shadows behind Calum and the women.

Who the hell was this Calum? He prayed to God Almighty that he wasna Catriona's husband. A jealous twitch of possessiveness flashed through Alexander, increasing his frustration not only with his bindings but even more so with his weakened condition. He wished he was at Catriona's side rather than strapped to this damned table, Alexander flexed his fists as he watched the two in their heated back and forth. He couldna make out everything said, but he heard enough to make him wish he could step in and bring Calum to his knees.

With a frustrated shift from side to side, he yanked against the bindings with renewed fury. Damn the pain. He had to get free. "Dammit all to Hell and back!"

Catriona appeared to be holding Duncan and the rest of his men back to keep them from seizing the bastard. Why the hell was the lass protecting the vile devil? *I'd no' be kept from snapping that whoreson's neck.*

"Take your hands off me, bitch!" The hard crack of another slap echoed across the hall and Catriona stumbled back a few steps, the light from the hearth highlighting her form.

"Kill that bastard!" Alexander roared, adrenaline and rage fueling his strength so his loud bellow risked shaking the foundations of the keep.

"She'll no' let them kill him," Graham said from his sickbed where he had shifted to an upright seated position. "'Tis doubtful she'll even allow them to thrash him. The man's her twin brother, ye ken?"

"Aye, but mayhap they'll have the chance to make him wish he was dead afore she's able to stop them." The knowledge that Calum was Catriona's brother and no' her husband gave Alexander a small bit of comfort. He strained to see, craning his neck to look around Graham. "Move your arse! I canna see."

Graham huffed out an amused snort as he slid out of Alexander's line of sight. "'Tis good to see ye awake and back to your pleasant self, brother. I'm glad ye're alive." He turned and studied the scuffle at the head of the hall. "Looks to be ended and appears that Magnus and Duncan are escorting the next chieftain of Clan Neal to his chambers."

Alexander strained to verify Graham's observation. The poor lighting in the room made it difficult to discern that the two hulking forms on either side of Catriona's brother were in fact Magnus and Duncan. He could, however, tell that the men were no' struggling o'er much to drag Calum's thrashing and cursing arse from the room.

A brighter flickering light in his peripheral vision pulled his attention back to the head of the room. Catriona stood consoling the young maid keening out uncontrollable sobs. A heavyset woman, holding a candlestick high, stood with a hand under Catriona's chin. She drew near to Catriona's face and angled her jaw toward the light. The old woman jerked her head back and forth with such fervor that her silver-gray braid whipped back and forth across her broad back. Alexander wished he could join them to see for himself how Catriona fared. The blow had popped hard like the shot of gunfire and when Catriona had stumbled back from the impact, she'd almost gone to the floor.

Straining against the damn straps binding his arms, Alexander made an oath to himself. An oath he looked forward to keeping. *By Heaven above and Hell below, Catriona's brother will rue the day he was born.*

After what was entirely too long, in Alexander's opinion, Catriona released the young maid to the care of the older woman and made her way back down the hall toward her pallet. Head bowed. One hand to her cheek. She walked as one publicly shamed and drowning in humiliation.

Anger. Disgust. Frustration. The unmistakable ache to comfort Catriona and right the unjust wrongs he'd just witnessed. All those things pounded through him. He had to help Catriona. He didna ken how but he had to find a way.

"Catriona," he called out in an urgent whisper, praying she'd harken to his call.

Eyes averted, she paused a moment at the foot of his bed then continued toward her pallet as though he'd not spoken.

"Catriona, please." He had to speak with her, give her what reassurance he could, some small bit of comfort.

"Aye, Master MacCoinnich?" She stood just past the foot of his bed, her back to him, head still bowed.

"Master MacCoinnich?" Her formal address pained him no small amount. "Alexander, to ye. Always. Ye ken?"

She pulled in a deep breath, lifting her bowed head and straightening her shoulders as she did so. But she remained turned away. "Alexander, then. What do ye have need of, sir?"

"I need ye to look at me, lass. I need ye to come close and let me see with me own eyes how ye fare."

Catriona's chin dropped, and she stared down at the floor.

"Please, Catriona. Grant me the relief I seek by knowing ye're well after battling with that worthless bastard." He paused a hair's breadth. "I would see so with me own eyes, lass. Please."

"I am well, Alexander. I assure ye."

"Then show me. Let me see for m'self."

Catriona turned and eased her way over to the side of his bed, keeping her face turned aside. Even in the dim lighting, he could tell her eyes shone with unshed tears.

"Untie me, Catriona. I beg ye," he said in a soft whisper he hoped would gentle her turmoil. He needed to touch her. Give her what little comfort he had the power to give.

Her mouth tightening into a quivering line, Catriona retrieved a small knife from the table beside the bed. Without a word, she cut the strips of linen away from his arms.

Sensing she was about to step away, Alexander took hold of her wrist and with a light persistent tug, pulled her closer. "I mean to punish that bastard for what he did. He had no right." He loosened his grip, slid her hand into his and brought it to his mouth. With the most reassuring look he could manage, he pressed a kiss to the silk of her skin and gave her hand a reassuring squeeze. "Brother or no', he had no right."

"I shouldha moved faster. I erred by thinking him slowed by drink. 'Twas my error." Catriona hitched in a shuddering breath and stared across the room, focused on where the scuffle had occurred.

Alexander reached up and brushed a finger along the curve of her jaw. When she turned toward him, he cupped her face in his palm. "Ye didna err, lass, and ye should ne'er have to gauge your movements by how fast a blow might be given. No man should ever raise a hand to a woman."

Catriona closed her eyes and swallowed hard, leaning her face into his hand like a wee kitten starved for attention. Without warning, she stiffened and drew away.

"Catriona?" Puzzlement filled him. Why had the lass reacted so? Had he imagined her accepting his touch? What had changed to offend her?

"Ye need your rest and so do I." Catriona gave him her back then lowered herself to her pallet. "Go to sleep, Alexander, and try not to tumble off the table since ye're no longer tied, aye?"

"Aye." He wouldna trouble her further with words—not this night. But as he lived and breathed, he would have the woman know he would tend to her brother later and Calum Neal, chieftain or no', would ne'er lift a hand to his sister again. He'd damn well see to it.

"Alexander?" Catriona's soft whisper rose from her pallet, surrounding him like a mist rising in the glen.

"Aye, lass?"

"I thank ye...for giving a care."

"'Twas the least I could do for the woman who kept me from death's door." He tried to make it sound as though his caring was nothing more than a polite repayment of all she'd done for him. But deep in his heart he knew, 'twas a great deal more than that, and that realization troubled him no small amount. If he allowed his caring for Catriona to grow, what would become of him and all his caring when it came time to leave?

CHAPTER 4

*C*atriona angled her chin to the left and tilted her head back. She lowered her handheld mirror to better examine the spreading bruise along her jawline. The salve of arnica had faded the angry coloring a small amount but not as much as she'd hoped.

Spoiled wicked bastard. Catriona flinched as she pressed her fingers against the angry purplish spot and worked her mouth open and closed. At least the blow had been glancing, or it wouldha broken bone or cost her teeth. She stared at her reflection in the small oval mirror framed in wood, pondering the mess life had become of late.

"I fear I can no longer protect them, Mother," she whispered to her downcast reflection. "Not from Calum."

Calum had grown too cruel and calculating. To maneuver his edicts to protect the clan, as Mother had done with Father's demands for so many years, would prove impossible. Once Mother had died, Catriona had accepted the task as her own. She'd been a bewildered fourteen-year-old lass, but she'd promised Mother, sworn on her heart even that she'd carry on the protection of Mother's clan. So, she'd done it. What had helped her the most was that Father's health had faded as soon as Mother had died. In fact, Gordon Neal had sworn his ailments were because of the curse

Margaret Neal had placed upon him with her dying breath. 'Twas rumored Mother had been a white lady. Catriona knew in her heart the rumors to be true.

If only I'd inherited her gifts. Catriona stared at the bruise along her jaw. *Oh, what a curse I'd place on dear brother.*

Calum wasna in poor health and his evil grew stronger every day.

Catriona placed the mirror face down on her dressing table, then pressed her hand atop it, closed her eyes, and whispered a desperate prayer, "Show me how, Mother. Show me so I dinna fail ye in the keeping of my promise."

A light tap on the door interrupted her. Catriona rose from the small upholstered stool, pressed a hand to the taut ties of her bodice, then hurried across the room and opened the door. "Aye?"

Jenny, Sawny's older sister and according to Cook, the best kitchen maid in the keep, stood with hands clasped in front of her narrow aproned middle, squeezing her fingers so hard that her knuckles shone white. Jenny's pale blue eyes rounded wide and Catriona heard her faint gasp before Jenny dropped her gaze to the floor and curtsied. "Sorry to bother ye, m'lady, but Mrs. Aberfeldy sent me to fetch ye if ye be well enough to come downstairs."

"Of course, I'm well enough. What a curious thing to say." Catriona joined the young girl in the hall and closed the door behind her with a firm thud. She would assume her normal duties as though nothing had happened. 'Twas the only way to keep the rumors held to a manageable level.

The keep was a community all its own—a giant beehive with every individual connected to the other. When excitement occurred, frenetic whispers hummed from the highest turret down to the dirt floor of the root cellar. If the gossip remained unchecked, it would seize control of the keep.

She smoothed her apron over her wool skirts, then checked her pockets to make sure she had her essentials. Knife. Kerchief. Aye, she had them all. With a decisive nod to herself, she hurried to catch up with Jenny. "Has Mrs. Aberfeldy seen to our guests and their breakfast?"

Jenny paused mid-step and gave her a sideways glance as though pondering what should or shouldn't be said. "All but one, m'lady."

"What do you mean 'all but one'?"

"The big one, Master Alexander MacCoinnich, willna eat nor allow anyone but yourself to see to his bandages and bedclothes—so he said." Jenny scurried faster. "He's another reason Mrs. Aberfeldy sent me to fetch ye." Jenny lowered her voice, glancing behind them as she slowed her steps then cast a fearful glance around the curve of the stairwell. "She fears he's gone mad with the fever again—or taken by demons. The man's ranting has grown verra loud."

Catriona hated that Alexander had witnessed last night's humiliating display of brutishness. His roaring battle cry and calling his brothers to arms had echoed off the walls. And afterward—she cleared her throat and hitched in a quick breath. His kindness afterward had triggered a tender fluttering beneath her breastbone she had no right to feel. Fool she was. The man would leave as soon as he healed. He was a mercenary. Mercenaries didna tarry anywhere verra long.

She couldn't resist the faintest of smiles. Aye, but Alexander MacCoinnich was an honorable man. She almost ran down the last of the stairs, waving Jenny toward the kitchens as she headed to the center of the hall. "Thank ye, Jenny."

Jenny responded with a curt bob of her head, then darted off to her duties.

The servants storing away the visitors' pallets and setting up the tables for the morning meal shot startled glances her way. Their gazes lingered over-long on her face. Catriona's jaw throbbed. 'Twas as though their stares were prying fingers poking and prodding her bruise.

She lifted her head and set her teeth. *Let them stare. I'm no' afeared.* She focused her attention on the cluster of individuals milling about Alexander's sickbed. If not for the fact that Alexander's ranting sounded quite lucid, angry but lucid, Catriona would have felt concern.

She clapped her hands and raised her voice to be heard above their arguing. "Oy! Oy! What be the problem? The din ye're making will surely cause an avalanche on the mountain. Quiet with ye now, aye?"

Alexander's kin split as clean as the Red Sea had parted for Moses. They stepped away from his bedside, relief shining on all their faces.

Catriona shooed them away. "Go now. See to your own meals. Your food grows cold." She drew closer to the bedside and fixed Alexander with a stern look she usually reserved for her little brothers when they misbehaved.

Such fire snapped in the man's eyes. Catriona could understand why Jenny and Mrs. Aberfeldy feared him crazed with fever or mayhap even riddled with demons. *Dark eyes just a shinin', they are.* Last night she'd thought them black or perhaps the richest brown, but that was in the shadows. This morning they were the deepest blue fringed in white—as though mimicking a night sky filled with angry lightning. "I would think ye'd want your dressings changed. Do ye not? Since your fever's broken, ye willna have to endure any more of Elena's poultices and if ye behave, we'll see to sitting ye up in a chair, aye?"

"I wish them changed by you. No one else." Alexander glared at her, then his gaze settled on her bruised jaw. "And I mean to horse-whip that bastard as soon as I'm able, ye ken?"

"So ye said last night." *And I'd pay a hefty bag of silver to watch ye, my fine warrior.* Catriona turned away, half-fearing her thoughts would show in her eyes. She pulled her small *sgian dubh* from its sheath within her pocket and set to cutting the dressing away from Alexander's shoulder. "I appreciate the sentiment, Master MacCoinnich, but dinna trouble yourself. My brother isna worth your efforts, aye?"

He caught her wrist and held it above the dressings she was trying to cut away. "I've asked that ye call me Alexander, ye ken?"

"Aye, that ye have, *Alexander*. I'll do my best to remember." The uncharacteristic heat of a blush warming her cheeks, Catriona busied herself sorting through the assortment of jars and bottles on the bench beside her. *Stop being the fool,* she scolded herself. Land sakes, ye'd think she was a lass mooning after a laddie. She plucked up a small jar from the bench and turned back to him, determined to stop acting so silly. "I've a salve for your wrists. I'm sorry the ties chafed ye so."

Alexander gave her a dubious look. "'Tis no' that rotted dung again, is it? If so, I'd rather leave them to heal in their own good time."

"Nay." Catriona smiled. Alexander's curled lip and wrinkled nose lifted her spirits. "Elena scented this one with ground rose petals. I swear it." She pulled away the waxed cloth covering the jar and offered it to him. "Smell." She almost laughed aloud when he tilted his head to a leery angle and gave the jar a hesitant sniff. All the while, he watched her as though she might fling the noxious mess at him at any moment.

He relaxed back into his pillows and nodded as he held out both arms. "Ye canna blame me. Would ye no' rather reek of roses than the manure that fertilized them?"

"Aye," she agreed, unable to resist an unladylike snort of amusement. She daubed the salve on his reddened wrists then massaged it into his skin. Such strength. Even relaxed, his forearms rippled with hardened muscle, so large and bulked she'd never seen such. Catriona cleared her throat and bent to the task at hand, very much aware of Alexander's steady gaze upon her.

"Be ye in a great deal of pain?"

Alexander's deep, gentle tone held so much concern, she caught her breath. Catriona set her jaw and forced herself to keep her attention focused on the man's arms. "Nay. Dinna fret yourself. I'm quite well. I assure ye."

"I dinna believe ye, Catriona." The way he spoke—so low and soothing—he shouldna do so. Not with a tone filled with such caring it threatened to set her to trembling.

She avoided looking him in the eye, turning away to return the jar to the bench. "Aye. I *am* fine, ye ken?" Her hands trembled as she wiped them in her apron and struggled to assume a calm, detached demeanor. "Do ye wish to try and sit up for a while?"

"Aye." Alexander flinched as he rolled to his side too fast for her liking.

"Hold fast now! Let me help ye." Catriona rushed to snug her shoulder up beneath his, wrapped her arm across his broad back, and held on tight. "Slow now. Slow," she crooned as she supported him.

Alexander groaned as he swung his body around and shifted to a sitting position. "Holy Mother of God," he growled out. He wrapped his arm around Catriona's shoulders and held her tight. He bowed his head, hissing at the pain through bared teeth.

"Whisky!" Catriona shouted to a nearby servant. "Now!" She held tight to Alexander. The heat of him. The feel of him clutched in her arms. *Sweet Jesu, what would it be like if such a man chose to court me? Nay, not only court me, but claim me.* She caught her bottom lip between her teeth and forced away the unseemly thoughts. *For shame! He needs healing. Not some moon-eyed maid.*

The servant scurried back to them with a bottle and handed it to Catriona. She plucked out the cork with her teeth and hurried to put the bottle to Alexander's mouth and tip it for a long, healthy draw.

Alexander gulped down the promise of pain relief. With a deep pulling in and huffing out of whisky-scented breath, he relaxed with a faint groan then sidled himself to a seated position atop the bed.

Catriona eased a step back but kept a tight hold of his arm, secretly wishing she still had an excuse to snug up close to him. What was it about this man that attracted her so? His strength? His honor? In the short time he'd risen from his fever, he'd shown himself to be...what? *A caring man.* Aye, that's what it was. Unlike most men in her life, this man cared for others more than he cared for himself. He even behaved as though he cared for her welfare and she feared such caring 'twould be her undoing.

Blinking hard against the troubling revelation, Catriona stretched out her foot to pull a small wooden stool closer and eased Alexander's injured leg up on it. By the amount of pain his movement had caused, she verra much doubted he wished to sit upright for verra long. They wouldna move him to a chair beside the hearth today. He'd gone too pale, and she feared he was about to retch or topple over or both at any moment. She noted the proximity of the nearest bucket and slid it closer, too.

Mrs. Aberfeldy appeared bearing a tray with a small teapot,

another bottle of whisky, and a shallow bowl of a yellowish-brown liquid. "He needs to get this broth into himself then drink Elena's tonic." She placed the tray on a small table beside the bed and gave Catriona a knowing look as she tapped a finger on the corked bottle of spirits. "He'll need the whisky to cut the flavor of the vile stuff. The devil himself couldna stand that concoction."

Alexander didn't respond. He sat with head bowed and eyes closed, hands clenching the edge of the bed and arms locked in place. A sheen of sweat covered his brow and his breathing came shallow and fast.

Catriona picked up the bowl of broth, moved in close, and pressed the edge of the shallow wooden bowl to his mouth. "Try to get down just a wee bit," she coaxed. She brushed his hair back from his face, then wrapped an arm across his shoulders and squeezed. "Just one good sip of the broth and then I'll give ye enough whisky to make ye sleep. I promise."

"Sister!" The bellow came from the front of the hall, near the outer doors leading to the bailey.

"Make him come here," Alexander said in a low, dangerous rasping tone without lifting his head or opening his eyes.

Catriona placed the cup of broth back on the tray then returned to Alexander's side. Concern flashed through her. She noticed he trembled the barest bit. "We need to lie ye back down, Alexander. I fear we've done too much."

"Nay," Alexander said with a deep, rumbling growl. "Make...him... come here."

She didn't have to take any action to do as Alexander asked because Calum already stormed toward them, marching in and out between the rows of tables, his cloak billowing out behind him. He halted at the foot of Alexander's bed.

"I demand ye make one of those useless maids tend to this man," Calum said in a brutish tone that boomed across the hall. His scowl twitched and his eyes narrowed as his gaze settled on her bruise. "'Tis unseemly for ye to do such. I'll no' have it, ye ken?"

"Make him come closer," Alexander whispered, his gaze still locked on the floor.

"What did he say?" Calum snapped, his focus whipping from Catriona to Alexander and then back to Catriona.

Was that fear she saw in her brother's eyes? Interest piqued, Catriona took a step closer to Alexander and set her hand to his shoulder to steady him. "He said, 'come closer.'"

With an arrogant huff, Calum stomped around Alexander's propped foot, took a stance in front of him, then shoved his face to within inches of Alexander's nose. "Close enough for ye?"

Lightning fast, Alexander grabbed hold of Calum's throat, curled his fingers around Calum's windpipe and squeezed. "If ye ever strike a woman again, especially this woman standing beside me, I'll rip off your bollocks and shove them down your throat, ye ken?"

Calum's face flared to an alarming shade of red and his eyes rolled back. He clawed and slapped at Alexander's arm and hand, gagging and gasping for air as he sank to his knees.

"Alexander, ye must stop." Catriona shoved her way between them, one hand flat on the center of Alexander's chest as she tried to make him listen before he toppled off the bed. "He's not worth killing your-self over. Ye're too weak for this. Please stop for your own sake. I beg ye."

With a jerking shove, Alexander booted Calum with his uninjured leg and launched him back across a bench. A grim, satisfied look settled across his face as he sagged sideways back down to the edge of the bed.

Duncan, Sutherland, and Magnus rushed to help Catriona get Alexander straightened and settled safe in the bed's center.

"I want that bastard gone!" Calum croaked as he clambered back-ward and rose from the floor, one hand held to his fiery red throat. "I want all of ye gone afore I return. Ye hear me?" He made a sweeping motion with one hand, pointing at Alexander and all his men as he staggered back toward the bailey doors.

"They are my guests and I bid them stay as long they like." With Alexander guarded by his brothers, Catriona shoved her way through the overturned furniture toward her brother. "The chieftain of Clan Neal has granted them sanctuary and ye ken as well as I that Father willna take kindly to your usurping of his orders. He willna tolerate ye making him appear a weak, indecisive chieftain."

"Ye will pay for this, sister," Calum sputtered as he yanked open one of the tall double doors and squinted against the icy winter wind that whooshed in around it. "I swear on Mother's grave—ye will pay."

"'Twas well worth it," Catriona said as she watched the door close behind him.

CHAPTER 5

"Are ye in need of anything?"

"Your company if ye be of a mind to give it."

Alexander kent verra well he was acting a stubborn, demanding arse, but he didna care. Nothing soothed him like Catriona. The woman was a balm to his soul and gave him a brief respite from the gnawing guilt of his failure to protect Clan MacDonald. He'd watched her all morning. She'd flitted in, out, and around the great hall like a wee sparrow tending her nest. 'Twas time she sat and visited with him for a while.

"I see." Catriona motioned toward Magnus and Graham where they sat on either side of him. Her expression told him loud and clear she was privy to his self-serving antics but was willing enough to indulge him. "Ye have your brother and your friend here visiting with ye. Is that no' company enough?"

Magnus barked out a laugh and rose from his seat beside the hearth. "Come, Graham. I believe they have dismissed us good and proper."

Graham stood and gave Catriona a polite bow. "Ye have the patience of a saint, m'lady, a true saint." He turned to Alexander and nodded. "I'd call ye selfish, brother, but were the situation reversed, I

canna say I wouldna do the same." He nudged Magnus as they meandered away. "Would ye no' druther the company of the lass to
Alexander?"

"Aye. I would at that," Magnus said in a loud voice as he glanced
back at Alexander and gave him a wink.

Alexander ignored them and motioned toward the chair beside
him. "M'lady." He shifted in his own seat, flinching against the pain
the movement stirred. He resettled the foot of his injured leg on the
pillowed stool in front him, damning the weakness for the shackle
it was.

His discomfort didn't escape Catriona. Perched on the edge of the
seat, she made to rise again. "I'll fetch your tonic. 'Tis nearly time for
another cup of herbs."

"Nay." Alexander stayed her movement with a touch to her wrist.
"Talk with me. Time with ye will ease the pain more than any herb."

Catriona's fair skin flushed at the compliment, twin patches of
rosy red highlighted her fine cheekbones and spread to hide the light
dusting of freckles across her nose. "I'm pleased to see ye've improved
much. Grown stronger and left your bed longer each day." Her mouth
tightened, and she grew serious, glancing down as her voice fell to
little above a whisper. "Ye will take leave of us soon, I expect?"

The more time spent with Catriona, the more disturbing
Alexander found the thought of leaving. Each time the unpleasant
subject reared its head, he'd push it to the back of his mind. He
couldna face that prospect just yet. He'd deal with that when the time
for leaving came. His heart lightened as the howling wintry wind
chose that moment to rattle the windows in their casings. "If ye feel ye
can bear our company, we would most certainly appreciate your
hospitality 'till winter eases its hold on the land." He nodded toward
the ice-encrusted windows. "'Twould be vicious hard traveling
through such as this."

"Oh, aye. 'Tis true." Catriona's quick agreement bolstered his
spirits even more. She leaned toward him, her sweet smile lighting up
her face. "Especially with ye and your brother weak as ye are from
your wounds. A wise man would delay any travels 'til spring. The

drifting snow in the passes can be verra treacherous." She glanced away, turning aside as though checking on the servants cleaning the candlesticks lined along the top of the whisky cabinet. "We can only hope poor Calum returns home safe from wherever he's gone." Catriona's tone did not convey the slightest sincerity or worry about her brother's welfare.

Alexander couldn't help but laugh. "Agreed."

Since she'd been the one to speak the devil's name, Alexander couldna resist prying. As they'd spoken each day, they'd worn through the words of polite niceties that were prim and proper, avoiding anything too personal. He tired of skating around the subject that truly piqued his interest. He wanted to know Catriona, and all that was her life. A pang of leeriness twitched through him. Was it ill-fated to get closer to the lass? Would that no' make his leaving all the more difficult? He swallowed hard and shoved the leeriness away. *T'hell with it.* He'd leave those worries for another day.

"*Tor Ruadh* is a fine keep," he said with a nonchalant wave of one hand toward the entire room.

"I thank ye." Although Catriona gave him a polite nod, Alexander didna miss the slight narrowing of her eyes accompanying her correct by society's standards response.

"I understand your father is quite ill." He'd ne'er been good at dancing around with words but he had to figure out a way to ask the woman why the blazes she hadna married and moved away from what appeared to be her own personal hell. He realized 'twas none of his affair but he wanted to know. Mayhap he could…help her. He'd heard rumors about Chieftain Gordon Neal and seen firsthand the cruelty of his son. Catriona still bore the fading bruise along her jawline that angered him every time he saw it.

"Father has been unwell for some time. Seems to have started when my mother died."

"Mourning can do that to a soul." Although Alexander doubted verra much that was what ailed the Neal chieftain—not if the rumors were true.

"Doubtful. Mother died a little over nine years ago. Closer to ten."

Catriona frowned down at her folded hands nestled in her lap. A controlled sigh escaped her. "Some would say paying for one's sins might cause one's health to fade." She cleared her throat and lifted her gaze, allowing it to follow the maids moving about the room sweeping and dusting. "But no matter. He bides his time in his rooms now, leaving everyone else in peace."

"Everyone but yourself." Perhaps he shouldna have said that, but the words sprang forth as though he had little control of them. A sense of thankfulness washed across him when Catriona didn't react, just acted as though she hadn't heard him. "I'm surprised Calum hasna claimed the chief's seat for his own." She must no' mind his prying. She hadna risen from her chair and stormed away. He had to find out more.

Her scowl shifted to a perplexed look as she stared off into space. Catriona gave the barest shake of her head. "Calum willna cross Father—no' even in his ever-weakening state." She turned and met Alexander's gaze. "He fears him, I think, even now."

Alexander reached out, slid his fingers under Catriona's forearm, then scooped up her hand and held it in his own. "Why are ye still here, Catriona? Why have ye no husband and children of your own?" There. He'd asked the question that had burned inside him, plaguing him more and more each day. He needed to know Catriona's story.

"I promised Mother I'd protect her clan." Catriona stared down at her small pale hand that disappeared within his grasp. "I swore to it on her deathbed."

"Such a waste," Alexander said then flinched. He'd not meant to speak the words aloud.

Jerking her hand away, Catriona tucked it back into her lap. "An oath is an oath," she said as she stared downward, head bowed as though in prayer. With a deep breath, she lifted her chin and gave him a look that sent a chill down his spine. "Besides—why would ye, a mercenary such as ye are, concern yourself with whether I'm wasted or no'? Ye will move on as soon as ye're healed and the snow melts. *Tor Ruadh* and all who dwell within it will be forgotten."

She challenged him. He'd pried into her secrets, stirred her defenses, and now she challenged him. Time to tread with care. He shifted in the chair, laced his fingers over his middle, then tapped his thumbs together as he proceeded with caution.

"Kindness is ne'er forgotten," he said. He dared to meet her irritated stare. "Ye saved my life and the life of my kin. How could I ever forget such a thing?" He'd never forget her. Her kindness. Her caring. Her courageous fire. He kept his gaze locked upon her, memorizing every feature. The lustrous copper of her hair. The creaminess of her skin highlighted with a dusting of freckles. Those tempting curves. Such enticing softness. Her scent. *Nay.* He'd never forget her so long as he lived. "I'm indebted to ye, Catriona, and I thank ye for all that ye've done."

She didn't say a word, just agreed with a polite nod and looked away.

They sat in silence for what seemed like forever, their conversation stalled. Alexander cursed his ineptness at social chatter. *If only I had Magnus's gift with the lasses.*

Catriona cleared her throat. "Ye asked a great deal about myself, Alexander, but ye've told me verra little about your own life." She gave him a smug look as though she'd baited a trap and felt sure he was doomed to step into it. "How did ye come by all those wounds that brought ye to my keep? Before ye woke from your fever, your brothers said ye were mercenaries but would no' explain anything beyond that. They said ye would tell me."

"Aye. We are mercenaries for hire. 'Tis true." He was too ashamed to tell her everything, but he'd tell her some. He owed her that much. "Unfortunately, with our latest quest, the odds were no' in our favor."

She watched him, silent as a judge. 'Twas clear she waited for him to continue so that she might weigh the truth of his words.

"We come from Islay," he said, staring down at his bandaged leg and the sickly bruised skin bordering the linen strips wrapped around his thigh. "Our clan, the MacCoinnichs, is gone." It pained him to say such a thing aloud but there was no escaping the truth. "We, my brothers and two cousins, are some of the few of a once vibrant clan that made the best whisky ye ever placed upon your tongue."

"What happened?" Catriona asked in a hushed tone.

"Putrid throat." He remembered the malady well. The aching. The fever and then the sweats. Feeling as though well-honed blades had lodged in his throat. "My brothers, my cousins ye've met here, and only a handful of others survived." He pulled in a deep breath and allowed it to ease out. "There wasna enough of us to bury the dead in proper graves. We did the best we could for them and remember them in our prayers, begging their forgiveness."

The soft, calming weight of Catriona's light touch on his arm urged him on. Alexander nodded toward his men where they sat gathered at one of the long trestle tables on the other side of the room. "The seven of us agreed to band together and survive." He shifted and looked at Catriona, his heart swelling at the compassion shining in her eyes. "The five or so others that withstood the scourge are scattered." He shrugged with a shake of his head. "I reckon they're settled now. Somewhere. 'Twas but a few distant cousins."

"I'm more than a little sorry for your loss." Catriona squeezed his arm, her gentle understanding a balm to the wounds he'd never tended. She soothed his soul, somehow eased the painful memories. "But take heart—ye have your brothers. The lot of ye could rebuild Clan MacCoinnich. Who tends the land ye left behind?"

"Campbells." Alexander spit out the word. "The king gave it to them when they discovered the fate of Clan MacCoinnich." 'Twas but another reason he and his brothers had jumped at the chance to serve the MacDonald of Islay, who was once known—and would always be known in Alexander's mind—as Lord of the Isles.

"M'lady?" A tall, stocky lass that looked stout enough to take up a sword and fight alongside any man came to a halt a few feet in front of them. "Mrs. Aberfeldy says Himself is ringing the bell for ye."

Catriona's demeanor transformed. Gone was the kind, hopeful young woman, replaced by a tensed lass with dread straining her features. "Thank ye, Leona. Tell Mrs. Aberfeldy I'll see to him right away."

The lass gave an obedient nod then lumbered off toward the kitchens.

"I must go," Catriona said, regret lending a heaviness to her tone. She rose from her chair, took a step forward, then paused and looked back at him.

Alexander held his breath, unable to read her or discern what she was about to do.

After stealing a glance around the room, Catriona darted to his side, pecked a quick chaste kiss to his cheek, and squeezed his arm again. "Ye can rebuild your clan, Alexander. Never give up hope when it comes to your kin." Then she turned and fled before he could react.

Alexander watched her scurry away, hand pressed to the side of his face she'd just kissed. "Never give up hope," he repeated in a whisper. Hope. What dangers and heartache could something as simple as hope bring to a man's life?

CHAPTER 6

"Nay, daughter. No light. Damn your callous heart! Ye ken how it pains me when I'm beset with the miseries. Bring me port and leave me be."

The stifling hot room reeked with the stench of rotting food, rancid wine and an overripe chamber pot. The thick noxious air spread a nasty greasiness throughout the space.

Catriona ignored her father's pleas and yanked the heavy velvet curtain aside. She secured it to one side of the double set of windows, fastening it with a braided rope looped around an iron hook embedded in the stone wall. If not for the winter storm howling outside, she would've push the windows open wide for the relief of fresh air.

With her basket balanced on her hip, she busied herself gathering empty bottles and soiled vessels littering the room. She spared a glance back at her sire. "The light of a winter morn is weak enough for your ailing, I reckon, and a bit a sunshine will aid in driving the miseries away." She paused in her tidying and nodded toward the tray she'd placed on the table beside his bed. "Drink the tea. Elena steeped it extra strong this morn. 'Twill help ease the ache in your head."

Gordon Neal, chieftain of Clan Neal, shielded his eyes with one shaking hand while he made a weak attempt at pawing his other hand toward the tray. "Nay, ye have set it out of me reach, Catriona. I told ye me ailing is fearsome today. Why must ye test me so? Damned, if ye are no' as malicious as your vile witch of a mother."

"Verra true, Father. Catriona thinks only of herself. How many times have I told ye of her wickedness?" Calum said as he entered the lavish unkempt chamber. He strode to the side of his father's bed and moved the tray to rest across the bleary-eyed man's lap. "There now. Drink your tea and eat your parritch whilst it's piping hot, aye?"

A slow-burning rage simmered deep within Catriona like a cauldron about to boil over. Even though the ugly bruise along her jaw had faded, her thirst for revenge had not. *Bastard.* Alexander might have brought Calum to his knees for the unacceptable behavior but she'd yet to have her turn at teaching him a lesson. He had surprised her with the hit. She'd no' allow him that advantage again. He'd best shield his bollocks well. She was no timid maid afraid to fight back.

A grunt escaped her as she hefted the basket filled with empty bottles and whisky skins over to Calum and dropped it square on his extended foot. Hard. With any luck, she'd smashed at least one of his toes. "Here. Take these to the larder when ye leave."

Calum wouldna dare lose his temper again and nor would he attempt any ill will toward her in front of their father. Father had looked almost fearful when he'd seen her bruise and sworn that Calum would be punished—horse-whipped, in fact. He'd mumbled something about Mother's curse gaining strength and becoming worse if he didna take proper recourse. *"Ye must never be touched,"* he'd mumbled to her on more than one occasion. Then he'd always add, *"Even though ye're sorely hated and reviled."*

Father had never attempted to hide the fact he despised her even more than he disliked his four sons. She figured that was the reason Mother had always bid her to lock her chamber doors. Perhaps Mother feared Father might try to kill his own children.

Father's threat of a horse-whipping had not only been futile, but ill-timed. Calum had escaped punishment with his absence from the keep for over a fortnight, closer to a month even. But if dear brother lost his temper again, she felt sure Father would remember and react accordingly. Catriona blew out a heavy sigh. So hypocritical since the son had learned his cruel ways from the father. Sober, Gordon Neal was a brutish, indecisive man concerned with appearances and what others thought about him and his clan. He'd grown to depend on Catriona's judgment regarding the managing and betterment of the clan but wanted everyone to think it was him. Drunk, Gordon Neal became vicious and tyrannical, treating everyone with the hatred and contempt he felt for himself.

"Damn damn damn." The Neal fretted and coughed, fluttering both hands above his bent shoulders as the entire contents of his breakfast tray dumped across the bed.

"And *that's* why ye dinna set the tray across his lap, fool." Catriona hurried to mop up the spilled tea and parritch before it soaked through every layer of her father's bedding.

Calum didn't respond. Just glared at her with contempt simmering in his eyes. He kicked aside the basket of empty bottles, strode over to the chamber door, and bellowed, "Orlie! In here now and tend to your master." He slammed the door closed and blew out a disgusted breath. "Christ, this room stinks. What the hell do we feed those lazy maids for if they canna tend to their duties?" Facing Catriona, Calum jabbed a finger at her. "And I'm no' the *fool* in this room. I have news about your guests."

A chill stole across Catriona, twisting a knot of dread in her middle and prickling gooseflesh across her arms. Calum looked even more cold and calculating than usual. She hadn't seen him since Alexander had choked him down to his knees. Where had he been and what in the name of all that was holy had he been doing? Calum had sworn revenge. Pray, what had he set in motion? She kept her brother in her sights as she gathered the upended teapot, bowl, and cup from her father's bed and stacked them on the tray.

"Dinna fill the tray over full next time and that willna happen, ye ken?" The Neal plucked at his linens with an agitated shake of his head. His thin legs worked back and forth beneath the covers, he struggled to scoot his skeletal frame closer to the edge and out of the path of the wet covers. He waved her away with an impatient jerk of his hand. "Leave it, girl, until Orlie comes. The bed be large. This edge be dry and the covers will dry soon enough. I'll just lie here 'til then."

"Ye'll do no such thing," Catriona said, knowing he'd soon berate her for leaving him to lie in soiled bedclothes if she followed his orders. She turned to Calum where Duff and Hew, two of the devoted miscreants sworn to carry out his every cruel whim, had taken their posts beside him. With a tight hold of one of her father's thin arms, she motioned toward his other arm. "Help me move him to his chair and one of ye see where Orlie's gone to and fetch him to change the bedclothes and get our chieftain dressed, aye?"

"I summoned the lazy wretch already. Did ye no' hear me? Where the hell is he?" Jerking a thumb toward the door, Calum sent Duff to find the servant then moved to his father's other side. A look of disgust screwed his usual scowl even tighter. "Judas! He reeks of piss."

"I couldna make it to the chamber pot, boy. Dinna disrespect me, aye? I still be chief of this clan and master to ye. Ye will do as I order or rue the day. I'm no' too weak to punish ye, ye insolent bastard." The frail old man, once tall and hulking, shuffled along between them, bent at the middle, his back humped between his shoulders. They half-led, half-carried him to his prized wingback chair that Calum had brought for him all the way from England. Once they'd settled him in the chair, the balding man hugged and patted his bony arms around his middle with awkward jerking movements. "Stoke the fire and bring me a dram. 'Tis bitter cold in here. Be ye trying to kill me with a deathly chill?"

Catriona fetched a clean wool blanket from the wardrobe, spread it across his knees, and tucked it up around his thin shoulders as she nodded toward the hearth. "The wrap will do ye. If we stoke the fire anymore, the soot will catch and burn down the keep as sure as we're standing here. 'Tis already hot enough in here to roast a goose."

She straightened as Duff and Orlie entered the room. Without an attempt to hide her contempt, she clasped her hands at her waist and allowed herself a weary sigh. "Orlie's here now to tend to him so speak your news, Calum. I can tell ye're fair bursting at the seams with it." *Better get it in the open and face it head-on.*

"I want him to hear this," Calum said as he pushed Orlie aside and took a stance in front of the Neal's chair. He pointed at Catriona as he spoke. "Ye ken it was seven men she tricked ye into taking in right in the dead of winter, aye? Seven, mind ye. Extra mouths to feed. And some so injured that our stored herbs and tonics verra likely willna last 'til spring. I grant ye she didna tell ye all of that, did she?"

"Not enough tonics?" the Neal muttered as he shifted his irritated squint-eyed gaze to his daughter. "Be the seven strangers drinking all our whisky and port, too?" The pale old man wet his thin lips and plucked at the folds of his blanket with trembling fingers. His head dipped and shook back and forth, stricken with the same tremors of his hands. "Why would ye trick me into doing such a thing, ye vile, useless girl? Why would ye risk the survival of our clan? We canna survive without our medicines. Be ye certain 'tis wise to house so many guests during the winter?"

It took every ounce of self-control that Catriona possessed to keep a civil tongue in her head. She knew damn well that the keep's supply of port, whisky, and ale was her father's primary concern. A plan of reasoning came to her as her gaze lit on a small worn bible, a carved wooden cross, and several unlit candles on a small table in the corner. "I did it for the sake of your soul, Father. Be ye forgetting your scriptures? 'Be not forgetful to entertain strangers: for thereby some have entertained angels unawares' Hebrews 13:2." With his fear of her mother's dying curse on his life and his diminishing health made all the worse by excessive drink, her father had become a very devout man when sober, fretting about the final destination of his soul with fear-filled obsession.

"There is that," her father admitted in a weak murmur, his worried gaze dropping to the floor. "But I hope we dinna run out of tonics," he added.

"Ye havena heard the worst of it," Calum continued. His voice rang with excitement, so much so that Catriona expected the fool to hop in place at any moment like a schoolboy tattling tales. "The men she took in are allies of the MacDonalds of Glencoe. Are they not, Duff?" Calum waited for Duff's dutiful nod of his shaggy head before continuing. "And remember we heard old MacIain was late in taking his oath of allegiance to King William. Ye ken what Lord Stair said could happen to clans who didna take the oath."

"Severe reprisals," the Neal said in a hypnotic whisper, his blood-shot eyes widening as he stared unblinking at the fire crackling in the hearth. "And Stair has the ear of the Court."

How could her father know so much about such things? The man stayed drunk and never emerged from his private rooms anymore, much to the relief of all in the keep. She couldna remember the last time he'd taken a meal in the hall. It had to be the elders' weekly visits to his chambers. They must be keeping him apprised.

I shall speak to them about such. It must stop.

Catriona patted a reassuring hand to her father's shoulder. "None of the men we took in have claimed fealty to Clan MacDonald of Glencoe. I'm sure there's no' a thing to worry after since Calum took Clan Neal's oath in your stead last October before the weather grew so fierce. King William kens well enough where our clan's allegiances lie." She shot a glare at Calum, willing her twin to shut his maw and stop worrying their father with such. The man would drink himself into his grave if he feared a reprisal from the king—any king, be it James or William. Her father's only true loyalty was to his drink. It pained Catriona to admit that her father was a fool, but she'd rather have him alive and the manageable chieftain of Clan Neal than Calum. *Better the devil ye know than the devil ye don't.* Problem was, she knew the devil that was Calum all too well.

"Ye have given her too much power," Calum said with a jabbing motion toward Catriona. His eyes glittered with malicious intent. "The clan thinks she speaks for yourself. They've no way of telling if they're following your commands or carrying out Catriona's whims."

"Perhaps the men should go," the Neal mumbled as he took his head in his hands and scrubbed at his temples with the tips of his thick, yellowed fingernails. He looked up at Catriona, confusion and worry fighting for supremacy in his eyes. "Daughter? Should they no' be put out to spare our own?"

"Nay," Catriona said without hesitation, placing herself between her father and her brother. She bent and placed a hand atop the arms of the chair and came nose to nose with her father. "If we deny them shelter now, 'twould be the same as committing murder. Do ye wish to bear such a stain on your soul when ye reach the gates of everlasting?" She knew this angle would win the argument. Her father had come to fear the wrath of Almighty God above all else—especially since he'd committed so many grievous acts during his lifetime and now tried to forget them with the deadly sin of gluttony, drowning his memories with the fermented fruits of the field or the vine.

"Orlie!" Her father shifted in his chair with a frantic jerking movement, glancing about the room until his focus settled on his personal servant. "I must dress and go to chapel. There is much to pray and ponder."

Orlie set aside the soiled bedclothes he'd stripped from the bed, gave Catriona's father a bobbing nod, then kept his gaze locked on the floor as he shuffled about the room gathering the items his chieftain needed.

Catriona knew her father might have good intentions, but he'd never make it down the steps much less past the great hall and its well-stocked cabinet of port and whisky displayed behind the chieftain's table. Catriona peered at him closer and the realization hit her. He seemed a great deal weaker this morning. Last night's emptying of bottles appeared to have been harder on him than usual. The thought pushed aside, she turned to Calum as she headed toward the door. "A word, brother?"

Surprisingly, Calum followed her without protest, even instructing Hew to close the door after they'd all entered the adjoining room that was the chieftain's solar. He took a stance in front of the small hearth and Duff and Hew resumed their posts on either side of him like well-trained dogs. Their brainless brawny bulk made up for Calum's tall, thin lankiness. The two men had followed Calum's every step even as children, comprising a most efficient bullying force more than happy to bring Calum's cruel ideas to fruition. As lads, the three had terrorized the younger children of the keep. As men, if given the opportunity, Catriona knew in her heart of hearts they'd torture and terrorize the entire clan.

Catriona also remained standing. She'd be damned if she'd sit and feed into Calum's illusion he was above everyone else and had the right to look down his bulbous nose at them all. Just as she opened her mouth to speak, Calum had the audacity to shush her and held up a hand.

"Before ye say whatever it is ye plan to say, I ask that ye allow me to speak my heart."

Instinct and experience sent a rush of adrenaline through her, tensing Catriona for whatever her brother was about to say or do. She strained to hold her tongue and refrain from any rash statements that might compromise her or the clan. She clasped her hands in front of her middle and gave him a nod. "Speak."

Calum gave her a half-hearted bow and a belittling nod. Wickedness glowed in his gaze like a poorly banked fire. "I feel I must apologize for our little mishap the other night."

"Mishap?" Catriona sidled toward the door leading out to the hall, not stopping until she'd reached the pillow-strewn settee angled in front of it. She didn't trust Calum as far as she could throw him and wasn't about to let herself get cornered with no escape. "I dare say striking me was no' a mishap." She rounded the settee and stood behind it, keeping it between herself and Calum. She folded her hands atop the cool satiny cushion of the lounging chair's curved back. "Ye meant to hit me. Ye know damn well that ye did, Calum."

"I daren't deny I was determined to deal the blow, but it truly was a mishap, sister." Calum cast a sly look first to Duff and then to Hew. "The hall was dark and ye most certainly startled me whilst I was attempting to punish that unruly maid. I didna ken it was yourself I'd hit until I had struck the blow. Your weariness from tending to those men along with all your other responsibilities has skewed your memory to be sure."

"We could fertilize the garden with those words, brother." Catriona gripped the cushioned back of the chair tighter, digging her nails into the braided binding tacked to the wooden frame. "Think me a fool?"

Calum's eyes narrowed. His ruddy face darkened to an even redder shade and his hands closed into fists. "I've given ye an apology. Behave like the lady ye're supposed to be and accept it, aye?"

Why was it so important to him for her to accept his apology? Calum had no conscience. Never had. Never would. Duff and Hew seemed filled with unusual interest in the conversation, too. "I'll accept your apology if ye'll agree to leaving our sire alone about our guests. I'll no' have ye worrying him, ye ken?" The longer she kept her father alive and well, the longer she could shield her clan from Calum.

"Your guests were there, Catriona. They fought at Clan MacDonald's side. *Against* men loyal to King William." Calum took a step forward, hands now relaxed and clasped in front of his middle as though he watched a baited trap with evil anticipation.

Catriona swallowed hard. The implications of what Calum suggested raced through her mind. The repercussions of giving aid to traitors of the Crown could decimate their entire clan. But Calum's smug, victorious look gave her pause. He knew how she felt about their clan. He'd watched her toss aside dreams of a husband and children to keep her oath to their dying mother. What if he was lying? *'Twould no' be the first time. He wants them gone because he fears them. Their strength. Their possible alliance with me. He fears me.* That knowledge calmed her, gave her strength. As a woman with four brothers, she couldna hope to be named chieftain. But if she had enough strong allies of her own, when Calum was named *Tanist* and made chieftain of Clan Neal, perhaps she could protect her clan by curbing his cruel ways, just as her mother had done with their father. She lifted her chin to a defiant angle. "Perhaps they were there. But they're no' hunted men. Ye ken as well as I that if the Laird of Glen Lyon was determined to seek and capture traitors, they wouldha already been here searching. Captain Robert Campbell wouldna risk angering the Earl of Breadalbane by allowing anyone to slip through his fingers."

"As ye've said yourself, dear sister, 'tis winter and snow is still verra deep in places—making travel much slower. But I assure ye, there are many routes still passable. Stair informed Breadalbane that he wanted Clan MacDonald rooted out. They will be here—eventually."

How could her brother know these things? How could he know the druthers and machinations of John Dalrymple, Minister for Scotland and Master of Stair? Catriona backed toward the outer door and took tight hold of the ornately fashioned latch. The cold hardness of the metal grounded her. "These men bear the name MacCoinnich, not MacDonald. They've claimed no fealty to Clan MacDonald." *At least, not the MacDonalds of Glencoe.* She prayed that were true. A long conversation with Alexander was most definitely in order. "I bid ye let things be. I'm sure they'll be gone come spring and the melting snow."

Calum smiled and closed the distance between them. He drew so close that Catriona retreated, opening the door and edging out into the hall. The urge to run was strong. Calum's smile was no' a smile of genuine happiness but an arrogant, sinister smile as though a devious plot had come to fruition.

"Spring." He nodded, a thoughtful look adding even more cause for her to worry as he strode around the settee and took hold of the edge of the door. He huffed out a silent laugh as he jerked the door free of her hand and swung it open wider. "Aye, I'll leave it be 'til spring. After your wedding."

Catriona swallowed hard as she stepped back, blinking at the disbelief flooding her senses. *Nay. I had to have misheard.* "Wedding?"

"Aye. Your wedding, dear sister." Then Calum shoved her the rest of the way out into the hall and slammed the door shut in her face.

Catriona barely heard her brother's infuriating guffaws over the roaring of her heartbeat pounding in her ears.

Wedding? Grabbing the latch with both hands, Catriona knew Calum had locked the door before she even tested it. What cruelty had Calum plotted this time? The knowledge of her brother's penchant for making other's lives miserable stoked the dread growing within her.

She could only imagine what sort of man he'd found to torment her. "Open this door, Calum! I demand it!" She pounded on the door, even resorted to a hard kick, succeeding in only hurting her foot.

Calum and his coconspirators just laughed all the harder, and the door remained locked.

CHAPTER 7

*S*omething had extinguished the fire in her eyes and she'd gone so pale even the dusting of freckles across her nose was difficult to discern. Rather than the usual purposeful grace and bounce in her step as she went about her duties, her actions were stiff and jilted. She behaved as though her mind was troubled, trapped elsewhere in a place she couldna escape. She'd been this way for days.

This afternoon, Alexander studied her with growing concern. She meandered between the tables in the great room. Mindless idle movements, gaze focused somewhere off in the distance while her hands worried with a bit of linen. Several times during her walk about the hall, she snatched the dainty cloth from inside her sleeve and dabbed it to the corners of her eyes after a furtive glance around to ensure no one looked her way.

Alexander shifted on the bench beside the hearth, keeping his bandaged leg stretched out along it and the other foot on the ground as he sat at the table studying Catriona. What had caused such a change in her?

He suspected that bastard brother of hers was responsible but she'd seemed well enough after the night Calum had struck her. She'd been the same lively Catriona he'd awakened to when his fever broke.

She'd even refused to speak of the incident, brushing his concern away as though her brother's behavior was naught more than a minor annoyance. Of course, that was when Calum had been away from the keep for most nigh a month. Catriona's melancholy had taken hold upon his return.

Nay. Calum had to have done something to quell her spirited nature, and Alexander was damn well inclined to find out just what that something was. When she came close enough, he reached out and touched her arm. "Catriona—lass, sit with me for a wee spell, aye?"

Catriona caught her breath and jerked her focus to him, batting her eyes as if startled out of a deep sleep. "Beg pardon?"

"Sit with me, lass," he repeated in a quiet tone as though gentling a skittish filly. He swung around on the bench and faced the hearth, repositioning his injured leg with a strained grunt. He patted the spot beside him. "Sit for a while. I'm weary of my kinsmen's complaining about being hemmed in by the Highland winter. Tell me more about Clan Neal and how your people came to be here so high upon Ben Nevis."

To be honest, he didna give a rat's arse why Clan Neal had settled in such a remote part of the Highlands, at an almost inaccessible point on Scotland's highest mountain, but 'twas all he could think of to say to convince her to sit. Something about Catriona made it hard for him to settle on words to share with her. No woman had affected him in such a way since he'd been a young lad foolish enough to think himself in love. He brushed aside that memory of so long ago. 'Twas different now. He was older. Wiser. He patted the bench again and smiled. "Come. Tarry and rest awhile. Ye deserve a wee respite after dealing with the lot of us and listening to our nattering to be on our way."

She paused, crumpling the linen in the hand she held fisted against her waist. The faintest of smiles flickered for a moment along the corners of Catriona's tempting mouth then she lowered herself to the bench beside him. Rather than looking at Alexander, she stared down into the dancing fire of the hearth. "Perhaps today's journey will ease your kinsmen's restlessness for a time since the weather's lifted and given them a chance to be out and about." She turned and gave him a sad, thoughtful smile. "I'm sorry ye werena well enough to join them. Ye must be as vexed as they are, what with being held prisoner by your wounds and the weather."

"I'm no' vexed." He did, however, possess a great yearning to brush away that reddish-bronze curl resting on the curve of her cheek, slide the silk of it between his fingers, and bring it to his lips. He pulled in a deep breath and eased it out, flexing his hands against the urge. "As I've said many times before, I'm thankful ye took us in, lass, took us in as though we were your own." Spurred on by her woeful demeanor, he slid his hand under hers, lifted it with a slow careful motion, and pressed a kiss to the silkiness of her knuckles. "I am grateful to ye, Catriona," he whispered, keeping her hand close and tucking it to his chest. "*More grateful than ye'll ever know.*"

The way she looked—so sad, so helpless, so in need of saving. He wished he could gather her up in his arms and tell her the same thing she'd repeated over and over to him when he'd been beset with fever. He wanted to tell her she was safe now and that everything would be all right. But how could he when he had no idea what had stolen the light from her eyes nor what he could do to help her? "What troubles ye, Catriona? Pray tell me so I can make it right. Ye've no' been yourself for days."

It had been weeks since he'd fought free of the fever and awakened to Catriona's caring smile and discovered genuine concern and kindness shining in the rich verdant green of her eyes. And he had no' failed to notice that whilst Mrs. Aberfeldy, Mrs. Bickerstaff, and the maids took turns tending to his brothers' healing and his kinsmen's other minor scrapes and bruises, Catriona alone tended to him. He had to admit, he liked that. Verra much.

Pulling her hand away with a nervous jerk, Catriona pressed her fists together in her lap and stared down at them. "Your brothers— Magnus and your cousins—what do they hope to find today? From what I overheard of their conversation, it didna appear they were going out for a ride just to clear their heads and breathe the fresh Highland air."

She was changing the subject. Again. Alexander shifted on the bench, pretending to resettle his worrisome leg but in reality, scooting closer to Catriona. He craved her warmth, her scent. The past few weeks in her care had made him need her closeness like a starving man needed food and drink. He tried not to think about how much he'd miss her when he'd healed enough to move on and return to his duties as a mercenary for hire in the Highlands.

"Where were they going? Glencoe, perhaps?" she prodded.

"Aye." Alexander nodded, an almost suffocating sense of doom filling him. A burning log popped and crackled in the hearth, shooting up sparks as it shifted deeper into the coals. "'Tis important that we give the Lord of the Isles an accurate account when we return." He forced away the troubling memories of all he'd seen, all the carnage and suffering he'd witnessed during the massacre at Glencoe. They'd failed in their task. Failed Clan MacDonald and the Lord of the Isles.

He reached for his tankard of ale and drained it. Rolling the metal cup between his hands, he stole a glance over at Catriona. The mere sight of her soothed him faster than a sip of fine whisky. The way the glow of the fire lit up her face. The graceful curve of her throat. Alexander wet his lips. How silky would her skin feel? How delicious would she taste? He shifted again and tugged at the folds of his kilt, verra much aware of the effect she had on him but not wishing to share it. 'Twas no' the time. No' when she was troubled so.

"The MacDonald, the Lord of the Isles hired ye and your men to fight against the king? Kill his men?"

The question hit him like a slap in the face. He'd already told her as much as a woman should hear about the battle. Mayhap more than she needed to know. She'd seemed relieved when he'd told her they'd no' sworn fealty to the MacDonalds of Glencoe. He knew what she thought, and he felt he couldna blame her for her suspicions. She thought him and his men to be traitors. Jacobites. And depending on the pay, sometimes they were—but he didna share that information with her. Catriona feared for the safety of her clan and he understood that. He chose his next words with care.

"Aye, the MacDonald of Islay hired us. 'Tis true." He watched the emotions flashing in her eyes, trying his best to read them. "He hired us to watch over his kin in Glen Coe. Informants advised us about the lawlessness of his cousins and in particular, their feuding with Clan Campbell, but no rumors ever mentioned an uprising against the king." He took Catriona's hand again and held it between both of his. "Never would I bring the king's wrath down upon your clan. I swear it."

Firelight flickered in her green-eyed gaze as she looked at him, searching his face as though he held all the answers she needed and so much more. What he wouldna give to pull her close and reassure her, to hold her in his arms until she believed the truth of all he told her. He could tell she hungered for such. He saw it in the way she held herself, her unconscious leaning toward him. The heart-wrenching need for comforting shone in her eyes. This rare woman had touched something deep within him, touched him with her attentiveness to his healing and the way she'd ne'er left his side whilst he was ailing. He'd ne'er received such caring before. Not even long ago when he'd thought himself in love. What he wouldna give to wipe away the sorrow weighing so heavy upon her and take care of whatever troubled her. A realization hit him. She hadn't reacted or responded to anything he'd just said. "Do ye believe me, lass?"

"Aye," she said in a subdued tone. With an awkward gentle pull, she removed her hand from his grasp and tucked it back in her lap. She sniffed and swiped her fingers across her eyes as she turned away with a quick shifting on the bench.

"Catriona?" He took hold of her shoulders and made her face him. "Ye must tell me what else troubles ye. Tell me. I swear I'll slay those demons."

Before she could speak, the large double doors leading outside to the bailey blew open and Duncan, Sutherland, Magnus, Alasdair, and Ian strode inside, stomping snow and ice from their boots and shedding their fur cloaks. Graham rose from a bench close to the hearth at the far end of the room and hurried to join them.

"Ye best see to them," Catriona said as she handed him the cumbersome crutch his injured leg demanded he use. "I'll leave ye to your men. I'm sure the lot of ye wish to speak in private."

Perhaps that was the way to ease her worries. Maybe if she learned that the skirmish they'd almost not survived wasna some ill-fated rising against the Crown, maybe then she'd return to the lively, full of fire Catriona he'd first met and wished verra much to know better. He caught her by the arm and pulled her back with a gentle tug. "Join me and hear what they have to say. I've nothing to hide from ye."

She studied him for a long moment then agreed with a graceful nod. "Verra well. If that's what ye wish."

"Aye, I wish it."

Alexander gimped his way toward his men, noting as he walked how Catriona curbed her steps to match his slow, hitching gait.

"Stay there, brother," Duncan called out to him as the men finished peeling away the extra clothing they'd worn to protect them from the weather. "Hearth, food, and whisky aplenty. I speak for us all when I say we seek all three after this day's journey."

With a subtle lift of one hand, Catriona flagged down a maidservant. "Food and whisky for the men, Maggie, and be quick about it, aye?"

"Yes, mistress." The young girl gave a polite bobbing hop then darted off toward the kitchens.

The men all settled at one long table. Alexander lowered himself to the end of the bench and propped his crutch against it. Catriona stood beside him, glancing at the full benches overflowing with the seven brawny men. The poor lass was uncertain where to go or what to do.

"Sutherland." Alexander thumped his knuckles on the table. "Fetch the lady a seat, aye?"

His youngest brother paused, arching a dark brow in a dubious *are ye certain, brother* look.

"A seat. For the lady. Now," Alexander repeated in a tone that left no doubt.

Sutherland hurried to pull a nearby, much shorter bench closer. He angled it to the end of the table beside Alexander. "M'lady?" With a polite smile, he held out his hand and helped Catriona maneuver her skirts between the table and bench.

"I thank ye." Catriona folded her hands atop the table. She sat ramrod straight and stiff as though she sat at her own inquisition and fully expected to receive a sentence of hanging by the neck 'til dead.

"What did ye find?" Alexander dove straight in. It had pained him with a deep burning regret to have to stay behind. He longed to see for himself the whereabouts of any survivors and what might be left for them to return to in the glen. The grim looks around the table knotted the already choking sense of failure tightening in his gullet. He and his men were good at what they did, the best, in fact, according to many who had hired them. But this time they'd failed, and the failure left a taste in his mouth as bitter as a bite of rotted haggis. "Well? Speak. I'll hear all of it."

"Gone." His cousin Alasdair finally spoke. "Burnt to the ground. The keep and every MacDonald croft in the glen cursed enough to be found by Argyll's regiment."

"I couldna even bury my Janet." Ian, Alasdair's younger brother, spoke in a tone filled with despair. "Nothing but ashes where I left her. Nothing." Janet had died in Ian's arms, her throat slit by a Campbell. "I set her a cairn with some of the keep's stones. I'll pray there whene'er I pass it."

Alexander scrubbed a hand across his face. The memory of Ian's loss on that godforsaken day fed into his nightmares. Raw and cutting it was. Still verra much real. His cousin's grief-stricken keening had ripped through all their souls with a heart-wrenching slash. Alasdair had stood guard over Ian that day, shooting any who dared interrupt his brother's grieving over his wife's lifeless body.

"I take it ye didna find any survivors at all, else ye wouldha brought them back here with ye?" Alexander spoke in a hushed tone, forcing the words out and dreading to hear the answer. Somehow, the recent dead and their troubled spirits filled the hall, clamoring to make their injustices heard.

"No survivors that we could find unless they're already sheltered somewhere else and no' giving away their location," Duncan said then took a deep draw from the short, squat round-bellied glass of amber liquid in front of him. "Those we did find had frozen to death." He stared down at the table, his face devoid of emotion. "We couldna bury them, what with the frozen ground, and the stones locked with ice. But we placed them together, the women, their wee bairns alongside them..." he paused and swallowed hard, bowing his head and closing his eyes, struggling to continue. "We covered them best we could and prayed over them," he finally forced out then drained his glass and poured himself another.

"May God have mercy on their souls," Catriona whispered. Tears flowed down her pale cheeks as she crossed herself and bowed her head.

"Aye," Alexander said. "A curse on Captain Robert Campbell." He fisted a hand on the table, clenching his fingers so tight every knuckle popped. What he wouldna give to have grasped Campbell's throat with just such a hold. "A curse on every Campbell born after him now and forevermore."

Catriona hitched in a startled breath. "Ye believe this to be the feud?"

"Nay. 'Twas made to look like a feud, m'lady," Magnus replied. "I was at Fort Smith on that fateful day and I returned there to search for any news of the attack. 'Tis rumored the Earl of Stair, John Dalrymple ordered the massacre, acting on behalf of King William."

"But ye can bet coin that Campbell and his men were more than glad enough to take part in it," Alexander interjected. "I'm certain the honorable Laird of Glen Lyon has already claimed MacDonald lands to pay off some of his debts. He left his colors flying there, did he not?"

Alexander had met Robert Campbell once. The man was a drunkard and a gambler, and an arrogant fool at that. Supposedly, he'd lost all his lands on ill-placed betting and was desperate to find a means of supporting his wife and seven children. What better way to support them than by stealing the lands of a rival clan under cover of king's orders?

"Aye," Duncan said. "Campbell colors were there." He took a long drink then thumped his tankard back to the table. "A curse on Robert Campbell and all his kin."

"Excuse me," Catriona said in a strained tone as she rose with an abrupt shuffling of her skirts and hurried to sidle her way out from between the bench and the table. "'Tis late and I'm verra weary." Her pallor had grown even more wan, and she looked as though she might retch at any minute. "Good evenin' to ye all." Without another word, she turned, caught up the folds of her heavy wool dress and nearly ran to the staircase.

"I knew we should nay have spoken in front of the lady," Sutherland said as he shot an accusing glance at Alexander. "Where's your sensitivities, man?"

Alexander ignored his brother, hefted himself up from the bench, and tucked his awkward crutch in place. Mind made up, he hobbled his way after Catriona. The stubborn woman would tell him her troubles if he had to stand outside her chamber door and beat on it with his crutch the rest of the night.

CHAPTER 8

*H*e lost momentum when he reached the stairs. *Damn leg. Blasted clumsy crutch.* He gripped the crude staff in one hand and studied the situation. 'Twas but one thing to do. He propped his free hand against the whitewashed wall of the stairwell. With a hopping lurch, he conquered the stone steps with his good limb while his wounded appendage dragged along beside it. A chamber door slammed above him. He hoped like hell it was on the second level of the keep and not somewhere higher.

Pausing a moment to catch his breath, he picked up on the sound of scurrying footfalls growing louder, getting closer. *Thank the saints. She's coming back.* He hitched his way snug against the wall and waited. Disappointment flooded his senses when Mrs. Aberfeldy careened into view.

The aging housekeeper caught her hand to her throat as she rounded the turn in the stair. "Master MacCoinnich! Ye gave me quite the fright." She scowled at him and pointed at his bad leg. "Ye've no business on these steep stairs! What with the way they wind and the narrowness of their rise, they'll do ye in for certain. What do ye seek? I'll fetch it for ye."

"Catriona."

'Twas best to be blunt under such dire circumstances. Alexander steadied himself on one step while propping his crutch on the tread above it. "Show me where she went or bring her here. I dinna care which ye choose but I will see her. Now."

Mrs. Aberfeldy studied him for a long moment. Her lips twitched, then clamped down into a stern line as her thin gray brows knotted into a fierce furrow in her brow. "'Twould be best if ye left her be, ye ken?" She sidled her way to the middle of the step on which she was standing, widened her stance, and folded her arms across her ample bosom. "Now hie thee back down to the hall and I'll fetch ye a bottle of the Neal's finest whiskey."

Alexander snorted out a laugh. The old woman might be stubborn but she didna realize she'd met her match. Mother had always claimed him to be the most strong-willed of the litter. "Have the kindness and good sense to move, Mrs. Aberfeldy, or I'll be moving ye m'self."

"Pshaw!" Mrs. Aberfeldy made an up and down sweeping motion with one finger. "Ye're in no condition to make such threats. Now, off wi' ye. I'll no' have the likes of ye bothering Catriona. She's enough burdens to bear."

The best weapon is surprise. He took in a deep breath, held it, then grabbed hold of Mrs. Aberfeldy's rounded shoulders and planted a hard kiss across her mouth. With a huffing grunt of determination, he set her to one side and shoved past her. 'Twas unfortunate he lost his crutch in the battle. It clattered all the way to the base of the stairwell, bouncing off each step with nerve-rattling accuracy. Alexander didn't allow such a minor setback stop him, especially while the dumbstruck housekeeper was no longer a threat. He continued hopping up the stairs whilst bracing himself against the walls.

Mrs. Aberfeldy called after him as he reached the head of the stair. "All the way to end of the hall. The verra last door. But I promise, she'll no' give ye entry."

"We'll see about that." Alexander huffed as he hopped to the right side of the hallway and planted a hand against the rough, chiseled coolness of the stone wall. As long as he could use the surface as a crutch, he'd do just fine, in fact, he gained momentum as he adapted an odd swinging hop down the passage. When he at last reached the arched portal at the end of the corridor, he snorted in a deep breath, then rapped his knuckles on the heavy oaken barrier.

Silence met his knock.

"Catriona! I beg ye let me in." He banged on the door, hitting it with enough force to rattle the iron hardware bolted across the boards. Another bang of his fist set the latches and hinges to clamoring louder. Still no answer.

"Verra well. Prepare yourself because ye leave me no choice." He grabbed hold of the handle and yanked so hard that the door banged open against the opposite wall then bounced back and thumped him, almost knocking him off balance.

"Sons a bitches!"

Another winding staircase rose in front of him. This one a great deal more narrow and steeper since it wound inside the center of a tower comprising the corner of the keep.

"Stubbornness is one of me strongest traits, ye ken?" He glared down at the steps, daring them to challenge him. With a hand propped against each of the walls, he hopped until he reached the top of the staircase where it opened out into a small landing and another closed door. He paused a moment, sagged against the wall beside the portal, and swiped the back of his hand across his sweaty forehead.

Holy Mother of God, I'm fair winded. His stamina had lessened a great deal while his wounds healed. Not moving from the wall, he banged on the door with his fist. "Catriona! 'Tis Alexander. Let me in."

Silence.

His ragged breathing echoed through the space. Alexander took hold of the door latch and pulled. Relief washed across him. "Praise the saints. No more stairs."

He'd come to a small circular room at the top of the turret. A welcoming fire crackled in the brazier in the center of the white-washed chamber lined with benches and pegs filled with cloaks and plaids. It was also empty. The urge to curse surged through him. "If that old…"

The outer door on the opposite wall of the chamber opened

inward. He forgot to finish his irritated rant as a hooded and cloaked Catriona pushed inside, failing to notice him standing in the doorway as the hood of her cloak blocked her view. She hurried to a bench piled with several pairs of gloves and sorted through them until she found a pair that suited her. As she slid them on, she straightened and turned to go back the way she'd came, facing Alexander with the movement.

"Holy Mary Mother of God!" Eyes flared wide, she stumbled to the side a few steps, both hands pressed to her chest. "Be ye trying to give me a fright that sends me to me grave?"

Alexander didn't reply, just hitched his way through the door and closed it with a firm thud behind him. He decided 'twould be more than prudent to block the doorway to the stair. With a determined thud, he settled himself back against the door. "No. I apologize for startling ye." He folded his arms across his chest. "But we're no' leaving this room until ye tell me what troubles have snuffed the light out of your eyes."

With a frustrated huffing that sounded a great deal like the hiss of a kitten, Catriona yanked off her gloves and tossed them back down on the bench before she removed her cloak and placed it on a peg beside the door. "Ye'll be leaving here soon as ye're able to travel, aye?"

He'd planned such but now that he stood looking into sweet Catriona's eyes, it pained him no small amount to admit to it. So he didn't. He could skirt a question just as good as she. He motioned toward a bench. "Shall we sit a while?"

"Sit?" She glanced over at the bench as though it were about to attack her.

"Aye." One hand supporting his balance by propping against the wall, Alexander hitched his way to the bench farthest from the door. Halfway to his destination, he paused. "I beg ye...dinna run. I canna manage those godforsaken steps again—no' just yet."

A quivering smile flickered across Catriona's face but a frown chased it away. "Where is your crutch?"

"I lost the damn thing halfway up here." Alexander lowered himself to the seat then held out his hand. "Sit with me, Catriona. Please."

Skirts rustling as she padded across the room, Catriona seated herself some distance from him.

"I willna bite, ye ken?" Although, if given the opportunity, he couldna guarantee that he wouldna nibble. He shifted on the bench and adjusted his man parts that had roared to life as soon as Catriona had pushed into the tower chamber. He patted the seat beside him then held out his hand. "Come, lass. Sit closer and tell me of your troubles. Mayhap I can help?"

"I verra much doubt that," Catriona said as she scooted across the bench until she sat beside him. Color now rode high on her cheeks but Alexander knew 'twas because she'd been out in the cold. Her eyes narrowed as she stared into the fire. "Ye never answered me, Alexander."

He breathed in deep, picking up on her beguiling scent of wood smoke, wintry wind, and young vibrant woman. "I had planned on leaving as soon as I was able." He reached out, took hold of her hand, and held it tight. "But I willna leave ye unsafe. No' after all ye have done for me and my kin. What do ye fear, Catriona, for that's what I see in your eyes, ye ken? Tell me, lass, so I might slay those demons that trouble ye." He set his jaw and decided to speak the evil he knew in his heart she wouldna wish to face. "Tell me true, Catriona, is it that damn brother of yours? I ken he's returned and ye've no' been right since."

Her tear-filled eyes flared wide for an instant. Catriona caught a trembling fist to her chest, hitched in a shuddering breath, then released it with a despairing cry. One corner of her lower lip trembled and the unshed tears welled up then overflowed, streaming down her cheeks. "Hell fire!" She swiped her fingers across her fair skin to chase the tears away.

He couldn't hold back any longer. Alexander pulled her into his arms, tucking her head to his chest and holding her tight. He closed his eyes as he stroked her hair. Hair soft as silky threads of a spent thistle weed, just as he'd known it would be. "It's all right, lass," he said in a crooning whisper. "I'll keep ye safe."

Catriona responded with more high-pitched sobs and a fist

thumping soft against his arm. Alexander smiled to himself when she burrowed deeper into his embrace, buried her face into his chest and howled. Whilst she still hadn't told him what ailed her, he considered this a good start. He rocked her back and forth with a gentle swaying, stroking her back, and making all the reassuring sounds he could think of until she cried herself out.

When her sobbing reduced to the occasional hiccupping sniff, Catriona eased herself free of his arms. She wiped her face with the backs of her hands and sat ramrod straight on the bench beside him. "I truly beg your pardon, Alexander. What must ye think of me?"

"I think ye be a fine braw, beautiful lassie in need of my help."

Catriona smiled but her lower lip set to trembling again. "Dinna make me cry anymore, aye? My head's fair throbbing as though about to burst." She pulled a crumpled square of white linen from her sleeve and dabbed it to her pitiful red nose. "I must look a sight," she added with a pat to her tousled hair.

"Ye're a bonnie lass, Catriona," he said and meant every damn word. He'd ne'er seen a lovelier, red-nosed, scarlet-cheeked, unkempt woman in his life. "Now talk. 'Tis time." He missed the loss of her warmth but made no move to return her to his arms. He sensed she needed space, a bit a distance to tell her tale.

"It appears I'm to be married once the snow melts." She knotted her fists in the gray-blue folds of her woolen skirts. "In the spring. Calum has arranged it." She turned and faced him with a bitter smile, malice glinting in her red-rimmed eyes. "With my father's blessing, of course."

"Married?" Her announcement hit him square in the chest, making it difficult to breathe.

"Aye, married." Catriona fixed her narrow-eyed scowl on the fire in the room's center. "Calum fears me. 'Twas an easy enough choice to be rid of me—save having me murdered and disposing of my body."

"And your father agreed?" Alexander could scarce believe it. 'Twas the strongest and most consistent rumor amongst all the servants in the keep, especially Mrs. Aberfeldy. Catriona had sworn on her mother's deathbed she'd never desert Clan Neal and leave them to the mercies of her father or her brother. The rumors also claimed her father couldna lead the clan without her.

"Father's not been sober enough for me to ask since Calum gave us the news of the match, but my brother assures me that my sire was fair pleased with the bargain he'd worked out *for the good of the clan.*" Her damp lashes fluttered fast as butterfly wings and despair sent a fresh volley of tears down her cheeks. "I canna bear the thought of it and yet I've no good choice of escaping it or figuring a way to protect my kin. If I refuse, and Calum allows me to do so, he'll never let me stay here. He's already said I'll be sent to the priory to spend the rest of my days confessing my stubborn ways to the sisters. And of course, when I marry, I'll go to my husband's lands. Either way—Calum is rid of me and will rule Clan Neal with none to hinder him with something as annoying as the conscience of a nagging sister."

Something akin to rage simmered dark and deep within him and the longer Alexander listened to Catriona and pondered her fate, the stronger the monster within him grew, until he came to realize the monster's name: *jealousy.* "How dare he. I'll no' allow it."

"And just how will ye stop it, Alexander? He's well within his rights and ye ken that as well as I. The elders willna take a stand against him. They've yet to name him *Tanist* but they fear him and his men too much to stand in his way should he force his claim of the chieftain-ship." She bowed her head and lifted a shaking hand to her brow. "All is lost. In a few short weeks, I am to become Jameson Campbell's wife." She covered her face with both hands, her shoulders trembling with pitiful sobs as she did her best to speak through the tears. "I'm told we shall live at Breadalbane's estate since Jameson Campbell is son to the earl and next in line to the title."

The shrewd bastard had not only rid himself of his sister, but he'd given her to a bloody Campbell, the clan noted for heeling to the king's whims better than any dog. Alexander pulled Catriona back into his arms. "I'll no' allow this to happen, Catriona," he whispered into her hair. "I swear it."

She shifted, lifting her tear-stained face to him. "I fear ye canna stop it."

Tracing his thumb along the soft, wet curve of her cheek, Alexander brushed away the tears and struggled to keep from telling her all the ways he intended to make her brother Calum suffer for putting her through such. Nay. 'Twould be wrong to discuss such vileness with this dear sweet lass. His gaze settled on her mouth. The precious parted lips he'd often thought about tasting.

'Tis time. He lowered his head and helped himself to the treasured sweetness she offered. His heart soared when she opened to him, inviting him in with hesitant flicking touches of her tongue. He dove into the taste of her, a heady mix of honeyed wine and desperate need. Her hands slid up his chest, and she wrapped her arms around his neck, holding him tight, as though she feared the kiss would end and he'd let her go. He laced his fingers into her hair and cradled her head in his palm as he trailed the kiss from her mouth down to the line of her jaw and along the curve of her throat. He'd been right. She brushed softer than velvet against his lips and tasted sweeter than any precious nectar. He'd known she'd be so, thought of it often as she'd tended to his wounds.

He paused at the neckline of her overdress, brushing his lips back and forth across her collarbone. A delicious aching to go lower thrummed within him, urged him to sample more, but he stopped himself. 'Twould no' be right. Not now. Not as vulnerable as she was. He lifted his head and pulled her close, tucking her snug beneath his chin and cradling her like the rare woman he knew her to be. She was too fiery a woman for the priory and he'd be damned if he stood by and watched her be given to a bloody Campbell.

"Dinna despair, Catriona, dinna despair. I will figure a way out of this."

"All is lost," Catriona said so low he strained to hear her. "My oath. My people…" She shuddered then keened out a heartbreaking cry against the base of his throat, her renewed tears hot against his skin. "All I sacrificed…all for naught."

Alexander shifted, pulling away so he could once more lift her face to his. "Dinna doubt when I say I will save ye from this fate. I swear— ye're no' in this alone."

She hitched in a shaking breath, despair in her eyes as she gave him a sad smile. "I've always been alone…and always will be."

"Not anymore," he said as he cupped her face in his hand and kissed away her tears. "Not anymore," he repeated against her trembling lips. "I swear it."

CHAPTER 9

"So ye mean to marry her yourself then? Ye told her as much, aye?" Magnus tore a chunky crust of bread in two and sopped the halves in the puddle of thick, dark meat drippings left in the shallow well of his plate.

"Lower your voice, man." Alexander paused as a kitchen maid set another board of meat and bread on the table, refilled their tankards, then moved on to tend to others. "Ye ken as well as I that I canna wed the woman."

Magnus looked up from his meal and frowned, staring at Alexander as though he thought him addled. "And why not? 'Tis obvious ye feel kindness toward the lass. I'll admit she seems a tad headstrong and set in her ways but I'm thinking a man such as yourself might need that in a wife."

"Aye," Graham said from Alexander's left, lifting his mug in a mock toast then taking a deep draught. A loud belch followed as he gave Alexander a knowing wink and thunked his tankard back beside his plate. "I agree. Marry the lass." He clapped a hand to Alexander's shoulder and gave him a friendly shake. "Ye've grown old, brother. Leave the fighting for hire to us." He leaned forward and nodded to

Duncan and Sutherland, sitting opposite him at the long table on either side of Magnus.

On cue, the brothers lifted their tankards.

"To Alexander's retirement," Sutherland said.

"Aye," Duncan agreed, then reached across in front of Magnus and tapped his mug to Sutherland's.

"Graham has the right of it, cousin," Ian said. "Get out while ye're able enough to father a brood of your own, ye ken? Marry the woman and take her somewhere safe." Ian sat at the other end of the table, off to himself, apart from the others. He spoke in a cold, somber tone without looking up from his plate, his knuckles whitening as he clenched his knife and fork tighter. "I lost my dear Janet by no' casting aside our warring ways and I'll regret it as long as I draw breath."

"What have I to offer a wife?" Alexander said in a strained whisper as he shoved his half-eaten meal away and fisted one hand into the palm of the other. "I've nothing more than my sword and pistol. No croft. No clan. What kind of life is that for a woman such as Catriona?"

Graham nudged a shoulder against his. "The Lord of the Isles promised ye land. The two of ye could build a life there. Claim fealty to Clan MacDonald, live on Islay, and fill it with a gaggle of sons and daughters."

"Aye," Sutherland said with an excited bob of his head. "Then we'd all have a place to rest our weary bones when we've no battle for hire."

"Do ye truly think Laird MacDonald will gift me land after what happened at Glencoe?" Alexander popped his knuckles and ground his fist harder into his palm. He'd lain awake most of the night trying to think of a way to save Catriona and her clan because she'd made it adamantly clear she was just as upset about breaking her oath to protect her people as she was about being promised to a man she'd never met. A man certain to be of questionable morals considering the fact that he appeared to be on good terms with her abhorrent brother. "And besides—Catriona wishes to save her people from Calum when the time comes."

"I'm surprised the wee bastard has no' already done his father in to lay claim to the chieftainship," Graham observed as he motioned for a refill by waving his tankard at a maid passing between the rows of long dinner tables lined on either side of the hall.

"'Tis my understanding he's no' been named *Tanist*," Magnus said with a meaningful glance around the room. He paused and waited for the maid filling their mugs to finish and move away. "Has Catriona spoken of anyone else that might sway the elders into being named as *Tanist* rather than Calum?"

"I asked her that." Alexander shook his head; the impossibility of the situation churned in his gut like a poorly cooked meal. "Her fifteen-year-old brother is well on his way to being as vile as Calum. Her two youngest brothers are naught but wee lads of nine years. She has no male cousins and knows of no one else in the clan the elders might consider."

"We shall figure this out," Alasdair said with a reassuring clap of his hand atop Alexander's shoulder as he rose from the bench. He bent close to Alexander's ear and nodded toward the head of the hall. "Battle readiness, cousin. There be the devil himself."

Just the sight of Calum sauntering toward them set Alexander's rage to a dangerous simmer that neared boiling over. He'd just as soon snap the whoreson's neck as to look at him. The only thing staying his hand was Catriona. She'd been clear enough, told him if Alexander or any of his men harmed Calum, her brother's blood would be on her hands just the same as if she'd done the deed herself. Alexander struggled to understand why that would necessarily be a bad thing but to Catriona, the thought of killing her own brother for the safety of the clan was unquestionably wrong. She'd explained that if she killed Calum, she felt herself to be no better than he was. Alexander huffed out a frustrated snort. Catriona was most definitely a more honorable person than himself.

"Men." Calum gave them an imperious nod while picking at his large, yellowed front teeth with his grimy thumbnail. Wiping the results on the side of his shirt, he sucked at his teeth as he meandered around their table. "I bring a warning for the lot of ye," he said with an irritating smirk.

"Have ye now?" Alexander shifted on the bench, sitting taller and flexing the hand that fit with such a comfortable grip around Calum's windpipe.

Calum didn't miss Alexander's intent. His eyes widened the slightest bit, and he cleared his throat. "Aye. I do." He took a stance at the head of their table, clasped his hands to the small of his back, and lifted his chin to a defiant angle. "I've received word we're soon to have more guests here at *Tor Ruadh*. Guests I'm sure will be most pleased to meet the lot of ye—if ye're still here when they arrive."

"Spit out your threat, man, or do ye mean to kill us with boredom?" Alexander winked at his brothers. If he couldna kill Calum, he might as well torment the man as much as possible.

Duncan and Sutherland each snorted out a laugh and Graham saluted his brothers with his tankard.

Alexander's cockiness faded when he spotted Catriona. She stood at the door of a small anteroom adjoining the hall. Distress colored her features an alarming rosy shade. Her clasped hands, knuckles whitening with her grip, trembled as she stretched to see across the room and those amassed at the tables. When her gaze alighted on Alexander, she rushed over to join them.

"Well?" she asked in a breathless tone, alarm flashing in her eyes.

"I havena told them yet, sister," Calum said in a sly, drawling tone. "They were too intent on their imbecilic jests to listen." He gave them a bored flip of one hand then made a gallant bow toward Catriona and retreated a step. "Perhaps they'll listen to yourself."

"Ye must leave," Catriona admonished, her hands crumpling and twisting a small bit of linen as though wringing the cloth might give her some ease. She locked eyes with Alexander and added, "All of ye. Leave and save yourselves. Afore it's too late."

Alexander rose from his seat. He planted a hand to Graham's shoulder, leaning heavy on his brother to manage his way out from behind the bench. He retrieved his smaller, much more convenient, knob-headed cane from where he'd leaned it at his side against his seat and limped his way to stand close to Catriona. It pained him no small amount to see her so overwrought, and he'd be damned if he deserted her when she needed him most. "Who are these guests, lass? Why do ye fear them?"

Calum rose to the tips of his toes then popped back down to his heels with an excited bounce. He folded his arms across his narrow chest and his knowing smirk deepened to an even more irritating level of repulsiveness. "Aye, Catriona. Tell your precious Alexander why ye fear the guests we're expecting?"

It was all Alexander could do to keep from lunging forward and snapping Calum's neck. He'd no' be stopped from finishing the job this time. With both hands propped atop his cane, he locked his arms in place, and gripped the polished wooden knob of the short staff with such ferocity 'twas a wonder it didna snap off. Jaws aching with the clenching of his teeth, he forced his focus on Catriona and waited.

Catriona wet her lips and swallowed hard. Her worried glance flitted across each of Alexander's men then returned to him. "A new regiment. Selected by the king himself to investigate the massacre at Glencoe." She dabbed the crumpled linen in her fist to her mouth as though she were about to retch. After a hard swallow and the clearing of her throat, she lowered it. "'Tis said they're searching for witnesses and traitors."

This didna bode well. They were not traitors—at least not this time. But they had fought against Campbell's men. They'd fought on the side of the MacDonalds. Alexander shifted his focus back to Calum. Something about the belligerent way the bastard was standing and the pleased with himself expression on his face spoke volumes. Alexander felt certain that Calum had a hand in making certain the king's men came to *Tor Ruadh*.

"The warmer days have the snow melting at a good pace. Several of the passes are open now—muddy and a challenge, for certain, but clear enough that the soldiers could arrive here within days." Catriona caught her bottom lip between her teeth, trembling as she stood there with brow furrowed and her face filled with worry.

Catriona looked at him with such desperation he wanted nothing more than to grab her up and take her with them. How could she ask him to leave? His men had risen from their seats around the table, standing at the ready to follow through with whatever he ordered. He stared at them for a long moment. He couldna risk their lives any more than he could risk Catriona's.

A featherlight touch to his arm pulled his attention back to Catriona. She stood closer, so close, he could feel the heat of her, breathe in the sweet beguiling scent of her. "Please. Ye must go," she whispered, staring teary-eyed up into his face. "I couldna bear it if anything happened to ye."

"Well, isn't that precious," Calum interrupted with a disgusted snort. "Ye belong to Jameson Campbell, Catriona, and the man was promised a virgin. Now step away and try to behave like a lady true to her betrothed, aye? Dinna shame our clan by acting the whore."

Alexander lurched a step in Calum's direction, lifting his cane to club the imperious smile off the fool's face. "Ye rude bastard. I'll teach ye shame."

"Alexander, no!" Catriona stayed the strike with an urgent touch to his forearm. "Please...ye mustn't." She drew back her hand, cradling it against her chest. With a graceful bow of her head, she stepped away. "Calum is right. I mustn't sully the Neal name." She paused a heartbeat with the fisted linen pressed against her mouth then cleared her throat again. With slow purposeful grace, she lifted her chin. An air of eerie calmness emanated from her. "I'll speak to Murtagh about horses and supplies for ye and your men. I think it best if ye leave at first light, ye ken? What say ye?"

If there was one thing, as both warrior and man, that Alexander hated more than anything else, it was the feeling of being backed into a corner with no hope of escape. And damned, if that was no' the exact feeling hammering through him at this verra moment.

He glared at Calum's simpering face, wishing the man dead on the spot. Clutching his cane so tight that the wood crackled in his grip, Alexander tore his gaze away from Calum and faced Catriona.

"I..." Alexander paused, his enraged rant defused by the merest hint of hope he detected in the wistfulness of Catriona's eyes. The lass was trying to tell him something. He didna know if it was her stance, the tilt of her head, or the slant of her mouth, but she wished to convey something of great import to him but wasn't able to because of Calum's presence. He'd bet his life on it.

"Aye," he said, struggling to hold his temper. "First light." He turned to his brethren and gave them a curt nod.

Calum fairly lit up as though he'd swallowed the sun. He stuck out his chest and preened a strand of his greasy red hair back from his face. "Good then. I suggest ye take the pass to the west. I'm told it's passable. Far safer than the east or the south."

Did the man think him a fool? The insufferable prig was most assuredly doing his best to send them into an ambush. Alexander drew in a deep breath and held it for a moment, struggling to keep from knocking Calum on his arse. He cleared his throat and forced himself to appear grateful. "The western pass. Aye. We will take your advice since several of us are still healing." He even managed a smile and a polite nod. "I thank ye for all ye've done for us and the hospitality of your clan."

Calum waved away his words as though they were flies buzzing about his food. "Aye, then. I'll leave ye to your preparations." He gave them all a long cold look, crooked nose wrinkled and lip curled as though he smelled a stink. Then he swung about and strode toward a double archway, waving down Hew and Duff as he went. "To my solar, gentleman. We've much to discuss."

The malicious pair, evil grins plastered across their faces, grabbed up their tankards and hurried after him.

As soon as the three men had left the hall, Catriona came to life, stepping forward in her distress and grasping hold of Alexander by his forearms. "Ye ken well enough to stay away from the western pass, aye? I've no idea what the wicked fool has planned but I'm sure 'twould be your end."

"I'm no' a fool, lass." Alexander took hold of both her hands and gave them a gentle squeeze. "I'll also no' be leaving ye here unprotected."

"He's quite gallant like that," Graham interrupted as he waved the others forward. "Come. We'll prepare whilst Alexander works out a plan."

"Aye," Magnus agreed, slapping a friendly hand to Alexander's shoulder as he passed behind him. "We'll be in the kitchens with the pretty maids. Fetch us when ye're ready."

Alexander could tell by the determined set of Catriona's mouth she was about to unleash quite the lecture. Before she could, he pulled her closer, close enough he could almost see the pounding of her heart beneath her tightly laced bodice. "I will kiss ye here and now, woman, in front of all within this room if ye dinna hear me out."

Eyes flaring wide and delicate auburn brows arched nearly to her hairline, Catriona gave a quick shake of her head. "Ye mustn't," she whispered. "Calum has spies among these tables. His allies are growing in numbers with each passing day. I'm sorely outnumbered, I fear."

"And that is the only reason the man has allies." For the sake of Catriona's pounding heart and ruby cheeks, Alexander eased back a step, putting a bit of space between them and regretfully releasing her hands. "He controls them with fear."

"Aye," Catriona gave a sad nod of agreement. "'Tis true but the fact remains, he controls them."

"What is it ye wished to tell me out of your brother's presence?" Alexander leaned on his cane, wishing he still held Catriona's hands rather than an infernal piece of wood. "Or did I misread your lovely eyes?"

"What I have to say depends on what ye have to say yourself." Catriona stole a quick glance around the room. "Ye bade me hear ye out, did ye no'?"

"Aye. I did." *Now, what the hell do I say?* He had no plan. No idea of how to save this dear sweet lass from whatever cruel fate her brother had plotted. For that's all that concerned him. He didna give a damn if the king sent all of Christendom after them. Alexander had been chased before. Caught even and tortured for it. None of that mattered a whit. All that mattered was Catriona and putting the fire back in her eyes. It was then he knew. A single moment of brilliant clarity. He cared for this woman and could never leave her behind. "Will ye come with me, Catriona?"

"Come with ye?" Words so soft. So hesitant.

"Aye. Come with me." Alexander held his breath, sending up a silent prayer she would agree.

Lips a hair's breadth apart, a hand pressed to the base of her throat, Catriona looked about the hall. "I…I don't…how can I?" she said, choking out the words with a sad shake of her head. "I canna desert the ones I swore to protect."

"Ye wouldna be deserting them." Hope stirred his adrenalin as a clear plan came to him. "Sometimes 'tis better to retreat in the heat of battle. Fall back to regroup and strengthen." Ever so gently, he reached out and slid his hand beneath hers, laced their fingers together, and squeezed. "Come with me to regroup and strengthen. We'll discover a way to overpower Calum and save your people. I swear it."

"How is that possible? How could we do that if we're no' here to guard them against his wrath?"

"Be honest with yourself, Catriona. Ye think ye can guard them? Alone? Look what he's already done to ye in a mere few weeks. Struck ye down. Betrothed ye to a man rumored to be as cruel as himself. Ye canna save them by staying here unless ye mean to drive a dagger in his heart while he sleeps or spike his favorite port with a good bit a poison."

"I canna kill him." She pulled her hand away and hugged herself against the words. "As much as I hate the bastard, I canna imagine taking his life."

"Ye're a better person than I." Alexander scanned the room, the sudden intense feeling of eyes upon them pricking the hairs on the back of his neck. "We should say no more here." He lowered his voice even more. "Go to your room. Gather only what ye canna live without then return to the kitchens, aye? Will ye do that, Catriona?"

She remained silent for so long that Alexander feared she would refuse. After what seemed like forever, she pulled in a deep breath and stood taller. "Aye. 'Twill no' take me long."

He resisted the urge to take her hand, every fiber of his being screamed to take her in his arms. But he couldn't. Not here. Not now.

Instead, he gave her a polite nod. "'Tis good then. Hurry, lass. We leave tonight."

CHAPTER 10

*H*eart pounding, Catriona burst into her room, hurried to close the door behind her, then leaned back against it to catch her breath. She shuddered. Thrilling excitement and choking terror coursed through her with equal ferocity. *Forgive me, Mother. I've no choice.*

She swallowed hard, struggling to control the anxious churning in her middle, the squeezing nervousness threatening to expel what few bites she'd eaten for dinner. She flexed her hands into fists then wiped her clammy palms against her skirts. With trembling fingers, she lit the candle on the entry table, then took it to light the other candles waiting on the mantel and the taper at her bedside.

What should I take? Should I don more layers to survive traveling in the snow? A thousand disjointed thoughts raced through her mind as she darted here and there about her room. Teetering on the edge of panic, she tapped her fingertips across the back of her favorite reading chair sitting beside the hearth, then along the top of the wooden frame of a half-finished bit of weaving. She might not see these things ever again. A smile tickled across her lips when it occurred to her in a brilliant flash of clarity: she didn't care.

Until now, life had felt as though she slogged through a muddy bog, trapped in one place until she drowned in complete numbness while those around her passed her by, achieving the milestones in their lives while the nothingness her life had become pulled her down until she felt like gasping for air.

And then Alexander had arrived.

She pressed her hand atop the worn leather cover of her book of Psalms on the table beside her bed. She closed her eyes and sent up a silent prayer. *Thank ye for sending Alexander.*

A resolute sense of calm swept across her. Catriona pulled in a deep cleansing breath and released it in a slow, controlled whisper of air. *I can do this and 'tis right I do this.* She hurried to the great mahogany wardrobe in the corner and yanked open the wide double doors. The sharp tang of cedar wafted into the room from the red-hued wood lining the cabinet.

Take only what I need to survive. Thankfulness filled her when the articles required seemed to jump at her from the shelves and pegs of the deep cabinet. She snatched up her fur boots, extra gloves, and heaviest cloak. "An arisaidh, too, and an extra pair of wool stockings."

She ruffled her thumb across the stack of folded skirts and chemises. One of each would do. The items piled in her arms, she carried them over to the bed. *I'll wear the boots.* She tucked her everyday leather slippers on top of the tight pile of necessities she'd placed in the center of her arisaidh. The corners of the generous wool plaid gathered and tied, Catriona expelled a satisfied sigh as she patted the snug bundle. It could be carried with little effort or slung across the horn of her saddle.

Aye. My saddle. She'd told Gaersa what she was about to do and sent her to tell her husband the plan. She felt sure she could trust Gaersa and Murtagh. Murtagh would get them horses trained to travel under such adverse conditions as shifting ground because of melting snow and mud.

Excitement building until it threatened to make her faint, she forced herself to hold fast and perused the room one last time. She stayed her hand before extinguishing the candles. Nay. 'Twas too early to darken the room. If anyone happened by after she'd left, the lit candles shining through the crack under the door would make them suppose she was within and if they searched further, they'd think she'd only left for a moment and planned on returning.

She donned her cloak, hugged her bundle tight against her middle, and covered it with the generous folds of the heavy wool garment. Mouth gone dry, she swallowed hard and breathed in a long, slow breath through her nose to settle her churning emotions. All would be well. Alexander would keep her safe.

Alexander.

The thought of him almost brought tears. Joyous tears. Tender tears. She hugged the bundle tighter and scurried out of her room. The whispering rustle of her skirts was the only sound in the hallway as she pulled the door closed behind her with a quiet thump. Rather than descending to the main floor and risking discovery, Catriona turned to the right and headed toward the stairwell housed in the corner tower. If she happened on anyone while descending through the tower, they'd think it normal since everyone knew she frequented the turret and side grounds at odd hours no matter the weather. They'd also pay no notice to her cloak or boots, thinking she only wore them against the cold during her odd habit of walking the parapet to clear her mind.

One hand against the roughness of the stone wall and the other hugging her bundle, Catriona slowed her pace on the winding staircase, guarding her footing on the steep rise of the narrow stone steps. She reached the base of the tower, then listened at the heavy outer door before opening it. All she heard was the wind rattling through the holly bushes surrounding the base of the tower. *Good.* She'd hoped it would be deserted since most of those looking for a private spot for an intimate meeting would seek quiet corners inside the keep and out of the cold on this frosty night.

She exited the tower. The narrow space between the wall and the dense leafy barrier of holly overgrowth running alongside the keep's walls caught her eye. The bushes were dense and tall. Father had ordered holly planted around every building and tower in the stronghold. The beloved plant was believed to be protection from lightning, angry fairies, and even witches. The glossy green leaves interlaced together made the hedging almost impenetrable. Mayhap, the lovely holly would protect her and bless her journey as well. If she kept to the space between the greenery and the wall, she'd leave no footprints in the mud and melting snow surrounding the small bit of ground between the curtain wall and the main building. She crept along the blocks of stone, squeezing into the space, the pointed leaves snatching at her cloak as she side-stepped her way to the back of the keep and the rear entry to the kitchens.

She paused at the corner of the wall, peeping around it and taking care to pay close attention to the shadowy area filled with the smoke pits and hulking contraptions of iron and wood used for preparing large animals for roasting. Many an evil could lurk in that darkness. A faint sense of relief wafted through her as the bitter cold wind rattled through the leafy spikes of the holly bushes. None were about. She kept to the shadows and made her way to the back entrance of the kitchens and slipped inside.

Catriona kept out of sight in a shallow space hidden by pantry shelving. She peered about and tried to differentiate the cacophony of sounds filling the busy room. Sweat trickled down her spine. Sweltering heat filled the place to an almost unbearable level. A steamy smoke hung in the air like heavy fog, rising from the still bubbling iron pots hanging in the fiery hearths and the sizzling fry pans on the great iron stove top inset into a stone ledge against the far wall.

Kitchen lads and scullery maids bustled about, scraping plates and platters into buckets, then stacking them in wash barrels by another hearth on the opposite wall where great cauldrons of boiling water bubbled over the red-hot coals glowing beneath them. Cook shouted orders. Lads flirted and teased the maids and the young lasses responded in kind.

Stretched up on tiptoes, Catriona at last found who she sought. Alexander and his men stood to the right of her hiding spot, closest to the pantry. Mrs. Aberfeldy emerged from the door leading to the more sizable of the two larders and the root cellar. She toted a bulging sack of supplies in each hand and several leather skins of whisky draped over each of her shoulders. Graham and Duncan rushed to relieve her of her burdens, parsing out the bundles among themselves and the other men.

A shiver of apprehension stole across Catriona, and she had to clench her hands into fists and press them up against her middle to stop the trembling. A clammy sweat peppered across her forehead and upper lip. She swallowed hard against the bitter bile burning the back of her throat. What if they found her? What if they discovered her and turned her over to Calum? She pressed a fist against her chest and swallowed hard again. If she maintained this inner discourse, she'd most assuredly vomit or faint—or accomplish both acts in rapid succession.

I can do this. I must do this. Her face hidden in the depths of her hood, Catriona crept out of her hiding place and scurried over to join the men. "I'm ready," she said, keeping her voice low and flinching as it faded in and out with the heightened tenseness of the moment.

Alexander rewarded her with a beaming smile then pushed his way through the group toward her. With one arm around her shoulders, he took care to keep her turned away from the servants and facing the wall. He snugged her tight against his side. "Mrs. Aberfeldy's supplied us well and Murtagh awaits in the stable."

A shudder of homesickness and the faintest stab of doubt pulled at her, making her heart ache. How could she leave Gaersa and Murtagh? How could she desert them? She twisted to look around past Alexander but he held her tight. "Nay, lass," he said in a low tone meant just for her. "'Twill only make leaving worse and stir suspicion. We daren't risk it. She loves ye like the daughter she's never had and wishes ye well. She bade me tell ye so, aye?"

"Aye," Catriona choked out around the lump of emotions threatening to strangle her. She sniffed back the tears and nodded toward the rear door of the kitchens that would lead them to the stables. "Let's be about this then, aye?"

Alexander responded with another reassuring squeeze of her shoulders as he gave a single nod to his men.

The six moved forward as one without a single word spoken

between them. Mrs. Aberfeldy turned away, face red and crumpling with tears as she hurried back into the larder. Head down, Catriona led the way to the stables, and they all rushed through the melting snow in single file behind her.

Once inside the stable, Catriona pushed back her hood. 'Twas only Murtagh, the horses, and Willie and Ferd, the stable boys, inside the coziness of the vast cave that nature had carved out of the side of Ben Nevis and the Neal clan had adapted into the perfect place to keep their horses safe through even the worst Highland winter. It smelled of clean hay, warm animals, and the slightest hint of fresh manure. With the number of horses stabled in the cave, it was all Willie, Ferd and Murtagh could do to clean out the stalls more than once a day.

Murtagh stood waiting in the large open area running across the front of the stable. Eight horses, saddled and ready, milled about behind him. Willie moved among them, double-checking their straps and reins. Ferd secured the supplies that Graham and Duncan passed over to him.

"Ye'll keep to the northern pass, aye?" Murtagh stated more in the tone of an order than a suggestion. "More snow there but passable." He gave the horse standing beside him an affectionate rub on its shaggy neck. "These lads love snow and mud even better. They'll get ye through whatever ye come upon with no trouble at all."

Alexander held out his right hand, nodding as Murtagh took it and gripped him by the forearm. "I am most grateful to ye."

Murtagh gave Alexander's arm a meaningful shake as he nodded toward Catriona. "Get her away from here and dinna bring her back, ye ken?"

Catriona rushed forward. "Hear me when I say I'll no' be leaving the ones I love to Calum's merciless ways. I'll be back as soon as I find a way to rid ourselves of him, I swear it."

Murtagh looked at her for a long moment, his face more lined with age and weariness than Catriona had ever noticed before. His beard was shot with silver and in dire need of a trim. Catriona smiled. She could just hear Mrs. Aberfeldy fussing at him to tend to his own grooming instead of spending so much time worrying after the horses' needs.

His already severe squint beneath his gray bushy brows drew in tighter until his eyes were mere slits glinting in the lantern light. He turned back to Alexander as though Catriona had never spoken. "Keep her away from here. The bastard will kill her for certain e'er she returns."

"I'll keep her safe," Alexander replied with a solemn nod. "I swear it."

'Twould do no good to argue with the gruff old man. She'd learned that long ago. Murtagh had been the father she'd never had, and she loved him. Even though the stoic, grumpy Murtagh had never displayed affection of any kind, she'd always known he'd cared about her. He'd shown his partialness to her in subtle ways. She'd never forget the time he'd selected the finest colt of their herds of rare warhorses, then raised it, and trained it for her use alone even though doing so went against her father's orders.

But she'd show him. As soon as she and Alexander had a proper plan of attack in place, she'd be back to save them all. She ached to throw her arms around him and hug him goodbye just as she had wished to do with Gaersa, but she knew it would pain him to no end if she did such a thing. Instead, she made her way to her horse, standing at the back of the group of strong, hardy mounts that Murtagh had handpicked for their journey. She almost wept when she spotted the wooden stool Murtagh had fashioned just for her and even marked with her initials so she'd be able to climb aboard the giant hairy-footed horses unassisted whenever she wished. It stood at the ready beside her horse.

Alexander and his men mounted up. Alexander gave Catriona a frowning glance and motioned her forward but the tight narrow space didn't afford the room needed to weave her large steed to his side at the front of the pack. A sense of being cared for warmed through her and set off an excited fluttery feeling in her middle. She was about to be free and embrace life. She waved him onward, under-standing he didn't like her position at the back of the herd but they'd made it this far. *I trust Murtagh and the stable boys. 'Twill be fine, I'm sure.*

The horses shifted and sidestepped in place with restless grumbling and snorts, ready and eager to be free of the stable and out in the open air. With Ferd's help, Murtagh unlatched the widest gate at the front of the stable and walked it open, swinging it into the frigid winds cutting across the outside paddock. They moved to one side, standing at the wide doorway as the horses filed out and turned toward the smaller, more concealed side opening in the curtain wall.

As she passed through the stable door, she touched her gloved hand to her heart then lifted it to Murtagh. He acknowledged the gesture with a single curt nod then turned away, motioning to the boys to man the gate and help him secure the stable. Just as her horse was about to follow the others out through the curtain wall, three sharp reports of gunfire split the frigid night air, exploding in rapid succession like a firing squad, and echoing off the side of the mountain.

Catriona reined in her horse and looked back. Terror closed icy fingers around her throat and squeezed. "No. No, it canna be so," she choked out, hot tears springing to her eyes but not blinding her to the horror in front of the stable.

Three bodies lay scattered across the ground, limp and lifeless in the golden glow of the lantern light shining out through the still open stable door. Dark stains spread around the crumpled forms. The heat of their spilled blood melted the snow around the bodies, turning it to a vile slush. Murtagh, Willie, and Ferd. Shot in the backs of their heads. Dead because of her.

Alexander shouted her name. Catriona heard him from deep within her terrified stupor, but was powerless to react. Her mount stood still, waiting for instruction. Those instructions weren't within her grasp at the moment. Catriona sat paralyzed by the barbaric end of those who had cared enough to help her, those brave enough to challenge Calum.

Duff and Hew stepped out of the shadows, arms crossed over their chests and cradling their pistols in the crooks of their elbows. The evil pair of miscreants fixed her with dual merciless grins as they saun-tered toward her with slow, menacing steps.

The ratcheting sounds of unwinding chains rattled across the bailey. A loud familiar thud sounded behind her, breaking her paralysis so she could turn. The raised portcullis of the curtain wall slammed shut as she faced it. Trapped. Catriona found herself trapped within and Alexander and his men were powerless to help her. The sturdy gate barred them from her, shunning them to the outer side of the wall. With a squeeze of her knees, she urged her mount to the gate, sidling up alongside the thick heavy boards spaced just wide enough to shoot arrows at an invading enemy. She could see Alexander on the other side, witness the anguish in his face. Despair engulfing her, she held out a hand, fingers widespread. Helplessness wrenched a keening wail from the depths of her soul.

"Catriona!" he roared, racing his mount back and forth in front of the gate.

"Save yourself!" she sobbed through the barrier preventing her escape. "Run," she screamed just as Duff yanked the reins out of her hands and held tight to her horse. The evil fool shoved the barrel of his pistol in between the bars of the gate and pointed it at Alexander. He paused, glanced back at Catriona and winked, then turned back and pulled the trigger.

CHAPTER 11

*N*o matter how close she sat to the fire, nor how tight she hugged her cloak around herself, Catriona remained ice cold and numb clear to the bone. She stared at the roiling glow of the red coals and the pale weak flames flickering in the tiny hearth. How had everything gone so wrong? Who had betrayed her? She closed her eyes as a fresh onslaught of tears and despair overcame her.

Murtagh. The unrelenting pain of his murder assaulted her with guilt and remorse. 'Twas her fault. If she hadna challenged Calum, dearest grouchy old Murtagh would still be alive. "Sweet Murtagh," she whispered between hiccupping sobs. "I'm so verra sorry."

And Alexander. If possible, even more pain seared through her heart. She prayed he'd dodged the foul Duff's bullet, prayed he'd been out of range and escaped. Calum's hellhound had crowed with glee after firing the shot, sworn he'd hit Alexander, and gloated about it every step of the way to this godforsaken room.

Perched on the slab of dusty stone protruding up from the floor around the small fireplace, Catriona leaned against the flat, round sandstones forming the walls of the narrow hearth and the chimney. No other light flickered in the small forgotten room in the northern-most wing of the keep, the part of the keep her parents had shared when Mother still lived. This part of the stronghold had been closed off for years. No one would look for her here. The tight, narrow room had more than likely been a tiny space for a maidservant.

A small cot, draped with a ratty, dust-encrusted sheet, took up one wall and a dented chamber pot squatted beside it. A tattered tapestry sagged down from the corner of the single window at the end of the boxy space; the glass cracked from top to bottom and smudged with so much filth little light, whether from moon, stars, or rising sun, filtered through it. A three-legged stool filled the small spot beneath the window. Candle stubs, squat and round but burned down to near uselessness, littered the floor along the wall. Perhaps, Catriona hadna been the first imprisoned here.

Keys rattled and clanked against the door.

Catriona pressed back against the stones of the hearth, swallowing hard as she watched what she felt was a demonic light flicker and dance its way toward her from under the door. It had to be Calum or one of his blackguards. No one else knew she was here. With a final heart-stopping metallic thud, the thick squat door swung open with a slow chilling creak.

"My dear sweet lass. What have they done to ye?"

"Gaersa!" Catriona sprang up from the floor, flinging herself into the aging housekeeper's open arms. "I'm so sorry," she sobbed against Gaersa's plump shoulder. "I'm so, so sorry about Murtagh."

"Hush now," Gaersa soothed in a voice broken and quivering with her own tears. "'Twas no' your fault, child, 'twas no' your fault." She patted and rubbed Catriona's back as the two held each other tight and rocked back and forth in their misery.

Gaersa took a gentle hold of Catriona's shoulders and set her aside. She reached just outside the doorway and fetched the small lantern hanging on the latch beside the door. Light held high, she looked about the small room, her mouth clamped into a scowling frown and her face drawn with weariness and sorrow. "I canna believe they put ye here. No' in this room."

Something in Gaersa's voice told Catriona that they once used this small room for something sinister rather than an innocuous resting place for a servant. "I didna ken this place. Not even when Mother lived."

Gaersa hitched her way to the window and placed the lantern on the small ledge. With a dismal sigh, she ripped the dusty coverlet off the small ramshackle bed, bundled it up and dragged it and the moth-eaten pallet beneath it into the hall. She turned back into the room and gave a sad shake of her head as she stared down at what was little more than a wide wooden bench. "This room is where your father found his pleasure when his drunken binges pushed his wickedness to even darker depths."

She motioned a bent finger toward a pair of rusty shackles hanging from iron rings embedded in the wall above the bed, odious *accouterments* that Catriona hadna noticed. "An evil monster, your father was." Her hand dropped to her side as she turned to Catriona. "Calum kens this place well because this was where his father trained him to be just as vile and cruel."

Gaersa's words made the room feel even colder and the damp mustiness hanging heavy in the air took on a more nauseating stench. Catriona pressed her fists hard against her stomach and struggled not to gag on the bile rising in the back of her throat. She had always known her father was even more cruel when he drank but she'd imagined nothing as depraved as this. Now she understood why Mother had become so inconsolable and enraged the night that Catriona had forgotten to bolt the door to her chambers and secure it even more so with a heavy bar drawn down across the inside of the door. She'd been less than ten years old at the time and had ne'er understood why Mother had always insisted she bolt and bar her door whenever she was within and not in Mother's presence. Now she knew.

A fearsome thought struck her. "Ye shouldna be here, Gaersa." She took hold of the old woman's plump arm and turned her toward the door. "I canna bear to lose ye, too. Go now and dinna come back."

Gaersa gave her a sad smile and shook her head. "Calum knows I'm here and he willna harm me."

"How can ye say that?" Catriona tried to move Gaersa with a firm but gentle push toward the door but the stubborn matron planted her stance and held fast. "He killed Murtagh just as sure as if he'd pulled the trigger himself."

"Calum willna harm me," Agnes repeated as she toddled just outside the door and fetched a cloth sack so bulging and full it almost became wedged in the small doorway. She pulled out bedding and blankets and spread them on the bed. Then she retrieved an even smaller cloth bundle and a wineskin from the bottom of the sack. "Bannocks and water. 'Twas all he'd allow me to bring up to ye tonight."

"He allowed it? Why?" Catriona could scarce believe her wicked brother hadn't just thrown her into the abandoned wing and left her there to die. She'd been more than shocked that Duff had even built her a fire before he'd left and locked the door behind him. "And how can ye be so verra certain that Calum willna harm ye if he sees all that ye've done for me?"

"Who do ye think tended to young Calum's wounds after his father finished with him?"

A cold, ominous knowing wrapped around her like a killing frost. "He hurt Calum?" When Gaersa had said they had used the room to teach Calum cruelty, she'd ne'er imagined that Calum had been a victim rather than a participant. She couldna bear to think of what her father might have done.

But now that she thought back over her childhood, she could almost pinpoint when it must have first happened. Calum would have only been nine or maybe ten years old. That was when his behavior changed. He'd been so different before then. She and Calum had almost been close. She tore her gaze from the shackles and looked Gaersa in the face. "But how did he get to him? Mother taught us to keep away from Father when he drank, taught us to bolt our doors whenever we went to our rooms."

Gaersa looked away, avoiding Catriona's gaze. "Your Mother gave him to your sire to keep ye safe."

What Gaersa proposed was unbelievable. "Nay." Catriona shook her head as she backed toward the window. "That canna be true.

Mother always favored Calum. Said he was the weak one. Spoiled him even."

"Your Father made her choose. I remember that night as clear as if it were yesterday. He grabbed up wee Angus and held his blade to the lad's throat. Little more than a bairn, he was, and just started to walking. He threatened to kill the wee babe if your *Mother* didna obey him and sacrifice one of ye to his games as he called them. Swore to her upon one of her most powerful curses in her grimoire, he did. Swore that whichever child she chose to spare, that child would be protected from him so long as he lived. 'Twas the dead of winter and he'd tired of the servants he'd already tormented and kent there'd be no fresh victims 'til they could hire new servants in the spring."

Catriona covered her ears and turned away. She couldna listen to any more, couldna bear any more pain, nor stomach any more suffering. Her splayed hand pressed flat on the cold cracked glass of the window, she shook with spasms of silent sobs, broken with dry retching.

"I'm thankful Alexander escaped this hellish place," she whispered as tears burned down her face. "I hope he rides as fast and hard away from here as he can go."

"Forgive me, lass. Believe me when I say, it breaks my old heart to have told ye these terrible things." Gaersa squeezed her shoulders then lifted the lantern off the window ledge. "But it was time ye learned the truth to help ye better understand your brother and why he does such cruel things."

"Understand him?" Catriona turned so fast she bumped the lantern and almost knocked it from Gaersa's hand. "I'm sorry for what Father must have done to him. Truly, I am. But I canna *understand* nor forgive the monster he is—no matter his past." No one could erase the cruelties Calum must've endured but nothing excused his perpetuating those cruelties on to others. "I love ye like a mother, Gaersa, but I beg ye, dinna return to this accursed room if your sole intent is to lecture me on turning the other cheek to my brother. I'd rather die and rot here than hear another word, ye ken?"

Gaersa acknowledged with a somber bowing of her capped head. "I understand." Her gazed drifted to the hearth as she held the lantern between her hands. "Calum has sworn to keep ye here until Jameson Campbell arrives and the two of ye are wed. Campbell has promised a strong alliance to Clan Neal in exchange for a wife and a dozen or so of our best horses, so ye should be safe from your brother's wrath for a bit."

What Gaersa said couldna be right. The old housekeeper must have misheard or gotten her information from an ill-informed rumor. Gordon Neal, her father, would never part with a dozen of his best horses. The herd of select and bred with the greatest care beasts had always been his pride and joy. 'Twas the one intelligent thing he'd ever done for the clan. The Neal herds were famous across Scotland and lusted after by many.

"I canna believe Father agreed to such," she said as she broke a stick across her knee then added it to the fire. Duff had left her little fuel. She'd have to make the stingy pile of spindly bits of branches last as long as possible. "I know Calum told him of the betrothal." With another stick, she stirred the fire. "He mentioned it. Seemed pleased because Calum told him he'd gotten Campbell to accept me with only a quarter of my dowry." She rose from the fire and faced Gaersa. "But there's no way he'd agree to losing his horses."

"He doesna have to agree," Gaersa said. "Your father is dead and Calum is now our chieftain."

"Dead?" Catriona staggered back then sat on the bed with a hard bounce, her knees gone weak with all that had happened. "When?"

"This verra night." Gaersa moved to the door, paused, then nodded toward the cloth of bread and the skin of water setting on the bed beside Catriona. "Eat, Catriona. Ye must keep your strength, aye?"

"For what reason?" Catriona snapped. "Why should I prolong this misery?"

The news of her father's death came as a watershed for the clan, barraging her with its own disturbing emotions: a sense of relief and finality but also chilling fear and dread. Implausible as it was, her situation had become even more dire. Calum had seized the chieftainship, ignoring the Neal elders and their advice. What would happen to the innocent people of Clan Neal now? Head throbbing and no tears left to cry, Catriona shoved the food and water to the end of the cot, sagged across the pallet, and curled up into a tight ball. "Dinna bring any more food, Gaersa. I dinna wish it, aye?"

Gaersa huffed out an angry grunt, then stomped forward and gave the spindly leg of the cot a hard kick. When Catriona ignored her, she latched hold of the footboard and shook the ramshackle bit of furniture until Catriona believed it would surely collapse beneath her. "I'll no' listen to such talk, Catriona Elizabeth Rose Neal. Ye've always been a fighter. Strong. Proud. Fearless." The old woman stepped back, her ample chest heaving as she gasped out her emotions. "Daren't ye make my beloved Murtagh's death be in vain, ye ken? Daren't ye give up now and abandon hope. 'Twould sully his memory and I'll no' have it." She stomped her foot and jerked the lantern higher, the spindly bit of iron and glass swinging from her fist. "Do ye hear my words? I'll no' have it! Ye are no' the first woman ever promised to a man she didna ken and I'll wager ye'll no' be the last. 'Tis no' the worst thing that could happen to ye, aye? Think of your poor brother and all he's endured."

Catriona sat bolt upright on the cot, rage fighting for supremacy among the storm of emotions roiling through her. She pointed toward the door. "Get out. I'll hear no more defending of poor Calum and his cruel choices. And I'll bear none of your heartless scolding about how I should count my blessings. The way I see it, I have little to celebrate this evening. My strongest of allies is gone, and those I thought I could trust have betrayed me." The hopelessness of her situation and the overwhelming sense of all she'd lost shook through her as she rose with both fists clenched and shuffled forward until she stood nose to nose with Gaersa. "Hope is lost, ye heartless old woman, and the enemy has won. Tell those who can do so to pack their things and escape this place, for God only knows what level of Hell waits for us here."

Gaersa backed up a step, eyes wide and double chin softly trembling. "Ye truly believe the MacCoinnich will abandon ye? Think ye so little of the man and his sense of honor?"

Catriona was no fool. Gaersa was but changing tactics in a weak attempt to return to Catriona's favor. No more. She'd ne'er trust Gaersa again. No' after the way she'd defended Calum's actions. "If Alexander has any 'sense' at all, he's already breached the northern pass and isna foolish enough to look back."

Life had betrayed her. Catriona trembled as she stared up at Gaersa. "Was your sole purpose in coming here to torment me? Ye regale me with my sire's cruel perversions, tell me to forgive Calum's ruthlessness because of his sufferings, and then hold out false hope about the only man who ever stirred my feelings?" She turned away from Gaersa and stared up at the moonlit window, then made a backward stabbing motion toward the door. "I told ye to get out. Leave me, Gaersa, and dinna come back."

Gaersa didn't respond but the sound of her footsteps shuffling out the door and its quiet thud when she closed it told Catriona that the old housekeeper, the woman she'd once trusted and loved as kin, had at last given her what she'd demanded: solitude.

As the keys jangled in the lock and the tumblers clicked and clanked into place, Catriona closed her eyes and bowed her head. With a hard swallow, she resolved to cry no more tears. Today had been a day of revelation and hard-learned lessons. Somewhere deep in her soul, she suspected Gaersa had been the one to betray her to Calum. She hated to think it was true but Gaersa's visit had planted that belief solid in her heart. If that were so, Gaersa had sealed the death of her husband and was just as much to blame for Murtagh's murder as Catriona.

Catriona stared down at her hands folded in her lap, remembering Alexander's oath to Murtagh to keep her safe. She replayed his anguished shouting of her name from beyond the gate and the terror she'd seen on his face when he had realized all was lost. Alexander had truly cared for her. And now he was gone.

CHAPTER 12

*H*e'd been helpless to save her as that grinning bastard had dragged her away. The sound of her screams echoed over and over in his mind, slicing deep into his soul and stoking his rage.

Alexander stared down at the keep from the secure outcropping he'd discovered at a higher elevation. Ben Nevis, the highest mountain in all of Scotland, might help fortify the Neal stronghold but it also provided innumerable ways to spy upon the clan and their movements.

From this vantage point, he could see most of the area inside the curtain wall but couldna quite see clear into the bailey to identify individuals as they scurried about, increasing the guard around the fortress. They held their torches high, unwittingly helping Alexander pinpoint their posts and count their numbers. Alexander found their behavior odd. Paranoid even. 'Twas a great deal of activity to protect a keep from as small a group as seven men. Alexander snorted out a satisfied grunt. Calum was afraid. Good. He should be.

Alexander's horse rumbled with a deep nicker, stomping in the cold night air then sidestepping all along the narrow plateau jutting out from the mountain. The lively animal was obvious in its ambivalence at being free of the stable. Murtagh had been right. The horses he'd chosen for their escape loved the snow and harsh weather of the Highlands.

Poor Murtagh. Betrayed by his own and now dead.

"We erred, brother. When do we go back to get her and make it right?" Graham asked as he sidled his mount up next to Alexander's.

"We need a solid plan," Alexander said more to himself than to his brother. He shifted in the saddle, the leather creaking in protest with every movement. "And we need to make haste." He nodded down toward the keep. "They're in quite a stir about something considering we're only seven of us."

Graham studied the scene for a long moment, his dark eyes narrowing into a scowl as the wintry wind whipped his black hair about his face. "Methinks additional things are afoot other than our attempt at freeing Catriona."

Magnus nosed his horse in between Graham and Alexander. "Have the two of ye a plan yet? Bloodlust runs high in this group at present."

Alexander stole a glance back at Alasdair, Ian, Duncan, and Sutherland. The sight of the men reminded him of the four horsemen from Revelations. Mother had bid him memorize that book of the Bible. Perhaps she had sensed his destiny. Aye. Mother knew him well. She knew his thirst for vengeance.

He acknowledged his restless kin with a nod and pulled his attention back to the keep below. "We dinna ken where they've taken her, nor what's been done to her." That thought alone nearly drove him insane.

"We need someone on the inside willing to give us information," Graham said as he sat taller in the saddle.

"Our *someone* was betrayed and now they've tossed his body outside the walls to the wolves," Alexander said, wishing that somehow, they could retrieve Murtagh's remains and give the man a proper burial—for Catriona's sake.

Graham leaned forward and gave Alexander a pointed look. "We have 'the Ghost,' brother." He glanced toward Magnus then returned his attention to Alexander. "And I believe there are at least two young maidservants working in Neal keep that would be more than happy to do his bidding."

"Aye," Magnus agreed with a shrug to shift his white-blond braid back from across his shoulder to his back. He pointed down the mountain with a casual jab of a finger. "I could slip in right about there. See the weakness where the outer wall connects to Ben Nevis? Take note the space between the blocks of the wall and the stones. A man could slip through easy enough."

Alexander studied the breach. "Aye, a man could slip through and make his way to the back hallways of the keep." He shifted in the saddle, worrying the reins between his hand. "But if anyone goes in alone—'twill be me."

"Ye are no' fast enough on your feet just yet," Magnus argued. "And ye've ne'er been quiet—wounded or no'. Ye canna run. Ye canna crouch nor climb. Ye'd be discovered in a matter of minutes."

Though his limp was vastly improved, Alexander grudgingly admitted that Magnus might have a valid point. But that didna change the fact he needed to be the one inside that keep, needed it more than anyone could imagine. Guilt at the mishandled escape burned through his veins like a raging fever.

"I can do more than ye know when the need arises." He kept his focus trained on the goings on below, wishing he could see within those walls, find Catriona. He pulled his attention away from the Neal clan's movements and turned to Magnus. "I have to be the one, ye ken?"

Magnus glared at him. His eerie blue-white eyes narrowed, and his blond brows knitted into a scowl. "Ye must use your head in this, Alexander. Not your heart," he said quietly. "Ye risk her life if ye dinna plan well and ye ken that as well as I."

"They said a regiment's coming," Graham mused as he rolled his shoulders and stretched in the saddle. He turned to Alexander. "Did Catriona say if her betrothed would come here or was she traveling to wed him? If she's traveling, we could steal her away then."

Alexander tightened his fists around the reins and leaned forward, his anxiousness and frustration building. "She never said. All she knew was that she'd marry in the spring as soon as the passes cleared enough for travel."

"The passes are clear enough now, I reckon," Magnus said as he backed his horse down from the narrow plateau and turned the beast toward the other men waiting on the trail to the northern pass of the mountain. He twisted in the saddle and looked back at Alexander. "Give me a few hours, Alexander. I'll find what we need to know to win this battle." A rare smile broke through Magnus's solemn countenance. "'Twill be my wedding gift to ye, aye?"

Alexander ignored the wedding comment. The fact remained he had nothing to offer Catriona other than freedom from her brother. He studied Magnus for a long moment. The waiting would be torture but after mulling it over, he realized he had no choice. He agreed with a stiff nod, scowling down at his still healing leg and cursing it. His other wounds healed and forgotten, already added to scars covering his body. He'd always healed quickly but this leg injury had sorely tested his patience. "Be quick about it, aye?"

"Aye." Magnus urged his horse down the narrow path heading down the mountain toward the keep.

Alexander turned to Graham where he waited beside him on his mount. "Take the men and find what shelter ye can that's close."

Graham nodded then turned his horse toward Duncan, Sutherland, Alasdair, and Ian. "Shelter. Close," he called out before reaching them. The four men splintered off, each of them taking a different direction. Graham took to the path leading toward the pass.

Dismounting, Alexander led his horse to the back of the plateau closer to the mountain. He found a spot out of the wind, large enough for both himself and the horse, surrounded by gigantic sprouts of stone jutting up from the earth like rows of great gray teeth.

"And now we wait," he said as he patted the horse's neck. He secured the animal's reins around the trunk of a twisted young tree. If he wasn't on the beast, he'd have to keep it tied. This close to its home, if it discovered itself riderless, it would eventually end up back at the keep. "I'll be back as soon as I see Magnus is safely through."

He walked back to the edge of the precipice and looked down.

Magnus's silver-white hair shone in the moonlight, making him easy to spot in his descent down the mountain. "Cover your hair, man," Alexander said under his breath. "They're sure to see ye from the turrets."

As if he'd heard him, Magnus's almost glowing mane disappeared. Alexander strained to follow his movements, barely picking out his form amongst the shadows. Magnus needed to hurry. In just a few hours' time, daybreak would be upon them.

Frustrated beyond measure, Alexander returned to his horse and sat on the edge of a boulder beside the beast. He'd ne'er handled idleness well.

* * *

CATRIONA STARED up at the ceiling, watching the shadows dance with the flickering firelight from the hearth. She peered at one particular crack in the plaster, not blinking until her eyes burned with the need for it. With the slow determination of a butterfly fighting to emerge from its chrysalis, her bull-headed sense of survival returned. There had to be a way out of this mess that her life had become. Had to be. All that remained was to find it.

She rose from the cot and set to pacing the length and width of the room. Ten strides from one end to the other and six strides across. Not even big enough for a proper tomb. She paused mid-stride. A tomb. Maybe that was her means of escape.

Calum adored pomp and circumstance but only if it focused on him. She harbored no doubt he'd dump their father into his final resting place with no funeral decorum at all. If she could convince Gaersa to intercede on her behalf, perhaps the old housekeeper could persuade Calum to allow her one last visit to her father's gravesite. 'Twould be expected for the chieftain's daughter to pay her respects and bid him farewell. Such an opportunity would free her of this godforsaken place and provide a means of escape.

But could she trust Gaersa?

Gaersa's demeanor when she'd shown up in the room had set off warning bells that the housekeeper had never triggered in the past. But why? Why would Gaersa betray her? They'd always been so close. Now that she knew Calum's history, she understood Gaersa's softness toward him. The old woman had always made excuses for him and tried to look the other way no matter what he did. But did that mean she couldna be trusted at all? Was it safe to seek her aid?

The shuffling of footsteps and rattling keys sounded out in the hallway. Catriona faced the door, widening her stance and lifting her chin. Who would it be this time come to torment her?

The metallic thud of metal entering the lock, the clinking of multiple keys on a ring, then the door latch jiggling repeated in sequence over and over. It was as though whoever was on the other side of the doorway attempting to open it didn't have a clue which key to use.

"Damnation and demon's balls," a young voice growled out in a low hiss on the other side of the portal.

Catriona rushed to the door and pressed her face close to the crack. "Sawny? Is that you?"

"Aye, m'lady. Me and Tom come to get ye out if we can find the right feckin' key."

A glimmer of hopefulness thrilled through her and brought a smile to Catriona's lips. Who knew her saviors would be a pair of young lads? *Praise be.* The keys rattled again, coupled with another string of curse words. Well, they'd save her if they could ever figure out which key to use.

"Are ye sure them's the r-r-right ones?" That was Tom. Poor lad. Such a stutter.

"Hush, Tom!" Sawny snapped in a loud whisper. "I lifted them from her own pocket, I did. These here are the only keys she had. Now hush up, soon as I get the door open, ye must take them and put them back in her apron afore she wakes up."

Catriona rolled her eyes and leaned back beside the door. This could take a while. Bless their little hearts. She massaged her temples, squinting against the pounding ache inside her head. No more tears. Tears did nothing but make your head throb.

After what seemed like forever, the latch clicked, and the door creaked open, revealing two wide-eyed young laddies. Sawny greeted her with a proud grin. "I told ye we'd get ye out."

"That ye did." Catriona hugged both the boys. She'd never been so glad to see those two ragamuffins in all her life.

Sawny handed the ring of keys over to Tom. "Hurry now. Her apron's hanging on the bedpost beside her pillow so step with care or she'll have both our heads on a plate just like she did Murtagh."

Tom took the keys, clamping them between both hands to keep them quiet. "G-G-Godspeed, m'lady," he said with a respectful bob of his head then bolted out of sight down the dark hallway.

Catriona sent a silent prayer after the young lad, begging for protection against his getting caught. She turned back to Sawny, something he'd said pricking her like a splinter. "Ye said Gaersa betrayed Murtagh. Are ye certain, Sawny, or could it be rumor?"

Anger flashed red across Sawny's freckled face and his blue eyes narrowed. "I heard her with me own ears, Mistress. She didna tell Calum herself but she as good as did and I wouldha warned Murtagh, too, if she hadna locked me and Tom in the pantry." He plucked at her sleeve with an impatient jerk as he held the lantern higher and side-stepped down the hallway. "We've no' much time. 'Twill be dawn soon."

"Lead on." Catriona grabbed up her skirts and hurried after the boy, wishing all the while they had more light. She didn't remember this wing. She didn't know what secrets the place might hold.

"Over here, m'lady." Sawny stood beside a stone archway that had a moth-eaten set of heavy curtains hung across it for a door.

When she swept aside the curtain, Catriona realized what it was: the garderobe for this wing of the keep. Still holding the rotting curtain to one side, she turned to Sawny. "The garderobe?"

"Aye," Sawny hurried to explain as he pushed past her and lifted away the wide board with the hole in the center. He pointed down-ward. "This shaft empties out close to a set of caves with passages connected to the stable's main chamber. Only me and Tom know about them. I figure ye can hide in them caves until that bastard—

begging your pardon, Mistress…" Sawny paused and gave her a polite ducking of his chin. "I ken he's your brother and all that but the man killed Murtagh." He took a deep breath and continued, all the while pointing downward at the gaping hole that had carried away human waste and whatever else was dumped down it. "But I figure ye can hide in them there caves until me and Tom find a way to get ye a horse so's ye can escape."

Pressing the back of her hand against her mouth and nose, Catriona peered down the chute. A thankful breath escaped her. It looked to be dry as dust—full of cobwebs—but dry and only smelled of dank, musty castle rather than the other aromas one might expect to find in the garderobe.

"This is the highest floor in the keep. Are ye certain the chute empties close enough to the ground so I dinna risk breaking my neck?" Her concern was valid. Some garderobe chutes were short runs that opened out at the same height of whatever floor they were on and the waste ran down the side of the castle.

"'Tis safe," Sawny reassured with a quick bob of his head. "Me and Tom tried it to be sure." He shuffled in place and gave a weak shrug of one shoulder. "We were looking for a quick way to get out and hide in case your brother…" his voice trailed off as he swallowed hard and shrugged again. "The servants he takes a liking to dinna always come back, so we wanted to make certain we had a way to escape."

So Calum had become just as vile as the monster who had created him. She'd known he was cruel and manipulative but, without a doubt, he'd reached levels she'd never imagined—nor did she wish to imagine such evil. Catriona pulled Sawny into a hug. "The both of ye, you and Tom, need to come with me. 'Tis wicked dangerous here and will be so until I rid the place of Calum."

Sawny smiled and his cheeks flamed red again but this time not from anger. "We have to get yourself safe first, m'lady." He held the lantern over the chute and held out his hand. "Keep your feet and your hands on the walls to slow your way down through the tunnel or ye'll end up rolling out arse over teakettle."

Catriona peered down the hole again and tried not to think about all the things that had touched those walls over the years. *I wanted a plan. I got a plan. Time to move.* She grabbed up her skirts and clambered into the hole, sitting on the edge of the great stone refuse tunnel. She swallowed hard and focused on Sawny as she wedged her hands against the opposite sides of the opening then did the same with her feet inside the tunnel on the walls. With her arms locked, she held herself secure and in place until time to begin her descent.

"'Twill be fine, Mistress," Sawny encouraged. "I'd never do anything to harm ye."

"I ken ye well to be loyal and true, dear lad, and for that ye have my gratitude." She looked down between her feet, said a silent prayer, then began her descent, inching herself from side to side with slow, calculated concentration. She glanced back up at Sawny peering down at her over the lip of the chute. "I'll see ye at the end of the tunnel, aye?"

"Aye," Sawny promised. "I'll be waiting there for ye to lead ye to the caves."

Then he replaced the board atop the hole and disappeared.

"I can do this," she repeated under her breath as she descended deeper into the darkness.

CHAPTER 13

"Your lady seems to have disappeared."

"Say again." Alexander halted mid-step of his pacing in front of the small fire burning at the back of the cave. Nerves raw as though he'd been skinned alive, he'd waited at the plateau until Magnus had returned and then the infuriating man had vexed him even more by refusing to divulge any information until they'd reached the cavern and the other men.

"Gone." Magnus stressed the word with a flamboyant opening of one hand toward the mouth of the grotto as though releasing a bird to freedom. "The keep was in such a stir to find her, I'd thought for certain that ye'd disregarded my advice and somehow swept the lass right out from under their noses." Magnus folded his arms across his chest and gave Alexander a scolding look. "Fair pissed at ye, I was for no' including me in your wee adventure."

"Gone," Alexander repeated, ignoring Magnus's uncharacteristic jovialness. What the devil was wrong with the man? Catriona's well-being was at stake here. "How the hell is she *gone* from there?" 'Twas all he could do to keep from throttling Magnus for giving him such disturbing information in such a callous way. "Spit out the details, man, afore I kill ye and if ye value your arse, ye'll adjust your attitude and lose the levity."

Magnus's rare, light-hearted humor evaporated like the morning mist seared away by the rising sun. "Forgive me, but I felt the news that the lass had so quick escaped them deserved a small bit of celebration."

"Celebration? We'll no' celebrate 'til Catriona is at my side, ye ken?" Alexander stabbed the air with a pointing finger aimed at Magnus. "Details. Now."

"The old housekeeper discovered her missing when she took her a bowl of parritch to break her fast." Magnus accepted a dried oatcake from Sutherland, bit off a hunk, and chewed a damn sight too long to suit Alexander.

Sensing Alexander's displeasure, Magnus hurried to wash it down with a swig from a skin of water. Nose wrinkled and lips drawn at what must have been the stale taste, he drew a small flask of whisky out from an inner pocket of his jacket and took a quick nip. His displeased look disappeared. "Two serving lads have gone missing as well. One of them had a sister working in the kitchens. I spoke with her. She thinks the boys helped Catriona escape. Said that her brother Sawny had sworn revenge on the entire clan for no' protecting old Murtagh and kent well enough that Catriona would help him see justice served."

Sawny. Alexander pondered a long moment, sorting through his memories at *Tor Ruadh.* The image of the red-haired lad always in the middle of some kerfuffle came to mind. *Aye. Sawny.* The memory triggered a sad smile. He remembered the lad and Catriona's exasperated fondness for the boy. He blinked away the thought and turned to study Magnus. "Where would they take her? She has to be close. They've no' had time to do anything but hide her."

"That I couldna discover," Magnus said as he paced alongside Alexander. "Ye said ye watched the keep the whole time, aye? Ye saw no one come or go?"

Alexander thought back, racing through all he'd seen during his watch. A heavy sigh escaped him along with a slow shake of his head.

Catriona had to be close to the keep, maybe even still within it. Hidden rooms and passages honeycombed most keeps. He felt certain Clan Neal's stronghold was the same. But where? While Magnus's report was frustrating, it spawned hope and a small amount of solace because Catriona was no' alone in her trials at present. She'd found a pair of daring allies. Then a disturbing thought occurred to him.

"Ye best go back and fetch Sawny's sister," he said to Magnus. "There's no telling what Calum might do to get information from her and that could verra well flush Sawny and the other lad out of hiding."

Magnus huffed out a low laugh as he took another drink from his flask. "The admirable lads already thought of that. Young Mistress Jenny had her possessions packed and was slipping out of the keep when I intercepted her." Magnus chuckled again. "Poor lass. I gave her quite the scare."

"Ye have that effect on women," Graham interjected as he sauntered forward out of the shadows and joined the men in front of the fire.

"Aye," Duncan chimed in from his post at the cave's entrance. With a teasing grin, he made a casual motion toward Magnus. "That pale skin and those eyes of yours. Women think ye're the grim reaper come to take them away."

Magnus ignored the men, directing his conversation to Alexander. "I made sure she was well beyond the curtain walls afore I left her. She's headed to kin near Fort William."

Alexander felt better with that knowledge but it still didna change the fact he was no closer to finding Catriona. He paced his way to the mouth of the cave, stepped out into the clearing, and studied the horizon. 'Twas already the eerie half-lit time between night and day. The in-between time that toyed with the senses, making shadows sinister and rocks and trees look like predators about to attack. The full light of the rising sun would be upon them soon.

Magnus and the other men joined him. "Well?" Graham asked. "Act now or rest during the day and wait 'til nightfall?"

"I'm going down there." No way in hell could he wait an entire day and the suggestion of resting was absurd. He turned to his men.

"Alasdair and Ian." He waited until those two stepped to the front of the group. No matter what happened, he'd keep his cousins together. Ian's stability was still a troubling uncertainty and Alasdair was the only one who stood a chance at helping his brother bear his grief over the loss of his wife and not go spiraling off the cliff into the abyss of insanity. "The two of ye hie yourselves toward Fort William. If a regiment's headed this way, they'll most likely come from that direction. Find them. Assess them. Then return here, aye?"

The brothers nodded and without a word, went to their horses, mounted and left.

"Duncan and Sutherland," Alexander said, adrenaline thrumming his voice into the low deepness of a drum call to arms. Warmongering excitement heated his blood as his plan set into motion. "Catriona's betrothed could be headed this way as we speak. Find Jameson Campbell. One of ye stay with him and one of ye report back here with your information, ye ken?"

"We could kill him," Duncan offered.

"Aye," Sutherland agreed as they turned to go to their horses. "He is a Campbell, ye ken?"

Alexander shook his head. As much as he agreed with his brother's reasoning, they didna need to kill the man—no' just yet. "No killing. Yet. Understand?"

Sutherland acknowledged the order with a lifted hand and a shrug. "Aye, brother. We willna kill him—yet."

Alexander watched his youngest brothers ride away then turned back to Graham and Magnus. "I intend to approach the keep from the farthest side where the curtain wall connects to the cave housing the stable. 'Tis the direct opposite from where ye entered, Magnus, and 'twas well out of my view as I stood watch. They couldha taken her there without us knowing."

Magnus nodded. "I would assume that where ye speak of should have the same weakness as this side. We should be able to breach it as easy."

"And us?" Graham asked.

"I ask that ye come with me," Alexander replied. "If ye will?"

"If we will?" Graham repeated with a narrow-eyed look. "Dinna be an arse, brother."

"Then to our horses, men," Alexander said. Every crunching step through the melting ice and snow layered across the clearing heightened his readiness for this battle. Bloodlust and thirst for vengeance pumped harder and a healthy dose of rage fueled the dangerous combination. Predatory anticipation pounded with every beat of his heart, tightening every fiber. He mounted his horse and took the lead down the winding narrow path.

I thank ye for this fine horse, Murtagh. May ye rest in peace. The beast needed little direction where to go. 'Twas as if he could feel what Alexander needed and complied without hesitation. Down the mountainside they went. With the greatest care, they picked their way around jutting crags of sharp-toothed boulders pushing up through the moss-covered soil like ancient fingers reaching for the sky. Alexander hoped to reach the level of the keep before dawn broke full upon them. They needed the safety of the shadows.

Alexander kept a close watch on the fortress, scanning the tops of the walls and peering at the arrow slits in the towers. Windows lined the turrets, looking like great dark eyes staring down at them. He saw no movement nor any lit torches. This side of the keep appeared to be unguarded.

They count on the safety of the mountain too much, me thinks. Alexander reined in his horse, pausing just before they reached the base of the keep where it connected to Ben Nevis. The terrain on this side of the stronghold was more harsh, covered with great chunks of granite and sharp spikes of stone. Slippery patches of mud trailed through the rocky landscape. Water from the melting snow puddled everywhere. The only color against the backdrop of dreary beiges, browns and grays painting the ridge and the wall of the fortress was the deep healthy greens of the holly bushes speckled with the vibrant reds of the plant's poisonous berries.

"This side of the keep appears unprotected," Graham observed as he sidled his horse to Alexander's left.

"Good," Magnus said as he brought his horse up on Alexander's right.

He pulled in a deep breath, then leaned forward, shifting in the saddle and studying the area. As he inhaled, he caught the slightest unexpected scent. He frowned and twisted to the left. *Smoke.* He lifted his nose and sniffed again, holding in the cold air and gleaning every clue it held. "There's a fire nearby. Smoke taints the air, and it's no' coming from the keep."

Magnus and Graham peered at him for a long moment then lifted their own noses and tested the air.

"Aye," Graham said as he turned to the left and nodded toward the place where the curtain wall snugged up against the mountain. "'Tis coming from that direction for certain."

Alexander dismounted but kept the reins of his mount wound around his left hand. With his right, he pulled his pistol from his belt and held it ready. "We'll ease that way then, aye?"

Graham and Magnus slid to the ground with soundless movements and quieted their horses. Graham held out his hand. "Give me your reins. I'll take the horses out of range and secure them." He gave Alexander a threatening look as he turned to go. "Hide here and wait for me, aye? Dinna ye start without me."

"Aye," Alexander grudgingly agreed. As much as he'd rather rush ahead, they needed to wait for Graham. Who knew what they might be up against and more guns and blades could verra well make the difference. He and Magnus took cover behind a monstrous outcropping of stones.

Magnus leaned back against the largest of the dark gray spires then squinted up at the sky. "He needs to make haste. 'Twill be full dawn in moments."

Alexander propped his boot on a small boulder and rested back against the shorter pile of rocks. "Aye. With Catriona missing they're sure to search everywhere. This side of the keep willna be unprotected long. If she's near, we need to find her first."

Graham popped into view from a different direction than what he'd taken, giving them both an adrenaline surging start.

"Dammit, man!" Alexander scolded in a strained whisper. "Dinna creep up on us. Do ye fancy getting shot?"

"I saw one of the boys." Graham grinned and jerked his thumb back over his shoulder. "Someone should tell the lad to cover his flaming red hair. 'Tis like a beacon amongst the dark colors of these stones."

"He was alone?" Alexander asked.

"Aye," Graham said as he turned and motioned for them to follow. "Out fetching wood, he was. Come. I saw where he slipped into the mountain."

"Lead on," Alexander said as he pushed away from his stony seat. They were so close. So close to finding Catriona. He wanted to roar and rush headlong to wherever Graham was leading. He forced himself to slow down and remain calm, gritting his teeth and clenching his jaws shut against making a sound.

Every step required the greatest care as they crossed the slippery path of mud and ice. With slow, steady movements, they climbed higher then angled to the right toward the direction of the keep. While winding through a smaller field of boulders, Alexander spotted their destination. Up ahead, in the side of the great imposing mountain, it looked as though the earth had taken in a huge deep breath and split its seams. An ominous dark crack gaped open just wide enough for a man to slip through.

Graham crouched behind a tangle of leafless bushes, their dried, knotted branches making an effective shield. He pointed to the opening in the mountain. "There." He looked back at Alexander. "We've no way of knowing what lies inside. Could be a passage or could open out into a cave. If the lads have weapons…"

"We'll disarm them without bringing them harm," Alexander replied. They were just boys. Little more than bairns. And they cared about Catriona just as she cared about them. He clapped a hand to Graham's shoulder and pulled past him. "I'll be going first, aye?"

Neither Graham nor Magnus responded, just fell in step behind Alexander.

Alexander paused at the opening, his back pressed against the stony side of the ridge. He leaned in close to the gaping fissure and listened. All he heard was a steady drip plunking into standing water then echoing throughout. He eased into the dark space, taking care where he placed his feet. Cave floors often held cracks large enough to swallow a man. He paused and allowed his eyes to adjust to the darkness. They wouldna be able to travel far without torches. The great hole boring into the side of the mountain was black as the Earl of Hell's waistcoat.

A pale light flickered off in the distance and the sound of shifting rocks echoed from up ahead.

"Are they coming this way?" Magnus whispered.

"Shh…" Alexander reached back and squeezed Magnus's arm.

"Dinna let Mrs. Aberfeldy catch ye. That old cow as good as shot Murtagh herself. She willna pause when it comes to shooting your-self." 'Twas one of the boys advising the other. Sounded like Sawny talking to the other lad.

The lights split into two flickering orbs, bobbing toward them in the darkness. Rocks tumbled and rattled, the loose shale shifting with each boy's steps. The second light halted then switched directions, retreating deeper into the inky blackness until it flickered out of sight. Alexander pressed tighter against the damp cave wall and motioned for Graham and Magnus to do the same.

"G-G-God's beard! We're f-found, Sawny!" The dark-haired boy turned tail to run but Alexander grabbed hold of the boy by the scruff of his shirt and yanked him back.

"Hush, boy!" One arm latched around the boy's chest, Alexander held tight to the lad's wrist to keep the wily scamp from hitting him in the face with the torch. "I'm Alexander MacCoinnich. Friend to Catriona."

"Sawny, r-run!" the boy screeched before Alexander could cover his mouth.

Alexander yanked the torch out of the lad's grasp, shoved the boy into Magnus's arms, and launched forward. "Hold him whilst I try to stop Sawny."

His speed hindered by the treacherous ground riddled with cracks, loose rocks and shelves of protruding shale into his path, Alexander forged ahead. The light up ahead grew stronger and so did the tang of smoke mixed with the unmistakable aroma of meat roasting over an open fire. "Sawny! 'Tis Alexander MacCoinnich! I mean ye no harm!" He prayed the boy would hear his shout through the panic his friend had stirred. "Catriona! Are ye there?"

"I am here, Alexander! I'm here!"

Something taught snagged across his shins then popped as though it had snapped. Alexander heard a great shifting rumble to his left that grew louder by the second. *The little bastards set a trap.* The searing pain in his weak leg triggered a groaning roar as he forced it into action. Alexander leapt across a wide crack in the cavern's floor, landed hard on the other side, and rolled to a stop. A jumble of loose rocks shot past him as he flattened himself against the wall and shielded his head as best he could with his arms.

"Sweet Jesu!" Catriona's desperate cry echoed through the cave. "Ye've killed him, Sawny. Your trap has surely killed him."

"I didna mean to," Sawny said in a panicked tone that squeaked and broke with the troubles of a young boy growing to be a man. "M'lady, I swear to ye, I didna mean to kill him."

"I'm no' dead!" Alexander shouted from the darkness of the ledge. He was, however, afraid to move. He'd lost the feckin' torch and couldna even see his hand in front of his face. "Bring a torch, boy! Now!"

Footsteps scrabbled toward him, sending a watershed of shifting rocks bouncing across the floor and over the edge of the precipice. A brilliant light appeared above him. The flames crackled and danced on the end of a crude torch made of pitch-soaked cloth wrapped around a chunky stick of wood. Alexander wormed his way out from under the ledge, scraping knees, elbows and shins in the sharp debris. The flaming light held high, Sawny helped him stand then positioned himself under Alexander's arm to support his weak side. "I had to set the trap. I had no choice. Ye ken that well enough, aye?"

"Aye, lad. I ken it well enough." Alexander took the torch from Sawny, peeled the boy out of his armpit and placed him in front of him. "Lead the way, boy," he said as he held the torch higher. As he lifted his gaze above Sawny's tousled head, he caught his breath. There was Catriona. A pure vision dearer than he'd e'er realized until that verra moment.

She held a flaming beacon in one hand while her other hand clutched an arisaidh about her shoulders. The fire of the flickering light lent a golden glow to her alabaster skin and deepened the richness of her auburn hair. Her pale lips were parted, and she watched with worry knotting her brow.

As soon as he reached her, Alexander shoved the torch into Sawny's hands then gathered Catriona up into his arms and crushed her to his chest. "I feared I'd ne'er see ye again," he whispered into the softness of her hair. Tossing her light to Sawny, Catriona's arms squeezed tighter around him and Alexander relished the urgency in her touch.

"I feared the same," she said with a soft, hiccupping sob as she lifted her face to his.

"Your eyes are a deeper green when ye cry," Alexander said, losing himself in her gaze with a gladness that rushed through him. With the tenderest of touches, he kissed away her tears then took her mouth with his, claiming hold of all the sensations she wrought in him and fueling the moment with all he hoped to give her in return. He needed her. Needed this. Her touch. Her taste. The feel of her safe in his arms. He'd never risk losing her again.

"A light wouldna be amiss to help us reach ye, Alexander."

"Aye there! Alexander!" The hollow sound of rocks scrabbling and bouncing toward them pinged through the darkness. "Alexander! Have ye forgotten us, man?"

Graham and Magnus's shouts finally broke into the wondrous place he'd discovered in Catriona's arms. With a great deal of regret, he ended the kiss, lifted his head, and found Sawny standing close by with a silly grin on his freckled face. "Lead them here, aye?"

"Aye," the lad said with a happy snort as he handed them one of the torches then headed to the mouth of the cave and Alexander's men.

"Ye've scraped yourself bloody!" Catriona said as she held the light higher and eased out of his embrace. "Come. The boys just brought in a bit a water. I'll clean ye up."

"Ever the nursemaid," he teased, already feeling the loss of her warmth and hating it. "'Tis but a few scratches. Nothing to worry after. I assure ye."

Rocks flying and steps thundering, Tom and Sawny ran past them and Graham and Magnus followed close behind. "Men coming!" Sawny called out in an urgent whisper as he paused and waved them forward. "Hurry! We must get past the second trap and douse the fires afore they spot us."

"Who?" Alexander asked as he latched hold of Graham's arm and yanked his brother to a stop.

"I dinna ken," Graham answered. "But they be from the keep. Young Tom spotted them headed this way. If they decide to explore the cave, we're trapped."

"Like hell we are!" Catriona's tone held the rage of a mother bear protecting her cubs. "This way—now!"

"Nay." Grabbing one of the torches, Alexander drew his sword, stepped across the great gaping crack at its narrowest point, and motioned for the rest to be on their way. "I'll run no more this day. Go to safety while I wait here to greet our guests."

"Nay!" Catriona called out to him. "Just reunited and now I could lose ye again? Nay, I beg ye. Come with us!"

Her words filled his heart to near bursting. He gave her his most reassuring smile and motioned for her to go. "Go now, m'lady. Keep safe. I'll return to ye once again as soon as tis clear and well to do so."

Before Catriona could argue again, he stomped out the light of his torch and placed it against the wall behind his heels. Sword drawn and ready, Alexander watched Graham and Magnus drag Catriona away. He watched them until the light of their torches disappeared and left him in complete darkness.

Voices came from the direction of the mouth of the cave and he heard the striking of flints to set fire to beacons.

He resettled his grip on his sword and steadied his stance.

"Come to me," he whispered. "Come to me now."

CHAPTER 14

"I canna believe we left him there. Alone in the darkness." Catriona jerked her wrist out of Graham's grasp, ran to the small fire next to the stone ledge, and hurried to douse it with handfuls of dirt and sand scraped up from the cave floor. Brushing her hands against her skirts, she rose from the task, worry and fear knotting her insides and making her heart pound. She whirled about and faced him. "How could ye leave your own brother? How could ye leave him behind?"

"'Twas what he wished and Alexander is no' afraid of the dark, m'lady." Graham lit a fresh torch off of Sawny's and scanned the cavernous room. "Are we well past that second trap ye spoke of, lad?"

"Aye," Sawny replied. "We should be safe in this section of the cave but we best move to the back so our torchlight will be a sight dimmer and less apt to draw notice. 'Tis my hopes they willna smell the smoke of the doused fire."

While her common sense knew Sawny was right, her heart screamed out a hearty, "Nay!" Catriona pulled away, heading back toward the passage they'd just passed through to reach the heart of the cave where they'd set up a camp. She would wait at the edge, in the

129

darkness, until she saw Alexander safe. Then she'd guide him through the maze of passages to reach the more secure section of the cave.

A strong hand closed around her upper arm and pulled her back with a firm, gentle persistence. She jerked about and faced Magnus. "Let go of me, sir."

"Nay, m'lady." Magnus gave her a respectful nod then faced her toward the others and walked her back to join them by a determined steering of her arm. "If I allow anything ill to befall ye, Alexander will have me arse." He nodded again with a faint smile. "Beg pardon, m'lady."

A howling scream, strong at first then fading away, echoed back to them from the passages. A chill washed across Catriona's flesh, standing every hair on end.

Still holding tight to her arm, Magnus gave it a reassuring squeeze. "Ne'er ye fret. That wasna Alexander."

"How can ye know? How can ye be certain?"

"He doesna scream," Graham interjected. "He curses, growls, rants and roars but I've ne'er heard him scream. Mam swore he was a bear in a past life."

"Aye," Magnus agreed. "Most definitely a bear." He placed Catriona at the center of their group, the two men and two boys flanking her, as he positioned her against the wall.

Catriona wasn't stupid. She knew well enough that the only reason he'd placed her there was to prevent her from escaping them and going to Alexander.

"What do we do from here?" Sawny asked, excitement making his freckled face glow like a beacon in the torchlight. "When do we attack and reclaim our keep from that bastard?" He gave a sheepish jerk of one shoulder in Catriona's direction. "Beg your pardon, m'lady."

"Aye," young Tom chimed in. "We n-need to clear the k-keep of the chieftain's vermin as well."

"'Tis no' their fight, boys," Catriona said as she hugged herself against the damp chill of the cave. "And we've no coin to pay them for battle." She wasn't trying to insult the men. They were mercenaries. Mercenaries were paid to fight. She had no money, no title, no land

and her head ached with the effort of trying to think of a way to save her clan from Calum. But so far, she'd come up with nothing. She pulled in a deep, stubborn breath and released it. But she would think of something. She wouldna desert her people.

The thunderous sound of tumbling rocks and layers of loose shale falling reached them. Catriona closed her eyes and sent up a silent a prayer. *Protect Alexander. Please. I beg ye. Protect him and keep him safe.*

"Damn ye, Sawny. That last trap of yours came near to endin' me."

"Alexander!" Catriona burst free of the group, raced across the room, and leapt into Alexander's open arms. Arms tight around his neck and one leg wrapped around his middle like a brazen woman, she hugged him so hard she trembled. "I feared ye lost," she whispered against his neck. "I was so afraid."

One hand burdened with the torch, Alexander tightened his other arm around her, holding her as close and hard as she held him. "All is well, dear one. All is well."

Catriona closed her eyes, soaking in the wondrous feel of him against the length of her body. His strength. His heat. With her face snuggled up against his neck, she inhaled, imprinting his delicious scent in her memory forever. She pressed a kiss to his throat, flicking her tongue to steal a shy taste of his salty-sweet flesh. Such behavior. Shame should fill her. Behaving like a low-born ill-mannered woman. She was a betrothed woman promised to another, but she didna care. Alexander was all that mattered.

"I'm so glad ye're safe," she said in a low tone meant just for him. With an embarrassed reluctance, she withdrew her leg from the unladylike position around his waist and stretched to put both feet to the floor.

Alexander kept his arm around her, his hand splayed against the small of her back and holding her close. He smiled down at her, his dark eyes smoldering with a fire that both excited and frightened her. "And now we'll be seeing to your continued safety. I'll no' risk losing ye again."

Catriona swallowed hard against the excited fluttering of her heart. Now this was how a man should behave. She patted a hand to the center of his hard chest, straightening the buttoned seam of his *léine* with nervous tugs. "I dinna wish to lose ye again either."

"Then let us make a plan." Alexander pulled her to his side and walked with her across the room of the cave to where the others waited. "Chieftain Calum's force is now less three men," he said to Graham and Magnus.

"When do we attack?" Sawny asked.

Catriona's heart went out to the boy, so intent on avenging his dear Murtagh. She wanted Murtagh avenged as well, but they had to go about it with great care. "Plan first. Then attack. And as I said earlier, this is no' their fight."

"It is now, dearling." Alexander hugged her closer, pride and so much more showing in his smile. "Catriona speaks with great wisdom." He nodded to Graham and Magnus. "We need to return to our cave and regroup. Discover what the others have found."

"'Tis broad daylight, brother," Graham warned. "And we canna be certain that the horses have no' been found."

"The way I see it, we've a bit a time," Alexander said. "They willna send more men to search this area until they miss the three that now rest deep in the heart of the mountain."

"The boys are quick and sly as mousies in a pantry." Catriona took hold of Sawny's arm and hugged him to her other side. "Tell them where ye put the horses. They'll find them if they still be there."

"Aye, we'll find them," Sawny agreed with a bob of his head. "Where they be?"

"Ye ken where ye were gathering wood afore the sun rose?" Graham asked Tom.

Eyes rounding with the revelation he hadn't been as stealthy as he thought, Tom gave Graham a solemn nod. "Aye."

"Ten paces higher up the mountain. A small plateau hemmed in by great chunks of granite speckled like a quail's eggs, ye ken?"

Tom nodded and motioned for Sawny to join him. Both boys, with torches held high, disappeared into the tunnels leading to the opening of the cave.

"I canna bear to wait here," Catriona said to Alexander. She'd had all the waiting she could stand. Body, mind, and spirit, while over-whelmed and thankful for Alexander's presence, craved action. She waved the men forward as she followed the boys. "Come. We can wait at the mouth of the cave. If anyone approaches, we'll be safe enough since we know the passages, aye?"

"We'd best follow her, lads, or we'll ne'er find our way out of this place." Alexander motioned for Graham and Magnus to follow.

With the utmost care to avoid additional traps and snags of Sawny's doing, Catriona led the men through the shorter of the several passages that led to the mouth of the cave.

"God's teeth, a thousand tunnels honeycomb this hell," Alexander said, his voice echoing throughout the tomblike space as he kept close behind her.

"Aye," Catriona agreed. "That's why I feared for ye when we left ye in the darkness."

"I noted the path ye took and relit my torch with the flint on my pistol," Alexander defended, sounding a bit insulted. He grunted and huffed with his efforts as they turned sideways to squeeze through a narrow to the point of being treacherous part of the pass. "Damna-tion, Catriona. Are ye certain this is the way?"

"Aye and for certain," Catriona said as the tunnel opened out into the small flat area at the mouth of the cave. She pulled in a deep breath of the fresh cold air and reveled in the sunlight pouring in. The cave had been a grand place in which to hide but she was more than ready to be shed of it. "See there?"

Alexander pulled her close. They stood together, waiting for Tom in silence. Catriona clutched her arisaidh tight and pressed her fist against the center of her chest. Alexander would have to be deaf not to hear the excited hammering of her heart. She swallowed hard, breath-lessness threatening to overtake her and her knees weak from emotions whirling through her.

Tom appeared at the mouth of the cave and waved them forward. "F-found'm! Come!"

"Thanks be," Catriona said with breathless relief as they all rushed to leave the cave. Blinded by the brightness of the day, she shaded her eyes with one hand as her gaze darted across the top of the nearby curtain wall and checked the windows of the turret. All looked to be unguarded but looks could be so deceiving. Calum had taught her that cruel lesson the last time she'd attempted to escape.

Alexander took hold of her hand, pressed a kiss to her knuckles, then gave her a solemn look. "Dinna let fear control ye, aye?"

"Aye," she whispered, helpless to speak any louder. She couldna make him understand how afraid she was that they were about to fail again—and if they did, Calum would kill them for certain this time.

"Do ye trust me?" He peered at her with such an intensity, she scarce heard him over the pounding of her heartbeat in her ears.

"Aye," she managed to whisper.

"Good." He grazed a gentle kiss across her lips, squeezed her hand again, then hurried them toward the trio of horses the boys had fetched.

Catriona knotted her arisaidh around her shoulders. Alexander's strong hands about her waist hoisted her into the air and settled her in the saddle. Alexander snugged in behind her, sending a thrill rushing through her. The breathless sensation grew as he pulled her back against the warm, welcome safety of his chest and wrapped his plaid about her.

Graham and Magnus saddled up and each of them pulled up one of the boys to ride behind them. A welcomed sense of relief settled across Catriona. The sight of Sawny, his freckled face beaming as he clung to Magnus's waist, made her smile.

A long, deep horn blast came from the top of the curtain wall, shattering the peacefulness and hope of the morning. The predatory hiss of arrows in flight shushed through the air alongside them as they urged the horses away in full gallop. Alexander curled her close against him and leaned forward, sheltering her as much as he could with his own body.

"To the west!" Alexander shouted across the narrow expanse of land separating the curtain wall from the mountain. "We must no' be followed!"

Graham and Magnus nodded, swerving their mounts from side to side as arrows punctured the ground all around them. Catriona held tight to the lip of the saddle, bent double over it as Alexander kept her sheltered beneath him. He had her tucked so tight in the curve of his body, she couldn't hazard a look about to see if horsemen followed or if it was only the bowmen from the curtain wall attempting to stop them. All she could do was close her eyes and pray.

They slowed as the horses turned and began the climb up the mountain. The agile beasts galloped around the piles of stones and dense hillocks of dried heather as if born to conquer such harsh terrain. They slowed even more, settling into a comfortable ground-eating trot. Alexander straightened in the saddle, pulling Catriona upright with him.

"Are ye all right, lass?"

Catriona squeezed the arm he held tight around her waist. "Aye. I'm a far sight better now that it's no longer raining arrows."

Alexander laughed, his amusement rumbling against her back in the most pleasing way. "Agreed. A storm of arrows is never a good thing." He reined in the horse as they reached a small plateau above the niche of the mountain cradling Clan Neal's keep. "No riders yet but I'm certain there will be soon." He turned in the saddle and waved down Graham and Magnus. "Keep to the west for a few more miles so they'll believe we're headed to Fort William, ye ken?"

Both men nodded and nudged their heels into their mounts to urge them higher up the mountain and westward.

"Are your other men safe and waiting for ye or have they moved on?" Relief had filled her to see Graham and Magnus unscathed from their recent escape but concern had dampened the sentiment when the rest of Alexander's kin had been missing. While they'd been at Neal keep, she'd noticed on more than one occasion that the group of seven men were a tight knit bunch—more loyal to each other than any clan and from the stories they told, they seemed to always travel as one.

"Whilst we fetched ye, the rest have tended to other matters we pray will show us the best way to help ye forever escape the clutches of your brother."

Catriona pondered this answer for a long moment, drawing in a deep breath as she drew her arisaidh closer about her. *Help me escape.* But what about everyone else? Her cheeks heated as the memory of both her father and Calum's deplorable behavior filled her with nauseating guilt. She couldna desert her clan to such a horrible fate. She swallowed hard and ground her teeth as she clutched the lip of the saddle tighter. Her mother shouldha killed her father during one of his drunken stupors. Killed the wicked disease at its source before it had consumed Calum.

"I have to save my clan," she said, shifting to look Alexander in the eye, praying he'd understand. "I canna leave them to Calum." She couldna bring herself to say more. She couldna bear the shame nor what Alexander would think once he learned the truth about her twin and how he'd come to be such a monster.

Alexander studied her for a long moment, dark brows knotted together, eyes narrowed, and black hair whipping in the wind. "Ye ken there's only one way to ensure that Calum is stopped and his followers dispersed?"

Catriona knew with a sick sense of finality what Alexander meant but she couldna put it in words. After all, her poor demented twin had become evil incarnate because of her. "I ken it well, Alexander." She looked away and swallowed hard, her throat aching, but she didna fear the onslaught of tears because she had none left to cry when it came to her family.

"Dinna fash yourself, dearling," Alexander said with a soft kiss to her temple. "We'll see this through and save all we can, aye?"

Catriona nodded and forced a smile.

"Besides," Alexander whispered against her cheek, his warm breath tickling her skin. "All that truly matters is that ye're back in my arms, aye?"

"Aye." She released the tensed breath she'd been holding and snuggled back against Alexander's chest. A sudden weariness made her ache to give up the battle and rest. How long had it been since she'd slept? So much had happened, she couldna remember the last time she'd actually closed her eyes and lost herself to the blissful oblivion of sleep. A long, hiccupping yawn overcame her.

Alexander cradled her head back against his shoulder and kissed the top her head. "Close your eyes, lass, and steal what rest ye can whilst we ride. I'll keep ye safe."

Safe. She relaxed against him and nestled her cheek more comfortably into the dip of his shoulder. Aye, she was most certainly safe from Calum now but how safe was her heart from Alexander? Her eyes popped open, and she caught her breath. He'd greeted her most ardently in the cave but could that have merely been his relief at finding her so he'd be rid of the guilt of losing her to her brother? She thought back to the keep and the tender moments they'd shared. He'd seemed truly fond of her but would that fondness grow into something more? Something strong enough to keep him ever at her side?

He's a mercenary. A man of travel. Catriona caught the corner of her lip between her teeth. She was wide awake now but slow to wish herself free of Alexander's arms and the thump of his heartbeat against her cheek. *I could travel with him. Tend to his wounds whenever he was injured.* The idea sounded laughable even to herself. What mercenary, what warrior for hire, wished to travel with a woman and all the trappings required for her to travel with him?

Nay. Alexander had no need of her. But since he was most assuredly a man of honor, he'd ne'er allow himself to leave her behind. A burden. She'd be a burden he'd grow to resent. Catriona closed her eyes again, squinting them shut against the burning signal of oncoming tears. 'Twas true she'd ne'er cry for her family ever again but she had tears a plenty left for Alexander.

CHAPTER 15

*S*he hadna slept nary a minute. Not even dozed. Her deep breaths had exhaled in soft, controlled sighs and the tensed way she held herself against his chest told him she didna give in to slumber. *Aye, but at least she stayed pressed close.* He took some small comfort in that.

Alexander snugged his arm tighter around her sweet softness and held her steady as he turned the horse in a northeasterly direction and headed up the steep incline. Graham and Magnus fell in line behind him. They'd wandered the mountain long enough. 'Twas at last safe enough to veer back to their cave. The Neal warriors had no' given chase.

Strange. If Alexander had been in Calum's stead, he would no' have hesitated to send riders to fetch back the escapees. Especially with the renowned horseflesh housed in the Neal stables. The horses Murtagh had supplied them were fine but they werena the best from the select herd bred by the Neal Clan. The stronger horses from the main herd wouldha overtaken them with little trouble.

An ill feeling, an ominous foreboding, settled like a stone deep in Alexander's gut. Why had Calum no' given chase? What was the man's plan? Calum Neal was a cruel bastard, but he was far from stupid. Alexander had surmised that much during his stay at *Tor Ruadh*.

"Riders up ahead," Graham called out, pointing toward two large horses and what looked to be a small, round-bellied mare.

"Riders?" Catriona pulled away from Alexander and straightened in the saddle, straining to peer over the arm he held snugged around her. "Neal riders?"

"Nay," Alexander said, instantly missing the warmth of her cuddled close against him. "'Tis Duncan and Sutherland." He paused for a long moment, studying the third rider on the mare. "And a priest." He blew out a heavy breath. What the hell had those two done this time?

"A priest?" Catriona shifted in the saddle, stretching to see. "Sweet Jesu, they've bound his hands and tied the reins of his horse to Sutherland's saddle." She looked up at Alexander. "Be they mad? Taking a priest captive?"

"Not mad—just a bit inclined to follow the path no' usually taken." Alexander reined in his horse and waited. He scrubbed a hand across his face and rubbed at the gritty corners of his eyes. He was damned tired and needed sleep. If these two were bringing more burdens to bear, he'd thrash their arses for them like he'd done when they were weans.

Duncan was grinning like a lad who'd just sampled his first whore and Sutherland looked the same. Alexander prayed this meant they bore promising news but with those two, one never knew. Their prisoner, the priest, looked ready to condemn them all straight to Hell.

"I dinna recall a request to take prisoners," Alexander said as Duncan's horse nickered a greeting to Alexander's mount and came to a halt in front of him. He looked to the priest and gave a polite nod. "Father."

The thin balding man dressed in dark, modest robes glared at him for a long moment then lifted his bound hands. "This is how ye treat a man of God?"

Alexander took a deep breath, gave Duncan and Sutherland a joint damning glance, then huffed it out. "Forgive my brothers, Father. They oft get a mite overzealous."

"A mite overzealous," the priest said, the pitch of his voice squeaking higher. "I dare say shoving a sack over me head while I'm at prayers and bagging me arse like a plump hen for market is a damned sight more than a mite overzealous!" He jerked his wrists toward Alexander again. "I demand ye untie me this instant."

Alexander shifted his attention to Duncan and didna say a word, just waited for an explanation.

"He's the priest what was traveling with Jameson Campbell." Duncan stole a quick glance at Catriona then returned his focus to Alexander. He leaned forward and lowered his voice as he jerked a thumb toward the holy man. "They were within two days' ride of Neal Keep. Coming for the marriage, they were."

"We figured if we kidnapped the priest, 'twould at least slow their plans. If we hadna stolen him away, even though ye've rescued Mistress Catriona and prevented a civil ceremony, they couldha done a marriage by proxy, ye ken?" Sutherland said with a smug nod.

Whilst their treatment of the priest left something to be desired, their reasoning was sound. Alexander looked back at the priest still holding his tied wrists aloft. "I apologize for the harsh treatment, Father. Once we reach our destination, we'll remove your bindings and do our best to be more hospitable, aye?"

The priest glared at him all the harder, setting his jaw and baring his clenched teeth as he dropped his tied hands back to his lap.

Aye. We are all going to Hell for certain. Alexander took the lead and urged his horse back to the narrowing path, tossing his words back over his shoulder. "How many rode with Campbell?"

"Near to sixty," Duncan said. "All armed."

"They even brought cannons. A pair of them loaded in wagons," Sutherland called out from farther back in the line. "To a wedding, mind ye. What the hell do ye need cannons for at a wedding?"

Catriona shifted in front of him. The poor lass had started to shake. Her pale hands trembled atop the horn of the saddle. "Calum means to make a strong alliance with the Earl of Breadalbane," she said in a quiet tone meant for him alone. "He swore to become the strongest outpost looking out across the glens." She shook harder and her voice fell even lower. "Jameson Campbell is the earl's successor and Calum considered myself and a dozen or more horses a fair trade for cannons and allies."

Alexander held her closer and pressed a kiss to the top of her head. "Ye be safe now, Catriona. Ye be no man's bargaining piece. Never again. I swear it." The Campbell troops and firepower complicated matters to be sure. But he'd faced worse. They'd merely have to adjust their tactics.

"But how will we ever overcome Calum against so many?" She shifted with a deep sigh and bowed her head. "Such impossible odds." Her voice quivered with her overwrought emotions. "I fear my people lost."

The fear and desperation in her tone fueled Alexander's determination to ease Catriona's pain and set things aright. He had nary a clue how to accomplish it all at the moment but he'd damn well sort it out. All he could do right now was hold her close and keep her warm. He pulled his kilt tighter around her. "Hold fast, dearling. I swear to ye all is not lost."

The horses slogged into the small clearing in front of the cave. With the sky cloudless on the early spring day, the snow and ice had reduced the ground to a muddy slush. Alexander dismounted then pulled Catriona down into his arms and cradled her like a babe.

"Sawny!" He paused until the boy looked his way. "You and Tom tend to the horses afore ye seek the fire, aye?"

"Aye, Master Alexander." Sawny waved Tom forward and the two boys gathered the horses by their reins and led them to a drier portion of the plateau hemmed in by an array of boulders.

Alexander carried Catriona inside the cave and lowered her feet to the dry slab of stone. With a brush of his fingers against the silky line of her jaw, he gave her a reassuring smile. "Fire. Food. Then sleep. Ye'll feel better and I promise ye, we'll win the day, aye?"

She didn't answer. Just looked up at him as though trapped in a trance. Her trembling smile and the sorrow in her deep green eyes came near to undoing him. She'd always been so strong but this situation had most nigh bested her. He lifted her hand to his lips and kissed it before leading her to a rock beside the coals of last night's fire. "Sit ye down and rest whilst I stoke the fire and get the lads settled, aye?"

"Aye," she responded with a soft dip of her chin. Her hand trembling, she pulled her arisaidh tighter around her shoulders and fixed a forlorn gaze down at the mound of ash-covered coals and blackened bits of burned wood.

With a stir of the coals, Alexander fed small sticks and dried moss to the faded embers until flames rose and crackled through the fuel. Larger pieces of wood soon had the fire blazing. He looked at Catriona, puzzling at her sudden withdrawal. She'd acted so happy to see him and yet now, she almost appeared as though she were sorry they had rescued her. Alexander shook away the thought. 'Twas mere weariness troubling the both of them.

"Warm yourself, aye? I'll be back anon."

Catriona nodded, leaning closer to the fire and stretching out her hands toward the flames.

Making his way to the front of the cave, Alexander made a spinning motion with one finger to turn his brothers around and lead them back outside. He stopped short at the sight of the scowling priest still sitting on the mare. "Duncan," he said with a weary huff. "Get the poor Father to the fire and untie him while ye are about it, aye?"

Duncan grinned then pulled the priest from his mount with an unceremonious yank and led him inside the cave.

Alexander turned and glared at his youngest brother. His irritation shifted from Duncan to Sutherland with the ease born of years dealing with the two and their antics. "Ye could no' have treated the priest any kindlier?"

"He knows more swear words than I do, brother." Sutherland accented the revelation with a defensive snort. "Dinna feel too sorry for the man. I promise ye, he doesna merit it."

Alexander dropped his chin to his chest and shook his head. "Any sign of Alasdair and Ian?" He lifted his gaze and scanned the surrounding area.

"No sign of anyone," Graham replied from a stone outcropping higher up the path.

Alexander pondered the situation as he studied the horizon, squinting against the bright blue of the sky. "If they rode all the way to Fort William, 'twill take more than a day to hear from them."

"At least spring is struggling to reclaim the land," Duncan said as he exited the cave. "'Tis almost balmy down in the glens." He clapped a hand to Alexander's shoulder and grinned. "Shall I see to finding a bit of greenery for your bride to hold whilst the priest hears your vows?"

Alexander came close to choking on his own air. Jerking away from Duncan's grasp, he stole a glance back into the cave to make sure his brother's statement had not been overheard. "Are ye daft? This is no time to jest about such."

"Who says I'm jesting?" Duncan said with an irritated frown. "Magnus, do ye no' think that would be the best way to keep the lass safe from both Campbell and her brother?"

Magnus nodded. "Aye. A good tactic indeed." He waved Graham down from his lookout and pointed at Alexander. "Do ye no' think that marriage would be a good start to clearing up this mess and repaying Mistress Catriona for all her kindness and hospitality?"

"Aye," Graham agreed then added with a grin, "She'll keep him in line the rest of his days."

"I told ye before, I have nothing to offer the lass." Alexander kept his voice to a low whisper. He'd not have Catriona hurt nor any more upset than she already was.

Duncan thumped him on the chest. "Ye've already given her your heart, man. 'Tis plain as the nose on your face."

"My heart willna feed her nor protect her from the cold." Alexander shoved Duncan and Magnus both farther away from the mouth of the cave. "We've already discussed this."

Magnus shoved him back. "Then what the hell do ye mean to do with her, Alexander?" Magnus thumped him again. Hard. "Ye've stolen her away from clan and home. Do ye mean to take her to some strange place where she kens nary a soul and dump her there to fend for herself?"

"Ye've meant to marry her since we started out. Admit it," Graham said with a shove against his other side. "Why else would ye bring her here?"

Why else indeed?

Alexander turned and stared back into the cave, his mouth gone dry as old bones. From this distance, he could just make out the light from the fire. The cavernous hole they'd found this high on the mountain was deep and generous. A chill ran through him. Caves. What sort of life was that for Catriona? Traveling hither and yon across the Highlands and sleeping in caves. What could he say to her? He had nothing to offer.

"Go to her, man," Magnus urged with a nudge against his back. "The words will come."

Feeling more fear and dread than he'd faced during any battle, Alexander stole one last glance at each of his brethren's faces. Every one of them gave him an encouraging nod.

Sutherland held up a hand. "Wait one more moment." He headed into the cave. "I'll drag the priest somewhere else so ye can have a bit a privacy to do your wooin'."

"Dinna drag the man!" Alexander knotted his fists, doing his damnedest to bite back the curse words threatening to roll off his tongue. *Christ Almighty. We're every last one of us headed straight to the hottest part of Hell.*

Sutherland and the priest emerged a short time later. The priest was wrapped in Sutherland's cloak but still looking sullen enough to damn them all. With his arm around the priest as he led him away, Sutherland thumped the poor man on the chest as he smiled up at Alexander. "He's got his prayer book and everything!"

Fixing Alexander with a very un-Christian-like look, the Father stumbled and mumbled something under his breath as Sutherland led him aside to a narrow ridge of stones.

With one last glance at his men, Alexander pulled in a deep breath and forced himself to enter the cave and make his way to Catriona.

"Where is Sutherland taking Father William?" Catriona rose from her stone seat and looked toward the mouth of the cave. "He told me to wait here but promise me he doesna mean to harm the man? Not a man of God?"

"Nay, m'lady." Alexander hurried to reassure her. That's all he needed was for Catriona to think them a band of soulless murderers. "Sutherland…" his words trailed off. What the hell should he say to her?

"Sutherland?" Catriona prompted, seeming a great deal more calm than when he'd first left her beside the fire.

Alexander made a mental note to thank the priest. He must've talked to the lass and eased her mind. "Never ye mind about Sutherland." Alexander waved away her words then took hold of both her hands and held them between his. Such a beauty she was. Alexander gazed into the deep green of her eyes and a calm knowing came over him. *Aye. This is the right of it. 'Tis surely meant to be.*

"Catriona." He took a step closer and cradled her hands to his heart.

"Aye?" Catriona said in a hesitant whisper, leeriness shining in her eyes.

"I would verra much like to take…" he paused. Nay. 'Twas no' how he should say it. He swallowed hard and started over. "If ye'd like to be…" He blew out an impatient huff. Nay. That wouldna do either.

"For God's sake, Alexander, what are ye trying to say?" She looked as though she was about to cry.

"Be my wife, aye?" There. He'd said it. He held his breath, every muscle tensed as he waited for her answer.

She ducked her chin, her unblinking stare locked on the floor. After a long painful moment, she lifted her gaze and gave him a sad look. "Ye dinna have to do that, Alexander. I'll be all right on my own." She squeezed his hands. "I care about ye too much to burden ye with such."

She cared about him. He caught hold of those words and held fast to them as he took a step closer, close enough that he felt more of her heat than that of the fire. "Ye are no' a burden, my lovely one. Ye would never be a burden."

She opened her mouth to speak but Alexander pressed a finger to her parted lips. "Hear me out, lass. I beg ye."

Catriona closed her mouth and hitched in a shaking breath before giving him a quick nod.

"I've nothing to offer ye." Alexander opened her hands and pressed them on top of his heart. "No hearth. No home. No clan." He folded his hands atop hers and pressed them against his chest. "All I can give ye is protection." His voice lowered of its own accord. "And m'heart and soul." With one hand still pressed atop hers in the center of his chest, he reached out with the other hand and cupped her face in his palm. "For all time, ye ken?"

Her mouth ajar a hair's breadth, she gazed up at him a long moment then raced the tip of her tongue across the opened seam of her lips, mesmerizing him with the motion. She hitched in a shaking breath and blew it out. "Ye swear I'm no' a burden to ye?"

Flinching against the stiffness in his weak leg, Alexander lowered himself to the floor and took a knee before her. He pressed a kiss to the palms of her hands then clasped them tight between his own. "On m'life and soul, I swear it."

The faintest of smiles quivered at the corners of her mouth.

Alexander held his breath, praying she'd know his words to be true and accept him. He didna have any idea where they would go nor how they would live but he did ken in his heart that they'd think it through and find a way. Together.

After what seemed like forever, she nodded and uttered a breathy, "Aye," then hurried to steady him as he rose to his feet. "I will be your wife, Alexander…for all time."

Fighting to restrain himself against the urge to catch her up against his chest and spin her around, Alexander brushed the chastest of kisses across Catriona's parted lips.

She smiled up into his eyes and squeezed both his hands. "Is this why Sutherland pulled poor Father William away from the fire?"

"Aye." Alexander returned her smile, sheer happiness coursing through him. "Poor wee man. We'll all be condemned to Hell I'm sure if he has anything to say about it." Lacing her fingers through his,

Alexander led her outside the cave where everyone was waiting. He nodded as he kissed the back of her hand then kept it hugged to his chest. "Catriona has done me the honor of accepting."

"Well done!" Magnus said.

Duncan and Sutherland unleashed a roar that echoed down the mountain.

"Fools!" Graham scolded. "Ye'll cause a feckin' avalanche."

They all went silent and turned and looked at the mountain rising above the cave. Thankfully, no such mishap occurred.

"Ye mean to marry this man?" The incredulous voice came from beyond the group close to the tethered horses. "This barbarian who leads a den of thieves that have no respect for the Cloth?" Grasping Sutherland's oversized cloak around his small frame, the priest marched over to stand in front of Catriona and gave her a piercing stare. Eyes so squinted they were almost shut, he leaned close to her. "Say the word, lass. I'll grant ye sanctuary and protect your virtue with the word of Almighty God. If they dare touch ye, they'll burn in Hell for all eternity." He turned and gave the warriors a smug look as though he'd just unleashed an invincible weapon and victory was nigh.

Alexander clenched his teeth to keep from laughing in the poor man's face. No sense endangering his soul any further. He squeezed Catriona's hand and waited.

"I do wish to marry this man," Catriona said, reaching out to rest a reassuring hand atop the priest's arm. "He's a good man, Father. I promise ye."

"Humpf!" The priest stood taller and resettled the cloak about his narrow shoulders. "We'd best be about it then before the sun sets and this air grows any colder." He reached inside his robes and drew out a small book with a worn faded binding and ragged cover. Still scowling, he lifted his long nose and glanced about the clearing, his damning gaze settling on each of the men. "Gather 'round then. Ye shall be the witnesses."

Graham, Magnus, Duncan, and Sutherland gave obedient grins and lined up on either side of the couple.

Licking the tip of his thumb, Father William opened his book and fluttered through the pages until he reached the desired passage. Holding it open in his palm, he traced a finger down the yellowed page then lifted his gaze and gave Alexander a stern look.

"Do ye..." Father William paused and scowled up at Alexander. "What be your full Christian name, man?"

"Alexander Grant Maxwell MacCoinnich." Alexander swallowed hard and tensed against the sudden urge to cross himself and draw his sword. There was nothing quite so dire and ball-shrivelin' as giving your full Christian name to a priest.

Father William turned to Catriona. "And your name, lass?"

"Catriona Elizabeth Rose Neal."

"Verra well then." Father William cleared his throat, leveled his shoulders, and continued. "Do ye, Alexander Grant Maxwell MacCoinnich, take Catriona Elizabeth Rose Neal to be your wife 'til death shall part the two of ye?"

A cold sweat stole across Alexander and he swallowed hard again. "Aye. I do so." Before the priest could continue, he turned to Catriona and held her hands tighter. The sudden need to make Catriona believe he did this of his own free will overtook him. "I have nothing to give ye but my heart and soul but I would have ye know that they'll e'er be yours. From this moment forward, we shall be as one 'till death shall end our years." His mam had taught him the oath long ago. Perhaps 'twas her spirit that had reminded him of the words. The words she'd said that his father had once said to her.

Catriona's lips parted and her eyes took on the sheen of tears.

The priest cleared his throat. "Verra good. Now, Catriona Elizabeth Rose Neal, do ye take Alexander Grant Maxwell MacCoinnich to be your husband 'til death shall part ye?"

"Aye," Catriona said without shifting her gaze from Alexander's. She squeezed his hands as she continued, "The first cut of my meat, the first sip of my wine, I vow shall always be yours. At night, only your name shall ever grace my lips and my smile is for your eyes alone each morning. I swear upon my heart and soul before all these witnesses here that I will forevermore cherish and honor ye through this life and into the next."

"Humpf!" The priest frowned at her for a moment then gave a noncommittal shrug. "A bit pagan, but I'll allow it." He huffed out an exasperated humming exhale as though trying to ensure he'd forgotten nothing. At long last, he cleared his throat, looked first at Catriona, then shifted his gaze to Alexander. "I hereby pronounce ye married. Two ye no longer be. Forevermore ye be one. Let no man put asunder what God hath done." He snapped his Bible shut, shoved it into the pocket of his robes, and studied each person of the group as though assessing their status of eternal damnation or ascension into heaven. Nostrils flaring, he huffed out a disgruntled snort then asked, "Where's the whisky?"

CHAPTER 16

*S*he had never hoped for a wedding night.

Catriona allowed her gaze to linger on each of the faces of the laughing males sitting around the fire. A warm sense of belonging, warmer than any flame or ember, engulfed her and made her smile. Here she sat. In a cave with no possessions but the clothes on her back. That thought made her smile, too, because she didna give a whit about belongings. Not anymore. Happiness filled her and she could never remember being this content before with her lot in life.

She stole a shy sideways glance at Alexander, then looked away with a quick turn of her head and sip from her cup when he caught her studying him. She both feared and hungered for his dark smoldering gaze that seemed to peer into her soul. He had the ability to unleash surges of heat through her faster than whisky. Even back at the keep, Alexander had always had the power to set her middle to fluttering and make her a little breathless with just a glance. But now...she drew in a shaking breath and swallowed hard. *Lord, help me.* The power he commanded now.

She swallowed hard. So, this was her wedding night. In a cave. With four mercenaries, two young boys, a priest, and her husband.

Husband. How could a mere word release such an avalanche of feelings?

She rolled her tensed shoulders and sat taller, attempting a covert yet casual search of the shadows of the large cave lit only by the fire. Aye, the space was large and the lighting dim, but how in heaven's name could they expect her to consummate her vows whilst bedding down among the group of men? She gave Alexander another quick glance. Surely, he'd no' expect her to...not with the men all around them.

Such barbarism. Her mother, God rest her soul, would spin so hard in her grave she'd knock the rocks from her burial cairn. Catriona bit back a silent bitter laugh. Her father wouldna give a damn and was more than likely too busy betting with the devil for sole ownership of Hell to pay her struggles in this world any mind. She blinked away the scandalous thought and took another quick sip of the whisky shimmering in the small tin cup that Alexander had retrieved from his pack and handed to her with a shy smile.

Magnus startled her as he stood and motioned for the others to follow. "Come. 'Tis time to leave the bride and groom to themselves. They dinna need an audience."

"But where will ye go?" Catriona cringed at the nervous squeak in her voice. The night held both excitement and fear when the men left them alone and she wasna...ready. She had never...well, she'd never. Not ever. Not even close. What if she did something wrong and Alexander found her wanting? She had heard of many a marriage where such things had occurred and the man had put the woman out.

"Ye canna sleep out in the cold," she called after them, struggling to keep the anxious desperation out of her voice.

The men and boys shared knowing looks among themselves. Smiling. Nodding. With much winking and nudging of elbows, they acted as though a prank they'd planned had gone verra well.

Magnus gave Catriona a polite bow. "We'll be fine, m'lady. We'll bed down with the horses outside the cave. There's shelter aplenty there thanks to Sawny and Tom and the night is mild compared to some we've endured, I assure ye."

Catriona folded her hands in her lap and attempted a nonchalant nod. Her hope of avoiding the inevitable lost. Her fate was nigh. "Verra well then. Sleep ye well."

Each of the men gave Alexander a pointed look as they filed out of the cave and took the two snickering boys along with them. Father William paused halfway, turned back as though to say something, then changed his mind with a quick shake of his head, waving away the thought as he turned and hurried out of the cave.

Catriona kept her gaze locked on the fire, finding it difficult to draw breath. Now, what was she expected to do? What would a wife do? She had no advice to draw from. Mother had ne'er told her about such things and neither had Gaersa.

"Catriona."

The way he spoke her name. So soft. Insistent and...possessive. She shivered. 'Twas like an intimate caress that made her long for him to come closer.

"Catriona." Even softer. A lover's whisper, or how she'd dreamed a lover's call might sound.

"Aye?" She stayed focused on the fire, hands knotted in her lap, concentrating on breathing. 'Twas true, back at the keep, whilst he'd been trying to console her about her betrothal, and in the caves after he'd found her, she'd shared his embrace and a few ardent kisses but this...what should she do now?

Alexander slid his hand under hers and nudged her around to face him. He leaned closer, slid a finger under her chin and lifted her face to his. "Do ye fear me, lass?"

His eyes, so telling. Need. Hunger. Yearning. So many emotions shone from those blue-black depths. Catriona hitched in a deep breath and released it with a slow, quiet hiss. "I'm no' afraid of ye...as such." She gave a nervous swipe of the tip of her tongue across her lips and dropped her gaze, mesmerized by the pulsing tick of his heartbeat at the base of his throat. His unbuttoned tunic revealed such a teasing expanse of chest, the swirls of dark hair across his muscles daring her to stroke her fingertips across his body just as she'd done back at the keep when he'd been unconscious with fever. She forced her focus back to the captivating pull of his eyes, relinquishing herself to the lure of the raging passion she saw storming within them.

"I dinna fear ye. It's just I dinna wish to disappoint ye." She highlighted the sentiment with an exasperated twitch of one shoulder.

Alexander smiled as though she hadna said a word then laced his fingers up into her hair. "Your hair has always beguiled me. Fiery as copper. Softer than any silk." With a gentleness that touched her heart, he freed her tresses from the ribbons and pins. The weight of her unruly mane tumbled down her back and flowed across his hands like liquid fire. He lifted a curl and brought it to his face, stroking it against his cheek and closing his eyes as though savoring the tress like a sample of the finest velvet. He opened his eyes, giving her a look that threatened to melt her where she sat. "Ye could never disappoint me, dearling." His tone was soft and coaxing. "Not ever."

"But I dinna ken what to do."

Alexander responded with nothing more than a kind smile and a gentle cupping of her cheek.

She wanted to be brave and do her best to be a good wife, but she had so little knowledge to go on. Her waning courage bolstered by the look in Alexander's eyes, Catriona fiddled free her knotted arisaidh and allowed the cloth to fall away from her shoulders. *Aye, that's good. Now...more.* She took a deep breath and with a shy hesitance, slid her hands up Alexander's bared forearms. A delicious aching sensation filled her, making the cave seem verra warm. She wet her lips again and found the courage to reach up and touch the dusting of more than a day's growth of beard darkening Alexander's usually clean-shaven jaw. The thick sable bristles had already begun to curl. They tickled against her palm.

"'Tis already soft," she said more to herself than him.

Without a word, Alexander rose, and eased her to her feet with him. He led her to a thick pile of pallets covered with a plaid and placed her beside it. After a long moment, he slid his hands up her arms and squeezed her shoulders, then bowed his head. "Forgive me for having no finery for ye. Believe me when I tell ye I'm truly sorry our wedding bed is so crude."

"'Tis fine enough," she whispered, touching his chest to steady herself after a sudden weakness seemed to overtake her knees and make standing a challenge. Gaining courage and praying he wouldna think her brazen, she smoothed her hands into the opened throat of his shirt and raked her fingers through the hair on his chest. So wiry. So tickling. She couldna get enough of the sensation, all muscled hardness beneath and tickling curls atop.

Alexander tensed and hitched in a breath as though startled by her touch.

"Forgive me," she said and moved to draw her hands away. 'Twas just as she'd feared. She'd made a foolish mistake and acted the whore rather than a wife.

"Nay," Alexander said in a low, rumbling tone as he took hold of one her hands and moved it lower. "Never apologize for your touch, wife. It inflames me, I promise ye."

Catriona caught her breath, not allowing herself to glance down. So rigid and hard. And it felt so much...larger. She'd seen his manhood when nursing him back to health but it had ne'er been like this.

He pressed her hand up and down the firm length of him with one hand while he laced his other hand up into her hair and tilted her head back for a gentle kiss. "This is what ye do to me, wife, and trust me, ye do it well."

Encouraged and burning with a strange wanting she'd never known, Catriona shoved aside his kilt and slid her hand down inside the front of his trews. With a hesitant touch, she grazed her fingers along the silken hardness of his member as she opened to his deeper, more urgent kiss. He tasted of whisky and need. The hint of wood smoke mixed with his scent of strong virile male created an exquisite combination that made her senses reel.

Alexander burned a trail of kisses down her throat, pausing long enough to yank loose the ties of her bodice and toss it aside before continuing his tasting and setting her flesh afire. "I want ye free of these clothes," he rasped against the tied front of her chemise as he undid the waist of her skirt and allowed it to fall into a pile of wool around her ankles. "I need the touch of your skin against mine. Please, Catriona."

Panic. Excitement. Apprehension. An avalanche of emotions crashed through her as she stepped out of her slippers then nudged them along with her skirt and bodice aside. She hesitated at lifting her chemise to remove her stockings. Did he wish her completely naked? The worrisome wondering left her as Alexander shucked his trews, tunic, and kilt and stood before her naked as the day his mother brought him into the world. She'd seen him naked before whilst tending his wounds but... *Merciful heavens. So big.* Concern filled her. She couldna help but wonder how this could happen without a great deal more pain than any of the women at the keep had ever mentioned when it came to sacrificing a maidenhead.

"Dinna be afraid," he reassured as he led her closer to the pallet and lowered them both to the plaid-covered bed. With a reassuring smile, he settled her back on the blankets then allowed his fingertips to trail across every dip and curve of her body as he rose above her. "I want ye, Catriona, but I want ye to want me as well, aye?"

"I...I do." And she meant it. She ached to arch her back, to meet his hand as he touched her, and rub him harder against her body. But she held herself still, fearing he'd think her a wanton whore. Sweet Jesu, how she wanted him.

He slid his hands down to the hem of her chemise and pushed it up to her waist. His gaze locked with hers, he brushed his fingertips across the auburn thatch of curls at the juncture of her thighs. He leaned over her, the heat of his breath tickling across her flesh. His warm, tender kisses trailed down her stomach as he moved lower, fanning the already burning ache about to explode within her.

Catriona gasped and shuddered, struggling against the urge to writhe beneath his touch. Alexander smiled down at her as he slid her stockings down her legs one by one then pulled them free and tossed them beside the bed. His warm calloused hands slid down the outer sides of her legs, down to her ankles, then tickled back up the insides of her calves, pausing at the tender flesh just above her knees. *Such delicious agony.*

He stretched out beside her on the pallet, treating her to gentle kisses as he tugged her chemise higher and whispered against her ear. "Your skin against mine. Our heat united. Please, Catriona. Would ye be willing? I swear I'll keep ye warm."

Keep her warm? That was no' one of her fears at the present. Catriona sat up, skimmed her chemise off over her head, then lowered herself back to the pallet. Her hands trembled as she crossed her arms over her breasts. Have mercy, she could hardly breathe as she eased herself back down on the blankets beside Alexander and looked up into his face.

"Such loveliness," Alexander rasped against her temple as he pressed the hard length of his body against her and with the gentlest of touches, slid a hand under her folded arms to cup one of her breasts in his palm. He eased himself over her and set to nibbling kisses across her collarbone and lower.

Catriona closed her eyes, cradling his head to her chest and filling her hands with his hair as he tasted and teased until she thought she'd surely die. She arched against him, luxuriating in the heat radiating from his body, no longer caring if she made a mistake as she slid her body against his. If this made her wanton, then so be it. It felt right. It felt damned good.

Alexander swallowed her groans as he trailed a hand up between her legs. She bucked into his touch, breathless, and writhing as he teased a finger up inside her. "'Twill be less painful this way," he promised as another finger joined the first and he hugged her close as he slid them both in and out, stroking and gyrating until all Catriona knew was that she needed blessed relief. Arching hard and fast, matching her rhythm to his, Catriona raked her fingers down his broad back, her moans growing loud but she no longer cared.

Covering her mouth with his, Alexander shoved his fingers deep with a quick thrust. Catriona felt a tearing. The burning rip caught her unaware, and she stiffened against the pain. She cried out but Alexander swallowed the sound, kissing her deep and long as he removed his hand and cradled her close.

Cuddling her against him, he soothed her with tender kisses along her jaw, nipping and tasting her throat and suckling her earlobe. He teased his fingertips across her with the lightest of touches, teasing them up and down the center of her torso then moved to stroke her side, cupping her buttocks and nibbling kisses around her breasts.

Catriona smoothed her hands down Alexander's back, pressing into his touch and arching against him. The aching inferno reignited inside her. The demanding need returned and grew stronger. She forgot the pain. All she knew was that she needed more. She needed Alexander. "I need ye," she whispered with a desperate gasp.

"Aye." Alexander rumbled beneath her hands with a purring groan. "'Tis time, indeed."

He rolled her beneath him, sliding his arms beneath her shoulders, and propping on his elbows as he nestled down between her legs. Catriona opened to him, wrapping her legs around him and arching to meet him.

Ever so slowly, he nudged his way into her, gentle but steady. "Relax, lass," he said with a kiss to her temple as he pushed deeper. "Relax," he groaned as he filled her.

So...so tight. Not painful but so... Catriona closed her eyes and committed to the wondrous array of new sensations. His smooth back under the palms of her hands. The ripples of his muscles as he moved. She hugged her legs tighter about him and matched her moves to his, thrust for thrust. The harder Alexander pushed, the more Catriona discovered she needed.

An exquisite shuddering stole her breath, bursting across her senses with such delight she reeled with the rapturous explosion, crying out as all thought left her and only excruciatingly wonderful delirium took over.

Alexander growled out a low rumbling moan, pounding harder and faster, then thrust deep and stayed there. Every muscle tensed, and breath held, he spasmed and jerked for the span of several heartbeats then collapsed atop her.

Chest to chest. Heart pounding against pounding heart. Catriona stared up into the darkness, still gasping for breath. So this is what it was. She tightened her arms around Alexander and snugged her cheek up against his head. What a wondrous pleasure to share with a husband. Her heart was most certain near to bursting. She'd never known this much happiness, never felt this cherished. A tear slipped down her cheek. She hitched in a quick shaking breath as she swiped it away.

Alexander lifted himself up, pressed a kiss to her forehead, then grazed another kiss across her tear-dampened cheek and immediately drew back. "Are ye all right, dear one? Did I hurt ye?"

He watched her closely and his expression made her heart swell. The man cared about her, worried about her well-being. Truly, he cared.

"I am quite well. I promise." She smiled up into his eyes and hugged her legs back around him, reveling in the rugged muscular manliness of him against her tender skin. She teased her fingers up and down his sides, pleased at discovering he was ticklish along his ribs. "I'm finding the cave to be quite warm with this wondrous new blanket I've discovered."

He laughed, stirring an entirely new array of sensations through her. "I'm pleased ye find me wondrous, m'lady." He kissed the tip of her nose and grew serious. "I dinna wish ye to regret your decision to marry me, Catriona. Not ever." He eased off her and rolled to the side, curling her up close against him and covered them both with the plaid. Cradling her in one arm, he traced lazy circles up and down her forearm, brought her hand to his mouth for a kiss, then peacefully tucked it to his chest.

"And 'tis my hope that ye dinna grow to resent me." There. Her fear was named and laid bare between them. Holding her breath, she shifted to watch his reaction. She prided herself on her skill to spot a lie.

"Why would ye say that? Why would I ever resent ye?" He pulled back a bit to better look her in the eyes.

"For becoming the weight around your neck that slows ye in your travels." A heavy sigh escaped her. "I ken good and well ye're a soldier for hire and no' accustomed to darkening the same threshold over long. I willna mean to but I fear I'll slow ye in your travels. Yourself and your kin will tire of dealing with me."

Alexander huffed out a silent laugh and shook his head. "Ye fear burdening me in my travels and I fear I've no place to offer ye to rest when ye're weary. We're a pair, are we not?"

"Aye. That we are." She reached up and brushed a finger against the scrub of his jaw. "Ye're a fine man, Alexander, and I thank ye."

"Thank me for what?"

"Many things," she mused aloud, as she watched the firelight dance across the walls of the cave. "Many things," she repeated in a whisper more to herself than to him. She couldna begin to name all the reasons she felt thankful for Alexander if she tried.

Alexander treated her to a long, slow kiss then lifted his head and gazed down at her with a tender look. "Rest now, aye?" He nuzzled the sensitive skin behind her ear and snuggled closer. "Rest now and perhaps we'll steal a little more pleasure in a few hours before everyone rises in the morning."

As tempting as he made that sound, she couldn't. Her mind reeled with too much that needed tending. "Where do we go from here?" she whispered. Catriona hated to keep him awake with her questions but her clan's suffering reared its ugly muzzle and set to nagging anew now that her head had somewhat cleared. "Fort William?"

He remained silent for so long and his breathing had settled down so low and steady she grew worried. Perhaps he already slept? "Alexander?" she repeated a little louder.

"Rest now, lass." He hugged her tight and pressed another kiss to the edge of her ear. "Alasdair and Ian should be back by tomorrow. They'll have been to Fort William and will tell us more about the regiment Calum mentioned and then we'll know."

"Know what?"

"How best to attack," he mumbled under his breath then droned off into a hissing snore.

Attack. *Aye. Attack sounds good.* That was promise enough to hold her 'til morning.

CHAPTER 17

"Ye canna go in there." Alexander shouldered past Alasdair to the cave. He took up a spread-eagled stance in front of the entrance and blocked it.

Weariness in the slant of his shoulders, Alasdair glared at him as though he'd sprouted a second head. "Ye deny me shelter and a place at the fire? What the hell's wrong with ye, cousin?"

Ian approached from the direction of where they'd penned the horses and thumped his brother on the back. "Perhaps his wife still sleeps. Best stay out here. There's a fire over near the horses. Come."

"Wife?" Alasdair repeated, scrubbing at the corners of his blood-shot eyes as though they burned with the need for sleep. "We were only gone two days. When the hell did ye have time to marry and how did ye manage to find a priest?"

"Yesterday." Alexander motioned toward his younger brothers. "Duncan and Sutherland provided the priest." The fresh memory of the captured priest with bound wrists triggered a clearing of his throat and forced him to add, "In a manner of speaking."

"Yesterday. I see." Alasdair seemed to struggle for civil words. "Congratulations," he forced out with a weak-hearted clap of one hand to Alexander's shoulder. "'Tis Catriona, aye?"

160

"Who else would it be?"

Alasdair opened his mouth and fisted his hand as though he wished to reply with more than words then stopped himself. He looked at Ian. "Show me to the fire, aye? I'm well past weary and no' in the mood for..." He bit off his words. Glare shifting to Alexander, he shook his head and fell in step behind his brother.

Alexander turned his head, training an ear toward the inside of the cave. Alasdair could pout like a greetin' bairn if he wished. Catriona needed her sleep. After a brief slumber, they'd awakened a few hours before dawn and further explored the pleasures of their marriage bed. Alexander hardened at the memory. Virginal, his new wife may have been but lore a'mighty, she was a woman of passion. The only sound emerging from the depths of the cave was an occasional rustling and a soft sigh.

He headed to the clearing of stone to the right of the cave where they'd tethered the horses. The men stood gathered around the fire in one corner of the sheltered space surrounded by boulders and chunks of stone that resembled the henges found in England and Wales. The horses munched on the horse bread that Murtagh had seen fit to stow in sacks tied to the saddles. With the heat generated by the shaggy beasts' bodies along with the fire, the area was quite warm against the chilly morning.

"Well, he can still walk," Graham remarked as Alexander joined them.

"Ye didna do it right then," Sutherland said as he motioned toward the entrance of the cave. "Best ye go back and try again. Ye dinna wish to leave your lady a wantin' and neither of ye should be able to walk after your wedding night."

Alexander ignored their jests and helped himself to a dried oatcake and a cup of whatever hot swill Magnus had steeped in the dented pot snugged into the coals of the fire. Magnus was a firm believer in herbs to strengthen the body.

Magnus's mother had been a renowned healer. A white lady respected by all until she'd angered the wife of a high-ranking noble in their village and fallen under a malicious accusation of witchcraft.

Tried and found guilty, her sentence had been barbarous. Alexander stared at the ground, almost flinching at the memory. They'd crushed the poor woman to death beneath a plank of wood laden with boulders. For most nigh a year after it had happened, Magnus had spoken verra little, never forgiving himself for not making it home in time to save her.

Alexander frowned down into the cup then took a hesitant sip. The fumes from the bitter drink made his eyes water as he washed down the bite of oatcake. He worked his tongue against his teeth and swallowed again. He'd have to lick a horse's arse to get the foul taste of that tea out of his mouth. "God's teeth, Magnus, what the hell are ye trying to cure us of this time?"

"Stupidity," Magnus remarked without looking up from the fire. He lifted the metal pot and smiled. "Another cup for ye?"

Magnus didna take well to criticisms about his teas.

"Damn, ye're a surly bunch this morn," Alexander observed with another flinching sip of his hot swill.

"None of us had the night ye had, brother," Duncan retorted then nodded at Ian. "And wait 'til ye hear their news."

Alexander sensed a looming darkness far worse than morning grumpiness. He turned his attention to Ian and Alasdair. "Ill findings?"

"Chieftain Calum Neal spoke the truth," Alasdair said. "The king's new regiment has already arrived at Fort William. Their sole duty is to search the Highlands for anyone who's even hinted at an allegiance to someone other than King William."

"And the leader of the regiment is rumored to be relentless," Ian added. "Everyone said the same thing. Some even mentioned Glencoe."

Glencoe. That failure still gnawed at Alexander's gut. "If the king had a scrap of humanity about him, he'd order those responsible for Glencoe hanged." Alexander moved to toss out what was left of Magnus's herbal brew, then stopped himself when Magnus cleared his throat and gave him a warning glare. "Who be the leader of this regiment?"

"We never heard his name," Ian said. "'Twas as though everyone feared to say it, as though he might appear like some evil demon."

"Ye ken that the order to erase the MacDonalds came from the king himself. 'Twas an example for all to see." Catriona stood on the plateau above them. The morning sun rose behind her, giving her a fiery halo as the wind ruffled through her still loose hair, fluttering the coppery strands about her shoulders. "Is the regiment headed for *Tor Ruadh?*" she asked.

The men stilled, all of them staring up at her with their mouths ajar.

It took Alexander a long moment to recover from the feeling that God had sent a fierce warrior angel of fire to advise them. He blinked hard, cleared his throat, and took a final swallow of the lukewarm muck left in his cup. He held it toward Magnus. "Some for Catriona, aye?"

"Is the regiment headed for *Tor Ruadh?*" she repeated as she climbed down from the stone shelf and joined them by the fire.

Alexander looked to Alasdair and Ian. "Are they?"

"Aye," Ian answered. He turned to his brother. "Set to leave in a week's time, was it?"

Alasdair nodded, scowling down into his own cup before taking a flask from within an inner pocket of his coat and sweetening the tea with whisky. "One hundred at least." After shoving the flask back into his coat, he turned to Duncan and Sutherland. "How many in Campbell's entourage?"

"Near seventy," Father William said without being asked. He held out his cup and nodded toward Alasdair's coat. "A tithe of your *uisge beatha* is most appreciated, my son."

Alasdair held out the flask to the priest as he turned to Alexander. "At least one hundred and seventy then all told."

"All armed and bringing a pair of cannons," Sutherland added.

"All to *Tor Ruadh?*" Catriona asked, accepting the cup of tea from Magnus with a polite nod then wrinkling her nose as she caught a whiff of the contents.

Alexander pulled in a deep breath and released it. "Aye, love. All to

163

Tor Ruadh." He shifted and let his gaze settle on the horses. The Neal horses and a safe stronghold in the Highlands. Renowned for their avarice and preening to play to the crown in hopes of favors, the Campbells wouldna hesitate to kill each other for such an opportunity.

"How can I save my people against such odds?" Catriona whispered with a sad shake of her head as she sank to sit on a nearby boulder.

Calum was no longer the sole nemesis of her people. Alexander went to her side and touched a hand to her shoulder. "I ken ye wish to save your clan for your father's memory but—"

"My father can burn in Hell. I do this for my mother. Clan Neal looked to her for guidance and as much protection as she could offer them from her monster of a husband. Upon her death, I swore I'd take her place as their protector and guardian and I mean to keep my word."

Catriona's passion wasna restricted to the marriage bed. Alexander stared down into her eyes, green as a Highland hillside in the summer. The determination and fire he saw in their depths disturbed him no small amount, twisting his heart and adding to the weight of the guilt he already bore because of Glencoe. They were naught but a few hiding on a mountain. Stealth and sly tactics had served them well in the past but they'd never fought against so many and there was no' the time to find allies to fight at their side. He blew out a heavy sigh and gave a slow shake of his head. How could they manage this?

"Dinna shake your head at me as though I'm a foolish child greetin' after something I canna have." Catriona jerked away from his touch, rose from her seat, and moved an arm's length away. "There has to be something I can do to stop this."

She kept speaking as though she were alone in this world and that grated on him no small amount. "Ye canna stop this alone, Catriona, and might I remind ye, ye are my wife now. Ye are never alone in anything ever again."

Catriona stared at the group of men as though seeing them with new eyes and finding them unbelievably naïve. "The lot of ye canna help. If ye return to *Tor Ruadh* with me, ye'll surely hang as traitors." She motioned toward the south. "Ye must leave the mountain." She pinned Alexander with a pleading expression. "Go to Islay. Wait for me there, aye?"

"Ye have lost your mind if ye think I'll be leaving ye to face this battle alone." Alexander pulled her to him and snugged her up against his side while pointing at his silent, wide-eyed men fidgeting with a growing uneasiness around the fire. "We've faced tall odds before and lived to tell the tale. Have we no' done so, lads?"

Graham grimaced then tilted his head to one side like a dog listening to its master. Magnus shrugged. Duncan and Sutherland looked at each other with brows raised and Alasdair and Ian fixed him with a dubious glare. No one answered.

Sawny jumped down from his perch upon a boulder and strode to Catriona's side. "I'll fight beside ye, m'lady. To the death, I will."

Stumbling over his own large feet, gangly Tom joined his friend. "Me, t-too, m'lady. I f-figure me and Sawny can help what wif all the secrets we ken about the k-keep. There's no' a passage or hidey-hole we havena explored."

Catriona gave the boys a trembling smile as she took hold of each of their hands then embarrassed them with a fierce hug. "Ye're my fine boys," she said. "Fine boys, indeed."

Alexander looked to his shame-faced men and the priest. "I know the lot of ye have the courage of these two boys. Are ye willing to at least sort out a battle tactic and do this?"

Ian rose to his feet. "The king's regiment willna reach Clan Neal for several days. How close are Campbell and his men?"

Sutherland stood, eyes narrowing as he spoke. "I'd say tomorrow. Next day or maybe even a day after that if the weather shifts and troubles them with a spring storm or two. The cannons are heavy and their wagons dinna take well to the muddy passes."

Alexander turned to Catriona. "How many *loyal* men does your brother have? Men who dinna serve him merely because they fear him?" If they could convince the people that loved Catriona to face their fears and fight, they'd stand a better chance at saving them.

"I canna say for certain." Catriona fixed him with a broken-hearted, frustrated glare. "Would ye make me a widow so soon? Please go and wait for me in Islay."

"We either fight for your people or we, as in yourself and I, travel to Islay to start life anew together. Which will it be, wife? Ye've no other choices." Alexander hated to speak so harshly but Catriona had to face the truth. If she returned to Clan Neal's keep alone, with no more than a pair of twelve-year-olds at her side, not only would she fail in her quest, Alexander felt sure that Calum would kill them all. "Need I remind ye that none of your people kept Calum from imprisoning ye? What do ye truly hope to accomplish alone?" She was being foolish, lying to herself, but he wouldna shame her by saying so in front his men. He lifted his chin and folded his arms across his chest, tensing as he awaited her decision.

She set her jaw and stared down at the ground, hands fisted at her sides. Alexander could plainly see she knew he was right and hated it. She finally looked up, fixing an irritated glare first on the boys, then shifting it to Alexander. "Fine," she bit out the word, then her clenched jaw softened a bit. "At least if we die, we die together."

Alexander wanted to smile but for the sake of Catriona's pride, he refrained from doing so. He nodded to Sawny. "Catriona told me how the two of ye got her out. Pray tell me there's a better way to spirit us all in other than the privy chute."

Sawny and Tom scowled at each other as though silently communicating their thoughts. "Ye think the caves?" Sawny asked Tom.

Tom paused and looked at each of the men and the priest, all of whom were now standing around them. He gave Sawny a thoughtful nod. "Aye. Through the c-cave and int-to the stable, then get them to the r-root cellar, ye th-think?"

"The root cellar?" Alexander didna like the sound of that. How the hell would a hole in the ground under the kitchens get them into the rest of the keep?

"But the old passage caved in," Catriona argued with a perplexed look at both the boys.

Alexander really didna care for the sound of that and from the looks on their faces, neither did his brothers.

"Who's side are ye on, boy?" Magnus asked Sawny.

Sawny gave Magnus a perturbed look then turned back to Catriona. "No' the old passage, m'lady. There's another. 'Tis a much older tunnel. Murtagh said the goblins of the mountains used it to bring their gold to the surface."

"Goblins of the mountains?" Sawny was talking about the legend of fairy goblins that were purported to have lived within the mountains of Scotland because they deemed themselves too good to behave like brownies and dwell in crofts or castles with humans. Alexander wished the lads would get to the point. "Spit it out, boy. We've no' time for stories that are better told at a hearthside gathering."

Sawny's freckled cheeks reddened and his mouth flattened into an embarrassed line. "The caves where we hid m'lady have passages that open into the back of the stable cave. From there 'tis but a few paces to the root cellar that lies between the stables and the kitchens." His face shifted to a darker red but his demeanor was no longer embarrassed. The young boy was enraged. "The root cellar 'tis where the bastards hid afore they killed Murtagh." His dirt-smudged jaw tightened. "But Hew and Duff dinna ken about the old passages at the back of the root cellar leading up into the keep. I can lead ye through them and find ye haven within the tunnels whilst Tom spreads the word through the village and amongst the Neal crofts scattered in our glen. We have allies there that couldna come to Mistress Catriona's aid because they didna ken of her imprisonment."

"Sound plan," Alexander agreed, saying it more than he felt it. The boy seemed determined to make them all believe Clan Neal would rally around Catriona if given the chance. Since they'd ridden north, up the mountain, to make their escape, he had no idea how many could be in the village or the surrounding crofts that Sawny spoke of. During his stay at *Tor Ruadh*, he'd not ventured outside the skirting walls due to his lameness and the weather.

He had another niggling concern. Who led King William's regiment? Who could strike such fear among the people that they wouldna even speak the man's name? This information could be vital. He looked to his brothers then to his cousins. "What say ye?"

Father William spoke up before any of the others could answer. "What will ye do once inside the keep?" The sprite of a man rose from his place beside the fire, rubbing the top of his balding head as though it were a wishing stone. "How will ye reclaim this lady's home?"

Sensing a spiritual lecture on the rise, Alexander lifted his hand to stave it off. "'Tis best ye dinna ken, Father. Dinna fash yourself. We'll be sending ye on your way. Your wee mare should have no trouble getting ye to Fort William."

The priest fixed him with an insulted scowl. "Ye'll do no such thing." He stood taller and squared his narrow shoulders. "I may be a man of God but that doesna mean I dinna ken how to fight." He paused and gave the entire group a cold, narrow-eyed look. "Ye seem to be an honorable group of men. I'll be fighting alongside ye and praying for your souls as we go, ye ken?" He turned to Catriona and pointed at Alexander. "Ye married a good man. Honorable. God-fearin'. Jameson Campbell is a heartless bastard that no priest alive could save from eternal damnation. I'm glad that I didna have to condemn ye to a life with that cur."

"My brother is the same as Campbell," Catriona said with a tight-lipped look. "The two of them can burn in Hell with my father and I'll thank ye to pray that we're successful in hurrying them both along their way."

"Aye," the priest agreed with a curt bob of his head.

Feeling none the better for the priest's mixed blessing, Alexander turned back to his men. "At nightfall, we move, aye?"

Graham studied the sky and checked the direction of the wind. "Aye. For now, the weather looks to be with us and with the dim light of the new moon, we'll be shielded and should be able to make it back to the caves without being detected."

"I'd feel a mite better if we knew who led the king's men," Magnus said, voicing Alexander's fears aloud.

"All we could discover was that he's no' the usual Sassenach," Alasdair said as he opened his flask and made his way around the group pouring a bit of the precious golden liquid into each man's cup. He paused when he reached Alexander and looked him in the eye. "'Tis said he kens our ways because he was fostered as one of our own before returning to his life in England."

Fostered as one of our own. Alexander frowned. That did not bode well. The man would know the ways they fought, stalking their enemies like they stalked their deer rather than lining up like a bunch of fools and walking toward one another to see who could shoot off their bloody heads first. He gave Alasdair a nod and lifted his cup to the group.

"To nightfall and the setting right of many wrongs."

"To nightfall," the group echoed.

"Amen," declared the priest, then downed his whisky and held out his cup for a refill.

CHAPTER 18

*S*he raked her fingers through her long auburn hair, wondering at the wisdom of choosing a perch on a ledge above the cave, open to the mercy of the endless wind, to comb out and plait her curls. 'Twas no helping it. She needed a brief respite from the males to ready herself for whatever the evening might hold. Even though 'twas a mite chilly seat, the bright sunshine did wonders for soothing her nerves.

"May I join ye?"

Alexander's deep, gentle voice not only made her smile but also stoked the simmering need she now felt whenever around him. She'd never dreamed that lying with a man was not merely the physical sharing of bodies but could also be the stitching together of hearts and souls—if the right souls were matched. After last night, she understood this verra well.

"Yes, husband." She so liked how that sounded. She did her best to suppress a shiver and concentrate on the over and under weaving of her tresses into a long, smooth braid that wouldna be in her way every time she moved.

Alexander lowered himself to sit on the ledge beside her. He sat as though mesmerized, watching her nimble fingers weave through her hair, his gaze following the plaiting motion of her hands.

"I like it better loose," he said in a tone that sounded more than a little sullen.

Catriona gave him a fleeting glance as she finished one braid and started on another. "It gets in the way when it's loose." She tossed him a shy smile. "I'll comb out the braids once our battle is done and we're settled, aye?"

Alexander sat staring at her for so long without speaking, she grew uncomfortable. She tried to ignore the feeling as she wrapped the braids around her head then tucked the ends into a tight bundle at the nape her neck. After securing it all with ribbons and pins, she dropped her hands into her lap and turned to him.

"What is it?" she asked. "I see it eatin' away at ye so ye might as well say it and be done with it."

"I dinna like ye going back there. I'd rather keep ye here where it's safe 'til all is said and done."

The worry in his eyes offset the stern set of his jaw. She'd forgive him much because of the amount of caring she saw glimmering in those dark eyes. "I must go. Ye ken that in your heart." She reached out and stroked the backs of her fingers against his close-cropped beard. "I'll be with ye and I know ye'll keep me safe."

His dark brows knotted together in a fierce scowl, Alexander caught her hand and brought it to his mouth for a kiss across the backs of her fingers. He hugged her hand to his cheek and gave her a look so filled with worry and apprehension, she wanted to gather him to her breast and assure him all would be well.

"I fear ye'll hate me when I kill your brother." He let go of her hand and looked away, squinting up at the cloudless sky.

She caught her breath at the cold harshness of his words, the words she wished he'd left unspoken so she might avoid facing for a wee bit longer what had to be done. "I willna hate ye, Alexander."

She didna add that she'd harbor a good helping of guilt-ridden hate for herself, though. She felt in her heart that Calum had to die, much as a wounded horse had to be put down to end its misery.

Calum would ne'er be right. He'd grown too settled into the evil generated from a past he couldna escape.

"It must be done," she said low and soft, more to herself than to Alexander. She gazed across the misty blues and grays of the mountains surrounding the soft greening of the glen below. She could hardly believe her own words. How had things come to this? Her plotting the death of her twin brother.

Alexander pulled her close, cradling his arm around her and resting her head against his shoulder. They sat just so for a long moment until Catriona had to pull away. She couldna help it. This waiting made her nerves raw and set her teeth on edge. She scrambled to her feet and hugged herself as she paced back and forth across the shelf of stone.

"I canna stand this waiting. The sun willna set soon enough." She clenched her fists then opened her hands and scrubbed the clamminess of her palms against the heavy wool of her skirts. She studied the path they would take down to the cave, then motioned for Alexander to rise to his feet and look. "The mist," she said once he stood beside her. "We should leave now. The mist will hide us."

Alexander scowled down at the vista below then limped to the far edge of the stone shelf and studied the path from another angle.

"Your limp is nearly gone." Catriona pointed to his leg. She could tell the thigh muscle didna fill out his trews near as much as the other, but the leg was strengthening and gaining better form.

Alexander tore his gaze from the horizon long enough to give her a suggestive wink. "Ye gave it quite the workout, love. Ye made it stronger." He winked again then grew serious as he pointed down the mountainside. "Ye're right. We need to make haste now afore we lose the mist."

He took her hand and together they made their way down from Catriona's perch and alerted the others.

"Ye're a wise woman, sister," Graham said.

Graham's kind words didna help Catriona's guilt about getting the men involved in such a dire venture that could end so badly. She acknowledged his compliment with a shy nod. "Let's just pray it keeps us safe, aye?"

They were saddled up and on the trail before the hour had passed. Catriona rode behind Alexander this time, arms tight around his middle. He'd insisted she ride this way so to better see the trail before him. Catriona recognized the lie for what it was. Alexander wanted her behind him because they were riding toward the enemy and he could better shield her if she sat behind him. She heaved out a sigh and rested her cheek against his back. No matter. She'd let him think she believed his lie. After all, 'twas well-intended.

None of them spoke as they wound their way through the white mist shrouding the mountain. The longer they rode, the more Catriona tensed, feeling as though she'd explode. 'Twas so difficult to gauge how far they'd ridden with Alexander's broad back blocking her frontward view. The only thing that eased her anxiety in the least was Alexander's muscles rippling beneath her hands and cheek and the reassuring scent of him she drew in with every breath. She sent up a silent prayer and a plea to her dear departed mother. *Keep him safe. I beg ye.*

The horse came to an abrupt halt and Catriona bit back a nervous squeak. She clutched Alexander tighter and waited. He patted her hand and spoke in a whisper. "We've reached the cave."

She could nary believe it since the trip down had seemed so much shorter than the trip up but then she remembered, they had taken a winding route up the mountain to throw any followers off their trail to keep their hiding place secure.

Alexander helped Catriona dismount then sent Tom scurrying to recruit any allies he could find. Catriona watched the boy until he disappeared from sight, her fist knotted tight to her stomach and her silent prayers following him. Surely to goodness, help could be found in the village and amongst the crofts.

"Catriona?"

"Aye. Coming." She hurried into the cave, pausing just inside the entrance to let her eyes grow accustomed to the absence of light.

"We've a store of torches inside a ways—if they didna find them,"

Sawny whispered as he eased his way deeper into the cavern. Flints clicked together several times, cracking blue sparks into the darkness with every hit. A torch burst into flames with a reassuring whoosh, highlighting Sawny's proud smile. He held the light high and motioned them forward. "Come. We've torches enough for everyone, and we'll need them since we're pushing through the belly of the mountain to reach the stables."

Catriona dreaded the journey but it couldna be helped. Sawny led the way, and she fell in step behind him since the two of them knew the bowels of the mountain better than anyone else. She'd often hidden here as a child whenever her father was in one of his drunken rages and now she understood why her mother had ne'er scolded her for such. She'd been much safer dealing with the dangers of the caverns than dealing with the dangers of her father.

They edged their way through the damp tunnels of stone, turning sideways to squeeze through some openings and ducking low to crawl through other passages until they at last reached an open space with vaulted stone ceilings that could rival any cathedral.

"This is where ye hid before," Alexander said as he held his torch high and looked around. "We've traveled longer than the last time and yet here we are. Have ye become turned around, lad?"

"Nay," Catriona said as Sawny gave Alexander an insulted scowl and a shake of his head. "This vault just looks similar, but if ye know it as we do, ye ken the difference. That's why many have died in these caverns."

Sawny waved his torch back toward the way they'd just come. "The ceiling. Note the swirls in those stones?"

Alexander and his men lifted their torches, studied the markings, then nodded.

"This is the room of the dragon," Catriona said. "Can ye make it out?"

"Aye." Alexander scowled closer at the marks covering the stones. "I see it now. Good way to keep your bearings."

"'Tis the work of the goblins," Sawny added with a wink and a snort.

Alexander waved toward an opening up ahead. "Move, boy. I'd like to reach the stable before nightfall to give us plenty of time to make our way to the root cellar when it grows dark."

If they all made it through this uprising alive, she'd ne'er darken the innards of the earth again, Catriona swore to herself. She breathed in a deep breath of the dank air, relieved when she picked out the faint scent of horse manure and straw up ahead. "We're nearly there."

"Good," Alexander said. "I'm tired of no' being able to see the fine bounce of your arse in these shadows."

The rest of the men chuckled. Father William snorted the loudest.

"Quiet now," Catriona scolded with a hissing shush. "If anyone's working at the back of the stable, we dinna wish to give ourselves away."

"We need to put our torches out and store them here," Sawny said in a hushed tone. He gathered up all the lights and stomped them out, leaving them in an inky blackness.

"Hold hands," Catriona ordered, taking hold of Sawny's hand in one hand and Alexander's in the other. "We dinna wish to leave anyone behind in the darkness."

"Amen to that," Father William said from the back of the group.

Ducking her head, Catriona squeezed past the boulder covering the exit and wiggled into the dimly lit stable without letting go of Alexander's hand. Alexander grunted and huffed against the confines of the passage, his broad shoulders and height complicating his entry. He finally shoved his way through and one by one, the rest of the men followed. They gathered in the wide space at the back of the rows of stalls, doing their best to move quietly amongst the straw and dried rushes scattered across the stone floor.

"Shinny up ahead and see what ye can see, aye?" Catriona urged Sawny with a barely audible whisper. She drew in a sniff and wrinkled her nose. The tang of rotting hay and stalls sorely in need of mucking filled the air. If Murtagh were still alive, someone's arse would be kicked and their heads would be on a platter. "I canna believe Calum is such a fool," she told Alexander. "Filthy stables make for weak horses."

"He's too weak a man to mind the business a chieftain must mind for the benefit of the clan." Alexander motioned for everyone to lower themselves to the back wall and sit while they waited. "Do ye think ye can persuade your people to accept a female chief?"

Alexander may as well have reached into her lungs and snatched out all her air. Catriona stared at him. "What?"

He gave her a slow, easy smile she barely detected in the low lighting. "Ye are damned and determined to save your people only to abandon them and leave them without a leader to guide and protect them? Come now, Catriona. Ye are so much wiser than that."

Was he mocking her? She swallowed hard and sat taller, lifted her chin and fixed him with a narrow-eyed look. "Nay. I'll be convincing them that their next chieftain should be yourself since ye are my husband."

Even in the shadowy light of the torch-lit sconces flickering on the walls, Catriona noted how Alexander's eyes flared open wider and his jaw dropped. Good. That would teach the man to mock her. 'Twas early in their marriage. She best get the rules set straight here at the start.

Sawny interrupted the lesson, scurrying back to them with his back bent to hide below the level of the stall walls. He made a beeline to Catriona, his face red and wet with tears. Catriona opened her arms, and he flew into them as if she were his mother. He shuddered in her arms, thumping her shoulders with his balled up fists.

"Sawny boy, tell me?" Hugging him tightly, Catriona looked over at Alexander for help.

Alexander patted the boy on his back and spoke in low, soothing tones. "What happened, lad? What did ye see?"

"I'm no' weeping because I'm sad." The boy hiccupped out sobs with great shuddering hisses of breath. "I'm feckin' mad as hell. The stable's a pigsty and from what I saw of the paddock and side-bailey beside the kitchens, 'tis no' much better. Dung and rot everywhere and we've only been gone a few days. 'Tis a disgrace. I'm ashamed of me clan and what they've allowed to come to pass." He shuddered with anger as he made a sweeping motion toward the stalls. "Murtagh's soul will never find rest as long as this remains."

Catriona gritted her teeth and pulled in a deep breath. She had to remain calm and whilst she was at it, calm the boy. "Shhh now, Sawny. We dinna ken what's been done to those within the keep. Calum may have locked them up." *Or worse.* But she wouldna say it aloud. Calum may have gone on a killing spree. They couldna tell for certain until they'd made their way into the keep.

Sawny pulled back and stared at her with a hatred far surpassing his years. "I want to be the one to kill him, m'lady. I beg ye. Let me avenge Murtagh. Let me avenge my clan."

"Ye canna kill anyone without a calm head and a well thought out plan, boy." Alexander gave Catriona a pointed look that said *I'll handle this.*

She agreed and nodded for Alexander to take charge.

"I want to kill him slow," Sawny growled out through clenched teeth, tears and snot running down his face. "I want him to suffer."

Catriona couldna help herself. She pulled a square of linen from her sleeve and held it out to him. "Wipe your nose and your tears and calm yourself. If ye be bleary-eyed with anger, ye canna see well enough to kill."

Alexander rolled his eyes and shook his head. "She's right, boy," he said with a huff. "Settle yourself so we can figure the best way to end the bastard."

Sawny blew his nose and after much cursing and hiccupping, he inhaled a great gulp of air then snorted into the crumpled linen again. "Forgive me." He waved the men closer around him then jabbed his thumb back toward the front of the stables. "I only saw two men staggering about the yard and both were heaving out what they must ha' drank last night. Smoke was coming from the kitchens so I'm thinking Cook and the scullery lads and lassies still be tending to those duties at least."

"Could we make it to the root cellar now, ye think?" Catriona stretched to look over the rows of stalls filling the cave. It appeared no one was in the stable but themselves.

Sawny nodded. "Aye. One by one. I can go first to be certain."

Catriona was touched by the twelve-year-old's bravery but he'd already experienced enough in his young life to earn him the title of man. She pulled him to her and gave him a fierce hug. "Ye watch yourself, aye? I canna bear it if anything happens to ye."

Sawny awkwardly pulled away, cheeks flaming and chin tucked to his chest. "I'll be fine, m'lady."

"Let's be on with it then." Alexander shooed the boy forward and followed close behind him. Catriona hurried to claim her place as next in line and the rest of the men fell in tow.

By the time they'd crept through the stable and reached the entrance, the outer paddock and bailey were deserted. The two men Sawny had seen were gone. One by one, they sidled their way along the walls, ducked behind barrels and wooden crates, then made a final dash across an open expanse of ground before disappearing into a small round door in the wall behind the kitchens.

The main room of the root cellar smelled of dirt, dried herbs, and the earthiness of potatoes, carrots, and turnips. Catriona ducked beneath fragrant bundles of dried rosemary, lavender, thyme, and sage as she followed Alexander and Sawny. With darting glances back at the entrance, they wound their way around the barrels and crates of Clan Neal's winter stores.

Once they reached the back wall, it took them all to clear away the boxes and crates covering a small arched door that looked as though it had been sealed shut with a thick layer of mortar.

"'Tis sealed shut," Alexander scowled at Sawny. "How long has it been since ye were in this set of tunnels?"

Sawny gave an impertinent roll of his eyes and retrieved an iron pry bar from the far corner. "Here. Ye see that wee hole in the base of the door? Shove this in that hole and push it to the left."

Giving the boy a narrow-eyed glare, Alexander took the bar and did as Sawny instructed. The seemingly sealed off door held fast for a bit then swung open into the tunnel with a great grinding and falling of dust.

"Ye see?" Sawny scurried back to the front of the root cellar then hurried back toting a lantern. He balanced it on top of a barrel, drew the flint box out of its base, and lit the taper within it. He snatched the lantern up by the bale, handed it to Catriona, and waved everyone forward. "Follow the mistress, I'll follow as soon as I make the root cellar appear as it was so no one will follow. I'll be right behind ye."

Catriona ducked her head and entered the tunnel, relieved to discover she could stand at her full height once inside. The outer wall of the tunnel was cold to the touch and dry but the interior wall on their right was wet with sweating rivulets of moisture. A cloying stench of mold and mildew filled the air. The floor was nothing more than dirt at first, but as they climbed, the tunnel became a stone staircase winding its way up into the castle and branching out like a system of veins just beneath the keep's skin.

Dim recollections surfaced as she held the lantern higher. "I know this place," she said more to herself than anyone else. Aye. She'd been here before. With Mother. She tried to remember why but could only bring back faded bits of the time gone by and it was more sensations than memory. The clammy odor of the tunnel. The chilled dampness of the air. Fear in Mother's whispers. Her trembling hugs. Catriona forged onward, giving up on trying to remember what had happened and instead using the memory to make her way to the second floor and the hidden doorway she knew awaited in the small sitting room of the nursery.

Aye. The nanny's room. The perfect place to plan the next step in their attack.

CHAPTER 19

*A*lexander didna ken which was worse: a small room bursting at its seams with braw battle-ready men or the feeling he had verra little control o'er the mêlée about to ensue. And then there was Catriona. His wife. He felt a tender protectiveness toward her like he'd never known for anyone and it scared the living hell out of him because here she sat, damn smack middle of the fray.

"The plan?" Graham nudged himself in between Magnus and Duncan and joined them in leaning back against the only wall in the tiny room bereft of furniture. Sutherland, Alasdair, Ian, and the priest perched on opposite sides of the shoddy narrow cot at the room's center, their backs butted against each other. Catriona and Sawny stood wedged in the far corner between the modest nightstand and the wall. Graham scrubbed his hands together before folding his arms across his chest. "I assume the chieftain, Hew, and Duff are the first we must handle, aye?"

"Aye," Alexander answered with a concerned glance at Catriona. He hoped she truly realized that her brother would die this day. "Calum and his guards first. Then we'll judge the future actions of the Neal clan and go from there."

"And when the others arrive?" Alasdair asked. "Campbell's group and the king's regiment?"

"'Tis my hope that enough Neals from the village and surrounding crofts will join the ones in the keep siding with us and we'll be able to hold them off long enough to reason with them and reach an understanding." Alexander surveyed his men and their fierce scowls. Their loyalty was unquestionable and for that, Alexander was thankful. "We have the advantage inside the stronghold and we know where its weaknesses lay because we've breached it ourselves."

"Noon is upon us. Calum should soon descend from his solar to eat his meal in the main hall." Catriona glanced out the narrow window they had all skirted to avoid discovery.

"Can ye be certain?" Ian asked. "Did your father no' make it a habit to eat in his rooms? I never set eyes on the man during our stay here."

"The man was dying," Magnus interjected. "That's why he ate in his rooms." He shifted his attention to Catriona. "Your brother be healthy but loves the drink as well. Think ye he'll descend for the noonday repast or wait till the last meal of the day?"

"Oh, he'll descend," Catriona said, a wry note of disgust coloring her tone. Her eyes narrowed and her jaw worked as though she were grinding her teeth. "He'll no' want to miss an opportunity to preen like a peacock in his new status as chief."

"What route will he take to the hall?" Alexander asked. Calum's chambers were here on the second floor but that didna mean he'd pass this room on his way down to his meal.

Catriona's scowl deepened then she elbowed her way out of the corner and shooed the men off the small cot. "Move."

"Move? Where?" Father William scuttled sideways, stumbling over booted feet and bumping into men.

"I dinna care, Father, but I need this linen to make a map." She motioned toward the cold hearth. "Pray, see if there's a stick of burnt wood I can use."

Sutherland squatted down beside the hearth, taking care to keep his sheathed sword vertical and out from under anyone's kilt. He dug around in the cold ashes of a long-ago fire and after a few moments, rose with a smile of victory and a chunk of blackened wood. He handed it over to Catriona who set to sketching out the floor plan of the keep on the linen across the bed. "We are here." She pointed to a mark then trailed her finger along a line and tapped on another open-ended square. "This is Calum's suite."

Alexander squeezed his way closer, committing Catriona's sketch to memory. He pointed to a horizontal line running between the two squares then veering off to the right. "This will be his route?"

Catriona nodded, eyes narrowing as she studied the crude map as though it led to treasure.

"We will flank them here and here." Alexander tapped on the linen, pointing to small open-ended blocks at intervals along the hall. He lifted his gaze from the sheet and looked at his brothers. "I want him dead afore he reaches those stairs."

"Sutherland and I will take out his pets," Duncan said with a nod down at the map. "They always follow a step or two behind the man, close enough to sniff at his arse."

"Daggers and swords only," Alexander said. "We dinna wish to announce our presence with gunfire."

"I get the first stab at him," Sawny said, bloodlust reddening his thin freckled cheeks.

Alexander understood the boy's need for revenge but they couldna risk it. "I know ye wish to avenge Murtagh, lad, but I've a better way for ye to accomplish that, ye ken?"

Sawny glared at him, a stubborn pout already pulling down the corners of his mouth.

Alexander handed Sawny his short sword. "I need ye to guard your mistress. I'm trusting ye to protect my wife. Will ye do that for me, Sawny? Can I trust ye to keep her safe?"

Sawny's demeanor changed with the swiftness of a blink. He shifted from a sullen lad to a proud, solemn young man. "Aye," he said with a downward jerk of his chin. "I'll keep her safe. I swear it."

Graham cracked open the door to the hallway, listened for a moment then looked back at Alexander. "Shall we take our posts then, brother?"

"Aye." Alexander stabbed the sheet with the tip of his dagger. "I'll be waiting here for Calum." Pointing first at each of the men and then to the sheet, he assigned them their positions. "Duncan and Sutherland, this door just past his solar. Dinna let those beasts get by ye. Alasdair and Ian, guard the base of the stairwell in case anyone harkens any cries to alarm. Graham and Magnus, take either end of the hall at the top of the stairs in case any of them make it past Alasdair or Ian." With seven men against three, Alexander felt sure that Calum would kneel before his Maker before nightfall.

"And what about us?" Father William asked.

"Stay here with Sawny and Catriona and pray we dinna fail." He took hold of Catriona's hand and pulled her to stand in front of him. "Swear ye willna enter the hall no matter what ye hear, ye ken?" He could tell by the look on her face that Catriona wanted to be in the fight's midst but he couldna allow it. He couldna fight at his best if he had to keep one eye trained on her. "Swear it," he repeated.

She stared at him for a long moment. So long, he felt for sure she was about to defy him and the first heated argument of their short marriage would ensue. "I swear it," she finally said in a strained tone then tiptoed and pressed an urgent kiss to his mouth. "Swear ye'll come back for me," she demanded, her lips and nose brushing his as she spoke.

"I swear it," Alexander answered, savoring the taste of her and wishing like hell there was a simpler way to do this.

They filed out of the room, all of them taking their posts. Alexander flattened himself into an alcove next to the doorway where Duncan and Sutherland waited to silence Duff and Hew. On his way to the stairwell at the other end of the hallway, Ian paused at Calum's door and pressed his ear against it for a long moment. Then he jerked away, gave Alexander a quick nod and sprinted down to his station.

The latch to Calum's door clicked. The squeaking of the hinges echoed down the quiet hallway. "They'll be here soon. Get those lazy bastards off their arses and get this place clean. I'll no' have the Campbell nor Crestshire reporting back to the king that I canna handle my clan."

Crestshire. Alexander knew the name well. Is that who headed the king's new regiment? A cavalcade of emotions surged through him. He would have to think more on what that news could mean to their cause as soon as they settled this chore. A dagger in each hand, he rolled the smooth hafts of bone in his palms, readying for the kill. He held his breath as the sound of footsteps drew closer.

Duncan and Sutherland sprang from their post. Duncan landed on Hew and Sutherland landed on Duff. The miscreants staggered and struggled, cursing and sputtering indignant roars as Duncan and Sutherland held fast until the two collapsed to the floor and went still.

Alexander stepped out of the alcove, blocking Calum's way as he spun around to escape Duncan and Sutherland approaching with their bloodied knives at the ready.

"Attack! Attack!" Calum shouted as he bent low and spun, kicking Alexander in his weak leg with a slamming hard thrust of his boot against the newly healed wound.

"Graham!" Alexander roared as his fickle leg buckled and took him down to his knees.

Wild-eyed and mouth ajar, Calum stumbled back a step then vaulted around Alexander and headed down the hallway.

Alexander rolled to a crouching position, flipped the daggers 'til he held them by the tips of their blades then let fly as hard as he could throw. One knife sank high into Calum's left shoulder and the other blade buried deep into the right side of his lower back. Calum kept moving, hitching his way down the hall.

"Graham, take the bastard! I've but nicked him." Alexander itched to fire off a shot but forced himself to hold fast. They could still finish this without the sound of gunfire stirring all in the keep.

Graham and Magnus charged toward the fray from opposite ends of the hallway but before they could reach Calum, the nursery room door flew open. Catriona burst into the hallway. She held the short sword that Alexander had given to Sawny raised high for a killing thrust.

"Mistress!" Sawny shouted, following close behind her, snatching to get hold of her.

"I mean to kill ye this time, bitch!" Calum screamed out an agonizing roar as he ripped one of Alexander's daggers out of his back. As Catriona charged him with her blade raised, he dove toward her and stabbed the knife low into her side.

Catriona cried out. The short sword fell from her hands as she and Calum tumbled backward and hit the floor together. With Catriona flat of her back, Calum reared back and stabbed her again before Alexander tackled him and the rest of his brothers closed in.

"Ye son of a whore." Alexander grabbed hold of Calum by the chin and the back of his head and snapped his neck with a hard jerking twist.

"Mistress, no...no...no!" Sawny knelt beside Catriona, rocking on his knees as his clenched fists pounded his agony against his legs.

Father William rushed to Catriona's other side and dropped to the floor beside her, ripping away pieces of his robe and using them to staunch the flow of blood gushing from her wounds.

Alexander crawled to Catriona and sank down beside her. Gently easing her head and shoulders atop his arm, he cradled her close as he scolded her in the softest tone he could manage. 'Twas the only way he knew to keep her conscious and stir her will to fight. "Stubborn woman. Look what ye've done to yourself by no' listening to what I told ye."

Face draining of color and eyes wide, Catriona struggled to speak as tears slipped from the outer corners of her eyes and trailed down her temples into her braids. "I'm verra sorry, husband," she whispered with a weak gasp. "I feared he was..."

"Shh..." Alexander kissed her clammy forehead then nestled his cheek against her. "I know what ye feared well enough." He caught Father William's eye, gave a pointed look toward Catriona's wounds, then locked eyes once again with the priest. *Tell me she'll live,* he mouthed.

Father William gave him the lightest of shrugs then looked skyward. "God's hands," he whispered then crossed himself.

"I'll get... I'll get," Sawny hiccupped from the other side of Catriona.

"Ye'll get what, Sawny?" 'Twas all he could do to speak in a civil tone to the boy. How the hell had Catriona gotten hold of the sword he'd entrusted to Sawny? "What, boy? Tell me."

Sawny lifted his red tear-stained face to Alexander then dragged his sleeve across his nose and face. "I'll run fetch the healer, Mrs. Bickerstaff. I willna let anyone stop me, I swear it."

"Can ye shoot a gun?" Alexander twisted and ripped his gun out of his belt. He handed it to Sawny, butt first, but held tight to the barrel until Sawny answered him. "Can ye shoot?"

"Aye," Sawny swore with conviction as he yanked the pistol out of Alexander's hand and rose to his feet. "I willna fail ye this time. I swear it on me mam's grave." He turned and bolted down the hallway.

"God go with that boy," Father William murmured as he kept both hands pressed hard on Catriona's wounds and returned to mumbling silent prayers, lips moving as he closed his eyes.

"Alexander," Catriona hitched out in a weak whisper.

"Aye, love." Alexander held her closer while his brothers, cousins, and dearest friend in all his life knelt around them. He softly stroked Catriona's cheek and her eyes flickered open wider. "Stay with me, Catriona. Dinna ye dare leave me in this cruel world all alone."

Catriona blinked, her forehead wrinkling with pain as she shuddered and coughed. "I'm here, husband, but I'm so verra cold."

Magnus stripped off his cloak quicker than any of the others could remove their coats and draped it across her. Father William kept his bloody hands in place under the cloak.

"Better, love?" Alexander pressed a gentle kiss to her temple, her salty tears wetting his lips. "Warmer now?"

"Aye," she whispered with a trembling smile as her eyes closed.

"What have ye done to ma wee lassie?" Mrs. Aberfeldy cried out as she emerged from the stairway and hurried toward them. Her steps slowed, and she faltered as she reached Calum's body. Her plump face wrinkled and twisted with grief. "And my poor laddie," she whispered. "God love him and forgive him."

With a shake of her head and clutching both hands to her breast, she rushed to Catriona. "His own sister," she whispered. "May God forgive him." Her distraught look hardening with determination, Mrs. Aberfeldy clapped her hands and stood as tall as her round body would allow. "Hie to the kitchen and tell Cook ye need the litter we keep in case someone falls ill." She grabbed hold of Sutherland by the ear and pulled him to his feet. "Hie with ye now. Run, boy! I'll no' have my dear sweet lassie lying on this hard floor to suffer her wounds like a felled deer."

"Old woman!" Knocking her hand from his ear, Sutherland looked to Alexander. "The old cow makes sense. I'll fetch the litter and we can move her to her bed 'til the healer gets here, aye?"

"Aye," Alexander agreed. He didna give a damn what they did. Only two things mattered right now: him staying at Catriona's side and keeping her alive.

Alexander ignored Mrs. Aberfeldy's continued squawking, intent on Catriona and stroking the silk of her cheek. "Open your eyes, sweetness," he begged. "I fear ye've left me when ye close them."

"I'm no' but resting," Catriona said with a soft sigh. Her eyelids fluttered open the least bit and she seemed to struggle to focus on Alexander's face.

"Once ye've healed," Alexander said, determined to keep her talking. "We need to be about the business of making a bairn or two. What say ye?"

A wan smile trembled on Catriona's lips as her eyelids dipped then opened wider. "Twins. A pair of boys. Aye?"

"Aye," Alexander agreed. "A pair of sons just might make up for your stubbornness and the scare ye've put into me this day."

"I didna think…" her voice trailed off and her eyes closed.

"Ye didna think what, love?" Alexander lifted her closer and stroked her cheek faster. "Catriona—speak to me, lass. Ye didna think what?"

To his profound relief, Catriona opened her eyes, looked confused for a moment, then smiled. "Fear. I didna think ye feared anything."

"Ye are wrong, Catriona," Alexander whispered as her eyes closed again. "I fear losing ye, m'love. I canna bear the thought of facing this life without ye."

"Always and forever, my husband. Always be with ye," Catriona promised in a breathy whisper without opening her eyes. "This life... and the next...swore it. Remember?"

"This life, Catriona," Alexander said, not caring that hot tears filled his eyes and burned down his cheeks. "Dinna give up on this life. I beg ye."

Sutherland burst from the stairwell with the litter clutched in one hand. A pair of white-capped maidservants scurried after him, their arms piled high with linens. Four scullery lads toting steaming hot kettles of water followed the maids. As the servants filed by, they spared worried glances at Catriona and Alexander, before rushing to the stairwell and ascending to the next floor.

With a clap of his hand to Alexander's shoulder, Sutherland gave him a grim smile. "The word of their freedom is traveling fast, brother, and all appear to be taking the news verra well."

None of that mattered now. All that mattered was Catriona.

Alexander bent and kissed her forehead then whispered against her skin. "I've got to move ye a wee bit, lass, so we can get ye to your bed, aye?"

A cold, icy hand of dread twisted his heart when she didn't respond. With a hard swallow, he pressed his face close to the end of her nose and her parted lips. He thanked God in Heaven above when he felt her breathing brush against his face. She yet lived. As long as she lived, he wouldna give up hope.

Sliding his arms beneath her, he eased her onto the litter. He walked beside her as Sutherland and Graham carried her between them up the stairs to the next floor. Mrs. Aberfeldy and three maids were already scurrying about the room. One stoked the fire while another swung more kettles from the irons on the hearth and set them to boil. The smallest of the three lasses ripped linens into bandages and stacked them on the table beside the bed.

Yanking the comforter and layers of blankets to the foot of the bed, Mrs. Aberfeldy waved the men forward. "Easy now, lads. Settle her with care."

Alexander shifted Catriona from the litter to the bed then stepped back. Father William stood at the foot of the bed, rosary beads in one hand, cross in the other, still mouthing fervent silent prayers.

"Out with ye now," Mrs. Aberfeldy took hold of Alexander's arm as she shooed the priest and the other men from the room. "Out with ye whilst I cut that dress away and get her ready for Elena."

"I'll no' be leaving, old woman." If she valued her life, the fickle housekeeper had best heed his tone. Catriona had told him she no longer kent where Mrs. Aberfeldy's allegiances fell. She wouldna tell him why she felt that way. Seemed almost ashamed to speak of it. But if Catriona didna trust the woman, then neither did he and he'd be damned if he'd leave his dear sweet love alone with her.

Mrs. Aberfeldy released his arm as though the touch of it burned her hand. Her eyes flared wide and reflected the alarm that Alexander had intended to instill in her. "Aye then," she said with a meek bob of her head as she lowered her gaze. "As ye wish."

Father William gathered the rest of the men and herded them all out the door. "Come, my brothers. We'll give our lady the privacy she deserves and say our prayers in her sitting room."

Alasdair and Ian left but Sutherland, Duncan, Graham, and Magnus stood firm, all with their attention trained on Alexander.

"What say ye, brother?" Graham asked.

Alexander nodded. "I'll be at her side but if ye'll stay close and pray for m'lady's healing, I'd be most grateful."

"'Twill be done," Graham said then the four men filed out the door.

CHAPTER 20

A soft rap on the door interrupted his restless dozing. He drew his pistol and dagger. Who dared? Without a sound, he rose from the chair beside Catriona's bed and pressed the back of one hand to her bare arm lying on top of the covers. Still cool to the touch. Good. No sign of fever yet. Old Elena had feared fever might set in due to the depth of the wounds. Tucking his dagger into the front of his belt but keeping his pistol aloft, he used his free hand to snug her arm under the covers and kissed her forehead before going to the door.

He paused with a finger on the latch then drew back and tightened his grip on the pistol. Clan Neal had yet to win back his trust. He would take no risks with Catriona. "Who knocks?"

"'Tis Munroe Neal, sir. I've brought the lady's brothers to see her."

Alexander paused. If memory served, Catriona's fifteen-year-old brother Angus had been Calum's shadow and well on his way to becoming as arrogant and cruel as his mentor. He glanced back at Catriona, unresponsive as she'd been since the ill-planned attack. "Visitors are ill-advised. Perhaps in a few days' time but no' today."

"Would ye be willing to come out and speak to us, sir?" Munroe asked through the door. "I ken ye dinna wish to overtax your lady or leave her, but if ye'd see fit to come out and meet with us here in the lady's sitting room for but a wee moment, 'twould be most appreciated."

Where the hell were his men? They'd camped out in the attached sitting room whilst he'd stayed at Catriona's side. Alexander heard the scuffling of feet and whisperings of muffled voices outside the door. He sensed ill-will a comin'. 'Twas a trap for certain. Alexander drew his dagger from his belt then cocked his pistol. He flipped the lock on the door with the tip of the sword and stepped back. "Open the door."

"Beg pardon, sir?" Munroe said.

"Open the door. I've unlocked it."

"Aye, sir." The door eased open into the sitting room, revealing a short, squat wizened old man and Catriona's nine-year-old twin brothers craning their necks around the elder's round body to see their sister.

Munroe Neal's watery blue eyes widened, and his bushy brows jumped near to his grizzled hairline. "S-sir?" His nervous stutter hissed and broke as his gaze locked on the barrel of the gun. "We mean no harm." He lifted trembling hands, stretching his plump fingers wide. He scowled down at the young boys inching toward the open door and yanked them both back behind him. "I bear no arms and neither do the bairns. I swear it."

"Graham! Duncan!" Alexander shouted, not trusting the old man or the young boys. He'd take no foolish risks.

Father William threw open the outer door to the sitting room and hurried to him. With a congenial nod to Munroe and the two boys, he pushed past them then stopped short when his nose came even with the end of the gun. His perplexed attention shifted to Alexander. "Alexander! Whatever vexes ye, man?"

"Where is everyone?"

"I told them to go walk about." He scowled at Alexander, pressed two fingers atop the gun barrel, and pushed it downward. "They've grown a mite surly from being cooped up. I told them I'd stand watch."

Alexander nodded toward the old man and two boys still standing in the door. "Ye failed, priest."

"I did not!" Father William drew himself up to his full scrawny height and fixed Alexander with a shaming scowl. "I searched them for weapons and asked them about their business before letting them in." He gave Alexander a quick up and down glare then huffed. "I thought ye might could handle an old man and two wee lads on your own. Shall I fetch your brothers to come and assist ye?"

"Dinna make me sin even more than I already have, priest." Alexander had never backhanded a priest nor cursed at one but at the moment his stains upon his soul were no' his greatest concern. Fraught with weariness and worry, he couldna guarantee his actions would remain civil toward anyone. He disarmed the pistol but kept it in his hand as he sheathed his dagger. "Stand watch and pray over Catriona, if ye would, aye?"

"Aye," Father William said with a conciliatory smile. He waved a hand toward the sitting room and nodded. "See to your guests. I'll watch over the lady."

Alexander entered the sitting room, closed the bedroom door behind him, then took a defensive stance in front of it. He folded his arms across his chest and cradled the pistol in the crook of his elbow where it couldna fail to be noticed.

"We'd never hurt our Catriona," said one twin, perhaps the one called Murray. With matching mops of flaming red hair and identical freckled faces, Alexander couldna tell the two wee imps apart.

"She's like our mam," the other twin said, puffing out his narrow chest and jutting his chin forward in the fiercest threatening scowl a nine-year-old could muster. "We came to make sure ye're watching over her proper or we'll be setting matters right, we will."

"Dougal. Murray. Mind your manners and go over there and sit whilst I speak with Mr. MacCoinnich." Munroe encouraged the boys with a slight shove in that direction.

Alexander returned the twins' glaring looks as though they were young men. He admired their bravado and remembered how Catriona had fussed over them like a mother hen. She loved them.

Trusted them. Perhaps in time, he would trust them, too. "Your sister is no' awake, but she rests easy and has no fever." He'd give them that. They had a right to know if they loved her as much as they seemed.

Both boys nodded, their fierce scowls shifting to expressions of worry.

Munroe stepped forward and gave Alexander a polite nod. "Munroe Neal, sir. I am the head of Clan Neal's elders and therefore 'tis my duty to extend our gratitude to ye." He glanced over at the young boys sitting on the settee then looked back at Alexander with a somber scowl. "Clan Neal has suffered a great deal over the years but thanks be to God, ye've rid us of the festering disease we've endured for so long."

Alexander studied the man. Head of the elders. A man of standing in the clan. He seemed to wish to be an ally, but that was yet to be determined. From what Catriona had said, the men of Clan Neal had always cowered, first, before Catriona's father and then before her brother. Alexander couldna fathom how they'd willingly live under such conditions. Why the blazes had they no' fought to better their circumstances? "Catriona has another brother." He'd say no more. He wanted to hear how Munroe addressed it.

"Angus is gone." Munroe folded his hands in front of his thick middle and settled his short, stocky stance as though he'd be there for a while. "He ran when he heard of Calum's death. We dinna ken where."

"If I learn ye are lying or hiding the boy so he can seek revenge..." Alexander paused and lifted the barrel of his pistol enough to highlight his words. "I shall hunt ye down and make ye rue the day ye tried to deceive me."

Munroe smiled. A smile that crinkled his eyes and made them sparkle. "Ye have my word that the useless cur has run with his tail tucked." He paused, fixing Alexander with a scrutinizing glance as he clasped his hands to the small of his back and meandered in a small circle in the center of the sitting room. "Would ye care to share your plans once Lady Catriona is healed?"

"I would not."

The old man threw back his head and laughed, his round belly bobbing up and down enough to make his kilt sway and his cheeks reddening with the effort. Once he'd finally composed himself, he faced Alexander and bowed. "I like ye, Alexander MacCoinnich. Ye are a braw man. Fierce. Protective. Canny."

Alexander didna trust compliments. They often shielded lies. "Is there anything else?" He motioned toward the door behind him. "I need to be getting' back to me wife."

Munroe grew quiet, his expression thoughtful. "I hope one day ye will come to trust me, sir, and realize I've only the best of intentions."

"That remains to be seen," Alexander replied, tapping the barrel of his pistol against his palm with a slow intentional pat.

Munroe gave him a curt nod and motioned for the boys to rise from the settee as he moved toward the door. With his hand resting on the latch, he turned back to Alexander and bowed. "I'll leave ye to your lady but I'll also leave ye with this: I shall be taking your name to the other elders as my choice for *Tanist* to Clan Neal."

"*Tanist?*" Alexander took a step forward but kept himself between Catriona's door and the elder. "I'm no' of Neal blood. Why would ye do that?"

"Ye've married the eldest daughter and the eldest son, the one still living, is as unfit as the two before him. This is Clan Neal's opportunity to heal. To thrive. To grow." Munroe lifted his chin and locked eyes with Alexander. "Will ye accept?"

"I will think upon your offer." Alexander refused to do anything rash, especially when it came to Catriona's people.

Munroe nodded. "I would expect no less from a wise chieftain." He turned to go, pausing a moment to glance back over one shoulder. "Good day to ye, sir, and know we're all praying for Lady Catriona's complete recovery."

Alexander didn't comment. Just watched the old man toddle away, herding the nine-year-olds down the hallway with him.

Tanist. Catriona had teased that she'd speak to the elders and get them to name him chief rather than claim the title herself and attempt to persuade them to accept a female leader. But was

Munroe's offer real? And would the other elders agree? Alexander snorted out a bitter huff. It had taken an outsider to rid them of the problem they shouldha tended to themselves. He had little respect for such men. They shouldha ousted both Calum and his father years ago.

Then what wouldha happened to Catriona and her mother? The puzzle of the Neal men's cowardice plagued him, gnawed at his gut like a dog worrying a bone. Surely, that could nay have been the only reason that kept Calum and his father in power.

"Alexander."

Father William's quiet summons came from the door at his back, sending a cold sweat across him. With slow, pained movements born of dread, he turned and almost collapsed to his knees when Catriona turned her head on the pillow and gave him a weak a smile. He rushed to her bedside, shoved his pistol into Father William's hands, then knelt and scooped up Catriona's hand.

"'Tis about time ye opened those eyes, m'love," he scolded in a teasing tone before pressing a kiss to her hand.

"I was weary," Catriona whispered then pulled her hand free of his and cradled his face in her palm. "Have I slept so long?"

"Long enough."

"But I'm better now." She eased in a deep breath, flinched, then eased it out with a slow exhale. "A mite sore, though."

"Aye." Alexander rose and poured a small amount of water into a cup. "Mrs. Elena said ye would be but the woman and her vile poultices kept fever and infection at bay." He slid an arm under her shoulders and lifted. "Naught but a wee sip for ye now," he said, matching the tilt of the cup to her swallowing. When she gave him a quick nod, he set the cup aside and lowered her back to the pillows.

Catriona lifted the covers then wrinkled her nose. "Shew! I fair reek." Still grimacing, she shifted her gaze to him. "How can ye stand to be in the same room with me?"

"Ye smell sweet as heather and the sparkling green of your opened eyes fair lifts me heart."

She gave him a side-eyed look as though he were a lad trying to charm Cook out of extra helpings. "Ye are a sweet talkin' liar, dear husband. I'll give ye that."

Mrs. Aberfeldy pushed into the room with Elena Bickerstaff and another suspicious smelling cloth-covered crock. "Saints be praised. She's back among us!" She looked to Alexander. "Have ye told her of the elders' decision?"

Alexander made a mental note to have Mrs. Aberfeldy sent off to England. The woman would be a fair weapon against the Sassenachs. She'd drive them into drowning themselves in the River Thames to escape her incessant meddling. He fixed her with such a glare she backed up a step and pressed her plump fingers to her lips.

"Ahh…beg pardon. I didna mean to speak out a turn." She looked to Mrs. Elena who rolled her eyes and shook her head.

"She's always been an eejit," Mrs. Elena said as she folded back the covers and peered under Catriona's bandages. "Looks good. I willna disturb the wounds for now. We can wait to put a fresh poultice on them til this evening."

"Are ye going tell me what Mrs. Aberfeldy is referring to or not?" Catriona pinned him with a fierce glare.

"It appears the elders have found a choice for *Tanist*."

Catriona's eyes widened and her smile grew so quickly that Alexander felt a wave of guilt wash across him. "Yourself?" she asked.

"Aye." Alexander gave Mrs. Aberfeldy a damning narrow-eyed scowl. "But I've no' accepted as yet."

"Why not?" Catriona cried out. "Ye would make a fine chieftain!"

Alexander pointed toward the door then nodded to the old women. "Out. The both of ye."

"But…"

"I said out." Alexander took a step toward them. "I've much to discuss with my wife and I dinna wish it to become fodder for the kitchen gossips."

"But…" Mrs. Aberfeldy repeated.

Mrs. Elena shot the housekeeper a dark look then took hold of her plump elbow and steered her toward the door. Shoving her into the next room, she paused to look back and nod at Alexander. "I hope ye find it in your heart to accept." Then she exited and closed the door with a firm thud behind her.

Alexander turned back and stared at Catriona for a long moment. There was no way to make what he had to say any softer so best say it and be done with it. "I'm finding it difficult to stomach being named chieftain to a clan of cowards."

"Cowards?" Catriona repeated, brow furrowed as though she didn't understand. "How could ye think us cowards?"

"Why did the men of this clan no' address the issue of your father, and then your brother? Why did they support such behavior? I ken your father was their kin and chosen by their elders, but only a coward stands by and allows their women such callous mistreatment."

"My father was no' their kin." Catriona spoke with a strange, detached calmness. Alexander recognized it for the shield that it was. If Catriona didna separate herself from the evil of her family's history, she'd lose herself to despair. She stared down at her hands as she continued, "Clan Neal is my mother's bloodline. They accepted her husband as their chieftain at her request since her father had no sons."

"That still doesna excuse keeping the tyrant in power."

"They did so to honor my mother. I can remember her saying so at different times over the years before she died." Catriona shrugged. "And when my sire happened to breed horses so renowned that even the sale of just one filled the clan's coffers, they were more than happy to look aside." She gave a sad shake of her head as she looked away to watch the sunshine streaming into the window. "Ye see, Alexander, 'twas no' so much cowardice as it was greed." She looked back at him. "They assuaged their consciences by telling themselves there was no harm in sacrificing a few for the betterment of the whole. My mother felt the same and I promise ye, it shames me."

The door vibrated with a hard knock.

"Who knocks?" A frustrated growl escaped him, doing little to assuage his frustrated desire to bellow and roar. *Hell's bells.* His wife had just awakened and they couldna even manage a simple conversation without being interrupted.

"'Tis Graham. I bear news ye need to hear."

Alexander yanked open the door and waved him inside. "What now?"

Graham's demeanor brightened when he noticed Catriona had awakened. "Dear sister, 'tis so good to see ye faring better."

"Thank ye, Graham." Catriona gave the barest nod toward Alexander. "Ye best tell him your news. He's no' in the best of humors."

"And rightly so," Alexander interrupted. "I canna even complete a private conversation with my wife." He pulled in a deep breath then expelled it as he scrubbed at his gritty eyes, burning for need of sleep. "What news have ye, brother?"

"Campbell is at our gates."

"Then by all means, keep them shut," Alexander said, torn between rushing from the room to prepare for pending attack and staying at Catriona's side to protect her. A solution finally occurred to him. "Where's the priest?"

"I am here and ready to guard your lady." Father William walked into the room, two pistols clipped to the leather belt he'd lashed around the waist of his robes, a shield in one hand, and a short sword in the other. "Go now and lead your people to victory."

Catriona held out a hand to him and he rushed to take it. "Ye are our leader and chieftain whether ye wish it or not." She squeezed his hand, giving him a look that melted his heart and made him wish to do nothing more than gather her up and hold her. "I beg ye, husband, accept and embrace the role."

"Is that what ye truly wish, Catriona?" It amazed Alexander that she wished to stay here and rebuild her clan after all the ill-will they'd seemed so able to accept. He couldna believe she wasna ready to shed them and start life anew. "Ye truly wish to redeem these people?"

"Aye," she said with a smile. "There are many good folk here worthy of being saved. I swear it."

"Then it shall be done," he agreed, a sudden weariness overcoming him. Who was he to fight such a mighty force as Catriona?

CHAPTER 21

"*T*urn your back, Father, I'll be gettin' dressed now."

Father William's eyes bulged open wide. Shock hiked his thinning brows to the highest point possible upon his shining pate. "Ye shall do no such a thing! Just awakened from days spent on death's edge? Ye must stay abed."

She moved to sit up and a gasp escaped her. Hand clasping her bandaged side, she cringed and bit the corner of her lip to keep from crying out as her body protested with excruciating jolts of pain.

"Ye see?" he said, shaking a finger at her and darting back and forth between the foot of the bed and her side like a wee squirrel scurrying for buried nuts. "Ye'll no' be tricking me the way ye did Sawny. Poor lad. Ye should be ashamed of yourself. The guilt ye rained down upon his young soul. Worried near sick about ye, I grant ye!"

That couldna be helped. She'd had to do what she'd done and given the chance, would do the same again. Granted, it had no' turned out quite as planned but she still didna regret doing her best to defend her husband. She'd never be a woman who cowered. She'd fight at her husband's side even if it meant her death. Someday young Sawny would understand.

"Turn your back or no', Father. Either way, dressed I shall be and going to my husband's side." She swallowed hard and steadied herself with deep breaths and slow exhales to calm the nausea churning in her stomach and tamp down the bile burning at the back of her throat. *I can do this. I'm no' some delicate lily in need of shielding.* Inch by inch, she scooted herself to sit on the edge of the bed then held fast to the bedside table until her head stopped spinning. She wished she could wash and remove the smelly bandages soaked with Elena's poultice but she feared she might cause the wounds to reopen and bleed again. "Hand me a clean shift, Father."

"I will not." Father William stood with his back to her, his nose lifted into the air.

"Fine," she snapped. "I'll get it myself."

"Stay there! I'll get it." Father William stole a glance back at her then stomped his foot. Returning to the bedside with her clothes, he fixed her with a fierce scowl. "If your stubborn arse hits the floor, ye'll set your wounds to bleeding for certain. Ye ken that, aye?"

Taking great care to keep his eyes averted, the priest first helped her with her shift then shook out a loose wool overdress that was more a body length apron than a gown. The garment was made to slide down over her head and tie underneath her arms at the sides. It was what she wore when the day's chores were certain to be a danger to her good clothes. He held it up for her approval. "Ye can wear this over your shift to keep ye decent. It willna rub your wounds as the waist of a skirt would."

"Good idea, Father." She bit the inside of her cheek to keep from crying out as she lifted her arms and struggled her way into the clothing. Clutching hold of Father William's arm, she eased her feet to the floor and stood. "Sweet Jesu," she swore under her breath.

"I heard that," Father William said as he held tight to her arm to keep her from collapsing to the floor. "Weak as a newborn kitten, ye are. Will ye no' see sense?"

"I'll be fine," she said more to herself than to him. "Now help me with the overdress. I think I can stand whilst ye put it over my head."

"Áve María, grátia pléna, Dóminus técum. Benedícta tū in muliéribus, et benedíctus frúctus véntris túi, Iésus. Sancta Maria, Máter Déi, óra pro nóbis

peccatóribus, nunc et in hóra mórtis nóstrae. Ámen." Father William repeated the Hail Mary in a sing-song voice, over and over, as he helped her into the heavy length of wool and allowed it to tumble down her body.

Orbs of flashing lights filled her gaze as she attempted to stand straighter. She grabbed hold of the priest's shoulders and held tight. Father William gave her a displeased look but didn't say a word.

"Tie the ties, Father. The longer I stand, the stronger I feel." God forgive her for lying to the priest but she had to get through this.

Father William rolled his eyes as he tied the laces loose on either side of the garment to grant her plenty of room for movement. "Ten Hail Mary's for your lie and a day of serving the poor, aye?"

"Aye, Father." Catriona took in a deep breath and released her hold on him, forcing her body to stand and balance itself. A wave of light-headedness pushed her back down to the edge of the bed. She'd forgotten the last time she'd eaten and that paired with blood loss had taken its toll. Her body's weaknesses refused to be ignored. "Dammit!"

"Child!"

"I have to get to the skirting wall. I have to be with Alexander." Her eyes stung with the threat of tears.

Father William scowled at her for a long moment, his thin brows wrinkling clear up to the wispy fringes of hair surrounding his bald head. "Alexander will have me crucified for what I'm about to do but I dinna have it in me heart to refuse ye."

"I shall name our first son William," Catriona promised, still struggling to control her ragged breathing and not pass out.

Father William paused at the door, "William Anthony Carmichael McBride, aye?"

"Aye, Father." Catriona closed her eyes. Father William's demeanor lightened her heart and made her burdens so much easier to bear. She made a mental note to ask the priest to stay at the keep. Clan Neal needed someone to guide their souls.

A short time later, the bedroom door creaked, prompting her to open her eyes. Father William was backing through the door, directing two sturdy lads as they brought an upholstered, straight-backed chair into the room.

Once they were well inside the room, the boys turned the chair and placed its back against the side of the bed. The taller of the two, the one called Mathy, gave a shy, polite dip of his chin in Catriona's direction then looked to the priest. "Good enough, Father?"

Father William studied the door then looked at the chair. "Aye, lad. Good enough." He hurried over to the great mahogany wardrobe filling one corner of the room and fetched Catriona's warmest cloak. "If ye find the strength and ye are still determined to do so, let's don your cloak and get ye seated."

"I can never thank ye enough for this, Father." With the help of the two lads, Catriona teetered to her feet, allowed the priest to drape her cloak around her, and help her walk to the chair.

Father William held tight to her arms as she held her breath against the pain and lowered herself to the seat. "If ye have a girl child, I wish her named Willa Antonia Catherine McBride, aye?"

That drew a snorting laugh and made Catriona grab her side. "Aye, Father, but I beg ye, dinna make me laugh."

"Hold tight to the arms of the chair. The lads will be as careful as they can but ye'll still jostle about a bit for certain." Father William motioned the boys forward and directed them to the chair. "One to the back of the chair and one to the front. Lift the feet and tilt her back a wee bit so she doesna slide out."

The young men complied. Catriona held her breath as they carried her through two sets of doors and out into the hallway. The farther they traveled, the more she trusted the young men and breathed easier as they headed to the front of the keep and the stairs leading to the parapet and the battlements above the great door built into the skirting wall. Still a bit lightheaded, Catriona had to admit that the throbbing in her side and her shoulder seemed somewhat lessened with her exertion. Catriona smiled. The thought of reaching Alexander's side as he faced Jameson Campbell surged newfound strength through her.

When Mathy pushed open the door to the parapet, Magnus met

them with pistol and sword drawn. Eyes wide and mouth ajar, he eased back, as though he'd just come upon a poisonous viper. After tucking his weapons away, he held the door open whilst they carried Catriona through it.

"I'm no' responsible for what Alexander does about this, Father," he said with a meaningful look at the priest.

"'Twas my idea," Catriona said, sitting taller in her makeshift litter and stretching to see over the wall.

"What in God's name is this?!" Alexander's roar echoed down the mountainside.

"Hail Marys all around, Father," Magnus advised under his breath as Alexander stormed toward them.

"I shall have each and every one of your heads!" Alexander shouted to the wide-eyed boys then turned to the priest. "And yours as well, Father!"

"Alexander!" Catriona clapped her hands together, flinching as she did so. "If it's anyone's head ye should have, 'tis mine and no others. Now leave them be and help me to the front battlement so I can see what we face."

Alexander glared a long, stern look at each of the boys, Father William, and Magnus then directed them down the parapet. "I would have a word with my wife," he said through gritted teeth.

None of them paused but took their leave as though their shirt-tails were on fire.

Catriona's flesh prickled as she lifted her gaze to meet Alexander's scowl. With his teeth bared and fists clenched, she couldna remember if she'd ever seen him this angry before—at least no' toward herself. "Now, Alexander…"

"Do ye wish to unman me and cut off me bollocks in front of your people? The verra people ye asked me to lead?" His tone was dark, low and rumbling, like a powerful storm building to a dangerous crescendo.

Alexander's perspective on what she'd just done dawned on her and the regret for showing him in such a poor light made her drop her chin and stare down at her hands knotted in her lap. She'd never meant to humiliate him. *How could I be so foolish?* Never one to think before she spoke or took action, she'd oft paid the price. But surely Alexander knew she meant him no harm. 'Twas merely her wish to show her support and stay at his side.

"Well?" he demanded as he resettled his stance in front of her.

"Forgive me," she whispered. She forced herself to look up and face his scowl. She deserved the imminent scolding. "I wanted to be with ye," she defended in a meek tone. "To help."

Alexander scrubbed a hand down his face, blew out a huffing growl, and turned to glare over the battlements. "Can ye no' understand that I canna defend either yourself or your people if my focus splinters? How can I plan with wisdom whilst pulled apart with worry about ye at my side?" He looked back at her and shook his head. "I ken ye are a strong woman, Catriona, and I admire that—I swear I do. But ye must stop defying me at every turn and so easily disregarding what I ask of ye or aye and for certain, I will grow to resent ye as ye fear."

He could never have said a worse thing in a thousand years. Catriona ducked her head again and blinked hard to stop the tears and rein in the hurtful pain that was so much worse than the ache from her wounds. How could she make him understand? They had reared her to always be the strong one, the one taking matters into her own hands. Of course, her doing such had oft gone afoul. Of that, she freely admitted. But if her actions risked pushing Alexander away…

She closed her eyes and refused to allow herself to cry. Marriage and good wifery was so feckin' complicated.

"I'm sorry," she finally said, pulling in a deep breath and lifting her head. "I will change, Alexander. It willna happen again."

Alexander stared at her for a long moment, weariness and worry deepening the lines in his face. "Can ye walk at all?" He pushed away from the battlement and came to stand beside her chair.

"Not far," she admitted.

Before she realized what he was about, he scooped her up into his arms and strode down the path of the skirting wall behind the crenelated parapet. He stopped behind one of the merlons so they were shielded as she peeped down through the adjoining embrasure notched into the wall to permit the firing of weapons. He sidled her closer so she could see down into the glen below.

"So many," she whispered as she clasped her arm tighter around Alexander's neck. "Why would he bring so many? 'Twas supposed to be nothing more than a wedding feast."

Jameson Campbell's men covered the rolling hillside in front of the keep like a swarm of teeming insects. Clan Campbell's tartans and flags hung from tall poles beside two rows of wagons filled with supplies and cannons, flapping in the wind as though whispering a warning of what might come to be. Tents dotted the landscape and more were being erected. At the far end of what couldn't be called anything less than an amassing army was the largest tent of all, Clan Campbell's colors flying on either side of its doorway and all around its sides.

"Duncan and Sutherland said sixty." Alexander blew out a disgruntled huff of air. "Me thinks their count was a mite shy."

"Father William might know more of what they're about."

Alexander shook his head. "I already asked the man, and he knew nothing. Said they'd barely speak to him since most of Campbell's men have converted and now consider themselves followers of the king's Protestant beliefs." He propped her atop the stone block meant for holding extra weapons and pointed to an impressive array of firearms, swords, and spears stacked beside the main tent. "Look there. Their intent is to claim this keep, lass. Every man ye see is armed and they have all those stores in addition to what they carry."

The sight struck fear deep into her soul, causing a pain that was much worse than her wounds. With their stronghold butted up against the mighty Ben Nevis, they could hold the Campbells off for a while—but how long? The only thing Catriona knew of warfare and battles was the havoc and loss they caused. She became aware of Alexander's gaze upon her. "What?"

"I shouldha ne'er brought ye back here," he said in a quiet, pained tone, regret echoing deep in his voice like the tolling of a death knell. "I shouldha listened to my instincts rather than my heart." Sadness and worry etched creases across his brow and narrowed his eyes. He breathed out a heavy sigh. "Ye taught me to love, Catriona, but now I fear 'twas all for naught."

"Love is ne'er for naught." She hugged an arm around his waist and pulled him closer so she could lean against him. "I dinna ken what the future may bring but I'm ever so grateful that I no longer have to face it alone."

Alexander stiffened and stood taller, throwing out his chest. Catriona eased back and looked up at him. His fierce scowl said more than any words. She hurried to look through the embrasure, down at the glen below at whatever had triggered such a reaction.

'Twas a great burly man riding the largest horse Catriona had ever seen. He wove the mount through the Campbell troops, making his way toward the gatehouse of *Tor Ruadh*.

"Jameson Campbell."

Catriona shuddered at Alexander's tone. It was a deep growling rumble filled with defensive fury. The predatory sounds of a raging beast.

Alexander turned and made a jerking summons with one hand. "Magnus!"

Magnus hurried to his side. "Aye?"

"Take Catriona to her chair and have the ones who brought her up here get her safe to her room whilst I go down to the gatehouse and greet our guest."

Magnus peered over the battlement, his pale eyes narrowing when he spotted Campbell. He stepped back, gave Alexander an obedient nod, then politely bowed to Catriona. "M'lady, I dinna wish to offend ye but we must make haste. I feel I must carry ye rather than help ye walk, aye?"

A sense of doom nearly drowning her, Catriona held up a hand to Magnus but before she could speak, Alexander interrupted.

"Catriona! Ye promised!"

"Aye," she said. "And I will keep my promise but surely ye'll no' deny me a kiss afore ye go to battle?" She couldna hardly breathe for the fear squeezing the air from her body. "I love ye, Alexander." She swallowed hard, struggling not to cry.

Alexander gathered her up and kissed her. A kiss so filled with need, sorrow, joy, and regret she thought she'd surely die when he pulled away. "I love ye, Catriona," he rasped out. "More than ye shall ever know."

She squeezed his arm then turned to Magnus and held out her hands. "I'm ready now but I beg ye, when ye return to Alexander, please protect him."

"I'll do my best, m'lady," Magnus replied as he picked her up, carried her back to her chair, then eased her down into it. "Ye have my word, I'll do my best."

CHAPTER 22

"*I*'m here for me wife," Jameson Campbell shouted from the back of his pale gray horse. He'd halted the mount several feet away from the tall pair of gatehouse towers and imposing portcullis of blackened iron and wood. "I bid ye grant me entry. Now."

"Rude bastard," Graham observed from his post at Alexander's left.

"At least he gets to the point," Magnus said from his position at Alexander's right.

Ignoring their commentary, Alexander took a step closer to the small open window of the gatehouse's main guardroom on the second floor of the right tower. The portal was at the perfect angle for greeting unwanted guests with a volley of arrows or gunfire while still being shielded from any return fire.

Might as well gig the man and see how long it took him to reach a full-blown rage. It always paid to know your enemy. "And who might your wife be, sir?"

"Catriona Neal," Campbell said with a surly glance up at the window. "Open your gates."

"Misinformed, ye are." Alexander watched Campbell, committing every nuance of the man to memory. "Catriona Elizabeth Rose is my wife and her last name is now MacCoinnich."

"Ye lie!" Campbell's face flared an angry red as he bared his teeth. "Where the hell is the Neal?"

"Gordon Neal is dead and so is his son, Calum."

Even from the second floor of the guard tower, Alexander could tell this tidbit of news shocked Jameson Campbell and threw an unsuspected kink into his plans. The man's eyes flared wide and his horse stomped and pawed from side to side as though ready to bolt.

"Who the hell are ye?" Campbell shouted. His hand lit on the gun clipped to his belt but he must've realized his vulnerable position because he jerked it away and fisted it back to the pommel of the saddle. "Your name, sir!" He bit out the words with such anger spittle showered down his dark beard.

"Alexander MacCoinnich, chieftain to Clan Neal."

A mighty roar went up from the battlements atop the curtain wall, echoing out across the glen below. "*Je ressuscite! Je ressuscite! Je ressuscite!*"

Je ressuscite. I rise again. The MacCoinnich battle cry Alexander had no' heard since the morbid sore throat sickness had decimated his clan and left naught but a handful of MacCoinnichs to walk the earth. He turned to Graham and Magnus. "And who, might I ask, taught them that?"

Graham grinned. "I dinna ken but ye must admit, it has a fine ring to it."

"I bid ye grant me entry, MacCoinnich!" Campbell shouted. "I dinna take kindly to being cuckolded nor cheated out of what is legally mine."

"Legally yours?" Alexander rested an elbow on the window ledge. "How are my wife and my land legally yours?"

"Betrothed to me, she was. Given by her father, the chief, along with Neal horses and the land upon which they graze."

"Show me the contract." Catriona had assured him Calum signed nothing because her brother never left written proof of anything that might hinder him backtracking on his word.

Campbell's mount stomped again and if Campbell's face grew any ruddier, the top of the man's head 'twould surely blow off. "I've no paper, ye bastard, as I'm sure ye already ken."

"Aye," Alexander replied. "And I'm no' in the habit of honoring the word of deceitful bastards—especially dead ones."

"I will take what was promised me," Campbell said with a brief glance behind him. "I've men enough to make this last as long as needed and force ye to open your gates without so much as a single skirmish. Ye ken that as well as I. Open your gates and give over. I'll grant the women and children safe passage to Fort William."

"Bastard," Alexander said under his breath. The Campbell's threat was not idle. With that many men securing the glen, he had the power to starve them out. Alexander had no' had the chance to assess *Tor Ruadh's* stores of food, water, and ammunition but he would do so at first opportunity, or at least send Duncan or Sutherland to tend to such. "Send our little brothers to size up how long we can last without opening our gates," he said to Graham.

Graham nodded and rushed from the room.

Magnus stepped up to the window, peering down as he folded his arms across his chest. "The elders might know if they ever brought any supplies in through the passages in the mountain."

"I was thinking the same," Alexander said.

"What say ye, MacCoinnich?" Campbell shouted.

Alexander cocked his pistol, took careful aim, and fired. The bullet hit where he intended. It splintered the wooden pole holstered in Jameson Campbell's saddle, the one bearing the Campbell colors, neatly cleaving the rod in two. The tartan flag sagged downward in a slow spiral like a felled tree then fluttered into the mud.

The battlements nearly shook with laughter, jeers, and roars, *"Je ressuscite!"*

Campbell's horse reared, pawing at the air, as Campbell jerked hard on the reins and turned it back toward his men. "If it's war ye want, it's war ye'll have!" he shouted as he kicked his horse and galloped away.

"Why did ye no' just shoot the man himself?" Magnus asked.

Alexander shrugged. "I probably shouldha killed the bastard but with the king's regiment headed this way, I didna wish to risk it. Campbells are too cozy with King William. I've enough to deal with at present." He thumped Magnus on the shoulder. "Keep watch whilst I try to discover how great our disadvantage."

He exited the guard tower and loped down the steps leading to the bailey. Once inside the keep, he spotted Sawny and flagged him down. "Fetch the elders and bring them to Lady Catriona's room. I need as much information about this stronghold as possible, aye?"

"Aye, my chieftain." Sawny took off at a run.

Alexander made his way across the main hall as fast as he could what with the Neal kinsman acknowledging their new chieftain with bows and curtsies and some even kneeling in his path and swearing fealty on the spot. At long last, he made it across the length of the room milling with people. He hurried up the stone steps leading to the private floors. Steps still pained him but he would no' allow his scars and old wounds to slow him down. At last reaching Catriona's rooms, he withstood the urge to burst into the innermost chamber. He paused in the sitting room to rap on the door.

"Who knocks?" Father William asked from the other side.

"Open the door, Father."

Latches clicked, and the door swung open. Father William nodded then moved to exit the room. He paused at the door. "I'll wait in the sitting room, aye?"

"Aye." Alexander pointed to the door. "Sawny's gathering the elders and bringing them here. I need to know as soon as they arrive, ye ken?"

Father William nodded.

Alexander closed the bedroom door and after a brief pause, locked it. 'Twas safer that way. They'd breached the fortress with ease. Who was to say a Campbell spy might no' do the same?

"I heard shouting," Catriona said from the bed. Propped among an immense pile of pillows with a tray across her lap, her color looked decidedly better than it had on the skirting wall.

"It appears Clan Neal has learned the MacCoinnich battle cry." Alexander traced the backs of his fingers along the curve of her cheek then bent to press a kiss to her temple. "The rose has returned to your fair cheeks. It makes my heart glad."

Catriona smiled and the flush on her cheeks grew even rosier. "I've had a bannock and forced down a cup of Elena's jaw-locking tea. Even though it has a fearsome taste, apparently, 'tis quite good for what ails me for I feel suitably refreshed."

"I remember that godforsaken tea." Alexander removed the tray from her lap and placed it on the table beside the bed. Taking care not to jostle her, he lowered himself to sit beside her. "I dinna wish to shake ye or cause ye pain."

"Ye are fine." She blew out a ragged sigh as she pulled him closer and pressed her cheek to his shoulder. "I need ye near whilst ye tell me your news. I see the worry in your eyes and I ken it must no' bode well."

Alexander wrapped his arm around her and drew her closer. With a tender kiss to the top of her head, he settled her back against his chest. "Ye already read me too well, wife." He rested a cheek on her head and idly stroked her arm. "The Campbell means to starve us out unless we surrender." He gave a light shrug as he traced a finger along the faint blue tracks of veins showing through the translucent skin of her inner forearm. "He's granted safe passage to the women and children of the clan if we give him what he wishes."

"Lying bastard," Catriona said with a low growl.

Alexander couldn't help but chuckle. "Aye. I agree." He took her hand and kissed it. "Which is why I bid Sawny gather the elders and bring them here. I need to know every secret about this keep. Our survival depends on it."

An earth-shaking boom sounded. Cannon-fire. Another bone-jarring boom split the air right behind it, even louder than the first.

Alexander ran to the window, thankful that Catriona's suite of rooms was situated toward the front of the keep and just above the height of the curtain wall. A perfect place to take in the glen's beauty. From this viewpoint, he saw no damage. "I see nothing from here." He turned to Catriona.

Eyes wide, face pale, and lips parted, Catriona appeared frozen with fear.

"I shouldha shot the bastard when I had the chance." Alexander growled through clenched teeth. He rushed to Catriona's side and took hold of her hands as Mrs. Aberfeldy and Father William burst into the room.

"Stay with her," he ordered before either of them could say a word. Then he bolted. He had to make it to the guardhouse.

Duncan met him in the stairwell, holding up both hands. "The whoreson's firing the damn things into the air. He's no' aiming at us at all. What's the bastard about?"

Alexander came to a halt and leaned against the white-washed wall of the tower housing the staircase. What a wily bastard Jameson Campbell was. "He means to rattle us so he can claim a keep that's still intact and not have to rebuild." He jerked a thumb upward. "Ensure plenty of wet sacks are at the ready in case he grows bored with making us deaf and decides to smoke us out."

"Aye," Duncan replied then took off at a run.

Alexander returned to Catriona's chambers just as Sawny and the elders were entering the sitting room. He motioned for them to seat themselves whilst he checked on Catriona. As he opened the door, he found her no longer nested in pillows but standing at the window. He gave both Father William and Mrs. Aberfeldy pointed looks. "Why the hell is she no' abed?"

"Dinna speak as though I'm no' here." Catriona turned from the window, slow but steady. She made her way to a chair, one that was plump and upholstered with satin of the deepest blue, and lowered herself into it. "How bad is the damage?"

"No damage." He pulled another chair over beside her and sat in it. "The bastard means to rattle us into surrender."

"I'll no' give that son of a bitch the satisfaction." Catriona's eyes widened at her own words and she pressed her fingers to her lips. "I mean…"

"I ken what ye mean well enough and I agree with ye." He motioned to the door as he looked at Father Alexander. "Would ye be so kind as to show the elders and Sawny in, Father?" He shifted his gaze to Mrs. Aberfeldy. "Ye may leave."

"Why, I—"

"Nay, woman. Come with me now. There's no time to argue." Scrawny Father William grabbed hold of the housekeeper's plump arm and forcibly led her from the room.

"I dinna trust that woman," Alexander said under his breath.

"Aye, Neither do I since her visit with me whilst they held me captive."

"Has she harmed ye?" Alexander rose, ready to string the old housekeeper up by her thumbs.

Catriona frowned at the closed door to the sitting-room, pondering the portal as though it held answers to questions she'd yet to ask. "Nay. But things she said and things that Tom and Sawny shared with me about her in the caves. I canna put my finger on it but I ken well enough that I willna share any confidences with her ever again."

Alexander reached out, took her hand, and gave it a reassuring squeeze. "Ye may always trust your confidences with me, love." He wished to hell this was all behind them so he and Catriona could get back to behaving as man and wife with their greatest worry being what they'd name their children.

At that moment, the sitting-room door opened. The three elders, Munroe in the lead, along with Sawny and Tom entered.

Sawny made a half-hearted gesture toward Tom. "I thought mayhap Tom could help. He knows the keep better than me."

"That's fine." Alexander nodded to the two older men standing beside Munroe. "Your names?"

"Jock Neal," said the taller of the two. The man looked like a great knob-kneed water bird with a long beak of a nose and a frame so thin he risked disappearing if he turned sideways.

"Cuddy Neal," replied the other man in a voice so soft that Alexander leaned forward to hear him.

Still holding Catriona's hand tight in his own, Alexander scanned the faces of the trio of old men and the two young boys. "I need to ken every secret this keep holds. Passages. Caves. Double walls. Jameson Campbell intends to starve us out so what ye tell me here today could be the key to our survival, ye ken?"

"Aye," they all replied in unison then Sawny stepped forward. "Me and Tom had an idea that might help sway the odds in our favor. Would ye care to hear it?"

"Aye," Alexander replied without hesitation. What could be more creative and devious than a pair of twelve-year-old lads itching to make a name for themselves in this world?

"We figure them c-cannons got a lot t-to do with ole Campbell thinking so high of himself," Tom said. Determination and fire flashed in the lad's dark eyes.

The boy's fervor surprised Alexander. This was the first time he could remember hearing the lad string together more than a couple of words and speak them whilst looking him in the eye. Alexander gave him a nod to continue.

Tom wet his lips as though his thoughts were making his mouth water. "The six of us c-could do it." He looked at his friend. "Daren't ye think so?"

"Aye," Sawny replied, his reddish brows knotted above his narrowed eyes.

"Do what?" Catriona shifted, her gaze flitting from Tom to Sawny.

"Clear our glen of the cannons," Sawny answered then grinned. "Oakie'll help us. Ye ken how he loves gunpowder."

"Who is Oakie?" Alexander asked, not entirely certain he truly wanted to know judging from the leery look on Catriona's face.

"Our f-friend," Tom supplied with a gap-toothed smile.

Catriona pulled in a deep breath and released it in a huffing sigh. "Young Oakie has always loved fire since he was little more than a bairn." Catriona seemed to be having a great deal of difficulty finding the words. She gave Alexander a pained look and a sheepish shrug as she squeezed his hand. "But he loves what it does to gunpowder even better."

"Aye," Sawny chimed in. "Murtagh nearly skint him when he blew up the fencing in the east paddock last summer. Said it knocked the horses off their feed for most nigh a month."

They intended to blow up the cannons. These boys and four of their friends. Alexander shifted to the edge of his seat, leaning forward with his elbows on his knees and clasping his hands in front of him. "The two of ye think ye can do this without getting yourselves killed?" He hated the thought of sending little more than children into such a dangerous situation.

"Master Duncan said he was f-fourteen when he took to f-fighting," Tom defended, astutely guessing what was giving Alexander pause. "S-Sawny and me be thirteen n-next month. Oakie and the others are b-bout the same. S-some a little older."

Sawny stepped forward and went down on one knee before him. "Ye have our fealty, my chieftain. Please allow us to defend our clan."

The boys' creativity and sincerity touched Alexander's heart. After studying them a long moment, he agreed. "Aye, lads. I trust ye to protect us but I'll be sending Magnus along in case ye have need of his wisdom." Alexander held up a hand to stay their protests. "No argument. And may God go with ye."

CHAPTER 23

"Ye willna hurt me. Please come." She drew back the covers. "Please lie with me." Catriona flinched as another round of cannon fire boomed, shattering the stillness of the night. The only peace they got was while the pair of cannons was reloaded or when Campbell's men went to take a piss or eat. She prayed that Sawny's and Tom's plan worked and soon. Her nerves were raw and the sound of cannon fire grated on her like a broken nail dragged across silk.

"Sweet Jesu! I'll be glad when this is over." She smoothed a hand across the sheets beside her and patted the bed again. "Please? Ye need your rest and neither the chair nor the floor will give it to ye." The stubbornness of her husband fair matched her own.

Alexander fidgeted next to the bed, eyeing the spot beside her like a hungry dog watching its master's plate. At long last, he blew out a low, groaning sigh, stripped down to nothing but his léine, and ever so gingerly slipped into bed next to her. "I dinna wish to shift ye or bump ye in my sleep. What if I cause your wounds to bleed? What if I hurt ye?"

"They didna bleed when I washed away Elena's noxious poultice. I'm sure they're well on the way to healin' completely and weren't nary as bad as everyone thought." She bit the inside of her cheek against a shooting pain as she scooted up into the crook of his arm and nestled her head into the dip of his shoulder. "I've so missed your warmth," she whispered as she slid her hand up under his shirt and rubbed it across his broad chest.

Alexander tensed beneath her touch and huffed out a groaning sigh that matched the first one. "And that's another reason I thought it might no' be prudent to share your bed."

Catriona slid her hand lower. His fine member had returned to the wonderfully long hardness of their wedding night and strained to meet her.

"Mayhap if I—"

"No!" Alexander grabbed up her hand and held it to the center of his chest. "We'll no' be doin' none of that until ye've healed enough so I dinna have to worry about loving ye straight into your grave."

"Well, fine." Whilst she agreed he was probably right, she most assuredly felt passion would do wonders as a pain reliever for her and a tension reliever for him. A terrible thought occurred to her, one she felt she must share. "What if we never share another joining ever again? What if Campbell overtakes the keep? If he's no' able to do so with the troops he's already amassed, he'll overpower us once the king's regiment arrives."

A bone-rattling explosion shook the keep. Dust filtered down from the ceiling, rattling across them like rain.

Alexander trembled beneath her hand then shook harder when his deep rumbling laugh broke free. "Well done, lads, well done."

"Ye're certain 'twas them?" Catriona shook herself and the bedcovers free of the dust and rose to go to the window to see. "I see fire and many rushing about down in the Campbell camp. Aye, they did it!"

"Good lads they are," Alexander said as he joined her and stood with an arm draped across her shoulders.

"Sneaky lads, ye mean." Catriona wrapped her arms around Alexander's waist and snuggled closer whilst still watching the Campbell camp attempt to put out the fires started by the demolition of their cannons. "Thank goodness they're on our side."

"Aye," Alexander agreed then swept her up into his arms, took her back to bed, and settled her in it before climbing in beside her. "Sawny swore he and his friends could disable the cannons and set fire to the gunpowder all in one fair swoop. Quick and crafty as foxes, they are. That boy's too smart to be a kitchen lad. Him and Tom both. We need to find a better place for him. I'm thinkin' he needs to foster with Magnus."

"A fine idea." She snuggled back to Alexander's side, content with the success of the evening. But far too quickly, new worries stained that contentment—seeped through it and spread like a deadly poison. "Now we'll truly feel the Campbell's rage," she mused aloud.

"Aye."

Alexander's tone worried her even more. In it, she heard the echo of her own fears and the weight of her own dread building within him. She reached up and pulled Alexander's face down to hers. "I need ye to love me this night, Alexander. I need ye to hold me and make me forget that we might die tomorrow. Please, husband. Ye willna hurt me. I promise."

Alexander rolled to his side and faced her, cradling her face in his hand as he tickled his thumb across her bottom lip. "I fear—"

"I dinna fear pain," she said as she watched the play of moonlight across his face. "All I fear is losing ye and having to go through the rest of this life without ye. Please, Alexander. Take away that fear for a little while. Please love me."

Alexander stared at her for a long moment, eyes dark and unreadable. Finally, he stripped off his léine, then gently rolled her to her back. With the greatest care, he started at the hem of her shift, moved it up her body, and helped her slide it off over her head. Catriona could barely breathe as he rose above her, propping himself on elbows and knees to protect her from the weight of him.

Catriona shuddered as she smoothed her hands across the tops of his shoulders and down his back. Words weren't needed between them. She saw his love for her in his eyes, felt it in his touch. He bent down and kissed her, tasting of both whisky and the honeyed wine they'd shared with their meal.

She closed her eyes and drew in a deep relaxing breath as he kissed his way across her collarbone, taking care to avoid the stab wound between it and the top of her rib cage. His warm breath fanned across her skin, making her nipples tighten and strain for his touch. He worshipped her breasts with mouth and hands, making it impossible to lie still. She wrapped her right leg up around his hips and stroked her calf across the smooth, muscular hardness of his back and buttocks.

He made to kiss his way lower, but she grabbed hold of the sides of his face and stopped him. "Nay, m'love. I want ye inside me now, aye?"

"Aye," he said softly as he repositioned his powerful arms on either side of her and nudged himself in between her legs. "I dinna wish to hurt ye," he repeated as he slowly pushed his way inside her.

Reveling in the way he filled her, Catriona stroked his sides with her hands and her right leg. 'Twas a mighty chore to keep her left leg still to avoid paining her lower side and the area around the other stab wound. She closed her eyes, losing herself in the intoxicating slow in and out slide of Alexander's ever so gentle thrusts.

"More," she breathed against his lips as he kissed her. "More, I beg ye."

Alexander rocked into her faster and deeper with muscles so tensed against hurting her that he trembled. He slid a hand under her, moving it down her back to cup her right buttock and squeeze.

"Yes," she encouraged as she slid both of her hands down to her husband's fine firm buttocks and squeezed. "Yes." The ecstasy grew. She was so close to reclaiming the delicious delirium he'd shown her on their wedding night. No pain could compete with this. "Yes!" she cried out as he pushed her over the abyss to where nothing existed but pure pleasure and mindless abandon.

Alexander groaned, thrusting faster, then locked his arms as he lunged forward, burying himself deep inside her to pump and spill within her. He tensed, then jerked and pulsed with another groan. Shaking his head as though struggling to recover from his own ecstatic fog, he shuddered above her, gasping as he bent and pressed his forehead to hers. "Did I hurt ye?" he panted.

"Only in the verra best of ways," she assured with a nuzzling kiss to his mouth.

With the greatest care to keep himself from brushing flat against her, Alexander pushed himself to one side and collapsed beside her. He snugged his head against hers as he gradually caught his breath and returned to normal breathing. "I canna believe two stab wounds didna prevent ye from making love to your husband."

Catriona rolled to her side, propped her head in her hand, and grinned down at him as she tickled her fingers across his chest. "'Tis your own fault, m'love. The ache I had for ye was fearsome. Much stronger than any cut of a knife."

"Ye're a rare woman, Catriona," Alexander said as he pulled her down for a proper kiss.

"Ye're rarer still, Alexander," she whispered. "And I thank God ye're mine."

He pulled her to him and settled her back to her resting spot in the dip of his shoulder. "I thank God ye're mine as well." He'd never admit it to her, but he'd needed this. The touch of her. The scent of her on his skin. He'd needed the ecstasy of spilling himself inside her and hoping like hell they'd seeded a son or daughter. A new life to fill her womb and round her belly. He needed hope.

She'd spoken rightly when she'd said they'd know Campbell's rage as soon as his men had doused the fires and taken stock of their stores. He brushed a kiss to her sweat-dampened temple and held her closer. At least they'd had this night. A smile curled across his lips. Stab wounds or no, she'd been determined to make love to him. What a braw fiery woman she was, and she was all his.

Her breathing had already evened out, and she'd gone limp beside him. Catriona only relaxed this much when she slept. He stared up at the ceiling, the gentle shift and flow of Catriona against his side as her breathing eased in and out calmed him. If only they could be this way forever, lying in one another's arms, their greatest worry being whether they'd planted the beginnings of a child and would it be a son or a daughter.

A light pecking tapped on the door, so light Alexander barely noticed it.

Ever so gently, he slid out from under Catriona, holding his breath and freezing in place when she stirred for a brief moment then rolled away from him and snuggled deeper into her pillows. Once her breathing had evened out again, he rose from the bed, yanked on his trews, and padded to the door.

He eased open the door and peered into the sitting room, dark with only a single candle burning on the round table in the center. Magnus stepped out of the shadows and motioned for Alexander to join him.

"You and the lads did well." Alexander kept his voice low as he eased the bedroom door shut without a sound.

"Aye. 'Twas the lads. Give them the praise." Magnus's tone was grim and filled with trouble. "Both cannons are ruined, warped by the explosion and heat of the fire. But it pains me to tell ye that one of the boys didna make it."

Alexander's heart fell. He'd feared such. He shouldha ne'er allowed a pack of lads who'd ne'er fired a gun nor wielded anything other than a kitchen knife or a crofter's plow, to do a man's job. "Who?"

Magnus shook his head. "The one they called Oakie. I could no' place the name until they reminded me of his looks."

"Were they able to bring him back so we might honor him with a proper burial?"

Magnus cringed as he scrubbed a hand across his mouth and made a face as though the entire situation tasted foul. "There was no' enough left of the boy to bring back. When they lit the fuse, it slipped free of the main barrel and Oakie ran to shove it back into the powder. The barrels shifted as he climbed across them and pinned his leg."

"Damnation." Alexander heaved out a groaning sigh, feeling as though he'd been gut-punched. "His family?"

"Only a father. No other kin."

"Let me dress and then see to the man. He needs to hear how grateful we are for his son's sacrifice. His boy was a fearless warrior."

"Aye." Magnus turned toward the door then paused. "Sawny also heard word of the king's regiment whilst we were in the Campbell camp."

"What word?"

"Two days." Magnus pulled the door open. "They arrive in two days."

CHAPTER 24

"No more word or any form of attack." Catriona studied the Campbell camp below as she and Alexander paced side by side along the top of the curtain wall. The clear skies and warm touch of the sunny spring day did little to brighten her disposition or ease the sense of impending doom crushing in from all sides. "It's been two days and still no reaction to the loss of the cannons." She shifted her attention to Alexander's scowling countenance, his eyes narrowed against the windy brightness of the cloudless sky. "What is his strategy?" Alexander had been in plenty of skirmishes. Surely, he'd ken Jameson Campbell's tactics.

Alexander gave a slow shake of his head, never taking his gaze from the glen below. "I think he waits."

"For what?" They paused at the wide landing atop the left guard tower. The battlements were higher here but the parapets atop had notches cut wider to permit the emptying of cauldrons of boiling water or fiery oil on intruders attempting to scale the fortress's walls.

"The king's regiment." He paused at a wider than usual crenel, rubbing a hand across the flat shelf of the notch as though he found it lacking. "Your brother mentioned the Earl of Crestshire on the day he died." He turned to Catriona. "Do ye know the man?"

"No. I dinna ken any Earl of Crestshire." Catriona leaned a shoulder against the wall, snugging her arms around her waist and tucking her arisaidh tighter about her. She ached with weariness. Sleep brought her nothing but troubling dreams colored by the fear and worry of her waking hours. She'd healed from the stab wounds with the swiftness found in good health. The occasional pains she now felt were hardly worth mentioning but the inability to rest wore her down. "Maybe he leads the king's regiment."

"Perhaps."

There was something about Alexander's tone that pulled her attention from Campbell's camp to him. "What are ye not telling me?"

"I canna be sure, mind ye, but I may know the Earl of Crestshire well."

Catriona couldn't tell from Alexander's tone whether that was a good thing or bad. "Be ye enemies?"

"If the man is who I think he is, we were once close as brothers." Alexander scratched his well-trimmed beard along his jawline, squinting one eye shut in the process. "But who's to say? Would the English allow a man who'd fostered in the Highlands to claim the title of earl and the estate that goes along with it? An estate that lays within a stone's throw of the palace?"

"I canna imagine what a Sassenach would do." Catriona fidgeted in place, tracing a fingernail along the mortar in the wall. She'd never done well with waiting. Patience was not among her scarce collection of virtues.

The deep, somber sound of a horn, followed by two higher-pitched blows traveled to them on the wind.

Catriona searched the horizon. Movement at the far end of the glen, close to the southernmost pass leading to Neal lands, caught her eye. She pointed just as Alexander leaned out over the embrasure and looked. "The king's regiment."

"In full force," Alexander said under his breath. "I dinna ken if the glen will hold them all."

Soldiers poured into the valley at the front of the keep, filling every space like ants swarming across kitchen scraps. Catriona's heart sank. She swallowed hard and did her best to bolster her waning courage to keep from dropping to her knees and weeping. All appeared lost. No way could they emerge victorious over so many. The Campbells and the English would obliterate Clan Neal, erasing them from the Highlands of Scotland. But even worse, she'd lose the man she loved and never see him again. She couldna bear the thought of what might happen to him.

"I shall go forth and speak to Campbell and the earl."

"You cannot!" Shock filled Catriona that he'd harbor such a notion. "Ye be our chieftain. We canna risk your capture."

Alexander pinned her with an icy stare that chilled her to the bone. "I willna send any more children to do the job I should do myself."

Oakie's loss still pained Alexander a great deal. He blamed himself for the boy's death, saying he never shouldha lost his good sense in the imaginings of young lads plotting to win a battle.

"Send Alasdair," she said. The man's nickname was the 'judge' because he had an uncanny talent for settling arguments and reasoning out differences. "Name him Clan Neal's solicitor."

With a gentle grasping of her shoulders, Alexander pulled her close, and gave her a patient smile that neared to breaking her heart. "I must go myself to meet these men." He gave her a conciliatory nod. "I shall take Alasdair with me. Ye've got the right of it there. The man is excellent at arbitration but I willna send him into the den of lions alone. 'Twould no' be proper and ye ken that as well as I."

Farther down the path running atop the curtain wall, the door to the guard tower swung open and Magnus and Graham appeared. Both men kept their attention locked on the glen in front of the keep as they made their way to where Alexander and Catriona stood.

With a perfunctory nod to Catriona, Graham cut straight to the point as he motioned toward the two armies below. "So ye're aware?" he said to Alexander.

"Aye." Alexander gave his brother and best friend a grim nod. "A meeting with Jameson Campbell and the Earl of Crestshire is in order with Alasdair accompanying as our clan solicitor. What say ye?"

"And the rest of us as your personal guard, aye?" Magnus added.

"And your wife," Catriona said, knowing Alexander would ne'er allow it—or at least he'd do his best to forbid it. But she had the right to be there. If Calum had no' betrothed her to Campbell, this standoff wouldha ne'er happened. "I dinna wait well so I'll have none of it, thank ye. I'll be at your side." She braced herself for Alexander's reply. "I'll no' have ye riding into the enemy's camp and I'll no' discuss it further, ye ken?" she added.

Alexander gave her a pointed look. The look said the discussion was at an end and had also veered dangerously close to breaking her oath to trusting him as chieftain. A different tactic would serve her better.

"Would ye consider allowing them, the Campbell and the Earl of Crestshire, to meet here? Within the keep?" She rested a hand to his forearm, praying he'd consider her request. "Then I'd know ye safe. I could remain in the gallery and watch over ye while ye met with them."

Alexander gave her a perturbed look and eased away from her touch. "Ye're saying ye'd be willing to stay in the gallery and no' chirp out nary a word whilst I speak with them."

"I dinna chirp," she said in a snappish tone before thinking better of it. With a hard swallow, she hurried to smooth any damage to the plan that her attitude might have caused. "I'd be most grateful, husband, if ye would allow this so I can see with my own eyes that ye're safe."

"Lady Catriona's idea holds merit," Magnus said.

Catriona made a mental note to name one of their children 'Magnus.' Of course, if that was the only way she could think of to favor people who'd served her well, she'd best hope for a keep full of sons and daughters. That thought sent a warm flush through her. She couldna think of a thing that would make her happier. A keep full of Alexander's children. 'Twould be wonderful, indeed.

Alexander turned and studied the forces below. "Think thee they would accept such an invitation?"

"If worded proper," Graham said.

"Alasdair and Sutherland are the best persuaders I know," Magnus said. "The both of them can tell ye to go straight to Hell in such a way that ye look forward to the trip. Shall I get them?"

Catriona noticed Alexander's knuckles whitening as his hands fisted atop the stone ledge. She could tell by his stance that whilst he wasna in full acceptance of the idea and was, in fact, fighting it, he couldna think of a safer option. She knew he realized that riding into Campbell's camp was a foolhardy thing to do. Which stirred another quandary: If they wished to invite the two men, how the hell would they do it without risking a life?

"How shall we extend our invitation?" Alexander asked.

Catriona caught her breath and stared at him all the harder. Was she so transparent? Had her husband read her mind? "Uhm…" As much as she wanted the plan to succeed, she couldna think of a viable option.

"Arrows," Graham said.

Another name for another child. Catriona smiled and agreed with a nod. Of course, arrows. They could wrap a note around the shaft and launch it into the camp without risking life or limb.

"A shot from that wee bluff overlooking their camp. Hit the pole in front of Campbell's tent easily. Ian could do it. I grant ye." Graham turned to leave, then paused and looked back at Alexander. "I'll fetch him, aye?"

"Aye," Alexander said. "Have our brothers pen the invitation and seek Alasdair's counsel as well. Tomorrow. Noon. We'll offer them a meal along with the conversation."

"It shall be so," Magnus said as he joined Graham and the two men set off to accomplish the task.

"I'll set Mrs. Aberfeldy and Cook to planning a fine repast." Catriona stretched to the tips of her toes and pecked a kiss to Alexander's cheek. "Thank ye, Alexander."

He darted an arm around her waist and pulled her snug against his chest. "I believe I deserve a proper kiss for bending to your wishes."

"Oh, do ye now?" Catriona pressed both hands to his chest, leaning back in mock refusal. While meant to be coy and teasing, the position had the additional benefit of pressing her lower half snugger to

Alexander, revealing that her husband was verra pleased to be with her. She couldn't resist a covert wanton wiggle against the delightful hard length of him, hidden from anyone who might watch by the fullness of her skirts whipping in the wind.

"Ye're a wee vixen, ye are," Alexander growled out in a low rumble right before he took her mouth and kissed her deep and long. "I'll never get enough of ye, Catriona," he whispered against her lips then kissed her again.

A wicked idea came to her as Alexander slid his hands down her back and cupped her behind through the layers of her skirts and squeezed. *Merciful heavens.* Perhaps a wee detour from her duties wouldna be amiss. After all, keeping her husband happy was a wife's primary function. Was it not?

"The benches in the tower room," she said in a breathless whisper against his temple as he pressed heated kisses to her throat. "We could...sit and rest a bit. Aye?"

"Aye, woman. That would please me well."

They hurried the few feet to the tower room. Alexander opened the door and held it for her.

With a stolen glance down the path of the curtain wall to ensure no one followed, Catriona darted inside and hurried to slide the iron bar across the other door to the staircase leading down into the keep.

Alexander stepped inside and locked the door behind him, then did the same to the door leading to the curtain wall. As he turned, Catriona rushed into his arms and resumed the smoldering kiss they'd paused whilst in their search for a more private place.

"I'm so glad ye wore your kilt without your trews this fine day." Catriona eagerly reached down with both hands and hiked up his kilt to rake her nails up the backs of his thighs and cup his fine sculpted arse.

Alexander rumbled with a low laugh as he gathered up her skirts and did the same, kneading her buttocks and sliding his hardness against her as he walked them back to the bench. "Shall we sit awhile, wife?" he teased as he positioned her astraddle his lap and lowered her down upon him.

"Most definitely." Catriona slid down his shaft, burying it to the hilt inside her. Settling into a slow rocking motion, she loosened the laces of her bodice just enough to allow Alexander entry to her bosom. She clutched his head to her chest as he kissed and fondled then suckled and squeezed some more, all the while riding his shaft at a steadily increasing pace.

The latch on the door leading up from the keep rattled, and the door bumped against the bar. "What fool bolted the tower door?" said the voice on the other side.

Alexander grinned and pressed a shushing finger to his lips as his other hand squeezed her buttocks and pulled her hard against him. Shifting on the bench, he met her thrust for thrust. Whoever was on the other side of the door could just be damned.

"We'll have to enter through from the wall," the irritated voice advised. "Come!"

A glance over at the door leading to the curtain wall assured Catriona that it was bolted, too, and they were free to finish what they'd started.

"Faster, woman," Alexander said with a barely stifled groan as he bucked beneath her.

"Gladly." Catriona rode harder, arching her back and holding tight to Alexander's shoulders. He filled her to perfection. So hot. So hard. Such fine exquisite strokes in all the right places. She bit her lip to keep from shouting as she increased the momentum then exploded with pure bliss.

Alexander rumbled with a low growl, clutching her buttocks tight as he emptied inside her, pumping and jerking with the effort. He arched so tense and hard with his pleasure he lifted her into the air. She sat astraddle him, feet dangling above the bench. His moment spent, he eased back down and pulled her to his chest.

"I'm verra glad ye needed to sit awhile and rest, dear wife," he panted into her hair as she struggled to catch her own breath.

The latch to the door on the side of the skirting wall rattled, and it bumped against the brace across it. "Son of a bitch! Who the hell locked all three doors?" The door thudded with the angry thumping of a fist. "Open this door! Whoever ye are! Open this door this instant!" Another thud, one much closer to the floor, shook the door. More than likely a kick. "I dinna ken who ye are, ye lazy bastard, but come out! Your shirking of your duties is over!"

Catriona burst into a fit of giggles, burying her face against Alexander's throat to muffle them as best she could. She couldn't quite place the voice on the other side of the door but she thought it sounded like Ranald, one of Clan Neal's best hunters and also one of their best fighters with a spear. She pressed a kiss to Alexander's salty-sweet skin. "Reckon we should make ourselves presentable and open the doors?"

Alexander smiled and winked. "As soon as ye've sworn that I've no' shirked my husbandly duties."

"Oh no, dear husband." Catriona squeezed him with her thighs as she gave him a slow kiss and teased him with her tongue. "Ye've no' shirked anything. I'm verra pleased indeed."

The door rattled and thumped again. "I fetched the chieftain's brothers! Ye best open this door afore we knock it down."

"Hold fast!" Alexander shouted. "Impatient bastard," he added under his breath.

Catriona shook with stifled giggles as she climbed off Alexander, fluffed out her skirts, and snugged the laces of her bodice. With a hurried pat to her hair, she retrieved her arisaidh from the floor and wrapped it back around her shoulders. She pressed her legs tight together, reveling in the warm wetness of Alexander's release and praying a wee bairn had taken hold.

Alexander stood and straightened his kilt then looked to Catriona.

"I'm ready." She gave him a smile and a nod. Aye. She was ready indeed. Alexander had turned her into a wanton. She'd be more than pleased to spend her days in their bed, loving the moments away. She wondered if many wives felt this way about their husbands.

Alexander strode across the room, unbolted it, and yanked it open to a very sheepish looking Ranald and a beaming from ear to ear Duncan and Sutherland.

"At work planning battle strategies, brother?" Sutherland asked, a knowing smirk on his face.

"At work makin' bairns," Duncan said under his breath with a snorting huff.

Catriona's cheeks heated as though on fire. She cleared her throat and lifted her head as she walked out the door and pushed her way through the group of men. "We were merely checking the strength of the doors in case of siege." She looked back at Alexander. "I say the tower room is secure. Aye, husband?"

"Indeed." Alexander caught up with her, offered his arm, then looked back at the three men still standing beside the opened door. "Good day to ye, lads."

CHAPTER 25

*A*lexander strode to the back of the stable, casting a glance into each of the stalls as he walked past them. The calming fragrance of fresh hay and healthy horses had replaced the earlier dank stench of mustiness and rancid manure. They had mounted additional hooks in the stone walls of the cavern turned stable and each held a lit lantern. The dancing yellow flames beat back the shadows, eliminating places to hide. Good. The space was clean and an enemy would struggle to find cover.

Magnus, Sawny, and Tom followed close behind. Alexander pointed to the opening in the back wall. The same opening they'd used in what now seemed like a lifetime ago when they'd snuck their way back into the keep. "I want this guarded or blocked. Well secured, aye?"

"Aye," Magnus said, glaring at the rocky portal as though it were a traitor.

"Tom and I checked the caves and the mountain pass. It doesna look as though anyone's been there but us," Sawny said.

"Good." Alexander turned and headed out of the stables, motioning for them to follow. Once past the paddock, he strode across the bailey, scanning the curtain wall to his left. With his attention on the wall, he plowed through a flock of meandering hens scratching and pecking at the ground. The plump birds flapped and fussed, scattering with a cacophony of insulted clucks and ruffled feathers.

The men and two boys reached the side gate and the flashback of their failed escape filled Alexander with a renewed burn of anger. Who had betrayed them that night and revealed their intent to escape? Whoever it was could still be a threat. He squinted up at the levers on top of the outer wall surrounding the keep. The control for the outermost gate was in the wrong position. It appeared to be open. He pointed at the levers. "I want the outer portcullis closed and the inner gate as well. We must take no chances."

Tom scrambled up the narrow blocks of stone embedded as steps in the skirting wall's side. Once he'd reached the lever that controlled the gates, he released the chains holding the outer portcullis open. The heavy gate, basket-like in its weave of wooden strips reinforced with iron bars and bolts, rattled down and hit the earth with a thud. The inner gate made of thicker planks banded together was already closed.

"Our men?" Alexander asked Magnus.

"Duncan and Sutherland are already in the gallery and placed to guard Lady Catriona as soon as she climbs the stairs and takes her seat. Well-armed with pistols and bows, they are," Magnus replied. "Graham and Ian have taken their posts in the hall and ensured men we trust guard the doorways."

"Alasdair?" Alexander asked as they walked through the bailey, circling around to the front of the keep. All had to be perfect before the earl and the Campbell arrived.

"Pacing." Magnus gave a shrug. "He'll most likely wear the floor of the main hall through."

Alexander understood. Nerves raw and teeth on edge, he prayed for wisdom. He was a man of the sword—not a man of negotiation.

A shout came from the front wall in the guard house's vicinity. The guard's bell sounded sending a cold sweat across Alexander's body. The enemy neared their gates.

"Greet them," he told Magnus as he strode up the wide slabs of stone steps to the main double doors of the keep. "I'll be waiting in the hall." He paused on the landing, one hand resting on the latch. "I trust ye to sound the alarm if ye sense the slightest need."

Magnus accepted his duties with a nod and pointed Tom and Sawny back toward the stables. "Guard the caves, aye?"

Both boys bolted off in that direction as though the devil himself was chasing them. They only stopped long enough to duck into the smithy and re-emerge with extra swords and several daggers tucked into their belts.

Alexander watched them go then yanked open the heavy door and strode into the hall. A glance upward gave him a glimpse of Catriona's worried countenance as she stood at the railing surrounding the upper gallery. "Back from the railing, Catriona, until they're seated with their backs to ye, ye ken? I'll no' have ye an easy target."

Catriona nodded but before backing away from the edge, she blew a kiss to him.

Alexander's heart swelled and the burning need to protect her made him pull in a deep breath. The woman owned him heart and soul and he loved her for it. "Almighty God, please help me save her and her clan," he prayed under his breath as he hurried to cross himself.

He scanned the hall as he strode down the length of the room. Spotless floors and both hearths swept and scrubbed within an inch of their lives. The smell of beeswax wafted about and the eye-burning scent of lye soap mixed with the smoky scents of roasted meat and herbs filling the air.

Banners hung at the sides of each hearth, both fireplaces crackling and bright with a cheery fire. Tartans of Neal greens, grays, and blues and sashes of MacCoinnich reds, greens, and blacks decorated the columns marching down either side of the hall. The chieftain's table sat close to the room's center, already laden with the best Clan Neal offered considering that winter had been long. Venison roasts surrounded by platters of carrots, parsnips, and turnips. Baskets of bannocks and loaves of brown bread. Crocks of butter and wedges of cheese. Bottles of port and wine stood at the ready.

The earl and the Campbell would be treated like respected guests and given the opportunity to act as such. Satisfaction filled Alexander. Mrs. Aberfeldy and Cook had done as instructed. His distrust of Mrs. Aberfeldy lessened the slightest bit.

Alasdair gave him an aloof nod from where he waited beside the table, hands clasped in front of him. The man was the picture of a self-assured solicitor. Alexander smiled. Alasdair filled the role well.

He turned and nodded to the men standing guard, then motioned for Ian and Graham to come forward. "I'll no' bear arms at the table and neither will Alasdair. Ye ken what to do, aye?"

"Aye," Graham said as both he and Ian nodded.

"We stand ready with pistols loaded should they forget their manners," Ian remarked with a glance toward the door. "They're here," he added in a hushed tone. Ian and Graham returned to their posts. Each widened his stance and settled a hand atop his pistol.

Alexander recognized Lord Crestshire as soon as he set eyes on him. He remembered the staunch man in full British uniform as Edward John Cunningham. But he would no' admit to such until he saw whether Edward remembered him.

Campbell stalked forward like a great angry bear reared up on its hindquarters spoiling for a fight. "MacCoinnich," he growled, his great bulbous nose pockmarked and wrinkling as though he smelled a stench. His unkempt mustache and beard twitched and shifted as he scowled and bared his teeth.

Alexander graced him with an imperious tilt of his head. "Campbell." Then he shifted his focus to Lord Crestshire and gave him a curt nod. "M'lord," he said, interest piqued to see the earl's reaction. He didn't have to wait long.

Lord Crestshire's mouth twitched at both corners and his eyes narrowed the slightest bit. Recognition flashed across his expression then disappeared just as quick as it came. He returned Alexander's greeting with a graceful dip of his squared chin. "Chieftain MacCoinnich."

Aye. Ye canny lad. Ye remember well enough. Alexander waved the men toward the table laden with food. "By all means, have a seat and enjoy the fine repast Cook has prepared for us."

Campbell glared at him, his face growing redder by the minute. "I didna come here to eat. I come to claim what is mine." He jabbed a finger toward Alexander. "The woman can go where she will. I've no use for a whore what will bed another man while promised to another. But I'll be taking all the horses and the land promised t'me."

Rage flaring hot and fast, Alexander shot forward and grabbed Campbell by his thick throat. Campbell struggled and spit to be free, drawing his dagger and raising it. Without easing his crushing grip on Campbell's windpipe, Alexander clamped his other hand around Campbell's raised fist and shoved his face within inches of the man's nose. "Insult my wife again and I'll send ye back to your clan in a box."

"I think not," Campbell hissed, arching his back and jerking against Alexander's hold. "Ye shall be too busy dancing at the end of the king's rope!"

"Release him," Lord Crestshire ordered but in a civil tone that in no way sounded like a command. "Aye?" he added in an almost perfect Scottish accent coupled with a lopsided grin.

"Aye," Alexander agreed as he gave Campbell a hard shove that sent him tumbling across the floor onto his arse. As Graham and Ian rushed to guard Campbell with pistols drawn, Alexander turned to Lord Crestshire and held out his hand. "So ye remember?"

Lord Crestshire took hold of Alexander's forearm, squeezing it with heartfelt greeting as he clapped a hand to Alexander's shoulder. "Forget the man who saved my life then took the beating I deserved?" He gripped Alexander's arm tighter and shook his head. "I think not. I shall never forget you, old friend."

"Ye canna take him!" Catriona swept down the gallery stairs, holding a pistol cocked and aimed at Lord Crestshire's chest. "I shall kill ye, I will. Ye'll no' take my husband to be hanged."

"The wily wench slipped past us, Alexander!" Duncan shouted from the gallery where he and Sutherland stood hanging over the banister as though about to jump. "Damned if she's no' as fast as a canny wee fox."

"Stand down, woman!" Alexander shouted as he stepped between Lord Crestshire and the gun. "God Almighty, dinna shoot!"

"And the lovely lady's name?" Lord Crestshire asked, looking as though he was having to hold his breath to keep from laughing.

Brows drawn and lips twitching in the sudden realization that perhaps she had not quite interpreted the scene with accuracy, Catriona lowered the pistol and eased the hammer forward to disarm it. She raised her chin to a defensive tilt and motioned toward Campbell still on the floor, pinned in place by Graham and Ian's pistols. "What was I supposed to think? Already attacked by a Scot? How was I to know the Sassenach would be a friend rather than a foe?"

Lord Crestshire stepped around Alexander and made a gallant bow. "Edward John Cunningham, Earl of Crestshire, at your service, m'lady."

Catriona eyed Lord Crestshire as though he were a dog that had just rolled in fresh manure. With a twitch of her shoulders and a defiant upward jerk of her chin, she belatedly remembered her manners and graced him with a half-hearted curtsy. "Catriona MacCoinnich, your lordship."

When her glare shifted and settled on him, Alexander could've sworn that his flesh burned. Lore a'mighty, the woman's protective fierceness flared hot and damned if he didna love her for it.

"'Tis all right, m'love. He remembers me," he said as he stepped forward and removed the pistol from her hand then passed it over to Graham.

"Obviously," Catriona said with a low warning hiss that greatly resembled the sound made by a wounded animal about to attack. She jabbed a finger at Jameson Campbell who'd risen to his feet with the rough-handling help of Graham and Ian. "But he still arrived with him."

"Let me assure you, dear lady, that I travel with my regiment. I am in no way partnered with Jameson Campbell." Lord Crestshire spared a glance in Campbell's direction. "The king's business is my only concern."

"He's a feckin' traitor!" Campbell shouted, backing them all up with his disgusting habit of spitting as he spoke. "He and his men. Every last one of'm was at Glencoe. Killing for the MacDonalds. Ask him if ye refuse to take my word for it."

Alexander clenched his teeth, biting back the words he wished to say. Edward might remember him but that didna mean the man wouldna complete the mission for which they had sent him. He squeezed Catriona's arm, willing her to do the same.

"I propose we sit and have a bit of food," Alasdair interrupted from his post beside the table. "Accusations are best handled on a full stomach. Do ye no' agree?"

"Absolutely," Lord Crestshire said. He gave Campbell a stern scowl. "All weapons. On the floor. Now."

"Here in the thief's den? Are ye daft?" Campbell glared at him. "How the hell did the king ever come to pick such a coward to lead his regiment?"

Alexander didn't attempt to hide the knowing smirk determined to creep across his face. If Edward was the same as he had been as a lad, then Campbell had just made a grievous error.

Lord Crestshire turned to Alexander, jaw working with the grinding of his teeth. His nostrils flared as he drew in a deep breath then released it with a long, slow hiss. "I assume your fine keep has a dungeon or someplace suitable for prisoners?"

"Most certainly," Alexander replied with a smile he couldn't contain. Aye, Edward had no' changed a damned bit. Call him a coward and rue the day ye were born.

"Good." Lord Crestshire made a dismissive wave of a hand toward Jameson Campbell. "Since I didn't bring my guards, would you be so good as to secure this man until I return to my regiment and send for him?"

"Aye. 'Twould be my honor." Alexander gave Graham and Ian a single dip of his chin. "Ye heard the man."

"Gladly," Graham said, taking hold of Campbell's left arm just as Ian took hold of his right.

Graham and Ian escorted Jameson Campbell from the hall spitting and raging like a wild boar being dragged to slaughter.

Duncan and Sutherland exited the hall behind them but turned and headed toward the gatehouse.

"Shall we dine?" Lord Crestshire asked as he pulled out a chair for Catriona.

Alexander came close to laughing out loud as Catriona shot the man a grudging look then lowered herself into the chair and scooted up to the table. Seating himself at the head of the table with Catriona on his right, he motioned to the chair on his left. "Sit, old friend."

Lord Crestshire took his seat then gave Alasdair a polite nod as he seated himself beside Catriona. "And ye are?"

"Clan Neal's solicitor." Alasdair gave a formal dip of his chin. "Alasdair Cameron."

"It pleases me to inform ye that there are no MacCoinnichs on my list," Lord Crestshire said with a nod first to Alexander and then to Alasdair. "Nor Camerons," he added. Then he paused, seeming to struggle with some unknown inner demon. "But I will have you know my regiment is sworn to make King William's presence not only known but very much felt here in the Highlands. I hope you understand but whether you understand or not…it is my duty."

Alexander filled Edward's cup, then Catriona's and his own before passing the bottle of port to Alasdair. He'd thought it better they dine without the servants hearing every word said. He still felt in his bones there was a traitor in their midst. "My understanding depends on your methods, brother." He'd used the word 'brother' with pointed intent to remind Edward of their childhood.

His wording worked as planned because Edward, Lord Crestshire, pushed up the sleeve of his red uniform and bared his muscular right forearm, revealing a thin white line marring the inner skin of his arm. The old scar gleamed with a silver-white sheen in the hall's lighting. "I still consider you a brother as well, Alexander. But not because of two young boys cutting their arms and swearing a bond with their blood."

He jerked his sleeve back down in place, brushed the wrinkles from it, then took a long sip of his port. "The scars you bear that were meant for me are a great deal more significant."

"What do you mean?" Catriona asked. Her puzzled look flitted back and forth between Edward and Alexander.

Alexander remembered that day and would just as soon not revisit it, but he held up a hand just as Edward opened his mouth to speak. If the tale had to be told, he'd rather do the telling.

"Edward fostered with Clan MacCoinnich for a brief time before the damned sickness destroyed us," Alexander said. "The both of us were only..." he paused, giving a slow shake of his head as he tried to remember. "Twelve or so?"

Edward nodded but remained silent.

Alexander reached out and took Catriona's hand, willing his wife to behave and play nice. "As I'm sure ye've already realized, Edward and I became fast friends, blood brothers even."

"Aye," Catriona said in a soft, patient tone. "Go on."

Unable to look anywhere other than down at the table, Alexander kept a tight hold on Catriona's hand as he spoke. "The last winter Edward spent with my clan was bitter cold. The loch had frozen solid, solid enough to slide upon. Or so we thought."

"He broke through," Catriona said with a hard squeeze of his hand. "Ye saved him from drowning."

"I managed to save him," Alexander said, struggling to keep his tone even and free of emotion. "But I couldna save the chieftain's daughter. She'd slipped too far under the ice and her skirts pulled her down fast." He paused and snorted out a disgruntled huff. He gave a sad shake of his head. "She was out of my reach and unable to move through her panic. I feared to swim too far from the hole in the ice. I feared I would become trapped and no' be able to find my way back to the blessed air."

Catriona sat open-mouthed, her free hand pressed to her chest and her eyes wide.

"Everyone knew I favored the lass, and that she favored me," Edward said, breaking into the conversation. "The clan blamed me for her death—said if I had truly cared about her I would never have done something so foolhardy as to lead her out onto the ice." Edward swallowed hard, regret and the darkness of self-imposed guilt etched in the lines of his face. "And maybe they were right."

"'Twas an accident, brother," Alexander said, using the same words he'd used to soothe himself for years. "A foolish pair of lads and a lass, all too young and free of worries to pay heed to caution or fear."

"The chieftain punished the both of ye for the accident?" Catriona asked.

"Beat Alexander until he was bloody," Edward said, lifting his downcast gaze to Alexander then shifting it to Catriona. "He nearly died because he lied to the chief to save me. Told the man he had been the one to coax Leannan out onto the ice and that I had happened by and fallen in while trying to save them. He knew the chief would have ordered my beating be more severe since I was an outsider responsible for his daughter's death."

Edward took another sip of port then turned back to Alexander. "I shall do what I can to shield you and your clan from the scourging. But know this, the Highlands are no longer a safe haven for traitors or anyone harboring ill will toward the Crown. His Highness has deemed it will be so for the good of all in the realm and I am sworn to see it through. Tread lightly, my friend, in everything you do, for your own sake and the sake of those you cherish."

A deep foreboding filled Alexander, churned in his gut like a great beast awakening. He brought Catriona's hand to his mouth and pressed a kiss to her knuckles before turning back to Edward. "Do what ye can but know this, when your protection falls short, I will no' leave this life quietly nor fail to fight for what is mine."

Edward gave a slow nod, his jaw tightening as he lifted his chin and leveled his gaze with Alexander's. "Understood."

CHAPTER 26

"*P*raise God we're at last shed of them." Catriona leaned back against him, hugging his arms tighter around her as they watched the king's regiment and Campbell's men leave the glen. A sea of red uniforms followed by a multi-colored mass of grays, blues, and greens exited out the narrow pass like water poured from a bucket.

"Aye." He pressed a kiss to the top of her head and held her closer, breathing in her sweet familiar scent and reveling in her soft warmth against him. He supposed he should feel happier. Jameson Campbell bound for the Tollbooth at Fort William and the regiment withdrawn without the slightest scuffle. Relieved, he should be.

But he wasn't.

Edward's warning of possible trouble on the horizon replayed in his head and the thought of a traitor, or traitors, still in their midst gnawed at him like a dog worrying an old bone. He would no' rest until he discovered who had betrayed their first escape, risked Catriona's well-being, and cost Murtagh and the stable lads their lives. Edward had spoken of a fragile balance. Too much was at risk. A traitor among them threatened destruction of them all.

"Ye be wool-gathering." Catriona pushed her way out of his arms, turned, and faced him. "What troubles ye, dear husband?"

She read him so well. He didna ken if that was a good thing or no'. Cupping her face between his hands, he sank into the sweet concern filling her eyes. "I fear safety eludes us yet." He wouldna lie to shield her. To do so would cause her more harm than good.

Catriona pulled away, her mouth tightening into a flat line as she glanced up at the sky and squinted against the brightness of the day. She pulled her arisaidh tighter about her, and strolled across the path to the battlement, returning her attention to the emptying of the glen. "If we keep to ourselves, surely Edward will let us be." She stared at the vista before her, the wind whipping her hair. "He said he'd do so as best he could." She tore her gaze away from the glen and pinned it on him. "Think ye he lied?"

"I've never known Edward to lie, but I do know he's loyal to a fault with whatever duty he's sworn to keep."

"Even if it betrays his conscience?"

"Even if it betrays his conscience," Alexander confirmed, grinding his teeth at the admission. 'Twas the one thing they'd always disagreed upon, even come to blows over once long ago. Edward followed orders—no matter what. Alexander had always felt it to be the man's greatest weakness of character. To Edward, extenuating circumstances didna exist. Orders were orders. Never questioned. Always followed.

A weary huff escaped him. "Truth be told, it fair shocked me when he said he'd leave us be as long as he could." Alexander only hoped Edward had at last come to the realization that life was no' a case of black and white. Proper choices came in a myriad of shades tinted by a man's heart, soul, and conscience.

"But he warned us to tread lightly." Catriona rested her hand upon the battlement and bowed her head. "He meant if we did anything to insult the Crown, he wouldna hesitate to destroy us, aye?"

"Aye." Alexander pushed away from the stone wall of the tower and joined Catriona at the low, crenelated wall surrounding it. "But at least his threat is out in the open and we'll see the danger full on before it hits."

Catriona scowled at him with a confused look. "What are ye saying?"

"We've a traitor here, Catriona. Somewhere." He encompassed the keep and the grounds with an impatient flip of a hand. "The night we tried to escape. Tried to free ye. Someone alerted Calum. Someone close to ye. Had to be someone close to ye." Scowling down at the courtyard below, he allowed his gaze to follow the repetitive movements of one of the serving lads loading armloads of wood into the pit for roasting meat. Back and forth the lad went from woodpile to pit, stacking the wood loose for when it came time to light the fire beneath the spit.

"Someone couldha heard us in the hall," Catriona defended.

Fair point. Alexander thought back but instinct told him no. "I dinna believe we said enough in the hall to give away our plans."

"Then someone in the kitchens." Catriona's voice fell, and she closed her eyes. "Or someone close to Murtagh."

"His wife, perhaps?"

Catriona shrank away. 'Twas a sure sign she too suspected Mrs. Aberfeldy.

"Aye, perhaps so," she said in such a soft, low tone he strained to hear her. She lifted her sad gaze to him. "I told her of our plan to escape and bade her tell Murtagh so he could ready the horses." She rubbed her fingers to her forehead as though trying to wipe away the memory. Catriona closed her eyes and shook her head. "But why?" She opened her eyes and stared at Alexander. "Why would she betray me knowing it endangered her husband's life?"

Alexander held out his arm. "Let us find out." They'd go to the hall and have the woman summoned to appear before them. The chieftain and his wife. Their first hearing and judgment as leaders of Clan Neal.

With a resigned sigh, Catriona hooked her arm in his. Together, they made their way down from the guard tower to the main hall and seated themselves in the ornate upholstered chairs on the dais beneath the Neal crest. Servants milled about the room, sweeping, dusting, scrubbing the flagstones.

Alexander motioned the closest of them forward. A young maid, her sleeves pushed up past her elbows, busy at her chore of scrubbing table tops with what smelled like strong lye water. Eyes flaring wide at his summons, she dropped the rag into the bucket and hurried to him.

"Aye, my chieftain?" she said in a quivering voice as she clutched her dark skirts with her reddened hands and curtsied.

"I bid ye fetch Mrs. Aberfeldy and tell her to make haste." Alexander gave the young maid an encouraging nod. "On with ye now."

The young girl's freckled cheeks flamed redder than the curls peeping out from under her white cap. She made another quick curtsy then shot off toward the kitchens.

"What will ye do to the woman?" Catriona asked under her breath.

"That depends on what she says." Alexander paused then took her hand and gave it a reassuring squeeze. "And your wishes."

"I wish for simple things. Happiness. Peace. And filling this keep with your babies." She gave him a sad smile as she returned his squeeze.

"Aye, love," he said soft and low. "'Tis my wish as well, dear one."

The breathless sound of huffing gasps, scurrying feet, and skirts rustling across the floor interrupted their discourse. Mrs. Aberfeldy emerged from the side hall close to the right of the dais at a full run.

"Are ye unwell?" she asked Catriona, gasping between words as she clapped both pudgy hands to her chest.

"Nay," Catriona answered in a quiet but firm tone. She tightened her hold of Alexander's hand and gave him a sideways glance as though asking for permission to continue.

Her need to be the one to do this shone in her eyes. Alexander gave her the slightest nod. The gleaning of the truth from Mrs. Aberfeldy would go a mite easier if he didna get involved. It also gave him the opportunity to observe the old woman's mannerisms closer.

"The night I attempted to escape," Catriona started then paused, took in a deep breath, and released it with a slow pained sigh. "The night of Murtagh's murder, who did ye tell of our plan besides Murtagh?"

All color drained from the old woman's face and her jaw slackened. Her lips parted in disbelief. She fisted both hands, flexing them in front of her waist, then finally clasped them tight together, her knuckles white with the effort. "Ye dare no' think... I didna betray ye, m'lady. I swear it."

"Someone did," Catriona rebutted, still speaking in a quiet tone filled with the strength of iron.

"Someone in the kitchens," Mrs. Aberfeldy said, still wringing her hands in front of her. "They saw ye with your cloak. Someone in the kitchens gave ye away. 'Twasn't me, m'lady. I swear to ye on me own grave."

"If someone in the kitchens had given me away, Calum would no' have had the time to plan how best to foil our escape the way that he did," Catriona said, sitting taller in her seat. "Someone warned Calum and he set his torment in motion before I ever reached the kitchens."

"Ye didna answer the question," Alexander said. The woman was lying. He could tell by the way she glanced about as though she feared someone might overhear her denials and challenge them. "Did ye speak to anyone other than Murtagh about Catriona's intent to leave?"

"I dinna remember," she said with a jerking shake of her head then stared down at the floor.

"How could ye, Gaersa?" Catriona asked, her tone filled with sorrow. "How could ye do such a thing t'me? To Murtagh?"

The old woman lifted her head, all of sudden looking so weary, it appeared to take all her strength to stand. "I didna mean to betray ye, Catriona." Her voice drifted off, and she looked away. "I swear I didna mean to."

"Name the person." Alexander shifted to the edge of his seat. He'd heard all the pathetic lies he could stomach.

Mrs. Aberfeldy bowed her head again and her shoulders slumped. She mumbled something under her breath. A single word.

"Louder," Alexander ordered.

247

"Orlie," Mrs. Aberfeldy said, tears running down her face. "I told Orlie."

"Who the hell is Orlie?" Alexander asked.

"My father's personal servant." Catriona frowned. "But I thought the man wasna able to speak."

"My brother could speak as clear as any of us," Mrs. Aberfeldy said in a subdued tone. "But your father's treatment of him over the years silenced him, making him speak only to the few people he loved and trusted."

"Are ye saying he betrayed me?"

Mouth drawn down into a sorrowful frown, Mrs. Aberfeldy gazed first at Catriona, shifted her focus to Alexander, then returned her attention to Catriona. "I should never have told Orlie. I wasna thinking proper when I did so." She gave them both a sad shrug. "Ye ken I've never been able to hold my tongue about anything I know. It's as though I'll die if I canna tell someone... anyone...especially when I know something of importance." She shrugged again. "Ye see, it...it makes me feel I matter when folk listen. Like I'm better. Folk take note of me when I have something to say. Something that no one else knows." She swallowed hard, looked down, then forced herself to raise her head and look them in the eye again. "I get so weary of being invisible. Please forgive me, Catriona."

"Why would Orlie go to Calum?" Alexander asked.

"Because he loved him," Mrs. Aberfeldy said with a heavy sigh. "And he feared for Calum's safety."

"What?" Catriona leaned forward, pinning Mrs. Aberfeldy with a stern, unblinking stare.

Mrs. Aberfeldy glanced around the hall then took a step closer. "Your father often paired them together. In his sick games. As your father aged and his ailments grew worse, he couldna perform as a man so he'd force Calum to do his perversions whilst he watched." The old housekeeper spoke in a low voice filled with shame. "Orlie said Calum was gentle with him. Wouldna torture him near as severe your father ordered. Orlie grew to love him for his kindness."

Catriona looked away, slumping back in her seat and covering her face with both hands.

Alexander took a light hold of Catriona's arm. Her pallor concerned him. She looked as though she were about to be ill and he couldna say he blamed her. "Send for your brother. I would speak with him about that night."

"I cannot, my chieftain," Mrs. Aberfeldy said, her face an emotionless blank. Before Alexander could demand why not, she continued, "Orlie hanged himself in his room on the night Calum died."

So the one who had betrayed them was already dead. But there was still Mrs. Aberfeldy. Alexander felt she'd betrayed them, too, and would do so again. The woman had admitted she couldna keep the slightest confidence. She was a danger, a threat they didna need.

Before he could speak his thoughts and reason out a solution, Catriona pushed herself up from her chair. He held his tongue and waited, wondering what his wife was about to do.

"Ye canna stay here, Mrs. Aberfeldy." Catriona gave a sharp shake of her head and motioned toward the door. "Pack your things and go."

Mrs. Aberfeldy looked as though she'd aged a hundred years. She gave Catriona a trembling nod as she twisted her hands together in front of her. "I understand," she said, then shuffled off toward the archway leading to the wing of the keep that held the servants' rooms.

"What a poisoned mess the evil in my sire caused," Catriona whispered as she watched Mrs. Aberfeldy leave the room. She turned to Alexander. "She lost my trust and understanding the moment she defended Calum and his evil ways."

Alexander stood and held out his hand. "Come. We'll walk a bit and visit the stable to clear our heads of this darkness. Sawny said your prize mare gifted us with a fine healthy colt this morning." Surely, seeing the sweet unblemished life would help raise Catriona's spirits. Whilst he understood her emotional distress, especially since discovering the depth of her father and brother's debauchery, Alexander hoped she'd find comfort knowing they had settled the problem of a traitor in the keep.

Catriona took his hand without speaking but graced him with a weak smile. They exited the keep and walked along in companionable silence for a long while. They strolled through the winding paths of the kitchen gardens where tiny bits of green were beginning to peep up through the clumps of black broken soil as though checking to ensure that winter had in fact gone before emerging any farther.

A gentle breeze lifted the loose tendrils of Catriona's auburn hair and fluttered them about her face. With an impatient flick of her hand, she brushed them aside and tucked them behind her ears. The sunshine set her hair afire, highlighting it with streaks of gold and shimmering copper. Her fair skin glowed in the fresh air of the sunny day. A creamier white than any ivory and seasoned with the faintest strip of cinnamon freckles across her nose and cheeks. She was a braw, fierce, lovely woman, and she was all his.

"I love ye, Catriona." The words left his mouth of their own volition and he was glad of it, rewarded by her pleased look and shy smile.

"I love ye as well, Alexander."

He pulled her into his arms and poured all he felt for her into a long, slow kiss. Her hands traveled up his chest. She held him tight and returned his fervor. Soft curves pressed against hardness. Heartbeat pounded against heartbeat. Growing breathless with need, Alexander raised his head and looked down at this woman who owned him heart and soul.

Fair skin flushed and lips parted, Catriona gazed up at him with half-closed eyes. "Ye've turned me into a wanton, husband. I canna get enough of ye." As if she feared he wouldn't believe her, she snugged her body harder against him.

Her words inflamed him and her actions made him ache with the need to take her. Alexander stole a glance around the enclosed garden, secluded in its position at the side of the kitchens but set well away from the area where meat roasted on spits or the great cauldrons rendered meat fat down into lye soap.

"I must have ye," he rasped against the softness of her jawline as he nuzzled at her throat. "Here. Now. Pray allow me, I beg ye."

"Never feel as though ye must beg, dear husband." Catriona leaned back against the stone wall surrounding the garden. With a slow deliberate move, she lifted her skirts and bared one leg.

Alexander charged forward like a bull released from its pen. He lifted her up against the wall, whipped aside his kilt and the mass of her skirts, then shoved in deep with a claiming growl. He kept her in place with one hand as he ground deeper then set to rocking, sliding in and out of the wondrous hot wetness as she held tight and clamped her legs around him.

Her nails raking down his back, Catriona shuddered and cried out as bliss took over, making her clench around him with searing wet spasms that pulled him in deep and hard, coaxing him to embrace his own release and spill himself.

Sagging into her, sandwiching her between his body and the wall, Alexander gasped for breath between tastes of Catriona's sweet mouth. "I love ye fierce, my wanton wife."

Catriona crossed her ankles at the small of his back and hugged him with both arms and legs as she gave him another kiss. "I'm glad of it and I love ye just as fierce." Then she gave him a wicked grin. "But if ye've torn the back of me dress on these stones, ye shall buy fabric for another."

"Well worth the price," he said as he squeezed the fine full cheeks of her arse, then withdrew with a deep regretful sigh, and lowered her to the ground. He stole another quick kiss of her sweet lips and winked. "Give me a son and I'll buy ye enough fabric and lace for two."

With a coy look in her eyes, she covered her mouth and gave a light cough as though struggling to hold back a smile.

"What?" He braced himself. What was the vixen up to now? Then a delightful thought hit him. "Are ye with child already?"

"'Tis too soon to tell," she said as she shook her skirts down in place. "Entirely too soon. But according to Elena, I'll know for certain within a sennight or so."

Alexander grabbed her up and spun her around, unable to contain the joy she'd just triggered.

"We mustn't celebrate too soon." She patted his shoulders and gave him the sternest look she could manage under the circumstances. "'Tis ill luck to celebrate before knowing for certain."

In his heart, Alexander knew she carried his child. A son for sure. "What shall we name him?"

Rolling her eyes in disbelief, she shook a finger at him. "Did ye no' hear what I just said?"

"Aye." Alexander couldn't suppress a proud smile. Excitement and joy grew within him, filling him to fair bursting. "But what shall we name him?"

Catriona folded her arms and lifted her chin to a challenging tilt. "William Anthony Carmichael McBride MacCoinnich."

"What?"

"I promised Father William," she said with a shrug. "Ye must admit, he's done much for us."

"And if it's a girl?" He couldna wait to hear what Father William had said about that.

"Willa Antonia Catherine McBride MacCoinnich," Catriona said. She gave him a wicked grin and added, "Has a certain ring to it, dinna ye think so?"

Alexander grabbed her up and held her close. "All I *think* is that I never knew I could love someone the way I love ye."

"Nor I," Catriona whispered as she brushed her lips across his. "Nor I."

EPILOGUE

"William and Willa?"

"She promised the priest." Alexander spared a glance back at Father William and Catriona where they stood beside the chieftain's table at the head of the hall. The pair bounced and jiggled back and forth, shoulder to shoulder in perfect sync, attempting to shush the caterwauling of his wee son and daughter. Twins. Not quite two months old and more than a little insulted at having water dribbled across their pates during their nap.

The closest thing he'd ever known to pure joy coursed through him even with the babies' howls echoing clear to the rafters and drowning out any attempts at a conversation among his guests. His heart couldna be an ounce fuller. If anyone had told him a year ago that he'd be happily married and the father of two braw, healthy bairns, he wouldha told them they were daft and had him confused with someone else.

Graham gave him a wink. "Twins at just a little over a year into your marriage. At this rate, brother, ye shall need a bigger keep."

The sight of Sawny bumping and darting through those gathered in the hall made Alexander forget whatever quick retort he had for

Graham. The boy looked harried and more than a little worried. What the hell had he gotten into this time?

Sawny came to a halt in front of him, stealing a glance around the room before he leaned in close and whispered, "Messenger. At the gate." He gulped in a deep breath and peeped around the crowd again. "A messenger from His Highness."

His Highness? What the hell did King William want? Edward's regiment had recently visited, and he had no' found them wanting. His old friend had seemed quite relieved that he could in full conscience report to his liege that all was quiet at *Tor Ruadh.*

"I shall go to the gate." Alexander forced a smile and nodded to the well-wishers gathered in the hall as he started toward the door. He did his best to appear nonchalant and not raise suspicion. He was more concerned about upsetting Catriona on their babes' christening day than he was about troubling their guests. She'd fretted herself into a frenzy planning this day. He'd no' have it go awry.

"Master Graham needs to go, too," Sawny hurried to say before Alexander had taken more than a step. "The messenger asked for him —not yourself."

Alexander turned to his brother whose smile had melted into a confused scowl. "What have ye done?"

"I've done nothing," Graham assured in a low, tempered tone forced through clenched teeth.

"Ye best join me." Alexander slipped out of the hall, then limped across the bailey, and headed straight to the guard tower. Graham followed a half step behind him, and Sawny brought up the rear.

A young soldier, wearing the king's red and looking to be a little older than Sawny, stood just outside the gate in front of one of the Neal guards. He held the reins of his horse in one hand and a folded bit of parchment bearing the ribbon and royal seal of King William in the other. Alexander could spot that ribbon and seal a mile away.

Alexander held out his hand. "The message?"

The young man gave a respectful dip of his chin. "Be ye Graham MacCoinnich, sir?"

"I am Graham MacCoinnich." Graham stepped forward then motioned to his brother. "This is Chieftain MacCoinnich."

"Beg pardon, sir." The young soldier made a curt bow, stepped forward, and held out the parchment envelope. "I am to escort ye, sir, as soon as ye've read the message."

"Escort me?" Graham gave Alexander a worried scowl. "Escort me where?"

"To Court, sir." The boy retreated a step and resumed his stiff-backed stance beside his horse.

Alexander pointed at the envelope, struggling against the urge to jerk it from his brother's hand, tear it open, and read it. "Read the damn message."

Graham ripped it open, his mouth tightening into a hard line as his gaze raced across the paper.

Alexander couldn't stand it any longer. "What does it say?"

"It appears the king requires my help with a most delicate matter." Graham looked up and fixed Alexander with a damning look as he crumpled the note. "Immediately."

If you enjoyed The Chieftain, please consider leaving a review on the site where you purchased your copy, or a reader site such as Goodreads, or BookBub.

If you'd like to receive my newsletter, here's the link to sign up: https://maevegreyson.com/contact.html#newsletter

I love to hear from readers! Drop me a line at maevegreyson@gmail.com

Or visit me on Facebook: https://www. facebook.com/AuthorMaeveGreyson

Join my Facebook Group - Maeve's Corner: https://www.facebook. com/groups/MaevesCorner

I'm also on Instagram: maevegreyson https://www. instagram.com/maevegreyson/

My website: https://maevegreyson.com

Feel free to ask questions or leave some Reader Buzz on https:// bingebooks.com/author/maeve-greyson

Follow me on these sites to get notifications about new releases, sales, and special deals:

Amazon: https://www.amazon.com/Maeve-Greyson/e/B004PE9T9U

BookBub: https://www.bookbub.com/authors/maeve-greyson

Many thanks and may your life always be filled with good books!

Maeve

EXCERPT FROM THE GUARDIAN

Read on for an excerpt from Graham MacCoinnich's story in The Guardian - Book 1 – Highland Heroes series

Chapter One
Kensington Palace - Spring 1693

*G*raham MacCoinnich eyed his surroundings, rubbing his hands together with slow, purposeful movements. Several grim outcomes had come to mind since receiving the strange summons from the crown. This situation had not been among them.

Graham shifted in place and pulled in a deep breath, hissing it out between clenched teeth as he stole another veiled glance around the small but opulent chamber—unoccupied except for himself. An ill-feeling permeated the air of what appeared to be a private library of the palace. Bookshelves lined each wall, laden not only with books but also all manner of useless baubles and trinkets, the likes of which Graham had never seen. Luxurious chairs and couches sat in clusters of twos and threes, crowding every available space. Tables littered with gilded boxes and cut-glass decanters filled to their stoppers high-lighted the cozy arrangements of gaudy furniture.

Graham wet his lips. He wouldn't turn away a drink about now. A bead of sweat trickled down his spine and settled in the crack of his arse. He didn't care for this place a damn bit. A chamber made for secrets. Dark. Ominous. The room reeked of deception.

He shifted positions again, turning with as nonchalant an air as he could muster. Places such as these always held spy holes, riddled with them, in fact. Someone watched him. He'd bet a barrel of fine MacCoinnich whisky on it. The king's personal guard had escorted him here with a rudeness that had come close to forcing him to teach the man better manners. Graham had managed to refrain. Barely. He still itched to put the insolent bastard in his place. But he wouldn't dare. It was too great a risk. After all, he was a Scot in the heart of hostile soil. For his own sake and the sake of his brother Alexander's new clan and young family, he'd behave. At least for now.

A quiet click to his right made him turn. A gold-inlaid, paneled door swung open.

"Come this instant, daughter. His Highness will join us presently. Your maid can fetch your journal later. We've greater matters at hand than the whereabouts of your silly sketches, and I will not be humili-ated by running after my progeny like an incompetent nursemaid." A tall man, once broad across the shoulders but now stooped with age, held tight to the hand of a fetching young woman. He yanked her forward with a rude, impatient jerk.

"Papa! I beg you—"

"This instant, Mercy! Heed me now. Not another word, do you understand me?"

The scarlet-cheeked beauty careened to a bouncing halt as her alarmed gaze fell on Graham. Her chin jerked to a prideful angle but her full lips quivered, and her slender throat flexed as she struggled to recover a calm, gracious appearance.

Graham's heart went out to the lass for suffering such an embar-rassment at the hands of her brute-of-a-father. He stepped forward with a warning glare at the man and lifted his fists to a more noticeable level. The old bastard best amend his behavior or rue the day he stepped into the presence of a MacCoinnich. Women were precious and meant to be treated with respect.

The lady's father made a weak attempt of jutting out his chin but took a half step back and cleared his throat.

Good. The old fool understood the warning.

Graham shifted his attention back to the sweet lass peering out from behind her father.

A rare vision. She had hair black as obsidian and skin fairer than any ivory Graham had ever seen. And those eyes. Fathomless. Curved as though smiling and colored the rich hue of a well-aged whisky reflecting the torchlight. A man could get trapped in those eyes, completely ensnared with the promise of discovering the rest of the lady's charms.

Graham wrenched himself free of her spell. Such a dalliance could prove dangerous. Not only was she a Sassenach but more than likely a noble judging from the looks of her father and her regal, genteel demeanor. The situation begged careful handling. He made a polite nod toward the beguiling lass and stepped between her and her intolerable father. "M'lady. Graham MacCoinnich at your service."

The lass curtsied and dropped her gaze with a coy turning of her head, but Graham didn't miss the glances she stole at him through those long, dark lashes. Aye. A fine, rare beauty, this one was.

Her father edged his way back in front of her. "Duke of Edsbury, sir." The man growled out the words in a low, huffing tone that said the name should impress Graham.

It didn't.

"Sir." Graham gave the duke that much politeness but no more 'til the man proved he deserved it. He'd march straight through hell's gates before he called the man *milord*.

Lord Edsbury's eyes narrowed the slightest bit and the crease between his twin thatches of bushy gray brows deepened. He stood taller, his spine stiffening into as challenging a stance as the man could muster. He might have been a worthy adversary at one time, a courageous lion, strong, and noble. But now the man moved with the hitched gait of one battling the ill health of overindulgence and advancing years.

"Papa." The word floated through the air as soft as a whisper, slipped between the two men, and hovered like a spirit.

The duke recovered his composure. The required shroud of polite court manners fell across him like a veil of mist tumbling down a mountain. He turned and took his daughter's hand, pulling her out from behind him to stand at his side. "Allow me to introduce you to my daughter, Lady Mercy Rowena Claxton."

"Honored to meet ye, m'lady." Graham graced her with a smile intended as a calming gesture and a truce. After all, it wasn't the woman's fault her father was an arrogant arse—and an English one at that. "Might I call ye Lady Mercy?"

"You may." Lady Mercy curtsied again and held out her hand, lowering her gaze as she waited for him to take it.

Take it he did. Graham relished the opportunity to graze his mouth across the softness of her long, delicate fingers. He knew well enough it was considered ungentlemanly to press his lips to the lady's skin rather than hover above her fine hand, but he'd never been accused of being a gentleman nor possessed the desire of gaining the title.

He took pride in his brazenness, breathing in her enticing fragrance as he drew a step closer. The earthy florals of a heather-filled glen paired with the intoxicating sweetness of a nervous young woman floated around her. What a treasure she was—sadly, a Sassenach, aye, but a treasure to be won and enjoyed, nonetheless.

She rewarded him with a deeper blush across her high cheekbones and an endearing gasp as she slipped her hand out of his grasp and tucked it to her middle.

"Damned, ill-bred Scot. I would expect no less."

Graham turned and laughed in Edsbury's face. "Aye, man. A Scot doesna leave a woman guessing after his intentions. They ken verra well when they're wanted." He returned his attention to the lady. As much as he enjoyed tormenting her pompous father, he wished the dear lass no unease. "Forgive me if I've offended ye, m'lady. I assure ye 'twas no' my intent at all."

Lady Mercy fluttered his words away with a gracious wave. "No offense taken, sir." With a modest lowering of her gaze, she retreated to a corner.

Were circumstances different, he'd take great pleasure in getting to know this lass better—despite her being a danger. The strange summons from the crown returned to the forefront of his thoughts and all levity left him. He turned back to the duke. "I assume your presence here means ye have a meeting with the king as well?"

Edsbury gave him an unsettling scowl, one that made Graham wish he could read the man's mind. "His Highness will be with us anon. Bentinck, Lord Portland, assured me of such."

"Bentinck?" Graham wasn't familiar with the name.

"The Earl of Portland. His Highness's Groom of the Stole." Edsbury gave a haughty sniff and looked at Graham as though he should be envious of the man chosen to wipe the king's arse after His Majesty took a shite.

King William's entrance cut off the less than complimentary retort burning on Graham's tongue.

"Your Highness." Edsbury bowed long and low, and Lady Mercy rushed to give the perfect, gracious curtsy.

Graham made the required respectful bow, then straightened and met King William's gaze.

The royal known for his heartless scheming and tenacity looked worn, far older than his forty-some-odd years of age. His Majesty appeared travel weary and ready for a drink and it was no wonder. The king wintered but a few short months in Whitehall or Kensington, traveling the remainder of the year and entrusting the everyday duties of ruling the kingdom to his wife, Queen Mary. He had proven himself more interested in the expansion of his empire and the battlefield rather than in the running of the kingdom. It was a rare occurrence for him to darken the doors of his own palace for more than a few days during the spring or summer months.

King William didn't speak for a long moment. Just stood there.

Motionless, except for the occasional shifting of his impeccably arranged long brown curls whenever he took in a breath. He peered at Graham, studying him as though weighing his merits to decide if he was lacking. After what most would consider an overlong stare bordering on rudeness, His Highness pursed his thin lips and gave a slow, imperious nod. He moved to sit in a luxurious chair situated on a raised platform near the entrance. With a lazy turn of his head, he shifted his focus to the almost invisible young lord standing beside his chair like a well-trained dog waiting for his master's command. "Pray tell, is there a reason our glass is bereft of port?"

The thin lordling's eyes flared wide with alarm, then he sprang into action, snapping his fingers at the pair of servants flanking the king's private entrance to the room.

The older of the servants bowed and bobbed as he hurried to snatch a decanter from the cabinet beside His Majesty's chair. "Sincerest apologies, m'lord, but Her Highness—"

Before the young, attending lord could administer a more severe reprimand, King William held up a bejeweled hand.

"We are well aware of Her Majesty's position on sobriety, but as you should know, if you wish to continue in our service, when we are present at the palace, it is our command and our rule. Not the Queen's inclinations."

"Yes, Your Majesty." Still bobbing and bowing as he scurried to fill more glasses, the addled servant waved his counterpart forward and gave a jerking nod toward Graham, the duke, and Lady Mercy.

King William took a slow sip from his glass, all the while continuing to study Graham.

Graham clenched his teeth harder and lifted his chin. Royal or not, he would not give the man the satisfaction of a Scot cowering at his feet. The ominous echo of a ticking clock filled the room. Graham felt the minutes of his life slipping away, and the feeling shattered his ability to curb his impatience. Time to end this waste of time. "Your summons appeared urgent." He gave a stiff nod. "How might I be of service to His Majesty?"

The king's gaze slid from Graham to Edsbury. "The Duke of

Edsbury is in need of your service, and it is our most adamant wish you see fit to accept the task." A sincere smile wiped the weariness from the king's long, drawn face as his attention settled on Lady Mercy. "Edsbury and his daughter, the lovely Lady Mercy, are our particular favorites here at court." With an affectionate tilting of his head in her direction, King William extended his hand and wiggled his fingers. "Come to us, child."

With the barest rustling of her full skirts, Lady Mercy hurried to the king and knelt at his feet, placing her fingertips up beneath his. She bowed her head, pressing a kiss over the jewel-encrusted rings sparkling across his knuckles. "My king," she murmured as she lifted her face to his and gifted the king with a reverent, adoring smile.

Graham studied the king as His Majesty gazed down at the lass, fully expecting to witness the signs of a lascivious royal sizing up his next mistress. But such lust was not there. Surprising. A genuine fondness filled the king's face. He gave Lady Mercy the adoring look one would expect from a benevolent guardian toward a most beloved charge.

"Explain to him, Edsbury," King William said as he kept his pleased countenance fixed on Lady Mercy. He took tight hold of her hand, steadying her as she seated herself on the small, upholstered stool beside his chair. "Your loveliness is a welcome balm to our weary soul, my dear. A welcome balm, indeed."

With a graceful nod, Lady Mercy lowered her gaze. "You are most kind, Your Majesty."

His patience thinning even more with this royal parlor game, Graham turned to the duke. "The task?"

Edsbury's jaw flexed. He took a fortifying sip of the dark liquid in his glass, then scowled down at the port as he swirled it in a slow, methodical circle. "Lady Mercy has a great interest in the flora and fauna of Scotland. The Highlands, in particular." He leveled an even sterner scowl on Graham. "My late wife's influence, I fear. I blame her for the indulgence of my daughter regarding such. And with both my wife and my son's untimely deaths, Lady Mercy appears to need a distraction from her grief or there will be no peace in my household."

He snorted, then coughed as though his words left a detestable taste in his mouth.

"Ye have my condolences, sir." Graham considered the man a rude cur, but he'd not be heartless toward him. 'Twas a raw thing to outlive a wife and a child. He'd witnessed such when cousin Ian had lost his wife and unborn child in the attack at Glencoe. "My *genuine* condolences, sir," he stressed.

Edsbury responded with a stiff nod.

"May they ever rest in peace." Graham raised his glass to Lady Mercy, holding it high as he gave her a respectful bow before downing the contents.

The duke responded to Graham's kind words with another jerking nod, then turned away, settling a long, studious glare upon his daughter still seated beside the king. He drained his glass, accepted another from a servant, then turned back to Graham. "It is Lady Mercy's wish to compile a book, an enhanced journal of sorts, cataloging the plants and animals of the Highlands. She wishes to dedicate it to her mother and brother since they were both avid lovers of nature."

"And she has our blessing," King William interjected with a look that dared Graham to argue. "We have vowed to see this journal properly published and added to all our libraries across the kingdom." The king gave Graham a menacing smile. "Hear this and mark our words when we say Lady Mercy has our royal sanction for this venture. We are certain you understand our meaning, do you not?"

"Oh aye, Your Majesty," Graham hedged. "*Your* meaning is quite clear."

Clear as a murky fog floating above the bogs. Whatever they were about to ask was an order, not a request. *That* part, he understood. But what were they asking? Had he been summoned here merely to describe the Highlands to a fetching Sassenach noble who more than likely had never set foot past Hadrian's Wall? What a waste of his time. Beguiling lass or not, he was no storyteller or some foppish bard. Why the hell had they chosen him? Time to sort this foolishness out. "What exactly is the task? I'm no' so much for telling stories of my beloved Highlands. My time is better spent patrolling them, ye ken?"

"I require a guide, Master MacCoinnich."

So, Lady Mercy could speak something other than the demure murmurings of a highborn lass seeking favor at court. Graham heard an underlying strength in her sultry tone and something more, something he couldn't quite put his finger on, but it drew him in just the same. Determined, she was. Aye, that was it. She might play the part of a shy lass but he'd lay odds the woman was sly and unpredictable as the wind. A thrilling, ominous shiver, a shudder of expectation shot through him. He relished a challenge.

"A guide, m'lady?" Graham took a step closer, noting the king's sharp-eyed perusal as he did so. "Surely, ye dinna mean to travel through the Highlands to make your wee book."

"That is exactly what she means to do," Edsbury said as he positioned himself closer to the king and his daughter, behaving as though he'd be an impenetrable barrier should Graham decide to attack. "And to do so safely, she needs someone who will not only guide her through the Highlands but also protect her." He widened his tensed, defensive stance and glared at Graham with red-veined nostrils flaring as though he smelled a stench. "Your reputation as a mercenary precedes you, sir. Are you not for hire?"

A warning tingle rippled through the hairs on the back of Graham's neck. The same instinctive alarm he always felt when danger neared. He'd best choose his words with care. He felt it clear to the marrow of his bones. With the king involved, if he failed at this, Alexander's clan could be endangered. King William had sworn to cleanse the Highlands of treasonous rumblings, and his edict played well into the hands of those seeking political gain and also wishing to settle old scores. The murdered MacDonalds of Glencoe lay restless in their graves as a testament to that.

Graham forced himself to appear a damned sight more relaxed than he felt. He even managed a congenial demeanor to go along with his polite half-bow. "Aye. I am a soldier for hire." He gave King

William a look he prayed the royal would understand. "For the right price and the right reasons."

King William rewarded him with a smug but thoughtful smile, one, gold-ringed finger twitching with a slow rhythmic tap atop the gilded lion's head carved into the arm of his chair. "Your loyalty is so noted by us, sir."

Lady Mercy rose from her seat beside the king, so graceful and lithe in the sumptuous yardage of her silk gown she seemed to float across the floor, suspended in the folds of rich purple framing her coloring to perfection. She eased closer to Graham, hands clasped in front of her in an almost pious pose. With a shy incline of her head, she flashed him a smile that Graham felt sure was meant to beguile him. "I would be most grateful if you would agree to this duty. My father assures me you shall be well paid for your services."

"Gold coin," Edsbury said, spitting out the words as though it was a struggle to say them. "As much as you can lift. Bags, of course. Both hands."

"Quite a sum." The generous offer made Graham even more wary. Was it truly that important to Edsbury and the king that the charming Lady Mercy be indulged and allowed to make her wee book rather than just disposing of the lass by marrying her off for political gain? There was more here, more than what had been said; damned if he could figure out what it was.

"Then you will agree?" Lady Mercy blessed him with a genuine smile and a look that stirred him in places better left unstirred by an English lass who was clearly a favorite to the king—especially if they were to be traveling through the Highlands. Alone.

Alone? Nay. Surely not. Graham cleared his throat and huffed away Lady Mercy's enamoring spell, shifting his attention back to Edsbury. "I need more details. How many will be in our party? I assume the lady has her own retinue accompanying her?" Royals traveled with herds of servants to see to their every need. If he was both guide and guard to all concerned, he needed to know the number.

"Myself and my maid," Lady Mercy said after a quick glance back at her father. "And a few servants to handle the horses and wagons, of course."

"And one of our own personal guards," King William added with a warning, narrow-eyed glare. "After all, parts of the Highlands are quite uncivilized. A lone man, even one with your rumored skills, could do little against a band of highwaymen."

Graham knew damn good and well why the king was sending one of his own. The man would be a bloody spy. If the king was so worried about highwaymen outnumbering him, he had a better solution. "My brothers, Duncan and Sutherland, might be available to join us." He turned to Edsbury and grinned. "Of course, they'll be wanting their own payment of gold."

The duke opened his mouth to speak, but King William cut him off. "We find your terms acceptable." He paused, gave Edsbury a hard look, then continued. "However, one of our personal guards shall still accompany you. We will not negotiate that point."

Three Scots against one red-coated Sassenach? Aye, that would do. Fair laughable odds it was and a great deal more acceptable. Graham settled his focus back on the lovely Lady Mercy, searching her expression for signs of guile or deceit. More was at stake here than the spoiled daughter of a duke getting her way. But what was it? Could the lass really just wish for a grand tour through the Highlands to honor her mother and brother? And why was the king so intent on accommodating the girl and her father? Graham understood the concept of favorites at court; but this...this was more than a little odd.

"Will you agree, sir?" Lady Mercy asked, looking like a child begging for sweets.

"Aye, m'lady. I agree to the terms set forth today." Graham accepted with a curt bow, then turned to Edsbury and the king. "My brothers can be here within a few days. All I need do is send for them. When shall I tell them we plan to leave?"

Edsbury sniffed and turned aside, glancing at the king before giving Graham a dismissive nod. "All shall be set in motion as soon as your brothers arrive."

"Do have them make haste," King William intoned. "We have little patience for waiting."

A warning. Graham acknowledged it with a bow, clenching his teeth to keep from saying more than he should as he turned and left the room.

ABOUT THE AUTHOR

"No one has the power to shatter your dreams unless you give it to them." That's Maeve Greyson's mantra. She and her husband of over forty years traveled around the world while in the U.S. Air Force. Now she lives in rural Kentucky where she writes about her beloved Highlanders and the fearless women who tame them.

maevegreyson.com

ALSO BY MAEVE GREYSON

HIGHLAND HEROES SERIES

The Guardian

The Warrior

The Judge

The Dreamer

The Bard

The Ghost

TIME TO LOVE A HIGHLANDER SERIES

Loving Her Highland Thief

Taming Her Highland Legend

Winning Her Highland Warrior

Capturing Her Highland Keeper

Saving Her Highland Traitor

Loving Her Lonely Highlander

Delighting Her Highland Devil

HIGHLAND PROTECTOR SERIES

Sadie's Highlander

Joanna's Highlander

Katie's Highlander

HIGHLAND HEARTS SERIES

My Highland Lover

My Highland Bride

My Tempting Highlander

My Seductive Highlander

THE MACKAY CLAN

Beyond A Highland Whisper

The Highlander's Fury

A Highlander In Her Past

OTHER BOOKS BY MAEVE GREYSON

Stone Guardian

Eternity's Mark

CPSIA information can be obtained
at www.ICGtesting.com
Printed in the USA
LVHW050721240722
724258LV00032B/843